HIGH REWARD

A Point of No Return Novel

Brenna Aubrey

SILVER GRIFFON ASSOCIATES
ORANGE, CA, USA

Silver Griffon Associates
P.O. Box 7383
Orange, CA 92863

Publisher's Note: This is a work of fiction. Names, characters, places, and incidents are a product of the author's imagination. Locales and public names are sometimes used for atmospheric purposes. Any resemblance to actual people, living or dead, or to businesses, companies, events, institutions, or locales is completely coincidental.

Trademarked names appear throughout this book. Rather than use a trademark symbol with every occurrence of a trademarked name, names are used in an editorial fashion, with no intention of infringement of the respective owner's trademark.

Book Layout ©2018 BookDesignTemplates.com
Cover Art ©2018 Sarah Hansen, Okay Creations

High Reward / Brenna Aubrey. – 1st ed.
ISBN 978-1-940951-63-8

www.BrennaAubrey.com

For Tessa, fellow dweller of the Lair of Brilliance 2.0

ACKNOWLEDGEMENTS

As always, thanks to my beta readers Kate McKinley and Sabrina Darby. Your long-suffering knows no bounds. Much thanks to Carey Baldwin for her expertise in the medical field and always kind willingness to share. Thank you to authors Lynn Raye Harris, Viv Arend, Natasha Boyd, Anna Zaires, and Cassia Leo for your enthusiastic and very vocal support of High Risk.

HUGE SHOUT OUT to everyone who reads, supports, shares and blogs about my books. I couldn't do this without you. If you liked the book the kindest things you can do are to review it and tell your friends.

Thanks to Sarah Hansen for the cover design and to Julianne Burke for the gorgeous promotional graphics.
Love my family. I'm so grateful for all their support. When I'm having emotional breakdowns while trying to puzzle out stories inside my head and sort out random imaginary people, you love me even though you don't understand. To my husband and our kids: You are my world I love you more than words can express. Always.

CHAPTER ONE
RYAN

*P*UFFY HEAD, BIRD LEGS. THAT'S WHAT WE CALL IT. IN weightlessness, your blood doesn't flow the same way as it does while under the influence of gravity. All bodily fluids pool differently. On orbit, you live six months of your life with your head stuffed up like you have a bad head cold and skinny legs hanging out the bottom of your shorts.

I run a hand over the soft tips of my crew cut. I always get my head shaved before working on station because I hate the way my hair sticks up in zero-g. It's lunch time, and I can feel my stomach rumbling. I've been running a complex science experiment all morning, and my head hurts from the deep concentration and the built-up fluids.

When I hit the Harmony module and the table where we eat our meals, Xander is already there, munching on a sandwich made with a tortilla, of course. We don't use conventional bread up here because it makes too many crumbs that float around, get stuck in machinery, and generally make a mess.

As I enter, I glance over at the only other occupant in the module—medium height, strong build, light brown hair. My best friend, Xander, is chewing thoughtfully on his folded tortilla—no doubt filled with his favorite, peanut butter and grape jelly—

and staring at the chessboard fastened to the wall above our general workstation.

"Did Marshall send you a new move?" I ask as I fix myself a quick burrito made of reconstituted beans and rice folded inside my own tortilla. I make sure to add *lots* of hot sauce. It's the most popular condiment up here since our sense of taste is muted from the excess fluid in our heads. Spicy food and other strong flavors are at a premium on station.

Xander doesn't answer my question. His schedule included some maintenance work on the water recovery system this morning. Last time I had to work on that, it was an exercise in frustration. But Xander is a much more patient person than I am.

"What's the word from home today?" I follow up with another question when he doesn't answer the first one.

He's peering at the board, cocking his head to study the new move. "Payday today. Haven't heard from Karen yet."

"She's probably out shopping," I smirk. Karen has sent him something every single day—sometimes twice a day—since he's been up here. Pictures of the kiddo, notes. Little videos, funny memes. Xander is downright spoiled. I might be just a tiny bit jealous.

So, she's a little late today. Is that why he's so down? He checks at lunchtime every day and usually is quick to share whatever it is she's sent him. But today, nothing.

I finish the last bite of my burrito and push off from our dining table—a workbench, really, covered with straps and patches of Velcro to hold everything down. Bouncing off the ceiling above Xander's head, I grab the nearest strap to hold myself there, reorienting so that the ceiling is now my floor. It

took time to get used to all of that the first time I was up here over a year ago, but now I'm a pro at it.

Xander never had much of a problem with it. Maybe it's his honed pilot's skills. I stare at the board for a moment, calculating his possible moves. This chess set is magnetic, so the pieces won't float away unless pulled off the board.

"They're going to have you in checkmate in five moves," I say.

Xander throws me an annoyed glance. "I'm playing against the pooled resources of the entire Marshal Flight Center. All that nerdy engineering power versus just me."

I shrug. "*You're* the one who challenged them..."

Xander huffs, his eyes drifting back to the board. He seems off today. Could he be that bothered by the fact that Karen's email hasn't come through yet?

He changes the subject by picking the old one back up again. "And I suppose *your* entire check is going right into your bank account for a rainy day or for that Harley you've been eyeing."

I push away from the ceiling and go to the bag on the wall where our "bonus" food is located. Pulling out a thick rope of licorice, I break it in half, floating a piece over to him. He catches it and begins chewing along with me.

"Naw. This month I thought I'd spend mine on hookers and blow." I chuckle, and Xander responds with a scowl. "Don't be jealous, just because the little wife has already spent all yours."

"Don't think you'll find any hookers or much blow up here."

I shrug. "The cosmonauts might have a stash of cognac over on their side." I nod toward the *Zvedza* module of the station, and we share a knowing look. *Officially*, there's no liquor on station. But NASA has zero control over what the cosmonauts can—and do—bring with them.

I watch him again for a moment, noting the unusual silence, the muted mannerisms. The spacewalk tomorrow has got to be what's weighing on Xander's mind. After our group dinner tonight on the other side with the cosmonauts, where we'll share food and stories, Xander and I will get ready for our sleep period and spend the night in the airlock. There, the pressure will be reduced, and we'll breathe pure oxygen to prepare our bodies for the harsh environment of space.

But Xander has never done a spacewalk before. I've done three. Apparently, that makes me enough of a veteran to be the EV1 for this one.

The added stress is that this extravehicular activity wasn't planned. The ammonia coolant leak was only detected three days ago. It took Mission Control a full day to examine the problem and another day to devise a plan and walk us through it. And after lunch, we're going to go through a complete dry run again for the next few hours.

"It'll be a piece of cake, you know. We're just going out there to do that one thing. Normally an EVA takes six or eight hours. We'll be out there ninety minutes, max. Not even long enough to wet your MAG."

He rolls his eyes. "God, Karen has been teasing me about 'astronaut diapers' ever since she found out about the EVA."

"She teases you about everything. I hope the sex is hot enough to be worth it."

Xander smirks. "It's definitely worth it."

I grin and wink. "I still prefer the single life and all the variety I get."

Xander laughs. "Not if Karen has anything to say about it. She's still determined to find you a wife. I give you six months max after we get home before you're tied down somehow."

Making a face at him, I reach for my water pouch, adjusting the valve on the straw. "Thanks for the warning to stay the hell away from Karen when we get home."

I squeeze a globe of water out of my drink pouch and catch it with a wash cloth as it floats away. Rubbing the damp towel over my hands, I eliminate the sticky residue of the candy we just shared. The wet towel gets clipped on my personal peg so that as it dries, the moisture will be reabsorbed into the recycled water supply.

I push away from the wall and glide toward the exit that leads to Node 1, where we'll run through our rehearsal of tomorrow's big feat. "Let's go, bro. Back to the salt mines."

With a laugh, he follows me.

I jolted awake, my heart pounding and my head splitting open with pain. Nope, no puffy head, no extra fluids. And I could very distinctly feel earth's gravity pulling down every cell in my body against the surface of my own bed in my Southern California home.

Blinking, I waited for the world to come into focus. I hadn't awakened with a headache in a long time, but last night had been a shitty night. I stared up at the ceiling, still startled by the aching reality of the dream.

Xander, as real as if he'd been sitting beside me and laughing with me seconds before. Rubbing my eyes through my eyelids, I try to shake the spooked feeling and calm the racing of my heart. *Fuck.*

I glanced at the clock to confirm my suspicion that it was late—almost ten a.m. And the bed beside me was empty. I ran my hand over the sheets, perceiving that they were cold. Gray had been up a while already.

And with the thought of her, all the background tension came rushing back to pile on the fresh hurts of having seen Xander for that brief snippet of time. In timeless slumbering moments, I'd relived a portion of the last full day of his life in such vivid, realistic memory—almost exactly as it had actually happened.

Some details had changed but those particulars had blurred with time...and with my desire to push that day, and the days that followed, into the furthest reaches of my memory.

My palms came up to rub my forehead as I willed myself—and failed, at first—to get out of bed. The memory of those moments with Xander was fading fast—too fast. I wanted to grasp those feelings and keep them close while simultaneously willing them to evaporate into a mist like liquid nitrogen at room temperature.

I hadn't dreamed of Xander in months, long months...not since the memorial. Why now?

I pressed my open palms to my face, then dropped them, forcing myself to rise from the bed at last. A good hot shower would drive the spooked mood away, the shaky feeling deep in my bones.

But behind this fresh pain was the ache that remained from the day before. I had held Gray in my arms the entire night. While I listened to her light breathing and her clicking heartbeat, I'd buried my face in her soft hair. The entire night my mind raced, and I only slipped into sleep at dawn with the question and no answers flitting through my mind.

Gray's father, the illustrious Conrad Barrett, had dumped a pile of shit in my lap yesterday, though it felt like weeks ago, now. *What on earth gives you the arrogance to assume you even deserve her?* And in that moment, I'd felt like the lowest, filthiest heap of dirt, knowing with every beat of my heart the truth of those words. Then, Barrett had given me the ultimatum—end this thing between his daughter and me, or suffer the consequences.

I'd willingly suffer those consequences. *Without a second thought.* I squinted and let the steaming spray of my morning shower cleanse my face and massage my stiff muscles. But it couldn't relieve the tension. Because deep down, in the not-so-back of my mind, I knew that it wouldn't just be me suffering those consequences.

And I still hadn't figured out yet what the fuck I was going to do.

But there was one thing I knew I *wasn't* going to do. I wasn't going to let that bastard win. I would *not* lose her. It wasn't even an option.

Minutes later, I was back in the bedroom, dried off and slipping into a pair of sweats and a t-shirt, wondering what she was up to. I could hear the distant sound of an appliance being used in the kitchen. My blender, maybe? No... it sounded different from my blender. A higher pitch.

When I entered the kitchen, it looked like a major malfunction had transpired in my home. Empty bowls, mixing spoons, measuring cups piled in and around the sink...all lined up like ancient, befallen monoliths.

There were pools of flour on the counters and on the floor. Cracked and empty egg shells were scattered around. Jeez. It looked like she'd mugged a baker at knife point in there.

"What the hell happened in here?" I asked before modifying my tone. She jolted where she stood before an unfamiliar kitchen appliance—a gigantic stand mixer that did not belong to me. I never baked, so why would I even have something like that?

Maybe she really *had* mugged a baker?

The mixer switched off, and she put a hand to her chest. "You scared the crap out of me. I didn't wake you, did I? I waited till I thought I heard the shower to start mixing the frosting."

But the frosting was *everywhere,* all over the counter and the backsplash in giant pink-red splotches like baker's blood. I almost laughed at the thought. Were I not already deeply melancholy from that recent dream—and not a little annoyed by the disaster that was now my kitchen—I might have laughed.

Her eyes widened, following my gaze across the countertops. "I'm going to clean every bit of this up, I swear!"

My mouth quirked as I looked back at her, cute, sweet and that clicking heartbeat racing a mile a minute. She was adorable as ever, and I was already itching to pull her into my arms again.

But she was also a sticky mess.

"Where did *that* come from?" I pointed at the huge mixer.

"It's mine. I grabbed it from my place on the way back from having dinner with Pari last night. I've been feeling the itch to bake, and since it's Pari's birthday this week, I'm making angel food cupcakes for her."

A smile tugged at my mouth despite my best effort to remain stern. She had pink frosting on her cheek and mixed in her blond hair. With powdered sugar dusting the thin halter top that clung to her breasts, I was finding it hard to look away.

She raised her brows up at me imploringly. "Are you mad?"

I moved up beside her and dipped a finger into the bowl and tasted the frosting. "Mmm. Strawberries."

She smiled tremulously. "Strawberry buttercream frosting. You like?"

I ran another finger over her soft cheek, collecting another bit of frosting there. "I love the taste of strawberry."

We held a long gaze. Her eyes widened, and she visibly swallowed.

"I haven't frosted the cupcakes yet, but I'll definitely save you some. You want coffee? I made a pot."

I could definitely smell the coffee, but glancing in the general direction of the pot, I could only see more stacked dirty bowls in front of it. "Exactly how many mixing bowls does it take to make a batch of cupcakes? And exactly what army are you baking them for?"

The timer on the oven chimed, and she hurried to it, burying her hands into brand new oven mitts that I was sure I'd only ever used once or twice. She bent to pull a cupcake tin—presumably also a transplant from her place—out of the oven.

Of course, from this angle, I got a terrific view of her ass in sweat shorts, and my eyes slid down her smooth, long legs. The cupcakes graced the air with the heady scent of vanilla, but my mouth was now watering for her instead. Already, in her sunny presence, the gloom of the morning was starting to fade away to a distant, dim echo. But I could still hear it. If only in the very back of my mind.

Drowning it out while burying myself in her? Win-win.

Gray slid a new cupcake tray full of batter into the oven and set the other one atop a trivet. As she fussed with pulling the mostly rather-lopsided-looking cupcakes out of the tray and setting them on a cooling rack, I moved up behind her and placed my hands on her hips.

"You have demolished my kitchen, young lady."

She flicked a glance over her shoulder at me before resuming her task. "Promise it will look good as new. It won't bother you if you go spend some time in your office. Go relax with a cup of coffee. When you come out, you'll never know this disaster was here."

I ran a hand over her round, tempting ass, lowered my mouth to her neck, and wasn't surprised when I tasted more frosting off her salty skin. Her hands faltered in their task, and her posture wavered as I sucked at her neck.

When I brought my mouth up to her ear, I said "I think I'm owed some compensation for the use of my premises."

Her head tilted up, but she didn't turn to face me. My hands wandered, sliding across her waist to her front. There I cupped her breasts, teasing her nipples to hard, tight points in seconds.

"Pancakes?" she asked with a wide smile, as if I wasn't currently rubbing her up in preparation for some good clean—and dirty—fun. "I suck at baking and my cupcakes are lopsided, but I make killer pancakes. I'll make you pancakes for breakfast tomorrow."

My hands slipped inside her tank top. And—surprise—she wasn't wearing a bra.

When my palms connected with her soft skin there, she let out an involuntary gasp, wavering against me. I bit her ear. "And if I don't want to wait that long?"

"Those cupcakes in the oven have fifteen minutes left, and I have frosting all over myself."

"Hmm. A problem..."

She finished her task of pulling the cupcakes out of the tin and turned around to face me where I had her pinned against the counter. My hands slipped out of her shirt, my fingers itching to touch more of her delicate skin. She looked up at me, raising her brows. "Raincheck?"

I think not. As if in answer, I pressed my erection to her leg, and her mouth opened. I said, in the firmest tone I could muster, "I'm not so flexible right now. My schedule is very...*rigid.*"

Then I put paid to my seduction plans, determined to change her mind in the most pleasant of ways.

CHAPTER TWO
GRAY

RYAN HAD HIS MOUTH ALL OVER ME—MY NECK, MY chest, my collarbone. Apparently, rainchecks weren't in his vocabulary. And if I hadn't been conscious of that batch of cupcakes currently in the oven, I would have happily followed him down that primrose path.

Because he knew just how to get my engine firing with a few short kisses and touches in all the right places. His own little personal and perfected launch sequence.

Suddenly his phone chimed with a text message from where it perched on the charging station. He seemed unfazed as he swooped in to land another kiss on my mouth. I pulled back, knowing if this continued for even a half a minute longer, we'd be burning cupcakes and causing all manner of other disasters in the kitchen.

Besides, delayed gratification and all that. A girl had to play hard-to-get *once* in a while. I really needed to get these cupcakes done and hadn't bothered to tell him I'd screwed up this batch of icing and would have to make another one.

I never claimed to be a baking expert. "Go check your text. I have to call Dad here in a second, anyway."

A strange look crossed his face—one that I couldn't pick up on before it vanished. "Your dad?" he asked in a low voice. "What does he want?"

I shook my head. "I'm calling *him*. To check up on him. He was out of sorts the other evening when we were out to dinner together, and I think he wasn't feeling well. I asked him to check his blood sugar, so I'm following up to make sure he did it."

Ryan took a tiny step backward but otherwise did not change his expression. His eyes roamed my face speculatively. Then he swallowed hard.

I frowned. He'd been acting weird since he walked in here and found me wrecking his kitchen. Was he actually angry rather than just feigning it? I reached out to put my hand on his chest and ask him. But at that exact moment he turned away from me and went to the phone sitting upright on its charging stand.

I'd been using mine to time my batches, so I went to it and opted to send Dad a text instead of calling him. When I looked up again, Ryan was gazing into his phone and beaming a huge smile. I mean *huge*.

I almost gasped when I saw it. He looked unconditionally happy in that tiny slice of a moment. "Did someone sext you or something?"

He glanced at me, eyes twinkling, and shook his head, wordlessly holding the phone up so that I could see. It was a close up shot of a child's mouth. All you could see were nose, nostrils, lips, tongue and teeth—or lack thereof in the case of one of the upper incisors. Clearly a young child's mouth.

"Someone lost a tooth?" I prompted, suspecting who that someone might be and hoping fiercely that I was right.

"AJ," he said. "Remember when you gave me the idea a few weeks ago to send him a picture? I sent him one of Noah and Hammer doing a sim at work."

I nodded, smiling wide. "Did he like it?"

"Yeah. We've traded a couple other pictures back and forth—no real message, just photos. I got to see a video of Boba."

I raised my brows. "Fett?"

His smile faltered as he looked down at the phone screen again, shutting the app he'd been using. "The Freeds' dog. A chocolate lab. Xander... He loved that dog."

Oh, dear. No, this was not the direction this conversation should be going in. I wanted to see his eyes twinkle again. I reached for the phone. "Can I see that picture again?"

He opened the app and handed me the phone. I looked at the picture again and laughed. And happily, he laughed with me. "Wow...first tooth lost. Tonight he gets his first visit from the Tooth Fairy. How fun."

Ryan's brow trembled just slightly. He was thinking about Xander again—or, more likely, still—and probably reflecting that Xander was missing this first milestone. "I know. I think you should send him a picture of you frosting a cupcake."

His brow went up. "What? I didn't even bake these."

I shrugged. "Technicality. Come on, I'll show you how to do one and then take a short video of you icing a cupcake."

He looked doubtful, so I walked over to the counter where my cupcakes had cooled after taking them out of the oven, grabbed a flat knife, and modeled for him. First, I dipped the knife into the pink frosting. It was thin, so it didn't really cooperate.

"That looks like shit." He laughed when most of what I'd glopped onto the knife had subsequently glopped onto the counter. I laughed along with him as he stared into the bowl I'd just mixed. "What the hell happened to this frosting?"

I shrugged, still determined to complete my task. "I think I screwed up the butter somehow."

He picked up the slip of paper that contained my discombobulated notes on the recipe. "This says room temperature butter. Did you do that?"

"Yeah, melted butter, I put that in."

He frowned at me. "Room temperature, Gray. Not melted. There's a difference."

I glanced up at him as the second glop hit the counter. "Oops, yeah I melted it in the microwave. It was liquid. Like the stuff you put on popcorn."

He shook his head. "Gotta be able to read and process those instructions quickly."

I shook my head. "Sorry I'm not a brilliant astronaut."

He grinned, swooping in for a kiss on my cheek. "Nope, just a genius. A strawberry-flavored genius."

I shoved an unfrosted cupcake at him. "You have some new directions now. Frost the cupcake."

He laughed at me. "I'm not using that defective frosting. We're whipping up a new batch and doing it right, or this is not happening."

I heaved a sigh. "But it would have been funny with the gloppy stuff. AJ's six. He would find that funny."

He shook his head, his lips thinned and curled grimly. "I only do my best work. Always."

In no time, we had set the old bowl aside and whipped a new—and much better looking, I had to admit—batch of reddish-pink strawberry buttercream frosting.

Then he cooperated while I filmed a ninety-second video of him frosting a cupcake. However, for the sake of drama and of amusing a little kid, he did purposely glop some onto the counter for extra comedic effect.

I clicked the off button and showed Ryan the segment for his approval. Then he promptly sent the video off to AJ, again with that wide smile. Perhaps he was thinking about the kid's reaction to his comedic attempts. I bit my lip, watching him.

It was beyond obvious that Ryan adored that child, which made it all the more sad to me that he hadn't seen him in such a long time. Maybe we'd have to work on that. Maybe they could Skype each other? *Baby steps, Gray. He needs baby steps right now.*

I pointed to his glop of frosting. "I'll clean the rest of this mess up but I'm not cleaning up *that.* That's all on you."

He stared grimly at the mess and then set the phone down. "You're right. I should definitely clean it up." With one large finger, he scooped up the mess and then reached out and smeared it across my cheek.

"Hey!" I said. "What are you doing?"

That sparkle in his eyes had returned. "Cleaning up," he said as he swooped in to lick the frosting off my cheek. I wiggled away, and his hands came up to hold my shoulders still, and he held me to him. His mouth slid to mine, and we were kissing.

He tasted like frosting and mornings and anticipation. I could feel the tension in his body and the way he sought to touch every bit of my body that he could with his own.

Just then, the timer on the new batch of cupcakes dinged loudly. I separated from him and moved to the oven, putting on the gloves again to pull them out. He'd kept me so distracted that I hadn't had a chance to put batter in the other tin again. I put the hot tin of cupcakes on the trivet and turned to grab the now-cool and empty tin.

Suddenly, I felt a cold sensation on my upper shoulder, just below my neck. I turned, and Ryan was right behind me. "What was that?"

"I think I accidentally spilled frosting on you. Here." He traced a path along the top of my shoulder toward my neck, and I involuntarily shivered. In response, his other hand came up and cupped my other shoulder and his head dipped down to land right where he'd put the frosting.

Right there. In *that* spot. He was licking and sucking, getting every last bit as his hands traveled down my arms, clamping around my elbows to hold me still.

"Accidentally, huh?" I rasped, my voice sounding alien to my own ears. Likely it was my aroused voice. And likely he knew exactly what it meant when I talked this way.

He was an expert at turning me on and doing it quickly. Zero to Mach 5 in seconds flat. Probably easier than flying his training jet. My panties were already wet, and my nipples were painfully hard and probably very visible under my thin tank top.

I cleared my throat. "I, uh." And cleared my throat again. "Have another batch to do."

Without a word he reached out and turned off the oven. "Let's hit *pause* on that little project for now," he said in that low, gravelly voice of his. *His* aroused voice. I knew that voice, too, and it usually seemed in perfect sync with the tight squeezing sensation in my belly and lower that screamed for his hands and mouth—and other parts—to ease the tension and bring release.

"You are a wicked, wicked man."

"This I already know," he said between more kisses on the back of my neck that sent electric shocks down my spine and wound that tension deep inside me even tighter.

I spun in his arms, and though I could barely reach it, I managed to scoop up my own dollop of frosting from the edge of the metal mixing bowl. He watched me then raised his brow to ask the unspoken question—*where are you going to put that?*

My answer? I grabbed the hem of his t-shirt and rucked it up, holding it just below his collar, then liberally spread the frosting across his upper abs. *Double yum.*

He sucked in a quick breath, and that was enough to get me diving right in. "Mmm. What kind of mess do we have here? Better start cleaning up."

The frosting was sweet, creamy. Delectable, really. Buttercream was delicious. Buttercream slathered across Ryan's rock-hard abs? Perfection. He barely breathed as I ran my lips and tongue across the ridges, crevices and the rest of the unique geography of his torso.

The best part was when he let loose that low growl in the back of his throat. It always ratcheted up my blood pressure to hear it. When I straightened, Ryan said nothing before scooping up more frosting and, instead of smearing it on me, he spread it over the lower part of his stomach, just beneath his navel.

I bent down and licked him clean, noting with triumph the way his sweats tented with his arousal. So, he could get me wet in seconds, and I could get him hard just as quickly—or quicker.

Straightening, I reached for the bowl, but he was too fast for me, beating me there. He dipped in another finger and scooped up yet another blob of frosting. And as I watched his stomach to see what part I would be licking next, he instead seized my tank top by the strap and yanked it down enough to expose one of my breasts. I stiffened, coming up against his arm as he slowly, gently spread the frosting across my tender flesh.

And even more slowly, he sunk to lick and suck the frosting clean from my skin. But again, he took his time, rolling his tongue over and over my nipple, sucking hungrily, each intake pulling my insides more taut, more strained, like his mouth had a direct connection straight down into my core.

By the time he lifted his head, the fierce ache between my legs and the fire smoldering in my belly matched the heat in his own eyes. As quick as I could, I darted my hand to the bowl before he could and dipped my three fingers in, scooping up the frosting and smearing it across his mouth. Then I jumped up, locking my arms around his neck and pulling his mouth to mine while I licked up every bit.

All our sticky parts were adhering to each other, and I giggled as I sucked the buttercream off his lips, feeling that same strung-out feeling I always got when eating way too much sugar too quickly. That, coupled with the cranked-up sexual tension, was threatening to make me dizzy.

Ryan straightened, pulling me off the floor, and my legs quickly looped around his hips as he walked us toward the nearest counter. I locked my ankles around the small of his back, and he crushed our chests together.

Then he halted, hesitated, appearing to look for a bit of uncluttered counterspace. When he couldn't find any, his arm darted out, and he roughly scooted metal bowls and plastic measuring cups aside, sending some of them clanging to the floor, spilling their contents.

"This is going to take forever to clean up," I said, my mouth against his mouth.

His eyes boring into mine, he growled, "It will be worth it." Then he pushed my butt onto the cold, hard granite counter. "Whenever I see, smell, or taste a strawberry, I always think of you."

I smiled. He really liked my strawberry shampoo, a lot. As if mirroring my thoughts, he ran his fingers—from the non-sticky hand—through my hair.

"Don't ever cut your hair. I love running my fingers through it."

"That is the best reason ever not to cut my hair." I laughed, opting not to tell him about that cute pixie cut I'd been contemplating. Maybe I'd postpone that for a few months instead.

Pulling off my glasses, I stretched to find a safe spot to rest them far enough away from the clutter. If I was going to have some fun throw down with Ryan, I needed to protect the eyewear. While I was stretched out, my shirt rode up from my waist and Ryan bent to kiss me there on my bare skin. "Don't tell me you found more frosting."

"That one was just in case." He grinned. In the next minute, in one swift action, he pulled my top over my head. I barely got my arms up in time before it was discarded onto the floor beside the dirty bowls.

"Mmm," he groaned, eyes fixated on my naked chest. "I love it when you don't wear a bra."

Before I could reply, he had his mouth on my nipple, licking and sucking while I ran my fingers through his thick, soft hair, my eyes closing.

I wasn't even thinking about the cupcakes anymore. They were the furthest things from my mind. Or the mess we had made—and were about to make worse. Somewhere in the next few minutes of frenzied kissing and touching, Ryan mysteriously produced a condom from the pocket in his sweats. He must have been planning his morning seduction from the start.

I was excited to break the news to him later in the week that, pending a follow-up with my cardiologist, we wouldn't need to use the condoms anymore. But I was saving that as a little surprise.

Mere minutes later, I was sitting on that icy counter, naked and he was spending a great deal of time covering every inch of my bare skin with his wet, hot mouth. Even with my breathing in stutters and my eyes rolled up practically into my head, I'd recognized the drive behind his insistence.

He'd been getting so much better about it lately, but I could tell that something was bothering him, and he was using one of his old fallbacks for comfort. Fortunately for me, he'd chosen to turn to sex instead of vodka.

I'd try to talk him through it later but for now, I was just along for the breathless, exhilarating ride.

And oh, what a ride it was. We ended up pushing more items off the counter. My hands clung to his perfectly muscular back as he drove himself into me over and over again.

When I hit my climax, I threw my head back and let out a long moan which only seemed to fire him up more. He hitched my hips closer to him and increased his rhythm in earnest. When he pushed himself in deep, he buried his face in my neck and froze, the contraction of his orgasm rippling through me, too. I locked my legs around his waist and held him there, close to me, as he came down from that high. And slowly his body relaxed and softened in my arms.

I pulled back and looked into his face. "You look tired."

He smiled wryly. "I'm sated. You always make me so hungry."

He kissed me then, and reluctantly I let him pull away, loosening my hold around him. I quickly pulled my clothes back on and used the bathroom. By the time I got out, he had the dishwasher half loaded with my cupcake debris.

And after a brief break to grab coffee and eat a bit of breakfast, we spent the next hour—he was a surprisingly efficient cleaner—putting the kitchen back together.

But he seemed quiet, contemplative, and that weird mood he'd come out with was clinging to him again.

I let it be for then, confident that I'd get it out of him soon.

Finishing the remaining batches of cupcakes, I frosted them and put on the final touches. He busied himself the rest of the day with studying some technical manuals for the upcoming launchpad tests in Florida, followed by a solitary workout and run in the canyon. Then he spent a few hours holed up in his office working on the book with his biographer and assistant, Lee.

I didn't see him again until dinner, which we enjoyed in the now-spotlessly clean kitchen. But we actually didn't get to have a real talk until we went to bed that night.

"What's it like when you're launching?" I asked. We lay beside each other in bed, both on our backs, our fingers laced together and hands resting above us on our elbows. His thumb rhythmically stroked mine. As was our habit when we talked in bed together, we stared up at the ceiling instead of at each other.

"What do you mean? It's like riding a giant explosion all the way to orbit."

I blew out a breath. "No, it's *exactly* riding a giant explosion all the way to orbit, but give me something here. Make me feel the experience. Give me a simile or something."

I turned my head to look at him, and he blinked a few times, rolling his lips into his mouth as he contemplated that. "It's like...an explosion..."

"Stop! That's such a male way to describe it."

He frowned and turned to me. "Well that makes sense since I'm, you know, male."

I rolled on my side and met his gaze. "What's it *like*, Ryan? I want to feel it. I'll never get to actually live it except what I can see in movies or maybe an amusement park ride. But you've actually been there. You've done it...what 99.999% of the human race will never be able to experience."

He took that in with serious blue eyes, then reflected another moment. "It's like losing control—no, it's like being *under* the control of this massive force so much bigger than you that you are inconsequential. You are nothing in its wake. You feel the engines all gimballing underneath you, jockeying to keep the rocket balanced. It's like being lost in a full-blown hurricane. Like riding a herd of wild horses all at once." He took another long pause while I hung on his words and pictured what he was saying to me.

"Like...looking in your eyes," he finally concluded, his voice dying out.

I gave him a look. "I was with you up until that last one."

His eyes narrowed. "I was being serious."

I reached out and put my hand on his cheek. "You're going to have to up your cheesy one-liner game. I'm not a cheap date."

"Cheesy one-liners?" His eyebrows raised, and I couldn't tell if he was feigning affront or if he was truly insulted. "First of all, that wasn't a one-liner to get into your pants, because—newsflash—I already got there today. And two, because...because I meant it."

His cheek bulged when he clamped his mouth shut as if preventing himself from saying more, something too revelatory. But there was something in his eyes, a flicker of emotion that speared me right through the heart and wrapped around my lungs, making it a struggle to breathe.

Oh.

Our eyes connected, and my heart jolted and—wait, were there prickles in the backs of my eyes? Was I tearing up from his words?

And had my flippant non-acceptance cut him off from expressing something even deeper?

They were incredibly sweet words. And I could tell from the earnest look on his face that he *did* mean it. I smoothed his cheek again.

"I'm sorry. That's a stupid bad habit of mine. To cut off anything that might be nice or flattering."

He mirrored my action, putting his large hand on my cheek. I swallowed, suddenly overcome with emotion. He whispered, "You haven't had enough nice things said to you throughout your life. I'm making it my mission to change that, Gray Barrett. Because you deserve nothing but the kindest words and actions for the rest of your life."

Okay, now an actual, real tear pooled at the corner of my eye, but I blinked hard so it wouldn't spill and give me away. I took his hand where it was still laced with my own and I kissed the rough, slightly hairy, very male back of it. "Thank you. I—" I. Love. You, I wanted to say. *I love you. Iloveyou. Iloveyousomuch.* The thought of those words escaping my lips made me simultaneously terrified and giddy.

Should I say it? Should I voice the words that were hanging in the air between us, anyway? Was that what he was hoping my response would be? I cleared my throat and gave my head a small shake, my tongue suddenly leaden.

And he leaned forward and planted a firm, decisive kiss on my lips.

When we pulled apart again, minutes later, we were breathing quickly. And he was staring into my eyes again with that look that was so intense it was like a probe straight through to my heart. Like he was searching to see what I was hiding.

But I knew, deep down, that he wasn't ready to see it. So I made the split-second decision to cut the tension with some humor.

"You *do* have cheesy one-liners, though. Even if that wasn't one of them."

He scoffed at me, settling back against his pillow. "No way."

"I imagine you haven't had to up your one-liner game because you've got so much else going for you but…let's see. *Let me take you to the Moon.* And what was that first one you used on me at the restaurant that day of the investors meeting?" I lowered my voice in an attempt to imitate him while holding my hand out in my best mockery of arrogant, cocky male. "*You can't handle this? Not every girl can…*"

He rolled his eyes and scrubbed his forehead with the palm of his hand while flushing. His embarrassment was obvious. He had been a jerk, so I didn't feel bad for making him pay for it a little belatedly.

"You'd just met me and you wouldn't shake my hand," he said. "It's not a defense for it, but..." His eyes flicked back to me. "Why didn't you shake my hand, anyway?"

Because I had a massive crush on you before I'd even met you, and you intimidated the hell out of me? No, no...too much information, Gray. I'd save those revelations for later. "My hand was sweaty. I was self-conscious."

He grinned. "Really?"

When I nodded, his grin progressed into a laugh.

"You still don't remember that wasn't the first time we met, do you?" I asked.

His features sobered as if I'd dowsed him in ice-cold water. "I'm not so confident you are truthful with that story you tell. I would *not* have forgotten meeting you."

I raised my eyebrows at him. "Seriously dude? That's where you're going to dig in? You know I'm in the right about this. I have witnesses who include all three of the men you work the closest with."

He rolled his eyes and muttered, "Conspiracy theory."

"It was at that happy hour mixer about a week or maybe two before the investors meeting."

He crunched up his brows in thought. "Uhhh. That time we all did that get together at the bar? You were there?"

I blew out a breath in mock disgust though I was not surprised. "How drunk were you, actually?"

He'd been at the bar when I'd entered, wearing jeans, a button-down shirt and a bomber jacket. Looking more delicious than every photo I'd ever seen of him—and I'd seen plenty.

As a bona fide space nerd, I was one of the few who could claim knowing who he was even before the accident that had made him world famous. The night we met, the bar had been busy—mostly with people from XVenture. This was Tolan's idea of company bonding—noisy, crowded, cramped and all.

I'd entered with Marjorie, the head of the health team and hopefully my soon-to-be boss, and a couple of the doctors who would work as flight surgeons. The group of us sat down at a big table across from the other three astronauts. Marjorie made introductions, and Kirill Stonov had stood and formally shaken all of our hands before beckoning the almighty famous and heroic Commander Ty from whatever was occupying him at the bar. From what I could tell, it was a bottle of beer and a blonde in a very short, tight skirt who was standing close to him and hanging on every word that came out of his mouth.

Kirill almost had to physically pull Ty away from that blonde who had made as if to follow him before Kirill waved her off.

"Marjorie, have you met Ryan Tyler?" the cosmonaut said. Kirill proceeded to give all of our names and Tyler's eyes skimmed over the four of us before tilting his head jauntily and making a two-fingered, mock salute.

"Good to meet all of you. Of course, I already knew you, Marjorie."

"Likewise, Commander Tyler," said one of the surgeons sitting to my right.

I laced my fingers together and straightened in my seat, opening my mouth to ask him a question when he stepped back and turned.

"Excuse me a moment, I have to go take care of something." He reached for his back pocket, pulling out a wallet, acting as if he was *going to settle his bill at the bar. Obviously, he'd bought the woman a drink—or was about to.*

She'd been staring at his back since the moment he'd left to come talk to us and ignored anyone else who tried to talk to her—like the dude right next to her who'd been trying to get her attention for the last five minutes.

When Ty turned back to the bar, her grin grew massive, and she actually did a little hop in her heels. Predictably, Tyler never came back to the table.

Nevertheless, we'd had a good time getting to know the other three astronauts, but it hadn't prevented me from throwing annoyed looks in his direction. He never even looked back, having forgotten about us two seconds after he'd turned his back.

Well, well, well. I guessed media reports had been more accurate than I'd been hoping.

When he left a few hours later with his new companion, I stared daggers at his leather-clad back so hard he must have felt them.

My stomach sank. Well, as they say, you should never meet your heroes.

And selling that arrogant jerk to my dad as the face of the new XPAC program was going to be nearly impossible.

What the hell were we going to do?

By the time I'd recounted the entire thing to Ryan, he had both hands over his face, the skin on his neck a shade of cherry red. He was too mortified with himself to even laugh.

I laughed, though, and encouraged him to do the same.

"I get it, you didn't think you had a lot to say to a psychologist and a couple of doctors. Your kind normally avoids our kind like the plague."

He dropped his hands and smiled lightly. "It's an unspoken astronaut rule that we never fraternize with the health team. Especially the shrinks."

I blinked a couple times, my mouth crumpling to prevent a smile. "Well that's another one you blew out of the water."

He laughed along with me, and when our gazes met, I could see that the laughter did not reach his eyes. There was something there, something heavy and a little dark. A sadness, perhaps.

I wanted to pull him into my arms and ask him why he was sad. Instead, he reached out to me, pulling me tightly to him. "Come here," he whispered, nestling me closely to him. My body melded to the shape of his, fitting him very close. "I'm sorry. I was a complete idiot for not noticing you then."

I tilted my head to kiss him on the neck and get a full whiff of his seashells and lime smell that always made my insides jiggle and tingle more than a little.

"On the bright side, it's given me something to tease and hold over your head all these months."

But that solemnity still clung to him like damp mist, and his arms tightened. "I love listening to your heart beat when it's so quiet it's the only thing I can hear."

And soon my eyes were heavy, and I felt safe and completely at ease in his strong arms.

My face pressed against his warm, solid chest. The last thing I remembered before drifting off were his words, merely a wisp of a breath into my hair like a breeze, like a premonition. *"I'm sorry."*

***

Sundays were becoming my favorite mornings...as long as I woke up in the arms of a sexy, handsome man, no matter how exhaustively he was sleeping.

I snuck kisses on him—his face, his neck, his arms—and he didn't stir. That was the litmus test of how tired he was. If he didn't move, even when tempted by the promise of morning sex, then he needed more sleep. And since he laid there like a log, I decided to make good on my promise of the previous day and make pancakes for breakfast while he finished sleeping in.

Ryan typically was an early riser but yesterday and now today, he appeared to have been sleeping very restlessly. Added to that, his melancholy seemed to have lasted the entire weekend. Was there an anniversary date that I wasn't aware of? Had something happened to remind him of the accident or pull at him?

He seemed genuinely happy to be in contact with Xander's family again. And as far as I knew, nothing terrible had happened on this date the previous year or earlier. It could be anything really. I'd just have to get him to tell me what it was.

And getting that man to open up involved some epic strategizing that would put Napoleon Bonaparte to shame. I decided to contemplate my plan of attack while making breakfast.

And as pancakes were one of exactly three foods I knew how to cook, I was in luck. I searched his cupboards and pantry for the necessary ingredients, happy to find them. There was even a bottle of maple syrup in the fridge, which clued me in that he liked them too.

So here I was, at the ripe old age of twenty-five, making breakfast for the very first man I'd...

I'd what? The guy I was sleeping with? The guy I was having sex with? My boyfriend?

None of those really fit.

I added flour to the batter, beating furiously to prevent lumps and being extra careful not to mess up the kitchen this time. I thought about our conversation the night before when I'd cut him off by laughing at something he'd said when he'd been so serious.

He'd said that riding a rocket was like being in a hurricane, on the backs of wild horses and like looking in my eyes. *Like losing control.*

Was that how he felt? And if so, did that mean he—he felt the same way as me?

Maybe he was afraid to tell me because I hadn't said it to him first. Maybe he was waiting for that.

The thought of telling him felt something like I'd imagine it would feel to jump out of a plane. Exhilarating. Terrifying. Potentially life changing.

I bit my lip as I stirred vigorously. Maybe it was because I always played it safe? Maybe *he* was afraid of scaring *me* off by telling me his feelings.

I stirred harder, banging the spoon furiously against the side of the plastic bowl. *Besides,* I wasn't even sure I'd be able to keep it inside much longer. It wanted to burst out of me.

Just then, I thought of the most ingenious way to tell him...

CHAPTER THREE
RYAN

I'M IN THE BAR AGAIN. IT'S HAPPY HOUR WITH THE NEW work colleagues. I really didn't want to come, but what choice do I have? I've been with XVenture roughly a week now and Tolan wants the astronauts to play nice with the rest of the team. I like bars well enough—and drinking even better, especially lately. But I've got to stay sober. This is a work thing after all.

Plus, after the motorcycle accident, I vowed to cut back on the drinking—even though I hadn't been drunk when I'd wrapped the damn thing around a tree. I *had* been speeding, though. And hot dogging—lost in the velocity. I'd come out of that incident without a scratch, lucky me. The bike however...

The insurance guy had almost started sobbing when he'd witnessed what I'd done to that Harley. I'd paid him extra to keep it quiet, but somehow, of course, the media had gotten hold of the info, too.

Now I'm here at my new job a week after that accident and hoping no one asks me about it. Besides this new group of people seem nice once they get over all the fawning and hero-worship that makes me want to put toothpicks through my eyes.

Hopefully, the XPAC will get our funding soon and we'll be able to train in earnest. Things are looking hopeful. I sip at my icy mug of beer and someone is talking to me—I hear a woman's voice but I'm not looking at her. I'm staring into my beer instead. Kirill taps me on the shoulder and speaks to me in Russian. "Come over to the table. There are new people to meet." I know this is where I'm going to meet Gray for the first time, but I know I don't know her yet so it doesn't make sense that I'd know.

And this doesn't feel like a memory. A memory I still don't have.

I roll my eyes and turn to say something to my companion, but she's not there. Turning back to Kirill, I see that he's gone, too. In fact, the bar is completely empty and utterly silent. I flick a glance at the table to see if Kirill has left without me. There's only one person sitting there.

I meet the man's eyes. He's definitely not Kirill—older, balding, thinly built and wearing an ill-fitting suit. He's looking at me with narrowed eyes and a hardened jaw.

I freeze, holding that hostile gaze.

Conrad Barrett. Fucking Conrad Barrett. The man who wants to steal from me the one ray of hope I have in this life. Yank it out of my grasp forever.

My entire body tenses, fists clenching, jaw clamping, and I stare back at him with an equal amount of heat. "Fuck you, Barrett," I mutter. "I'm not giving her up."

He shakes his head. "How badly do you want to fly again?"

"Go ahead and pull out. You'll be ruining her dreams, too."

His brows raise. "I'm not the one ruining her dreams. It's you. You ruin everything. And everything you touch breaks, turns to dust. *Dies.* I want you far away from her."

"Yes," a third voice says, though I wasn't aware there was a third person in the room with us. I jerk my head to the left, and he's standing at my shoulder, staring into my eyes. We're in our EMUs without the helmets on, but our heads are wrapped up in our Snoopy caps.

My throat seizes when my eyes meet his golden hazel gaze. *Xander.*

I look around again and see that we're no longer in the bar. I'd recognize the white plastic walls of the station anywhere. And the smell—a mixture of perpetual new car smell and the faint traces of garbage and human body odor.

The realization hits me like a brick, and I'm weightless again, floating beside my best friend. I should be happy to see him. *Happy.*

But he's not smiling.

"Ty," he says in a quiet voice, one of restrained emotion. "What the fuck are you doing?"

I blink. "I'm—I'm—" My mouth opens and closes again a few times as I search for words.

"You promised," he shoots at me again, his words clipped and penetrating, like bullets from a gun. "Don't your promises mean anything?"

"I'm going to do it, man. I'm going to fly again. For you. I've thought about that promise every day—"

Xander's gaze is flat, devoid of emotion—devoid of belief. In the next second, the walls around us have vanished though we're still weightless. Now we're outside station though neither of us is wearing a helmet.

There's a gorgeous field of stars behind Xander—a darkness that can only be perceived when we have crossed the terminator and are on the night side of the planet. Otherwise, the brilliant earth below drowns out all the stars. But I can see them, which means that it is night. Which means that it is—

"*Dark*," Xander speaks the word aloud as if it is right out of my head. We aren't tethered. We're drifting out. Station is getting smaller and smaller. "You never used to be afraid of the dark. Why are you now?"

And before I can answer him, he belts out another question. "Why are you so afraid—all the time?"

"Please. Forgive me." My voice comes out as nothing more than a strangled whisper.

He shakes his head. "Stop all this bullshit." Then his jaw tenses and his face flushes. He jerks a hand up toward me. "What did I die for, Ty? Huh?"

There's a vise around my throat and I can't breathe, though I'm gasping. We should be dead already. I look around. Station is another speck among the stars, and Earth is a distant, blue sphere.

"Don't look away. Look at me." But when I do, I see that he's having trouble breathing. His voice is hissing, gasping, the way he sounded over the comms when it was near the end. When he said goodbye forever.

He coughs violently. "What did I sacrifice my family for? I gave up everything for you to live, so you could come back and, what, fuck around?"

Xander's words and behavior, the stare in his haunted eyes, are so unlike him and yet so much him at the same time. The eyes are hard as rock and devoid of emotion.

Dead.

Dead like him.

I sucked in a frantic breath and came awake coughing, gasping as if I really had just been floating through a vacuum with no protection. The room spun as I sat up, trying to figure out why there was no moisture in my mouth. I stared at the far wall and his eyes stared back at me like an image burned into my brain.

Sweat dripped down my forehead as an arc of pain stabbed through my head, pulsing in sync with the beat of my heart.

Without hesitating another second, I fought through the covers on the bed and pulled myself out, stumbling to the bathroom where I first splashed an inordinate amount of cold water on my face.

And as I did so, the words ran through my head. *Just a dream. Just a dream. It was just a dream. Just a dream.*

What are you doing, Ty? That question cut through all the rest of the noise. That question, asked in Xander's accusatory voice. If anything, the pain in my head blossomed into a full-blown migraine headache—the kind I only got when I was on orbit due to the carbon dioxide air scrubber not functioning properly on the station.

As if in reality I had been there, the headache was a reminder.

I jumped into the shower and cranked the heat up to skin-flaying lava temperature—high as I could tolerate it. Squeezing my eyes shut, I shoved my face under the direct spray.

What the fuck was I going to do?

Barrett's narrowed eyes. His single question. His threats.

Everything you touch breaks, turns to dust. Dies.

My heart was still racing from seeing Xander again—a mixture of joy at being there with him, like the dream from the morning before, but blended with the obvious disgust in his voice. The same disgust I felt for myself.

I pulled my face out of the spray and leaned my head back. The pain drilled its way into my temples. I grabbed the soap and worked rotely through my hygiene routine while I thought.

I was putting off the inevitable. The decision.

I wanted to ask her what I should do, but doing so would only be passing the buck. I'd be dropping the responsibility on her.

And it would throw a bomb into the middle of her relationship with her father. I'd already been responsible for destroying one father-child relationship—Xander's and AJ's. I couldn't do it again.

Because in the end, she *would* hate me for leaning on her. For passing along to her the hard choice that had been thrust at me.

I was alone in this decision. And Xander's eyes accused me every time I closed mine.

Since I couldn't stand being in the dark anymore, I wondered how long it would be before I wouldn't even be able to close my eyes. Could a man die of self-imposed sleep deprivation?

I pressed my hands hard against my eyes.

Was I man enough to do what needed to be done?

Quick and dirty. Rip off the bandage, Tyler. Just fucking rip it off in one sharp tug.

The thought of how much it would hurt to tear off that particular bandage left me gasping for air. It wouldn't just sting for a few minutes. It would fucking eviscerate me.

Dark dread pooled in the pit of my stomach, where indifferent, stony determination congealed.

I couldn't do it.

But I had to.

Yes, I knew I *would* do this, but I'd fucking hate myself forever. Even more than I already did.

Probably more than humanly possible.

Fuck.

CHAPTER FOUR
GRAY

I WAS ALMOST READY TO BRING MY MAD-GENIUS PLAN INTO fruition in the kitchen. A thrill zinged through my heart as I took the bowl over to the heated pan on the stove and ladled in a small amount of batter. I'd learned this trick while recovering from my last surgery in the rehabilitation center. My nurse had given me a few cooking lessons.

I flicked my wrist, smiling at the perfectly heart-shaped pancake. *Yes!*

Repeating my feat, I made a whole stack, perfectly sized and shaped, and loaded them on a plate. Then I turned to the breakfast tray I'd prepared earlier, set up perfectly and ready to go.

I folded the cloth napkin into a U-shape and set it on the breakfast tray to the right of the plate, smiling at my work.

And, as I'd heard the shower going, I knew he was awake.

Picking up the tray, I crept into the bedroom and balanced it on its stand atop the comforter, angling it to optimize how he saw it the first time he looked.

Faster than you could say *HolyShitThisIsScary*, Ryan opened the bathroom door and entered the bedroom again wearing only his underwear. *Perfect timing.* Like I'd choreographed it.

"Hey," he grunted at me, then turned to go into his closet—presumably to grab some clothes. I frowned. What the...?

He was supposed to walk straight toward me, come take me in his arms adoringly and gaze over my shoulder at the breakfast I'd so painstakingly prepared for him.

I frowned, folding my arms over my chest. Then I positioned myself directly in front of the tray, waiting.

Minutes later, he reentered the room fully clothed in jeans and a t-shirt. His hair was wet and disheveled. I doubted he had even brushed it after he got out of the shower.

Typically, he didn't shave on the weekends, so his whisker growth from Friday morning was now dark on his cheeks and jaw.

But beneath that, his skin was pale as paper and he looked exhausted.

Like he hadn't slept at all.

I frowned. "Did you have a rough night?"

He blew out a breath and ran a hand through his wet hair as if to flatten it. "You could say that."

"Hopefully you can be cheered up with a nice fat stack of..." I moved aside to throw my hands out, waggling them jazz-hands style, indicating the tray. "Pancakes! As promised."

He was silent as he took in the place setting, blinking several times. Meanwhile, my heart thumped a mile a minute.

Because with this gesture I was saying a whole lot more.

On the tray, using the pancakes as the center piece of my message, the utensils and the folded napkin, I had spelled out the words I (heart) U.

I'd done it. There would be no doubts now.

Gray, the girl who always played it safe, was jumping out of the plane, trusting that her parachute would open at just the right time.

I clenched my fists as he studied the tray, digging my short nails into my palms while I waited for his reaction.

When it came, it was a study in the expressiveness of his handsome features.

First there was uncomprehending amusement. Then sudden realization. Then shock, his jaw dropping, brows raising. He swallowed, his mouth closing, thinning.

"I don't..." he shook his head.

"It's a message. From me, of course. It shouldn't be hard to figure out."

Still studying the tray, he went a shade paler, if that was possible. His features clouded but not enough to conceal the clear internal struggle.

And that's when I realized I'd screwed up.

Gray had jumped out of the plane, and now she was yanking the ripcord to her parachute.

It wasn't opening.

Ryan's eyes closed, and his own fists clenched at his sides.

I gulped at the air. So, he didn't feel the same way. It wasn't the end of the world, was it? I held out an imploring hand. "It's okay, Ryan. You don't—I mean, I wasn't expecting you to say it back. I just thought—"

He took in a deep breath and opened his eyes to look at me. And what I saw there...

What I saw there sent my innards into a full plummet. Falling. Down. Down. Down.

My breath hissed out of my lungs. I blinked, feeling slightly dizzy.

"We can't do this," he rasped, jamming his fists into his pockets. "This is over. I'm sorry. It's not—"

I shook my head, holding out a hand. "Do not say 'it's not you; it's me.' *Don't...*"

Those blue, blue eyes of his held mine in a vise grip. I couldn't tear them away, even as my own threatened to fill with tears.

"Gray. I'm sorry. But this has to end. And it has to end now."

I would not cry. I was the expert at keeping my tears in. I'd grown up perfecting the technique. I could do this...

I tore my eyes from his, swallowing the bitterness at the back of my throat and turned. Calmly picking up the tray, I turned and walked out of the room and back to the kitchen. Without a word, without a thought, I dumped the pancakes from the plate straight into the garbage as his words turned around and around in my head.

I wanted to argue with him, but that look in his eyes had made it clear.

There would be no changing his mind. And I should have fucking known better. Well at least he didn't do it over the phone, so I guess I was a very wobbly and miserable one-up on Suz, the trainer-with-benefits.

Pari had warned me weeks ago as if she'd been able to see what was coming, see what I couldn't. Maybe because she was a player herself, she could identify with Ryan. She had some special insights to what made him tick that I did not. However, I doubted Pari would be so cruel as to string someone along for weeks and allow them to develop feelings for her.

But she'd known this might happen and she'd warned me.

And I hadn't listened.

I cursed my own past arrogance and stupidity. My vain belief that I, Gray the almighty psychotherapist-in-training, had all the answers.

I stood staring down into that trash can for way too long, the plate and fork frozen in the air above. What the hell should I do now? My mind was numb, like I'd just been hit and was trying to recover. What were my options, really?

Well, it was obvious. The first thing I needed to do was *leave*.

Sucking in a deep breath, I put the dishes in the sink. He could clean up the mess, for all I cared. Then I went to the guestroom where most of my things were and pulled my suitcase out from under the bed.

My insides twisted into a familiar deep freeze as I gathered my things and robotically packed them into the case. My mind, however, was a thousand miles away.

And the only question it was asking—on repeat to the beat of every movement I made—*Why? Why? Why?*

I don't even know when he appeared in the doorway. I just turned my head slightly to grab a new pile of clothes and spotted him out of the corner of my eye. I jerked my head in his direction and our gazes met. He looked...

What was that look? Partial hurt, partial relief? Was he relieved?

I stepped back from the suitcase and turned to face him, my arms folded over my chest, my chin high. My eyes sparred with his deep blue gaze.

I wasn't going to grovel.

No matter what my heart wanted me to do, he'd never see me beg. A girl had to keep her pride.

I drew in a long breath through my nose. He tore his eyes away first, nodding to the suitcase. "I'll help you out with your stuff when you're ready."

It was delivered in a low, flat voice, but it hit me like a slap. My throat seized, and I could hardly even breathe. I wanted to scream, cry, fall on the floor, and punch his face all at once.

Fuck emotional maturity. *Fuck it all to Hell.*

I wanted to stomp my feet and have a full-blown tantrum. Instead I just stood there, my arms locked in the grip of each of my hands.

"This is what you want," I finally muttered in a small voice. It wasn't a question.

He frowned. "I'm sorry?"

"No, you're not." I shook my head and cleared my throat, speaking in a more forceful voice so that he could hear me. "This is what you want. What you wanted my reaction to be."

His features froze, and they reminded me a bit of a blank wall. His blue eyes hardened, and silence rang out between us, clashing through the air like the cacophony of church bells.

He finally took a deep breath. "I don't want to hurt you."

"It's exactly what you want. What better way to get me out of the way? To stop this whole *babysitting* thing? You start something between us and then end it just as abruptly. Push me aside as easily as you did Suzanne the trainer—"

I cut myself off when he visibly stiffened, his hands once again clenching so hard that the veins on his forearms bulged. He took one step into the room and stopped. "That's *not* what this is."

"Do you mind telling me exactly what this *is*, then? Because from where I sit, it seems like a very concerted effort to get rid of me. I mean, what better way to eliminate me as someone you'll ever have to work with directly?"

His brow crumpled, and his gaze intensified. "I wasn't using you. I wasn't—" He shook his head, muttering to himself as he ran a hand through his hair.

"But you want to take my things to the car. You want me to go."

He closed his eyes and then opened them again, looking deeply into mine. "Yes. You need to go."

I stood frozen for a moment, hardly able to collect my thoughts, hardly able to work around the fresh hurts he heaped right on top of the slightly older ones. Like a compost pile.

But if I did this, if I walked away, I'd be compromising everything. I'd be quitting the work that had been important to me in the first place. Ryan Tyler had succeeded in getting under my skin—in more ways than one—and getting into my brain. Perhaps it had been a concerted effort to try to control me.

Or maybe it had been a game, and he was just the player who had let something go too far and now had to end it.

I went back to my suitcase, grabbed the stack of underwear, and put it back into the drawer I'd just emptied, following suit with my t-shirts and socks.

"What are you doing?" he asked after quietly watching this production for a few minutes.

"I'll tell you what I'm *not* doing," I grabbed three pairs of shoes and plopped them back on the floor of the closet. "I'm *not* leaving here."

He blinked a few times before reacting. "You have to. I'm asking you to."

I turned to him and jerked my hand in his direction, pointing a stiff finger at him. "It's not up to you. I'm here because XVenture and the future XPAC have a vested interest in me being here. In making sure you behave yourself. I've obviously screwed up big time over the past few weeks, and that's on me. But I'm. *Not.* Leaving."

His chin came down and his eyes narrowed, his hand gripped the doorjamb until his knuckles whitened. "Under the circumstances, it's best if you don't stay," he said in a low, almost dangerous voice.

I reached into my back pocket, whipped out my phone, and held it out to him. "How about I dial Tolan's number and you explain that to him right now? You have my permission to tell him all about the *circumstances*."

His brow trembled again as if he was completely confused by my behavior. Nevertheless, he did not touch—nor did he even look at—my phone. Instead, he just watched me, frowning. As if I confused him.

Fine. Let him be confused. With a disgusted sigh, I stuffed the phone back into my jeans. "Since I'm not going to need your help taking this to my car, you don't really need to stand and wait for me to finish. I'm sure you have work and things to get done today."

With that declaration, I pulled out the last bit of my remaining things, threw them onto the bed, and then very pointedly shoved my suitcase back under the bed. Then I turned my back on him and began to refold the clothes I'd dumped out.

When I turned and looked minutes later, he was gone.

I fell onto the bed with a soul-rending sigh and stared unseeing into the open closet for a long while, replaying that entire conversation in my head. And then rewinding to the previous conversation in his room and the moment he'd seen the pancakes. And then rewinding to the conversation before that, lying in bed beside him, staring into his eyes.

Him telling me that looking into my eyes was like losing control.

I blew out a long breath, pleased with my strength, that my ability to hide the tears was still intact. It was my superpower, really, honed from a childhood where I'd been determined to keep my parents calm, keep them from panicking.

Even when I felt the keenest of fears, the deepest of sorrows that I couldn't go out and run and play with the other kids, or even when I was hurting, physically or emotionally, I'd kept it in for the sake of my parents. To keep them happy. To keep them from falling apart.

I may have been the sick one, but I was never, *ever* the weak one.

And Ryan would find that out too.

***

One of my modern psychology idols, Elizabeth Kubler-Ross, defined grief in five stages. And when you lose someone, whether by death or rupture of a relationship, a person suffers all of them at one point or another. Sometimes many times over.

And though I'd like to say that having that knowledge and my training might have helped me to handle things better, I know it's never that easy.

First Stage: Denial and the Search for Answers

I spent way too much time that night staring up at the blank white ceiling—ridiculously unable to turn off the light until I'd forced myself to do so. I'd grown used to having it on all night in the short month since I'd started sleeping beside Ryan in his bed. But now I'd been viciously yanked back to my old life. And I—unlike him—had no problem with the dark.

So out of spite, I turned it off as soon as I realized what I was doing. But I stared up at that ceiling unable to believe he'd heartlessly break things off without even the blink of an eye after my admission of love for him. I swallowed, remembering how hard it had been to summon my courage to admit to my feelings in the first place. And I'd done it in such an indirect, nonthreatening way for fear of scaring him off.

Ha!

How could I have been so wrong?

I was quick to remonstrate myself for not having seen this coming but at least I didn't cry. No, no, I wouldn't cry.

I got next to no sleep that night, as strung out as I was on these thoughts. My eyes had finally closed about thirty minutes before my alarm went off.

But I already knew the house was empty. Ryan had left an hour before that, just as sunlight started to touch the eastern horizon.

I checked my phone, hoping to see a text from him. But...nothing.

So I got ready, feeling hollow, aching in every bone of my body.

But I had work to do. And I wouldn't let this stop me.

CHAPTER FIVE
RYAN

THAT GODDAMN BANDAGE METAPHOR. FUCK THAT noise.

It wasn't like ripping off a bandage. At all. It *was* like ripping out an organ with my own bare hands, *digging* it out. A bloody and vital organ. Not a kidney. I could live a lifetime with only one kidney. Maybe the liver? Would the removal of the liver cause a person to slowly die a prolonged and painful death?

No, I wasn't actually dying. But sometimes, I literally felt that way. Like medieval torture evisceration. It felt like how I imagined it might feel to be hung, drawn, and quartered.

Slow torture.

And the last thing I wanted to do was to sit at a table in a room full of bright lights beside XVenture CEO Tolan Reeves and the chief designer of our Phoenix space capsule, facing the clicking shutters and questions from the media.

But I'd gotten here nice and early for this. Though I hadn't succeeded in fooling myself that it had nothing to do with getting away from her. Since the breakup, I'd spent the last few nights practically climbing the walls of insomnia and insanity. I tossed and turned knowing that she was just a few rooms away from me curled up in her bed, all alone and thinking I didn't give a fuck about her.

Every night, I had to stop myself from busting through the door into her room and pulling her into my arms, whispering my apologies and making everything right again. I was slowly growing obsessed with the thought of it.

So obsessed that I'd barely prepared myself for this stupid press function I now found myself at the center of. We'd just made the official announcement about the test flight, and now the media wanted their pound of flesh.

The banner on the table where we sat bore the logo of the XPAC—XVenture Private Astronaut Corps—the X featuring the exhaust trails of two rockets crisscrossing. Before us, beyond the bright lights, were several dozen of the most dedicated space press.

I laced my fingers tightly in front of me and focused on the journalist asking the next question.

"How does NASA feel about you defecting to the commercial side, Commander Ty?"

I responded by rote and without hesitation. "My relationship with NASA remains positive and productive," I lied glibly. In truth, there was no relationship to speak of. But Victoria had prepared me well for this press conference. She was *very* good at her job. She stood off to the side, scoping the press from her vantage point and typing notes into her phone. On the table beside my arm, my mobile screen lit up.

Victoria: Tabloid reporters here. Brace yourself for some Keely questions. Came the text.

I looked up into bright lights, a video camera, and some flashes. Catching a glimpse of a slender blond figure in the back of the room, I hesitated. Suddenly, the tie around my neck felt tight, and I was swallowing to work moisture into my throat.

It wasn't like I didn't see her often enough—at work, at least. I'd perfected how to avoid her at home. Leave before she did, get home just before sundown, stay in the opposite side of the house than the one she occupied. Only occasionally did we cross paths in the kitchen, but aside from exchanging a few glances, we never spoke. At work it was only in passing—the lunch room, a hallway, various meetings with dozens of our closest colleagues. It sucked.

And yet as much as I tried to avoid her, I still looked forward to seeing her every damn day.

But every time I *did* see her, it was like reopening the same self-inflicted wound, feeling every bit of that missing organ. The soreness of something vital that had suddenly been stolen. That's what it was.

She was right under my nose, and yet I *missed* her.

I forced myself to focus on the next question. "Any statements on your new relationship with Keely Dawson, Commander Tyler?"

I flicked a glance at Victoria who had a snarky smirk on her perfectly red lips as if to say, *I told you this was coming. Always trust me.* I sent her a knowing wink and returned my canned answer— prepared by her—to the reporter.

"I'm here to speak about the new crewed test flight. I'm very excited about it and would rather not give the time over to my personal life. That gets plenty of stage time as it is. While other private space companies are sending insects, old cars, and flight test dummies into space, we're sending living astronauts. And quite frankly, I'm excited about that. And you should be too. I'd like to turn the focus back to where it belongs."

Grumbles and loud whispers filled the room, and a few more hands went up. I fielded some more questions about the technical aspects of the launch that would be happening in just over eight weeks.

"Will you find it difficult to go back up again, considering what happened on your last mission?"

My fists tightened, and I froze, considering the question. Of course, I'd prepped for it, but the reality of having it thrown out there, with the lights and the clicking camera shutters, made my mind skip. Peripherally, I was aware that my phone was lighting up—likely more texts from Victoria.

I ignored it. After sucking in a deep breath, I fought to keep my voice calm. "The truth is that I've wanted to go back up ever since the last time, so I'm grateful for the opportunity. I'm also grateful to be able to dedicate this flight to the memory of my best friend, Astronaut Xander Freed."

The thought of the flight, despite its horrifically high cost, sent a cold thrill through my gut. It was excitement tinged with a little dread and some doubt, if I was being honest with myself.

I'd never doubted what I wanted. And I've never *not* gone for it. My eyes flicked back to that figure at the back of the room only to note with disappointment that she was gone. A door nearby was slowly closing.

I sucked my lips into my mouth and wet them, focusing on the next question and trying not to roll my eyes when it came up. "Will Keely be getting a role in the upcoming film being made about your life and the space station accident?"

Later, Victoria would commend me for my lack of sarcastic answer.

They'd be getting their eyeful of me and Keely together next week at a movie premiere, anyway. But it still annoyed me that they cared more about the "scorching love affair" farce we were putting on rather than the possibility of moving humankind out of low earth orbit and back into space travel once again after nearly fifty years of doing nothing.

Whatever. The press conference was finally behind me. Thank God.

It was time to get on with the rest of my day. It would be another long one as I strove to avoid my ubiquitous housemate while struggling not to go insane with wanting her at the same time.

Yeah. Such a tall order called for double workouts.

But first, I had a brief team meeting followed by rounds of rigorous flight training simulations with the entire astronaut team.

The day consisted of hours upon hours of us rotating, round-robin style, moving through checklists and then recording our data. By the time early evening hit, we'd wrapped up our last sim and were preparing to leave for the day.

Noah started his harping...again. He leafed through papers attached to his clipboard and frowned. "Is there a reason we keep putting off the lights-out board test?"

To be fair, none of us was in a great mood after a very tedious motherfucking day. The repetitiveness of what we were doing was beyond annoying, and we were all mentally and physically exhausted.

I shoved my laptop into a bag along with a folder full of my latest batch of checklists. They'd only been printed out that morning and were already covered with sticky notes and penciled-in comments suggesting changes.

Noah had directed his remark at me, so I replied. "The lights-out test is not crucial. Especially at this time. We need to get that de-orbit burn sequence down several thousandths of a second before we start all the what-if scenarios."

I avoided his gaze, zipping up my laptop case. We wouldn't talk about the real reason I was avoiding a test that was conducted completely in the dark—a test that helped rate the functionality of back-up systems should the main electrical system cut out. There was no telling what might happen if I was locked in a contained dark space with no way to get out. And I didn't want to find out in front of the other guys.

Noah threw me a weird look as he packed up his own bag. "Can we at least get it on the calendar? It's really messing with me that we are leaving such a simple test undone when we are covering everything else so meticulously."

I shrugged, turning my back to him. I was *not* about to get into this now. "Not for at least another few weeks."

"Hope that leaves us some time before the flight," he muttered between his teeth.

I didn't say anything, pretending to be distracted by something on my phone. Noah started muttering under his breath, and Kirill waltzed in to save the day, slapping him good-naturedly on the shoulder. "Relax dude. Where is your chill? What you need is hot woman and to get laid." I all but laughed at Kirill's apt command of Southern California slang, complete with his Russian accent.

Noah arched a brow at him. "Easy for you to say. I'm not the one who's regularly banging the hot actress."

Kirill grinned. "Try not to be so jealous, Noah. Not everyone can be so sexy the women won't leave them alone."

Hammer appeared on the other side of Kirill. "He's too sexy for his shirt..." he started to sing.

"He's too sexy for his brain," I muttered out the side of my mouth, and Noah snickered while Kirill joined in singing with Hammer.

"That's right. I'm so 'sexy.'" Kirill said with, hilariously, his signature misplaced air quotes. It mystified me how Kirill, who could fly every machine imaginable, held officer rank in the Russian military, and had the equivalent of a master's degree in aerospace engineering, could not grasp the subtle art of the air quote.

Granted, he wasn't speaking his native language. I was nevertheless certain that if air quotes existed in Russian, he would have fucked them up in his mother tongue, too.

I stuffed the last of my shit in my bag, and with a laugh and a grin, I turned down the guys' invitation to go grab drinks. "I'm beat," I said. Though in reality, I was headed to the gym for a workout since it would be too dark to run when I got home.

Kirill caught up with me before I got into my car.

"Ty, wait up," he said, speaking Russian as he usually did when we were alone. "Let's go watch a movie, hey? That one about the bank heist looks good."

God, a movie. I hadn't been in a theater since before the accident. I didn't even want to chance what might happen. Maybe they weren't dark enough but I didn't want to risk it.

"Kirya. I'm going to go home, swim for a bit, and then sleep like a log," I said, amending my evening plans on the spot.

He corrected me with the more current slang term for going to bed, chiding me once again that I spoke Russian like his grandpa.

I shook my head with a grin. "Because I learned it from *my* grandpa. Night, Kirya. See you tomorrow."

He put a hand on my shoulder. "I'm worried. You seem not yourself."

I shrugged. "If you're out here on a scouting mission for the guys, then you can tell them that I ended things with Gray. No need to keep checking up on me."

He frowned but gave a curt nod, putting his hands in his pockets and gazing out at the surrounding horizon in the parking lot. "I am sorry about that. Before. Come, we can go get a drink, at least."

I shook my head with a jerk. Of all the people I'd discuss this breakup with, the macho Russian would not be my first choice. Odds were, he'd use it as a way to torment me for the rest of my life.

"I'm focused on the flight. I don't have time for anything else."

He sobered. "Good. That is sensible. I should do likewise."

My brow twitched, but I left it at that. Did that mean Keely was in for some bad news soon, too?

God, that was all I needed. Avoiding the girlfriend who wouldn't move out of my house and being forced to spend time with the fake girlfriend who would be nursing her own breakup. It sounded like the obstacle course from Hell.

As far as I could tell, Keely and Kirill had been casual, but who knew? Kirill typically lost interest in the women he was seeing after a short period of time. I said nothing, though. Kirill's business was Kirill's, and he was a big boy. Even though he'd seen fit to interfere in my own personal life, I would not reciprocate.

He knocked once on the hood of my car. "Maybe things will be back to normal soon. Just us four guys. Having fun together. Hanging out."

Kirill had a group of friends—fellow Russian expats—that he hung out with regularly. I knew he wasn't lonely. But I nodded. "Yeah, we're just stressed out these days with the flight coming up. Sometimes when we're going at it hard like this, we need a break from each other."

He nodded. "Da. Eto pravda." Then, he repeated himself in English. "This is true. Have good night, Ty."

I nodded. "You, too."

I watched him go, crossing the parking lot before I put the key in the ignition and turned on the car. I thought about how much I enjoyed working with these guys and solving the puzzles and the bugs in procedures and checklists. The camaraderie. The excitement. These days I loved everything about my job except for the actual thought of going up in that rocket again, in spite of what I'd told the world at that press conference today.

But I'd do it, because that's what I'd promised I would do. I'd get through this somehow.

I scrubbed my face with my hand and started the car, heading home, simultaneously hoping to avoid and yet to see my houseguest.

Maybe she'd be inclined to discuss the press conference—or anything—instead of maintaining her weird, calm silence.

She was heading out to the deck with her e-reader just as I finished my laps in the pool. We crossed paths right in front of the glass doors that led inside.

As I was blocking her way out, I stepped aside, still dripping, and she quietly thanked me, avoiding my eyes.

A knot tightened in my throat. I stood, toweling myself off as she moved past me to go sit at the railing, positioning herself to watch the moon rise in the east. It was almost full and just kissing the horizon over the canyon. I turned and watched her for a moment.

As if detecting my observation, she turned around to look at me. There was no animosity in her face. Just that same, quiet calm.

She'd been like that since Sunday morning. No emotions. No crying. No sad speeches. No guilt trips. Not even hostility. Nothing.

It was like whatever was between us had never happened.

Except it *had* and I couldn't forget it. And I was starting to resent that she appeared to have put it behind her so easily.

Still waters ran deep. And Gray's waters…well I'd had no time to plumb their depths, to discover all the hidden landscape underneath that placid surface. She surprised me at every turn. Even at a time when we theoretically had no relationship at all. Even now.

Those serene features. No anger. No sadness. At least none that I could detect.

She cleared her throat. "Did you need something?"

I shook my head. "No, I'm good. Have a good evening."

She froze, as if confused at how to react to my words, then slowly nodded. "You too."

I turned and stepped through the door, trying to grasp at ideas on how to get her the fuck out of here. If we had to share a roof until the test flight, there was no telling what might happen.

Cold war. Mayhem. Hopefully not murder. And in all probability, a relapse—one that involved me, her and a whole lot of naked, sweaty fun.

After a shower and change of clothes, I checked my phone and found another picture—a Karen and AJ selfie. Underneath, the caption read, *We're coming to California!*

I blinked and then processed.

Lately I'd been staging amusing photographs, most often involving photos of AJ's school picture posed in strange places to make him laugh. Taped inside our capsule simulator while we were working; fixed onto my steering wheel during the drive home; sitting on a rock at the beach; taped to one of our model Rubicon III rockets.

I'd just about exhausted what limited creativity I possessed. Gray would probably have had a wealth of ideas. But as with everything else, I had to remind myself at least a dozen times not to ask her.

Nevertheless, the entire exercise had served to remind me that I was seriously lacking fun in my life. The old type of fun, the fun I had when I was close to Xander's family and my friends in Houston.

I replied, *That's great! When?*

A few minutes later, I got the answer. *Next week.*

I responded that I was happy to hear it and looking forward to seeing them. Then I tucked my phone away, sobered by the fact that the first thing I wanted to do was go tell Gray they were coming. But that constant ache, that hollowness inside, reminded me that the less I said to her, the better.

I needed a bit of a break from that empty feeling. Slipping into my living room, I approached the wet bar, careful to ensure that she was nowhere near and was unable to see me.

I told myself I'd pour one shot. Just one. To help me cope a little with this shitty day, this shitty week—soon to be shitty month. Soon to be the next long string of shitty days that would blur one into the other.

But as I uncapped the bottle and poised it to pour into a shot glass, I spied the little Sharpie hash marks she'd put onto the bottle.

My breath escaped jerkily, and I recapped the bottle, leaving the vodka undisturbed.

Her crafty plan had worked. I hadn't touched the stuff since the day she'd marked the levels—over a month ago.

And now I was just not going to do it out of stubbornness. But I realized how clever she had been in even that, too. I ran a hand through my hair, bending my fingers and pulling at the roots, wincing slightly but not from the dull pain in my scalp.

I was finding it hard to breathe, thinking about her. I was finding it hard not to go out there and sit beside her under the moonlight. Except now it was dark, and I couldn't stand the thought of being in the dark, even if it meant I could be close to her.

And really, I couldn't even brave the dark for her, my clever, beautiful girl—not mine, but *mine*. If I couldn't brave the dark for her...

I'd never deserve her at all.

CHAPTER SIX
GRAY

I MISSED HIM. SO MUCH. BUT I WAS TREADING A THIN LINE here, trying to be a calming influence still, trying to be emotionally mature. Trying to be accommodating of the fact that I had willfully chosen to stay and live under his roof even after a romantic breakup.

I was aware that he might be under some distress.

But I, too, was nursing wounds.

So that night, I watched the moon rise pale and silvery, bathing the dark canyon below in deep purples and the darkest shades of gray. I wondered when I'd transition to the next stage of grief.

It had only been a few days, yet I was still pathetically weeping into my pillow at night when I could no longer hold it in, waking up every morning with stinging eyes and a sore nose.

I told myself it would pass soon, right? Time could only dull the pain, as with a physical wound.

The next step, justified anger, was right around the corner.

And I happened to turn that corner the following afternoon, as a matter of fact.

When I got back from work, I rushed to get some time in the pool before Ryan returned for the day. But I had to search for my swimsuit. Nothing was where it was supposed to be because of the hurried packing and unpacking job I'd done when Ryan had asked me to leave.

I wanted a swim, goddammit. But the suit was evading me under a pile somewhere.

Thus, I lost my temper.

In my frustration, I indulged in a full-blown tantrum.

Second Stage: Anger

I broke my glasses. Not accidentally. No. I stomped on them. I was frustrated. Or maybe I was pretending the glasses were Ryan's face.

That crunch was oh so satisfying until I realized my backup pair was also broken. That teeny tiny little screw had fallen out of them, and I had meant to take them to be repaired and never got around to it.

Crappity crap. I went for a dip anyway, to calm myself down, to take out my anger on swimming laps, and to brainstorm a solution to my sudden eyewear issue.

It came to me as I was toweling off. I'd use duct tape. I found it easily in one of Ryan's utility drawers and ripped off a small section of it, returning to my room.

Apart from looking like crap, I'd fixed them up almost good as new. I made a face at myself in the mirror. I looked like Harry Potter after a particularly trying summer with the Dursleys. Maybe I'd start a trend.

Now if only I could force myself to forget about what an idiot I was to get satisfaction from the crunch of those lenses under my shoe as I pictured Ryan's skull.

Not that I'd actually crush his skull, of course.

But imagining it helped a little.

With the glasses issue temporarily resolved, I took a shower to get the pool water out of my hair and off my skin.

But seeing as Ryan wouldn't be home for hours yet, I dressed and followed up my dumb stunt with an even dumber one.

One right out of the *Beginners Guide to Stalking* handbook.

I wandered into his bedroom.

In all honesty, I'd left a couple things in his en suite bathroom, so it started innocently enough, grabbing my stick of deodorant and some make-up remover.

On my way out of the bathroom, I slowed when walking by the bed. Ryan always made the bed. Always. Without a wrinkle, the sheet and comforter pulled perfectly straight and tight. It must have been all that time in the military when it had been drilled into his brain.

I reached out and touched his pillow. Then, like any perfectly sane, non-stalkery woman, I bent down and buried my face in it, inhaling his smell deeply and feeling that perfect rush of emotions wash over me. Memories of his kisses, his hands on my body, of waking up with my body pulled tight against his.

I set my things aside on the nightstand and sat down on the bed, pulling the pillow into my lap so I could hug it while getting a few more good whiffs.

It smelled like *him*. Seashells. Lime. The smell of his skin, his hair.

In spite of everything, I still worried that he wasn't getting enough sleep without me there to help him.

I missed feeling his body next to mine in bed. Our affair—I refused to label it a relationship—had only lasted a few short, amazing weeks, but I'd grown used to sleeping beside him very quickly. Too quickly.

I'd lost my heart even quicker than that.

When tears prickled the backs of my eyes, I stopped, forcibly replacing the pillow and willing some sanity back into my brain. But no, apparently I wasn't ready for that yet.

Instead I went into his large walk-in closet. What I was hoping to find there, I had no idea. I just knew I wasn't ready to leave his room yet. All his clothing in there was laundered, so it didn't smell like him, but I fingered some of the shirts I'd once enjoyed taking off of him during frenzied make out sessions. Unbuttoning the buttons slowly, kissing my way down his solid torso.

I ran my fingers amongst all the different textures of fabric, wondering why Elizabeth Kubler Ross had not written about temporary insanity in her treatise on the stages of grief.

My hand stopped when I reached a thick, utilitarian material at the very end of a long line of clothing on hangers. Royal blue, adorned with patches—most notably the dark blue rectangular patch edged with gold and bearing the Eagle and Trident emblem of the Navy SEALs. Beneath, in the same gold, denoting an astronaut from the Navy, was his full name, *Ryan Tyler*.

There were several of them hanging beside each other, including the plain one he'd been given to wear the day he'd fulfilled a Make-A-Wish Foundation promise. With him, we'd all toured the Space Center in Houston with an adorable, young cancer survivor, Francisco.

Without even thinking about what I was doing, I pressed my face to his NASA flight suit. Of course, it didn't smell like him. Likely it had been laundered since he last wore it. When I pulled back, I traced the ISS Expedition mission patches with my fingertip. Another minute passed, and I was out of my own clothes and zipping up his flight suit around my body.

It was huge, of course. Ryan was a lot taller than me and had a muscular build. I swam inside that thing, but I had to admit, ill-fitting or not, it gave me a massive thrill to wear a real live astronaut flight suit. I ran my hands over the material again, imagining it was my own perfectly fitting suit and I'd just returned from a mission to the ISS.

Rolling up the pants and the sleeves helped a bit, along with grabbing one of his belts and fastening it around my waist. I made my way back to his bedroom to look at the full-length mirror on the bathroom door, turning this way and that.

Sure, I'd been feeling like crap, but this was a sudden glimmer of happy in the middle of my day. I hugged myself and then straightened as if at attention. As if posing for the cameras in the press.

Why yes, indeed, I was merely aiming at being the best darn flight psychologist out there, but they insisted I train as an astronaut for the first trip to Mars. I flicked my head arrogantly in the mirror and laughed at myself.

When I heard the key turn the bolt lock in the front door, I froze. Any other time and I would have laughed at the deer-in-the-headlights look on my reflection in the mirror. But right now, I was both a stalker and in a potentially very humiliating situation.

Oh shit. Oh crap. Oh—all the other swear words besides the scatological ones!

My eyes flew to the clock as I hurriedly jerked the zipper down my front to get out of it before he saw me. He was a little early, but not that much. In all my daydreaming, I'd lost track of time.

Exactly what my plan was, I had no idea. My brain had apparently stopped functioning, frozen, like the damn zipper once it hit my waist and the belt. Panicking, I unzipped the top and pulled out of the sleeves before undoing the belt. But in the middle of all this, I decided I didn't have enough time to undress, redress and hang up the flight suit before he came in the door—and ultimately into his room to change.

He was only seconds from catching me in his bedroom wearing his clothes.

My skin boiled at the thought of that level of embarrassment. It would be off the charts. So I did the most logical thing that popped into my frenzied brain and dashed out of his bedroom at a full run, hoping to make it back into my room before he opened the door and saw me wearing his flight suit.

Alas, my spontaneous plan B—run and hide—was not to be.

As I was racing through the front living room, headed for the hallway where I'd been staying, I had to pass right by the front door. And as I did so, I tripped on an unrolled pantleg and went flying.

In my rushed panic, I had not pulled the top of the jumpsuit back on again. Therefore, I now had rugburn all across my chest. And of course, my upper body was completely bare.

I blinked, reaching out in front of me for my glasses that had leaped off my nose—probably in disgust for me, at this point.

Suddenly, a pair of black shoes came into view right in front of my face. Big black shoes.

Man-sized shoes.

Then a hand joined the shoes at my sight level as Ryan bent to pick up my glasses and placidly pass them to me. I reached up and took them, feeling my skin burn with embarrassment along with the friction burns from the rug.

I mumbled my thanks through my humiliation, then cleared my throat as he undoubtedly took in the scene before him—me sprawled across his living room floor, half-naked with his unzipped NASA flight suit hanging off me.

"This, uh, this isn't what you're thinking."

"It isn't?"

I sucked in a breath, trying to figure out how I could sit up without fully exposing myself, though that thought was pretty dumb. Less than a week ago we'd had sex on his kitchen counter and I had no problem being naked in front of him then.

There was an awkward pause while I waited, facedown on the floor, trying to figure out how to leave the room with my dignity intact. *Way too late for that, Gray!*

"So, uh, what am I thinking?"

My face burned hotter, and I didn't answer. A few seconds later, he seemed to detect the strong *go away* vibes I was mentally sending him. He had to step over me to go to his room, but he did it without further comment.

When his door closed, I stood up and raced to my guest room and hurriedly removed the flight suit. Carefully folding it, I then dressed in something else—eschewing a bra on my poor, tender nipples. My yoga pants and t-shirt from earlier were still on the floor in his closet.

I was sitting on my bed, fidgeting and deciding on a sudden stay-in-bedroom fast for the rest of the night, when he knocked lightly on the door.

Licking my lips, I didn't answer, still struggling for something to say.

"Gray," he said through the door, "I have your things here."

Without a word, I scooped up his folded flight suit and his belt and went to the door. I cracked it open just wide enough to make the garment exchange, then started to close it.

Ryan's hand shot out to hold the door open. His eyes narrowed.

"Are you okay?"

I cleared my throat and willed myself in vain not to blush. "I'll live."

"Can I...can we talk?"

My eyebrows shot up. Well that was something. He finally wanted to talk?

I checked my watch as if I had a million pressing appointments instead of some reports to write for work the next day—not more than an hour's worth of work.

"Uh, yeah, sure. Give me a minute. I'll meet you in the kitchen."

Minutes later, after I'd gone to the bathroom to calm down and splash some cold water on my face, we sat across the dining room table from each other. He'd pulled a beer out of the fridge for himself and, without asking, handed me a cold Dr. Pepper.

He wanted me out. I could tell by the way he was looking at me, the way he was acting. This was not a reconciliation. This wasn't even an explanation—which he still owed me. It was an expulsion.

I popped the top on my soda can and took a sip while he twisted the cap off his beer bottle and set it aside without bringing it to his mouth. Then he laced his long fingers in front of him, elbows on the table and he studied his hands. He spoke without looking up but with measured words I was certain he'd repeated to himself several times beforehand.

"Gray, we have to come to some kind of understanding."

I blinked, failing to look at him. "I'm really sorry. I shouldn't have gone into your room or put on your flight suit. I wasn't being stalkery, I promise. I just—"

"Gray," he reached out his hand on the table to get my attention while the words spilled out of me faster than I could pronounce them.

I looked up at him. His face was serious but not stern. "I don't care about the flight suit. You can have that one if you want."

My brows pinched together, suddenly feeling struck with the pain of this situation. I shook my head and mumbled a miserable, "No, but thank you. That's kind."

He sighed. "Okay, but there is something else I want to talk to you about."

I sat up. "What's that?"

His deep blue eyes flicked up to mine, and I could see it— every single barrier was up. He was well shielded. "About us living together like this… Before I say anything more, I want you to know that this wasn't calculated. I didn't start this in an attempt to manipulate you."

Oh, I wasn't going to make this easy for him. No way. I rested my chin on a fist and fiddled with the metal top on my soda can, bending it backward and forward until it snapped off. "Why *did* you start this, then?"

He did this strange sort of slow blink, like his eyes closed, held for a beat, and then snapped open again. Then he swallowed. "I was attracted to you. I sensed you were attracted to me. There was chemistry."

"And that's not the case anymore?" I angled my head to emphasize the query, and he shifted in his seat.

It didn't take a PhD in Psychology to recognize that he instantly regretted initiating this conversation. That just made me less likely to let him off the hook.

"I'm still attracted to you," he said in a low, flat voice. "But there's more to it now. Feelings are involved."

"Oh? You mean you have feelings?"

His jaw tensed. "I was talking about your feelings."

Ouch. Shields up indeed...

"Oh, okay. So, you don't have feelings?"

He gave another long pause. "I didn't say that."

I frowned. "But they aren't the same feelings as mine."

He pulled back from the table and leaned against his chair back, looking stiff and very uncomfortable. "I don't want to talk about feelings right now."

His clear agitation told me we were getting close to something he wanted to avoid—or too far off the track from what he initially wanted to discuss. Or both.

Without letting go the sigh I desperately wanted to release, I decided to cut to the chase. "So, does that mean you're not going to tell me why you broke things off between us?"

His eyes flickered off to the side, and his brows crunched together. It was a strange expression until his face flushed, and I could easily tell that he was fighting anger.

I blinked, mystified. Was he getting pissed at me for forcing this? For not allowing him to deliver his canned speech and then shove me out the door?

But when he looked back at me, it wasn't with anger in his eyes. It was something else. Maybe he was frustrated. But not at me.

I shook my head, confused.

"Gray," he gruffly whispered, and the way his voice trembled when he said my name plucked at my heart. "The last thing I want is for you to question or second guess yourself. You did nothing wrong."

Gritting my teeth, I fought my own wave of frustration. "How can you think that I won't question myself? You know that's impossible. Especially if you won't give me any answers."

His fists balled on the table in front of him. "I'm fucked up right now. You know I am. I can't do this. You deserve better."

I shook my head in protest. "But we were working on that. I was helping you..." My voice died out at the stone-cold expression on his face. "I thought I was, anyway."

He swallowed. "I need to keep my head in the game for all this training, the test flight, and the stuff with Keely. All of it. I can't get distracted." He shook his head, looking away.

"So I was distracting you?"

He bent his head to run a hand through his hair, his eyes twitching in irritation. "Yes," he huffed.

My throat tightened and prickled with tears that really wanted to surface. But I wouldn't allow them to. The man was already riddled with enough guilt and thoughts of himself as being irreparably broken. I couldn't add my own distress and sorrow to the load he'd willingly taken upon himself.

I frowned, knowing that it took two to start something. And I'd been perfectly aware of his brokenness long before we'd started our romantic liaison.

I'd gambled that he'd get better, maybe. Or maybe I'd just made the fatal mistake of not thinking things through.

I'd gambled, yes. And I'd lost.

"So now you want to talk about me moving out," I finally said in a low voice.

His troubled brow smoothed, and he darted a look up at me and away.

"*But,*" I continued, "there's the problem that I'm expected to stay here and keep you from relapsing. Tolan expects it. My father and the other investors expect it."

I saw that strange wince and flash of anger again before he quickly looked away, as if forcing himself to calm down. For lack of anything better to do, I grabbed my soda and sipped at it. He stared off into space for a minute or two before visibly shaking himself and turning back to me.

"I have house guests coming next week," he said quietly.

Well, *that* wasn't what I'd expected to hear. I hesitated, nodding for him to clarify.

"Karen Freed. She's also a consultant on this new film, and the studio asked her to come out for interviews. When she told me, I invited her and AJ to stay here. And since the little guy doesn't have school for another month and a half, they're going to be here a while."

I opened my mouth then shut it and then opened it again. "That's great. I'm so glad that you're in a place where you can..." My voice unexpectedly faltered, though not quite into a sob. That place he was at where he could reach out to Karen was the exact same place he was at when he had dumped me and was now giving me my packing orders.

Fighting the tremble in my emotional control, I swallowed my own grief. I could be happy about this big step in his progress. "It's good that the two of you are talking again."

He looked down at the table between us and I noticed how tightly his hands were balled into fists, knuckles whitened. He had the most attractive hands. Large, long fingered, defined veins. I blinked before I allowed myself to go down the primrose path of remembering what those hands could—and did—do to me. Because it was over. With all of this, he was reassuring me of just that. There was no hope. This would not resume.

I blinked. "I have a feeling you aren't just telling me this so I can clear some space on the bathroom counter for your other guests."

He shook his head. "I think there's a lot you can be doing for the program. And you have your own life to get back to."

Another weight dropped into my gut, a sudden, heavy loneliness instilled by those words. *Your own life.* My life...without him in it.

"You're thinking that Karen can fill in for me?" I asked softly.

His brow looked puzzled, and I gestured jerkily with my hand as I clarified. "I mean for keeping you from, uh, relapsing on your lifestyle."

He said nothing just held my eyes with his piercing gaze. He had that look again as if trying to solve a difficult puzzle. Then he slowly nodded.

I took a deep breath, overwhelmed with a mixture of emotions. I had no real strong desire to stay here and continue the awkward evasion we'd been managing over the past few days. But I didn't want to say goodbye either.

I didn't want this to be the end.

And I sure as hell didn't want to keep sitting at this table and continue this conversation.

I stood. "I'll talk to Tolan in the morning and see if that will satisfy him."

"I can do it. You don't have to—"

I held out a hand to stay the argument. "I'm fine. I'll do it."

His eyes fell to the table again. Before I said or did something I regretted—like dissipating into a blubbering puddle on the floor—I put the can in the recycling bin and returned to my room.

To lick my wounds in silence and with my well-practiced stoicism.

At first, open wounds are raw and vulnerable, susceptible to the elements. But soon, according to the body's natural pattern of healing, a scab forms, protecting the mending skin underneath while scar tissue formed. Soon the tissue is as good as new, if a little worse for wear. And eventually the scar tissue is less sensitive than the original skin it has mended.

Experiences seemed to work the same way.

And heartbreak.

I made two promises to myself: I'd try my best to get over hating him for breaking my heart. I'd also fight to get over hating myself for giving him the opportunity to break it in the first place.

Time will heal this, a voice told me at the back of my head. The voice of my reason. My thinking self.

But deep down, I knew it wasn't as simple as that. Not when it felt like a part of myself was missing. And the wound it had left behind was raw and sore.

CHAPTER SEVEN
GRAY

O N MY WAY TO WORK THE NEXT MORNING, I GOT A phone call from my dad. Since I was still slogging through morning traffic on the 22 freeway, I answered the phone through the buttons on my steering wheel.

"Dad, hi. I'm on the way to work. What's up?"

"Dinner's at my house this week. Saturday night if you can make it."

"Sure, sounds good." I laughed and couldn't resist a tease. "You cooking?"

"I'm inviting a guest. Remember Aaron Thiessen? He called me last weekend and wanted to chat. I remembered how well the two of you hit it off when we ran into him at that frou frou restaurant last month. He was asking you all those space questions, so I thought it might be fun to invite him to our dinner. We can chat about old times."

I tensed, smelling a set up. And I hardly had many "old times" to talk about with Aaron. I'd been at college most of the time when Dad was his mentor. It wasn't at all like that close friend-of-the-family relationship I had with Tolan.

I frowned. "Uh, okay. What do you want me to bring?"

"Just your beautiful self," Dad replied as if he'd been anticipating the question.

This was so unlike him. He usually kept his nose out of my personal social life—especially my love life which, until recently had been next to nonexistent. *Weird.*

We chatted for another couple minutes before I hung up, puzzling over the strange new development, but also relieved for something to get me out of Ryan's tension-filled house for an evening.

Because now, it seemed we were just counting down the days until Karen Freed and her son arrived and I left, pending XVenture's approval, of course.

I found myself having that discussion over lunch that day, after texting Tolan the moment I'd arrived at work. I'd offered some Chinese takeout from one of our favorite nearby restaurants as an incentive for him to pencil me in, and he'd agreed to meet with me while we wolfed it down.

Making it past his assistant with the warm and fragrant bags of food, I almost laughed when I noticed Tolan waiting at his desk, chopsticks already in hand. The only thing that would have been funnier would've been finding him wearing a big bib over his knit shirt.

His chopsticks were slightly different, metallic and flat Korean chopsticks. It made sense that he'd prefer them, because his mother was Korean—and possibly the most adorable woman I'd ever met.

I pulled out my wooden disposable chopsticks from their paper wrapper and held them out, fencing style. *"En garde.* Winner takes all the wontons?"

"Hell no. Cough them up, girl." He snapped his two chopsticks together loudly, imitating hungry jaws. In response I plopped the bag onto his desk, and he started digging through the white cartons to find his favorite dishes.

"Don't snarf down all the spring rolls, please. Save at least one for me," I huffed.

He already had one box open, lo mein noodles bunched between his chopsticks just inches from his mouth. "I'm sorry. Did you actually want to talk? I was just planning to pig out."

We spent the next few minutes happily consuming our food with lots of lip smacking and murmurs of approval coming from Tolan's direction. He was a brilliant man—one of the smartest and most visionary that I knew—and I'd been acquainted with a lot of smart people.

But Tolan had nurtured a vision since his early years, brought himself up from a middle-class background, an immigrant to the US as a young teen. Despite our fifteen-year age difference, we'd bonded when he'd studied as a mentee under my dad. We'd both been space freaks and had attended space events together—lectures at the planetarium, a couple shuttle landings at Edwards Air Force Base, astronaut memoir book signings, even several space exploration conventions.

He'd taken me out to Florida to watch the very last launch of the space shuttle *Atlantis* at Cape Canaveral in 2011. Having impressively pulled strings, he'd been able to get us seats in the VIP section to observe it.

It would stand out as one of the most memorable events in my life.

"Ahh, that was so good," Tolan said as he sat back a few minutes later. He was an unusually fast eater, for which he was teased constantly. He patted his belly. "I might have to undo my belt, Gray. Just warning you."

I raised a brow. "Please wait till I'm gone and exercise a little self-control with your food consumption."

He shook his head. "Not my fault. You're the one who dangled Chinese food in front of me. I'm like Homer Simpson and donuts with Chinese food."

I smiled serenely but didn't say aloud what I was thinking. *That's what I'd been counting on, Tolan.*

He reached out and wiped his mouth with a white paper napkin imprinted with the restaurant's logo, name, and address in red. "So, what can I do you for?"

I shrugged. "Just wanted to chat and catch up."

"How are things going with Ty? Any better?"

We hadn't talked in-depth about the situation since those first few weeks when Ryan had been belligerent and very crabby about my 'babysitting assignment.'

Tolan was not privy to all the goings-on since then, much to my relief.

"Well, about that..." I began slowly. "I was thinking we could ease up on how closely he's being watched."

Tolan did not seem surprised or even the least bit curious about this observation. He dropped his soiled napkin in the waste bin and reached out to sip at his water bottle. "Yeah, your dad more or less said something like that when I saw him last week."

I blinked. Last week? Tolan had talked to my dad last week?

"Dad was here last week?" I'd have known, wouldn't I? He definitely would have stopped by to say hello at the very least.

Tolan shook his head. "Not here. Across the street. We had a little meeting at Happy's. Anyway, he was saying he was concerned about you not being able to finish up your clinical hours. Said he wasn't as concerned about Ty now that he was going along with his fake relationship. He hasn't mentioned that to you?"

Struggling to hide my reaction, I kept my features placid instead of showing my surprise. "Not yet. I have dinner with him on Saturday."

"Well personally, I trust your opinion. We'll give Ty a little breathing room if you think he's up to it. Especially so you can get back to your own life."

I almost rolled my eyes. Yeah, my big, fat exciting life. What a joke. Thousands of calories of ice cream consumed by the pint while listening to sad love songs. *Couldn't wait.*

"So you know, Xander Freed's widow and son are going to be staying with him starting next week. I think he'll be in good hands with her. Besides...besides...."

I couldn't even bring myself to say it.

"Is he doing better?" Tolan prompted.

I nodded slightly. "Yeah. No drinking, no partying." We wouldn't talk about the other stuff. The PTSD, the paralyzing fear of the dark, the lack of sleep. And the penchant to want to keep punishing himself for being *broken.*

Tolan nodded. "Good. Then why don't you just stay until Karen Freed gets here? And please, will you invite her out here if she has time? I'd love to meet her and her son. I'll give them a VIP tour."

I nodded. "Yeah, sure." My insides tightened up, and we chatted for a few more minutes about his life. Tolan and his girlfriend were starting to get serious, and he wanted a little psychology advice about some of the big milestones...like when to pop the "three-word phrase."

Best advice? Don't do it with a stack of fucking heart-shaped pancakes. I bit my lip to keep my comment unspoken and did my best, as usual, to provide the good listening ear.

The next day, I finally met up with Pari, whom I'd been semi-avoiding since Ryan had dropped the bomb on me the previous weekend.

I'd left her birthday cupcakes and a card on her desk early on Monday morning, and she'd left a gorgeous thank-you note on mine a day later.

But I hadn't really wanted to talk about this mess with anyone. Not yet, anyway. Maybe deep down I'd been hoping it was temporary.

But Pari was unavoidable. We crossed paths, and I had to put on a fake smile, which she saw through immediately.

She pulled me into an alcove. "You have been hard to get a hold of," she said, nodding to me with expectant eyes and a wide smile. Then she lowered her voice. "How are things going in the astro-love pad?" She waggled her thick dark brows at me. "Or should I call it the *launchpad?*"

I shushed her. "It's not going."

Pari's brows buckled. "What happened?"

I blew out a breath. "I don't want to talk about it now, okay? I promise I'll tell you everything this weekend, or better yet, come by my house next week. I'll be back there then."

Pari mulled this over for a moment before slowly nodding. "Are you okay?"

I bit my lip. "I will be. I'll tell you later."

Her face fell. "Okay. I'm so sorry."

We hesitated, looking at each other, and then I took a step in the direction of the cubicles I shared with other members of the health team. It was almost quitting time, and I had work to gather so I could get it finished at home. "How about you? Are you okay?"

She nodded then looked down, a little smile on her face. I caught it all, halting in my tracks.

"What's that smile?"

"Well, I was going to tell you what was going on with me, but I feel bad now for sharing good news."

Staring at her expectantly, I folded my arms over my chest. "Spill it."

"I listened to your advice and... Well, I summoned my courage and talked to Vic."

In spite of my own misery, I smiled. I'd been hoping for a positive outcome between her and Victoria ever since she'd originally told me about their tryst. "I'm so glad. It went well, I take it?"

She nodded. "I think so. We're going to talk some more over dinner, maybe this weekend if either of us gets a free minute."

We turned to continue walking in the same direction. "Please let me know how it goes, if you want to share. And you know, don't hesitate to tell me something good that's going on with you, even if I'm sad, okay?"

She nodded, still eying me speculatively. "Promise me we'll talk when you're ready? You can't be the one who listens to everyone else's troubles and yet never gets time to talk about your own, you know?"

I returned her smile with my tight one. I'd hug her, but Pari was not a hugger and I respected that.

From work, I went to a nearby coffeeshop and did most of my side work there, avoiding going back to the house too early.

Still smarting from Ryan's "get out" talk, I didn't feel like packing up my things just yet, and I wanted to run into him even less.

On Saturday, I made the long slog to LA for dinner at Dad's house. And I found myself, quite awkwardly, on what could only be described as a surprise first date. I hadn't been on many first dates, to be honest, but they'd never gone well. And a first date that my dad not-so-stealthily tried to set up was beyond the typical realm of awkward.

Dad owned three homes; one back in Pretoria, Illinois, his home state, an apartment in Manhattan, and his California home, which was a modest ranch-style house in the upper-middle-class Los Angeles neighborhood of Los Feliz.

None of these dwellings gave away the fact that he was one of the richest men in the country. No ultra-modern smart home on a lakeside retreat like his acquaintance, Bill Gates. No flashy Frank Lloyd Wright replica on a waterfall like his good friend Mark Chandler, CEO of one of the biggest hedge funds in New York. And no sprawling San Fernando Valley ranch in Hidden Hills like his former mentee, Tolan Reeves.

Dad had purchased the LA home for our family when we'd had to move out here for my medical issues at the age of eight. I'd lived there through many of my formative years because it was near one of the best children's hospitals in the country. My family's moves—and many of the major incidents that had shaped us as a familial unit—had often centered around me and my health.

Aaron Thiessen was already at Dad's house when I arrived with the freshly baked bread and bouquet of flowers for the table. And I knew I was in for a long night when Dad called me into the sitting room where he and Aaron stood in front of the wall of photos of me.

Yeah, that's right. He had an entire wall of photos that had been taken of me throughout the years, from infancy through that wonderful period when I'd been cursed with the trifecta of braces, horrible skin, and thick-framed, break-proof glasses. There were a couple of hospital photos with some of my favorite doctors and nurses. And of course, there was the snapshot of my first trip to Disneyland after my last valve replacement, looking ready to take on the world after having finished my secondary education at sixteen.

"She had the grades to graduate valedictorian if she'd graduated from a high school."

Oh, ugh, Dad. Stop.

"What's going on in here?" When in doubt about how to act in the ultimate awkward situation, play dumb, I always say.

Aaron straightened from bending to look more closely at the picture of me holding up some weird *object d'art* for my fifth-grade art project. "Gray! Good to see you again so soon." He approached, and before I could stick my hand out for a shake, he bent and kissed my cheek.

He was in his early thirties, a very successful man of average looks and build. He did not lack a shrewd business eye, though I'd always thought him amiable and easy to get along with. He didn't have a cocky-jerkwad bone in his body. Quite the opposite of a certain male whose company I'd been keeping of late.

"Welcome to Casa Barrett," I said, turning to my dad. "Whatever's cooking sure smells amazing. Did Mary leave something for you in the oven?"

"Her lasagna. I know it's your favorite, so I asked her special." Dad approached, taking me in his arms in a tight hug and a particularly showy kiss on the cheek, which was strange because he wasn't known for openly displaying affection—even for his only kid.

"Well, I brought your favorite sourdough bread, so that will go perfectly." I smiled. "I haven't had her lasagna in ages. I'm drooling already!"

Dad turned to Aaron. "She doesn't actually drool." And Aaron obediently laughed, shooting me a grin.

I blinked. *Oh, Dad. Just no.* It sounded like he was trying to sell a used car. "How about we eat? I'm starving." And before my dad could amend the statement, I jerked my head toward Aaron with a snarky smile. "I don't actually starve myself, either."

Dad chuckled. "You're so funny. I always tell people how funny my girl is."

I resisted the urge to look up to the ceiling in supplication. I was going to have words with him later. Possibly not pleasant, respectful words, either.

Dad had a plain white table cloth and the red holiday napkins on the dining room table for some reason. Everything was done up fancy like for a holiday—likely by Mary, his housekeeper, before she'd left for the day.

I dug into the still-warm sourdough, slathering it with soft butter and passing it along while we dished out helpings of lasagna from the casserole on the center of the table. To my utter shock, Dad re-entered the room with an uncorked bottle of red wine.

"Doctor's orders, I have to lay off the wine, but I have this for the two of you to share." He bent and poured us each a glass as formally as if he were a sommelier at a five-star restaurant. I wanted to scowl, but I didn't. Damn, he was laying it on thick.

Dad chattered on good-naturedly about business—in between extolling my virtues. Then suddenly, only ten minutes into dinner, he wiped his mouth and stood. "I just remembered. I need to make a very important phone call. Ahh... Where'd I leave my phone?"

"It's in your front shirt pocket, Dad."

"Uh, yeah. Well, I'll be right back." He hesitated before leaving, stopping to refill our wine glasses before disappearing. I cringed inwardly and avoided Aaron's gaze.

As soon as he stepped from the room, Dad began very loudly. "Ah, hello there. Yes, it's Conrad. Conrad Barrett. I have to make this short because my very beautiful daughter is here with me having dinner." *Mental face palm.*

Then he closed the door to his study, and mercifully, the rest of it was muffled before fading into nothing. I reached down and grabbed the remainder of my piece of bread and began to shred it nervously into little bits.

"I'm, um, sorry about that."

Aaron set his fork down and looked at me with a smile. He was not a bad looking man. Maybe a bit younger than Ryan. His hair was much lighter, and he was about four inches shorter than Ryan. Not in nearly as good shape, but he had a nice smile. Although, admittedly, it didn't light up everything around him like a class O star like Ryan's smile did.

Oh, ugh, Gray. Stop it. Stop it right now. I did not need to be comparing every man I met or spent any amount of time with to probably the most incomparable of men out there. In Pari's own belief system, I had committed the unforgiveable sin of falling in love with the first and only—to date—man I'd ever slept with.

She was right. It was a mistake. A *big* mistake.

But try as I might, I couldn't train my mind to go elsewhere. I made a mental note to apply some cognitive behavioral therapy to the problem when I had the time and inclination to do so. If I learned to pinch myself every time I thought of him, I'd either end up with a strong aversion to thinking about him or a severely bruised arm. Most likely the latter.

For his part, Aaron looked extremely amused. "I'd be mortified on your behalf, Gray, but I think he's being kind of adorable."

I rolled my eyes. "Adorable is *one* word for it. I have no idea why he's suddenly decided that I need a date."

He smiled. "Your dad's never been one to meddle but... Who knows? Maybe he just thinks you're working too hard."

I shook my head. "But he never thinks his mentees work too hard, am I right?" I raised my brows at him.

"Absolutely."

"And when you love your job, you never work a day in your life."

Aaron put his elbows on the table and pressed his fists to his chin. "So, tell me more about your job. I've been fascinated since I heard you talking about it at the restaurant last month."

I tried not to frown at him. If Aaron was feigning interest in hearing about XVenture merely for my benefit, then he was doing a remarkably good job of acting. Dad was gone for another hour at least and we ended up moving to the couch in the sitting room and talking while I answered his questions. Neither one of us touched another drop of wine, thank goodness.

"Humankind was born of Earth, but it was never meant to die here," I said, picking at a loose fiber on the back of Dad's threadbare but very comfortable sofa.

Aaron sat facing me with his back pressed up against the opposite arm of the couch. He mulled that over. "That's a profound thought."

I laughed. "I can't take credit for it. It's a paraphrase from the movie *Interstellar*. But a good point is a good point, even if the source is from a script and uttered by Matthew McConaughey. We were meant to explore, to go out among the stars. To survive and find a way to help our planet sustain our growing population."

He laughed. "I'll need to add that one to my watch list. You are full of surprises, Ms. Gray Barrett."

"Are you filling his head full of space and stars?" Our heads jerked in Dad's direction. Neither of us had heard him enter the room. "I just checked the table. Neither one of you touched your wine."

I gritted my teeth and was as nice as possible to Dad, but I soon found myself making excuses and truthfully yawning. It had been another long, emotional day, and I still had work to get done.

But Dad insisted on packaging the leftover lasagna for me, calling me into the kitchen to do so. "I don't suppose you want to take that wine."

"It's an open container, Dad. I can't. Just stick it in your fridge."

He threw everything into a secondhand grocery bag, one of those thin plastic ones, then cursed and doubled up when he saw that it could barely hold the weight of its contents. Dad flicked a gaze up at me. "See you in a week or two? You'll be all moved out and back at your apartment by then, right?"

I frowned at him. How the hell did he know that I was moving out of Ryan's place? Had Tolan told him? But when?

Then it occurred to me, something Tolan had said at lunch earlier in the week. "Dad did you have a meeting at XVenture last week?"

Dad frowned. "What? No. I haven't been there since they did that nice tour for the investors."

"But you saw Tolan, right? At Happy's?"

A strange expression crossed his face, and he glanced up at me sharply. There was fear in his eyes. Raw fear. *What was that about?*

He turned his face away quickly and fussed with the bag. "Yeah, I had lunch with Tolan last week. No biggie."

I leaned forward to ask him another question, when he snatched up the bag and headed out of the kitchen.

"Aaron will help you out with your things."

I didn't need the help but accepted it without comment, trying not to roll my eyes. Dad's weird behavior certainly was puzzling. Had he met with Tolan to tell him he was pulling the funding from the XPAC program? No, Tolan would have surely mentioned that to me.

What else could it be? There was obviously something about that meeting that Dad didn't want me finding out. He was so flustered, he forgot to give me his customary kiss on the cheek goodnight.

Aaron was a good sport about escorting me unnecessarily to my car. Just as he shut the front door, he said, "Sorry, Gray but there is not a chance in hell that I'm disobeying Conrad's direct orders about helping you out."

I blew out a long breath. "Please don't tell me he ordered you to ask me out or something."

He laughed. "Not at all. He doesn't have to order me to do that. Will you go out with me sometime?"

I swallowed and straightened, looking into his face. He was a really nice guy, and I'd enjoyed talking with him. But was I really ready for this? To move on to someone else so soon?

I took a deep breath to turn him down when he held up a hand. "Don't say anything now. But can I call you? We'll just go out for coffee or something. Nothing big."

I tilted my head and smiled. "I can do that."

He grinned. "You've inspired me to learn more about the space program. I'm going to watch *Interstellar* before I talk to you again. Any other good ones I should hit?"

I nodded. "Definitely *The Right Stuff*. Not to be missed!"

"Got it."

"And let me know how much more you want to know. Tolan is going to do a tour of the XVenture facility for some friends sometime in the next few weeks. I can get you in on that."

His face lit up. "I'd love it. Let me know."

He put my bag of food on the passenger seat as I climbed behind the wheel. Thankfully, it was dark, because the less he saw of my messy interior, the better.

I pulled out and drove the hour and ten minutes to Ryan's house, uneventfully until the last five minutes. As was normally the case when driving through the hills at night, the wildlife came out in droves. I normally took the curves and hills slowly, but I was so distracted as I thought about my dad's weird behavior. All of it had been so bizarre, from the strange set up date, to knowing that I was moving out of Ryan's place, to the way he'd reacted when I'd asked him about meeting with Tolan at Happy's last week.

As I ran everything through my mind, I almost didn't see the little possum that darted into the road then froze and played dead when captured in my high-beam headlights. I pounded on the brakes, the tires squealing.

The food Aaron had put on the seat went flying, and the contents of the leftover box Dad had fixed for me splattered all over the floor. The rich smell of tomato sauce, basil and garlic assailed my senses.

With a groan, I maneuvered my way around the little guy, hoping he'd make it out of the street in time to avoid the next car. I pulled into Ryan's driveway, entered the front door, dropped my stuff in the living room, and beelined it to the kitchen to grab a trash bag and a roll of paper towels.

I could easily see what I was doing due to how brightly lit Ryan kept his grounds until around midnight or so—I guess in case he was needed outside. In any case, his phobia of the dark helped me out this time. And surprisingly, he wandered out after a few minutes and caught me on my knees mopping the muck out of my car.

"You left the front door open."

I shoved a goop-laden bunch of paper towels into the trash bag and tore some fresh ones off the roll. "I'm sorry. I was in a rush to get this cleaned up."

He glanced inside the car then muttered. "I can help you. Let me go grab a couple things."

He headed to the garage, returning a few minutes later with a battery operated wet-dry shop vacuum and a bucket.

After sucking the mess up into his vacuum, he filled the bucket with some soapy water and sponged out the fragrant mess.

"My car is going to smell like an Italian bistro for months," I said as I finished wiping out the wet floor. I sat back and looked at him but avoided his eyes. "Thank you for your help."

"So, did some hobo upchuck in your car or something?"

"They were leftovers." I squinted up at him. It was hard to see his face as he was backlit by the brilliant house lights. "From dinner with my dad."

Ryan scowled, bent stiffly to scoop up his bucket and vacuum, and disappeared into the garage again. I puzzled, looking after him. What was the scowl for? Was he mad at me?

And if so, why?

And more so, why did I care?

I set my jaw and closed my car door, walking the garbage bag full of the remains of dinner over to the garbage can, trashing it.

He appeared from the garage again at that moment. "Your old man needs to be more careful about where he puts your leftovers in your car."

"Oh, he didn't do it. Aaron did, but he was careful. I just had to brake really hard for a possum."

His head snapped in my direction, his voice clipped. "Aaron? Who's that?"

I turned to him to ask him if he was seriously jealous, but I didn't have to ask. His face said it all. *No that's not confusing at all for me, Ryan. Keep acting like a possessive cave man a week after you've dumped me. That will make things so much easier to understand.*

I folded my arms over my chest and shrugged. "Someone who mentored with my dad a while back. He was also a guest at dinner."

Even in the evening lighting, I could see the color darken his face. He really was affected by this. *I didn't say I don't have feelings,* he'd said. But what, exactly *were* those feelings?

"I didn't say his name to make you jealous, Ryan. I was just explaining what happened with the leftovers in the car."

He stiffened. "What makes you think I'm jealous?"

I huffed out a half snort before controlling the rest of my reaction. "The way you're acting."

He ignored that and plowed on with more questions. "Does your father do that a lot? Set you up with his mentees?"

I licked my lips. "He's never done it before, no."

"*Before*...but he did it tonight? That bastard needs to stay the hell out of your life." His voice was decibels louder than normal and tight, full of hostility. His hands clenched into fists at his sides.

What the hell was going on? First Tolan and his weird little revelation, then Dad and his super abnormal behavior. Now Ryan's outward and renewed animosity toward my dad.

Was it all related?

"Are you dating this man? Aaron?"

I blinked, pulling back in disbelief and holding my hands out. "Wait, wait, wait a minute. Hold the phone. Are you asking me a question that is clearly none of your business?"

He froze, put his hands on his hips, and then, after his gaze warred with mine for several tense seconds, focused on the ground between us.

We stood like that for a moment while the night sounds continued indifferently around us—a slight breeze rustling the branches and leaves, the crickets and frogs from the canyon, the distant and constant hiss of the freeway. He took in a deep breath and let it go, giving me a curt nod. "I'm sorry. You're right. It's not my business." But the way he said it made the words sound as though they had been squeezed out of him.

I frowned. Something nagged at the edge of my thoughts, probably as a result of the weird information I'd collected this week. "Did, uh, did you tell Tolan last week that I was moving out?"

He shook his head. "How could I tell him something I didn't even know myself at that point?"

True enough, but I'd had no idea if he'd planned the breakup ahead of time. I'd like to think that he hadn't. I'd like to trust my belief in the best part of him. That he wouldn't have carried on even while planning to send me packing. I'd like to think the idea had only struck him on Sunday.

But it had been so abrupt. So sudden. *Triggered by something.*

I decided to play a hunch and see how he'd react in his vulnerable state. "Tolan and my dad met at Happy's last week. Were you there, too?"

Ryan appeared to stop breathing at that point, the color draining from his face. He didn't move a muscle, nor did he say a word.

But I had my answer. My dad had met with Tolan. And Ryan had been there, too.

It didn't take a genius to figure out what the subject of the conversation had been. I sucked in a long breath and let it out. It made sense; the abruptness of Ryan's actions, the weird first-date set up Dad had tried to pull off tonight, Dad's knowledge that I'd be moving out of Ryan's house, and that fear in his eyes when I'd brought up his meeting with Tolan.

"Did my Dad tell you to break things off with me?"

Chapter Eight
RYAN

I STOOD FROZEN, STARING AT HER LIKE AN IDIOT, A CLAMP closing around my throat. What could I say in response to that honest, straightforward question? So like her. So *her*. But I couldn't. I couldn't.

Instead, I blurted, "You're changing the subject, but that's fine. We won't talk about this anymore."

Then I did what any red-blooded American hero would do. I turned tail and ran. Well not literally. I sauntered quickly into my house as if I really had a place to hide from her and her question.

No, I wouldn't hide. That wasn't *me*.

But it actually was. I was hiding so much. Hiding from everyone around me. My colleagues, my closest friends. And all that I was hiding from her. *Her.* The person I least wanted to hide anything from.

I ran a hand through my hair as I crossed the threshold into my house, considering how I'd approach this. Maybe I could regroup then come back to this conversation later—better yet, tomorrow.

She grabbed my arm with both of her hands and yanked. Hard.

It didn't hurt, but it was enough for me to notice her. I spun and faced her.

Her face was white, her eyes wide, her jaw slack with disbelief. She was always so steady. A rock, really. To see her revealing this much was jarring.

Even the day I'd broken up with her, the calmness with which she'd flipped that suitcase closed and told me under no uncertain terms would she be leaving the house had almost bowled me over.

That even voice that hardly shook. No tears. No accusations. No yelling.

None of the usual.

It was just another way in which this particular woman was so uncommon. I swallowed. No need to torture myself with what I'd thrown away. Having her meant turning my back on everything else I cared about. And I'd made that choice already, hadn't I?

I wouldn't change my mind.

"Tell me," she bit out between clenched teeth.

I pulled my arm out of her grip. "There's nothing to tell."

She shook her head. "Don't lie to protect him, Ryan."

My eyes darted to her, and I blinked. Keeping my own raging emotions in check was a challenge, but not one I wasn't up to.

"I'm not lying. You're under the false impression that your father can tell me what to do. Ending this was my decision. Not his. Not Tolan's. *Mine.*"

She absorbed that with a frown, but I knew this wasn't over. I folded my arms and waited for her onslaught.

"Making a decision under duress is not a decision of your own free will," she said quietly. Even now, I could detect only the slightest struggle. Fuck, she was good. I'd once joked to myself that she was a secret Vulcan because of her uncanny perceptiveness that felt like mind-reading.

With this ability to control her negative emotional reactions, maybe she was a Vulcan in more ways than one.

"He threatened the program?" she asked when I didn't reply. "End it or he'd pull his money?"

I met her gaze. "I had a choice. I made the choice. I want to fly, Gray. I *need* to fly again."

Her eyes widened, and I could see it there, easily—the hurt, the betrayal. Mixed with a touch of disgust. Or maybe that was just what I was feeling for myself because of the statement that I'd left unspoken.

But she'd heard it all the same. *I chose to fly again over having you in my life.*

"You don't know what you want. Or what you need," she said in a quiet voice. A voice that left no doubt she was certain of her opinion.

"I know what I've promised. And I'm sorry, but I never made any promises to you."

She bit her lip. "So why didn't you just tell me all this on Sunday? Or for that matter, why didn't you tell me before you had sex with me on your kitchen counter?"

I sucked in a breath. In typical fashion for her, just like that first day she'd shown up at my house and I'd been canoodling with the trainer, Gray was pulling no punches.

Because I knew what I had to do but I didn't want to give you up, I wanted to say. I chose to be a callous asshole instead. "I didn't see the point. I dislike the man intensely, yes, but I have no right coming between his relationship with his daughter."

Her hand came up, pointing stiffly at me, her eyes aflame, cheeks flushing. Perhaps the closest thing to anger I'd ever seen in her. "And *you* had no right to make decisions with him about *my* life without *my* input."

"It wasn't just your life. Or mine," I answered quietly, my heart beating like I'd just run laps in the canyon. Perhaps hurting a little, too. Like some invisible hand was squeezing it, making it harder to breathe. "What about the other astronauts? What about everyone involved in the program? Your boss, your colleagues. What about Tolan?"

She pressed her lips together until they practically turned white. Now that I'd had a minute to calm down, to find some words to explain to her what I'd been thinking when I'd made my decision, I could take the time to just study her.

She handled upset and disappointment with unparalleled grace and strength, but I could still see the pain in her eyes. Pain that *I* had inflicted and that I had no wish to continue. I could also witness in her features the dawning realization of how utterly fucked up this situation was.

Conrad Barrett had laid down the law. A law that neither one of us could afford to break.

She pinched the bridge of her nose above her eyeglasses and sucked in a deep, noisy breath. "I'm so pissed at him right now."

"You can't tell him."

The hand dropped to her side, and she looked at me—looked right through me, actually. Her eyes were like lasers cutting right through my body, leaving deep wounds even as they cauterized my flesh.

"I'll decide how I want to handle this. Just as you've made your own decisions, the ones you excluded me from."

Fuck.

She stepped back, holding up her hands as if surrendering. "No decision is ever set in stone, Ryan. Just remember that." Then she cleared her throat, dropped her hands, and said in a voice so void of emotion it was almost dead, "I'm done."

She turned and calmly collected her things from the sofa while I watched, trying to think of what to say. I was still standing there like a fool five minutes after she left the room.

Scrubbing my face with my hand, I decided then and there that I wouldn't do the thing I wanted to do most at that moment—follow her to her room, pull her into my arms, bury my face in her hair. Kiss her. Hold her.

Tell her it would be all right.

Because it wouldn't be all right. Not for her and not for me, either.

I spent half that night pacing the floor in my bedroom but not from the typical fear of closing my eyes to the darkness. No, this episode was fueled by rage.

I was trying to fight the killer instinct that burned in my blood. I wanted to go on a murder spree. Target number one would be Dear Old Dad. I could break his neck in his sleep, easy. Number two would be this Aaron creep who better *not* have touched her. Maybe I'd take my time with that one.

Fuck. I let a breath go, and in spite of myself, I laughed, too. It was ridiculous, but damn if I wasn't feeling possessive as hell. Possessive of what I did not have.

Great going, Tyler. As if you weren't fucked up enough already. Now this woman had me tied in knots and chasing my own tail.

And though I knew damn well I didn't deserve her, it hadn't stopped me from wanting her.

The next day, Sunday, I left the house early, desperate to get away from her—and from my own thoughts. Not only would I have found it too difficult to look her in the eye again after the things that had come to light the night before, but the thought of watching her pack up her things and leave my house forever was about to drive me half insane.

So to get my mind off it, and to practice some great visualization during target practice, I went to a gun range with the guys. It was a long drive. Gun ranges were much harder to come by in Southern California than they'd been in Texas. But we had certifications to keep up on, all of us. Whether or not we'd been assigned to NASA in the meantime, we all still belonged to the nation's armed forces.

Happily, I had a new showpiece, a rare find—a Sig Sauer P210 Target pistol—to show off.

"Where the hell did you find that?" Hammer's eyes bugged the moment I pulled it out of its case. "These things are impossible to find in the States." I handed it to him, and he went over every inch of it. The other two guys bent over his shoulders to take a look.

"I guess being an American hero has perks that keep on giving," Noah said in a flat voice.

Without even dignifying Noah's shitty comment with a reply, I spoke to Hammer. "Don't get your drool on it. It'll rust." I snickered at his open display of lust over my newest firearm. "Did the Air Force even teach their fly boys to shoot a gun?"

He replied with a single finger, straight up into the air, and I laughed my ass off.

Kirill got revenge on Hammer's behalf not too much later, because in my distraction, I was shooting like shit today.

"Look," Kirill said, holding up my target to examine how far off the mark I'd been. "Ty is shooting like half-blind old woman."

"Fuck you," I said, snatching the thing back from him. It was embarrassing, really. I'd been a marksman on my team while I'd served as a special operator for the Navy. And I usually won any competition among my astronaut colleagues or came damn near close. Not today. Good thing I didn't have any money riding on it today.

"Hmm," the cosmonaut continued. "Perhaps it's this German piece of shit you're shooting with."

"No way, Kirya. That's a sweet piece," Hammer said. "I shot just fine with it."

I frowned down at my target before crumpling it up in my tightened fist. Not even visualizing Conrad Barrett's smarmy head in the middle of that circle had helped.

In disgust, I pulled off my goggles and ear protection and sat and cleaned my guns in silence while the guys continued to rib me.

"Loser buys the beer," Noah said with a slap on my shoulder. And I did just that.

When I came home, I saw that Gray had just returned from taking a carload of her things to her house. She'd purposely left the packing to after I'd left, most likely to prevent me from offering her help.

She wasn't speaking to me, apparently, because when I asked her a question in the kitchen, she turned around and left like I'd never said a damn thing.

Tonight would be her last night here. The thought of it made me ache with the loss and the uncertainty. Even while she hadn't been next to me in bed this past week, having her in the house had brought me some comfort—though I'd never admit that to another soul in a thousand years.

And I'd miss her, goddammit. I already did, in truth. I would have loved to have planned a special dinner or taken her out. The fake girlfriend was filming movie scenes on the other side of the country. If I were seen with Gray, even for a goodbye, it would cause a scandal.

I couldn't stand the roving thoughts anymore. Marks on the bottle or not, late on Sunday night, I grabbed that bottle of vodka and downed three shots in a row. It didn't make me feel any better.

But it had numbed me enough to summon up the courage to turn off the light. I'd made the decision on the day I'd broken things off with her—the day I'd had that dream. Since then I'd heard it over and over in my mind, asked in his voice. *Why are you so afraid—all the time?*

I decided I'd fight to get over this. Move past this. Be able to function as an adult once more. And most importantly, I'd make good on all the promises I'd made to him. If I couldn't do right by Gray, at least I could by Xander.

And I needed to prove to myself that I didn't need her like a crutch to help me get through the night.

So I sat beside the lamp in my bedroom and dimmed it slowly over a period of twenty minutes until I was in virtual darkness, my hand on the switch. I remembered the things she'd taught me and tried those—mindful deep breathing, focusing on the physical sensations of my body occupying space around me. Even visualizing something pleasant—her smile filled my mind's eye and then faded, replaced by Xander's haunted features. My breath seized, suddenly ice cold, and I flipped on the light.

I reached over and grabbed for her pillow—the one she'd used when she'd slept in my bed until the past week. I tucked it into my closet every day so that my housekeeper wouldn't change the pillowcase. I held it to my face and breathed in deeply, taking comfort from her smell.

It took me a while to calm down, but I promised myself I would do this every night until I could fall asleep in the dark.

***

As luck would have it, Gray was in the middle of grabbing her last things from the house on Monday afternoon after work when my guests for the rest of the summer arrived.

I'd taken off work early to greet Karen, who had insisted on driving herself from the airport since she was renting a car. I was working in the garage, trying to salvage my poor, wrecked bike, when Karen pulled in.

Wiping the excess grease off my hands, I made my way onto the sunlit plateau at the top of my driveway, blinking in the bright light. A nondescript white sedan—clearly a rental car with out-of-state license plates—greeted me.

No sooner had the car shut off, than the rear passenger door flew open, and a brown-haired boy of about six years old flew out of the back seat, running straight for me. He looked like he'd almost doubled in size since I last saw him, and my heart pinched to know I'd missed so much of his life.

"Uncle Ty!"

My gaze flew back to the car, where a petite and very attractive brunette was extricating herself from the seat belt and exiting from behind the wheel.

I swallowed a sudden lump in my throat to see them again. Xander's family was now here with me. Would he smile if he could look down on the scene right now? Or would it just make him angry?

I bent and scooped the boy up in a bear hug, overcome by true joy at seeing him again. "Who is this tall kid? I don't know any tall kids," I said gruffly.

His hands hooked around my neck. "It's me, AJ!"

I placed him back down on the ground with a grim shake of my head. "Nope. No way. AJ is like half your height. He's a little kid. You're a big boy."

"Ty!" he said, his smile revealing a gaping hole where his front top tooth had been. "It's me. I grew."

My mouth thinned, and I put a hand to my chin as Karen approached, her smile equally huge. "Hmm. Fake news. Not possible. Nope." I shook my head again. "Don't buy it."

"Mom. Tell him it's me."

She put a hand on AJ's shiny hair. "I'm afraid it's true, Ty. Boys grow, and they grow fast."

"KareBear," I said with a grin, leaning forward to kiss her on the cheek. She returned the kiss, hugging me tightly. When I pulled back, I noticed Gray watching us from the doorway. With a stiff gesture I waved her over.

"Karen, you met Gray in Houston."

Gray approached, her hands laced together in front of her. I avoided looking into her face or looking at her any more than I had to. These were her last moments at the house, and that thought was leaving me with a cold sense of foreboding.

"Karen, hi," she said, holding her hand forward to shake. "Great to see you again in person. I feel like I know you so much better because of all the texting."

I frowned at that. The two of them had been texting? About what?

Karen's smile widened. "I'm so glad I got to see you. I hope we aren't kicking you out of the house."

Gray laughed and waved toward me. "No, he's doing it, actually." I froze, but both the women seemed to take it as a joke. One quick glance into Gray's lovely face, and I noted that the laughter did not reach her eyes. No, those green eyes showed sadness, hurt, and yes, lingering anger.

"I'm happy to give you some space. I'm sure you have tons to catch up on," Gray said, reassuring Karen without another look at me. Then she bent. "And you must be AJ. I've heard lots about you."

AJ's eyes widened. "What did you hear about me?"

"Well, I heard that the Tooth Fairy visited you recently."

AJ nodded enthusiastically. "She brought me three golden one-dollar coins."

"Wow," I interjected. "Tooth Fairy is paying good dividends these days. She must really be hitting the big time."

"What do you want to do while you're in California? When you're not working, of course," Gray said, straightening and self-consciously adjusting her glasses. She'd addressed her question to both of the newcomers. I had no idea why I was so surprised to see how well she took to people she hardly knew. It was her strength, and a big part of why she was so good at her job.

"The beach," Karen answered.

"No! Disneyland," AJ said, sending a pointed look at his mother.

"Yes," Karen said with a weary sigh, as if she'd heard the request a few hundred times before that. She put a hand on her son's shoulder. "Definitely Disneyland, as promised."

Gray's smile widened. "Well I have good news, AJ. I think you'll have plenty of time to do both. And then some."

AJ's grin grew wider, and he looked at me. "Will you come to Disneyland with us, Ty?"

I opened my mouth to answer before Karen interrupted. "Ty has lots of work to do, AJ. He's, um, he's got a test flight coming up."

AJ's face clouded, and he grew quiet. In response, Karen tensed.

Gray reacted quickly, appearing to have picked up on his mood immediately. She extended her hand to him. "Hey guess what AJ? Ty has four bedrooms in his house to pick from. Want me to show you so you can pick yours out?"

AJ's eyes widened, his previous sullenness vanishing. Karen looked immediately relieved. He took Gray's hand, and she led the boy back into the house.

Karen smiled after her. "She's so sweet. She's been a good friend to you?"

I swallowed. *Friend, yeah.*

And by the tightness in my chest, I knew she was so much more. So much more I didn't even want to begin to examine for myself, much less discuss with Karen. The less said the better, so I merely nodded.

Karen turned back to me. "Are you in love, Ty?"

I blinked, suddenly spooked by the feeling that Karen had read my mind. I sent her a puzzled gaze, hoping that would be enough to cause her to elaborate.

"Keely Dawson. The two of you are all over the news back home."

I took a deep breath and let it go, relieved that my secret feelings for Gray—whatever they were—remained preciously secret. "Oh, that."

Her brows shot up in surprise.

"It's fake, Karen. It was something that XVenture asked me to do to help—to spruce up my image, I guess. Keely makes me respectable."

Karen's mouth dropped, and she had a strange look on her face. "Oh. Wow. They do that? I mean, I heard rumors that things like that are done in Hollywood, but I always just assumed they were strange Hollywood rumors. That's...." She shook her head in amazement. "I can't believe they got you to agree to it. That is so not your thing."

I shrugged one shoulder. "You're right. It's not my thing at all. But hey, it was the only way I'd fly again. So here we are. I had the right incentive."

She nodded, her smile faltering just a little. "I watched your press conference last week. Congratulations on the flight."

But given the tone of her voice and the pasted-on look of her smile, I could easily tell that she was not so thrilled that I was going up again. With good reason, considering that the last time, her family had been virtually destroyed.

Clenching my jaw, I opted to change the subject.

Glancing at the door where AJ had disappeared minutes before, I asked, "How is he doing?"

She followed my gaze but took a long time to answer. My eyes scanned her face, and she looked worried, genuinely worried. Uh oh. That wasn't good.

"He's having trouble. It's been a very difficult year, especially for him."

I'd been out here for over six months now. And not there for them. "I'm sorry," I said quietly.

She looked at me and smiled. "Don't be. We're going to have fun, right? We can't wait to explore. Are you sure it's okay for us to stay here with you for so long? We aren't going to cramp your style?"

I laughed. "I don't have much style to cramp these days. The partying and all that is behind me."

I'd known Karen a long time, since we were all teenagers. We'd hung out constantly in college. And I could tell that while she wanted to believe me, she was waiting to see the truth of my words with her own eyes.

Just then, AJ came bursting back through the front door. "Mom! You have to see this house. There's a swimming pool. I already picked out my room. You should get yours, too."

I raised my brows. "Yeah, better rush and get one while you can. Never know when someone's going to swipe it out from under you." My breath let out suddenly, like a punch to my gut, when Gray appeared in the doorway just behind AJ. Karen left my side to follow AJ into the house. Gray stepped aside, smiling

"Oh, by the way," she said to Karen. "Tolan Reeves, our boss at XVenture, asked me specifically to invite you and AJ to come tour company buildings and the factory where the rockets are made. He said he'd give you the VIP treatment."

I raised my brows, not having heard that news before. Then I realized this must have been the conversation where she'd found out that Tolan and I met with Conrad Barrett last week.

Gray gave AJ a fist bump then disappeared, returning a minute later with a box and a backpack slung over her slim shoulder. I hurried to take the box from her, which she handed over to me without resistance or comment, or eye contact, for that matter. I encouraged AJ to show his mom around the house while I helped Gray out with her things.

We walked out to the street where she'd moved her car, and I lowered the box into her trunk. My eyes landed on that blue and white toiletry kit that she'd brought with her that first day she'd shown up at my house. That was the day she'd cut her hand and scared the shit out of me that she was going to bleed out right in my kitchen.

It felt like years ago because it felt like I'd known her for years. But it had only been two short months before, almost to the day. My entire insides sunk when the trunk of the car thumped closed. And there was a tightness in my throat.

She stood there, beside me, staring back toward the house. Eventually her gaze flickered up to meet mine. "Thank you," she said in a low, even voice.

"I should be thanking you," I said flatly. "For all of this, for straightening me out. For getting me to reach out to them again." I nodded toward the house to indicate who I meant.

She shook her head. "I didn't do those things. *You* did. I'm proud of you."

My eyes locked on hers and I forced moisture into my throat, clearing it.

She took my breath away when she smiled sadly. "Goodbye Ryan Tyler. Be kind to yourself."

She backed away, but I reached out and grabbed her wrist, holding her where she was. I didn't move otherwise. I just needed a moment—many moments, in truth. I needed to prepare myself for what it would do to me to watch her drive away. Fuck, this was hard.

"I don't know..." I began in a shaky voice until it faded away.

"Yeah, you do. You do. And when being around them gets too overwhelming, promise me—promise me—you'll talk to someone."

To someone, but not to her. That's what she left unspoken. I couldn't lean on her anymore.

I nodded solemnly. "I promise."

She nodded too, then stepped forward again. "Can I give you a hug?"

Without speaking, I pulled her toward me. She rose on her tiptoes, and her arms encircled my neck. I bent my head and, though I ferociously fought the urge, I lost. My nose went to her hair, breathing her in. Her strawberries and mint scent. A country field in summer. As fresh and nourishing as she was.

If all the other shit I'd been through in the past year wasn't going to do it, this just might break me.

I couldn't breathe when she pulled away, turned, and slid into the driver's seat. I stood there, looking after her long after she'd driven down the street and out of my sight.

Out of my life.

And I had little idea whether seeing her again practically every day at work would make it feel better or worse.

Chapter Nine
Ryan

THURSDAY NIGHT, JUST OUTSIDE A GLITTERING VENUE IN Hollywood, I was getting icy glares and a cold shoulder from my fake girlfriend. We awaited our turn at the curb before exiting the limo for the premiere of a movie I had no interest in watching, nor did I even recall its title. It was a hot night in late July and I wasn't looking forward to stepping into the heat in my monkey suit. Summer nights in Southern California, unlike those of Houston, cooled off quickly. But not quickly enough to make this god-awful tuxedo feel any more comfortable.

Having just flown in from the location of her new movie on the east coast, Keely looked perfect with her red hair styled into an elegant updo. Add to that her flawless skin, gorgeous bone structure and a fantastic smile. She was exactly the type of woman I went for—*before.*

Flashing cameras and cheering fans would, no doubt, greet us the moment we stepped out of the limo. They'd taken to calling us "Tyley" which sounded unfortunate to me, but Victoria, our public relations specialist, had beamed over it. Apparently, the nickname had denoted ultimate success for her scheme.

Keely ripped her eyes from the window and met my stare. "Don't even think about it, Tyler," she said in a gruff voice.

I blinked. "What?"

"You and me. That's never gonna happen."

My brows crunched together. "What makes you assume I was thinking that?"

She froze, holding my stare for a few long and tense moments, mouth slightly open. Then she pulled her eyes away, picking at her designer gown as if finding a stray thread. "Well, in case you *were* thinking that, it's never gonna happen. I have too much respect for Gray."

Had she and Gray been talking to each other? I knew that they'd been friendly. It wasn't hard to believe that they'd hit it off. Keely was an affable woman—not really full of herself at all.

But had Gray been confiding in Keely? It seemed so unlike her.

"Have you been talking to her about me?"

A cinnamon-colored brow arched up, and she opened her mouth to speak when an usher opened our door and bent to speak with us. "Are you ready?"

I exited the car once the usher pulled it wide enough for me to step out. Then I bent to extract Keely, who had replaced her skeptical doubt with a brilliant smile that lit up the place every bit as much as the camera flashes. She grasped my arm and molded herself to my side in every way. I tried my best to gaze adoringly at her for the cameras.

"Have you heard from her in the last couple days? How is she?" I hadn't caught any glimpses of her at work since she'd left my house earlier that week.

"Do you care?" She held up a hand, waving to a cluster of groupies clumped on the sidewalk, furiously trying to capture her attention.

I fought the desire to roll my eyes. *Jesus.* I herded her down the red carpet a little more harshly than I intended. "I wouldn't ask if I didn't care."

She threw me a sidelong glance. "Why did you do it then? If you care?"

I took a deep breath and let it out, trying to release some tension that was building. The woman was infuriating me. I'd asked a simple question and expected a simple answer. "It's complicated."

Yeah, *complicated.* That was one word for the whole fucked-up situation.

"We've texted back and forth a few times. She didn't tell me much. Just said you were no longer seeing each other when I asked."

"How about a kiss for the cameras?" a paparazzo asked just as we hit the head of the carpet. Keely had finished posing alone in her designer gown while folks oohed and aahed and clicked away. I tried my hardest not to look bored. I couldn't manage an adoring stare, though.

With that, Keely turned to me and immediately pointed her face up toward mine, and I pecked her obediently.

Cameras clicked, and photographers scoffed. "Kiss her like you mean it, Commander Ty."

I raised my brows at Keely, and she nodded. I closed my eyes and dove in for something a little livelier, more passionate. All fake.

I'd kissed Keely several dozen times for the benefit of the cameras, and this time was no different. But instead of a glamorous and perfectly manicured redhead, I pictured a slender blonde with mussy hair and lips to die for.

Or at least lips that I'd die to taste again.

I remembered her smell, the feel of her body against mine, and the sound of her voice. I deepened the kiss, opening my mouth to hers, plunging my tongue inside. It didn't make the ache go away. It didn't make anything feel better.

And when I pulled back and noted the confusion and flush on Keely's face, I realized it hadn't made her any less upset with me, either.

"Wow, that was some kiss!" One photographer commented as he clicked away, and I laughed uncomfortably.

Keely grinned. "Damn straight! That's what I keep him around for."

As soon as we were out of earshot, which was moments later, she added. "Clearly you weren't kissing *me*, though."

I winced slightly and turned away. She squeezed my arm. And after a long beat of silence between us, just before entering the doors of the auditorium, she said, "I'll find out how she's doing."

I cleared my throat and rasped under my breath, "She needs a friend."

She frowned as she studied my face then nodded before we entered the building.

Fortunately, the house I went home to was not as empty and hollow as I felt inside. With AJ and Karen to fill up my spare time, it helped keep me from losing my mind.

In the evenings, we took AJ to the park, had dinner together, and sometimes watched a movie. Karen would get AJ ready for bed and read to him while I cleaned up. It quickly became a comforting routine.

That weekend, we went for a walk in the canyon, exploring the countryside. I barbecued AJ's favorite meal, hotdogs and corn on the cob for dinner.

"When can we go to Disneyland?" AJ asked his mom.

"We'll get there, I promise. I have to find out what days the studio wants me next week. And Gray texted me. She says the tour at XVenture is on Tuesday." I tried not to wince whenever I heard her name pronounced. I managed it almost every time, but it still took conscious effort.

AJ turned his eyes on me. "Does that mean I get to see you at work?"

I grinned and ruffled his hair. "Me and Noah and Hammer. And we have a cosmonaut friend you haven't met yet, Kirill. He's a cool guy, too."

"Maybe they can come to Disneyland with us, too."

"You can't do Disney in just one day. You know that, right?" I said. "There are actually two parks there. The Magic Kingdom and California Adventure."

AJ shoved the last bite of hotdog and bun in his mouth, then proceeded to talk around the bite with his mouth full. I couldn't help but laugh. "I want to go on the rollercoasters, but Mom hates them."

I smiled. "I'll take you. There aren't that many over there, though. California Screamin' is pretty fun. You even pull 4.3 G's on the launch sequence."

"Ugh. You and Xander and your roller coaster love," Karen sighed. "Clearly AJ takes after you two and not me."

"He's a boy. Boys like their thrills. Maybe you'll grow up to fly planes like your dad."

AJ very visibly paled but said nothing, just shaking his head. Karen shot him a worried look, a frown creasing her brow. Our eyes met but I didn't say anything.

Every night that AJ had been here, he'd woken up within an hour or two of falling asleep screaming and inconsolable from bad dreams. His mom would spend an hour or so in there calming him down again until he gave in to exhaustion.

Every night this happened...for months, so Karen had told me. It had to be taking its toll on her. We hadn't discussed it yet, but the sheer exhaustion I saw in her eyes and her pale features was enough to reveal that truth to me.

A little later, AJ was ushered to bed through the usual routine—bath, pajamas, teeth brushing, and a story read to him. Since cleanup was quick this evening, I volunteered to read the story so that Karen could finish her glass of wine in peace.

When I entered the bedroom, Gray's old bedroom, in fact, I hesitated. AJ was in bed, his green Orbit plush toy, the mascot for the Houston Astros, tucked in beside him.

"Hey, champ. I hear we're halfway through *Harry Potter and the Sorcerer's Stone?*"

He nodded, his eyes already at half-mast. The hike must have worn him out.

Listlessly, he handed me the book. I opened to the bookmark and read only one page before the kid was fast asleep.

Karen was finishing her wine when I made it back to the sitting room.

"Thanks. I bet he was so thrilled to have you tuck him in."

I shrugged. "He was pretty exhausted. He was out after one page."

Her brows twitched in surprise and she nodded. "Good. Maybe we'll have a nice quiet night tonight."

I sunk down on the couch next to her. "Do you get many of those?"

She grimaced at me, then pointed to the half-full bottle. "You want some? This stuff isn't going to drink itself."

I shook my head, and she didn't push it. She did, however, pour herself another glass and sip at it thoughtfully.

"How was the movie premiere?" she asked. "I saw pictures on Twitter. You and Keely make a cute couple."

I rolled my eyes and leaned my head against the back of the couch. "Please. Not you, too."

This rear sitting room overlooked the canyon. The sun had gone down, but the sky was still light. Karen commented on the beauty of the sunset. "Mmm, I could get used to California. Never thought I'd say that."

I grinned. "You've only been here a week. Wait 'til you have to drive in traffic or fight crowds at the shopping malls."

"*You* seem to be enjoying it out here." She smiled and tilted her glass up to her lips.

I blinked and pushed myself back into the corner of the couch, turning toward her. "I love California. Can't beat the weather anywhere."

She nodded. "Yeah. You never miss Houston?"

I gulped. "I miss all my friends there, former colleagues. But I needed to leave."

Her dark eyes flicked up at me and I registered the hurt easily. "There's no denying that your life was certainly taking a dark turn. I'm proud of how you've turned things around. You've been working hard."

I'm proud of you. Gray's sad smile immediately popped into my mind. The wisps of blonde hair stirring in the breeze. In spite of her anger at me, in spite of the pain I'd inflicted on her, in spite of it all, she had still asked for a hug and wished me a sweet goodbye.

I forced the image away and looked back at Karen. "It's nothing compared to what you've had to work through. You're doing an amazing job with him. You've always been the best mom."

She tilted her head and smiled. "This single parenting thing really sucks. I think every single parent deserves a fucking medal." Then she sighed, setting down the half-empty glass. "On the other hand, I thank God that I have him. I'd have gone off the deep end if I hadn't had to hold it together for him."

I looked away, knowing I should have been there for her too, to help with AJ. Instead I'd been able to indulge myself and dance dangerously close to that deep end. She'd never even had that option.

"I should be able to get out to Houston more once we pull off the test flight. We've got joint training planned at some NASA facilities. And—and I want to see you and AJ more."

She leaned forward and put her hand on mine. "We want to see you, too. I'm so glad we didn't leave things that messy way the last time we met in Houston."

I inhaled deeply and let it go. "Yeah, so am I."

She opened her mouth to say something, but she was interrupted by a soul-wrenching, ear-splitting scream coming from AJ's bedroom. She shot off the couch and headed down the hallway.

I followed quickly behind her at a loss for what I could do to help but not willing to leave it all in her hands.

Karen flipped on the lights in the bedroom and sat beside him on the bed.

"Daddy," he said softly. "He was right here in my room."

My breath froze, and I felt like I might suffocate. Oh shit. I'd had dreams like that. Dreams that were so real that they spooked me down to the bones. Down in the core of my body, something shivered with fear and pain.

This poor kid.

Karen was hugging AJ, pulling him close to her and whispering into his hair while he whimpered. "I saw him standing right there. He said I couldn't come with him. Then he was gone."

"I know, bud. I'm so sorry."

"Why? Why did it have to happen?"

I took a quick step back from the doorway. *Shit.* I couldn't listen to this. My movement, however, caught AJ's eye, and he looked over at me.

"Ty!" AJ said, pushing away from his mother and holding both his arms toward me.

I hesitantly came forward. "Yeah, champ. What do you need?"

"I need you," he whimpered. As I came closer, he stood on his bed, and then jumped into my arms, molding his head to my shoulder. I held his small body to my chest and my heart melted, my throat closing. Karen stood, and our gazes met over his shoulder.

She stroked his hair. "It'll be all right, buddy."

"Ty was there. Ty was with him...when he died," the distraught kid mumbled into my shirt. I stiffened, still like a statue. Determined to bear these moments as my own part of purgatory. Maybe after all was said and done, I'd be cleansed of it, this ever-present guilt. This *shame*. It burned.

"AJ," his mom said.

But I tilted my head toward Karen. "I got this. Go relax."

With a grateful smile, she nodded, then lifted on tiptoes to kiss AJ who barely seemed to notice. Then she quietly left the room.

I held him for a long time without moving or saying anything, hoping maybe he'd fall asleep like this. But finally, after a big sniff, he sleepily asked, "Will you stay with me? Until I fall asleep?"

I gently laid him down on the bed. "I'll sit right here. But we can't talk, okay? Or else you won't fall asleep."

AJ gave a wide yawn and rubbed his eyes with his knuckles. "Okay, but I don't need the light on. Can you switch it off? I'm a big boy." Another spear of shame stabbed me then. The six-year-old boy was fine in the dark while the thirty-five-year-old man was terrified of it.

I hadn't consumed any vodka to fortify me, but I was determined to do what he asked, even if it meant just gritting my teeth and pushing through.

I went shakily to the doorway and opened the door to allow some residual dimness to leak in from down the hall. Then I flicked the light off and moved back to the kid's bedside. AJ promptly grabbed my hand with his little one, and I held it, focusing on being there, being strong for him. Doing the things I should have been doing all along.

Fortunately, he was asleep in minutes while I sweated it out in the dimness.

But there was no numbing this pain, this realization that the child was suffering without his father, while *I* existed when I shouldn't. How could I look either of them in the face again, knowing what I knew?

I'd been a full decade older than AJ when I'd lost my dad, and it was pain I would never forget. I couldn't even imagine what this little champ was suffering, but I could empathize. I could remember the day we'd gotten the news. Mom and Dad had been divorced for a few years, so I was his next of kin, his sole surviving heir.

We'd received the news in person from his SEAL team members. One had answered Mom's questions while I tried to breathe, the news not quite sinking in that Dad was never coming home again. Never going to call me on the phone again and wish me luck at my next water polo match. A chaplain that had accompanied them had sidled up to me and put his hand on my back. "Are you okay, son? There's no shame in letting it out."

But I'd shaken my head and held it inside.

And every night I missed him. We'd never been able to do that summer-long National Parks camping trip together, the one he'd promised me we'd do when his latest deployment was over. I stuffed down that old sorrow, the realization that it had been almost twenty years since I'd seen him, talked to him, heard his voice.

My eyes roamed AJ's innocent face. I had no idea what memory he clung to—the color of the tie on the man who told him his dad wouldn't be coming back? The sound of his mother's sobs? The first bouquet of flowers to arrive or the taste of one of the many casseroles that had no doubt started appearing at their doorstep before the first twenty-four hours had passed?

I took in the shape of his young cheeks, still round with baby fat. Still so innocent. Too innocent to be dashed into the harsh waters of this cruel, cruel world.

Was he already forgetting Xander now? Could he remember the sound of his voice? The way the stubble on his dad's chin felt when he rubbed it against AJ's babyish cheek?

Soon the child's breathing was even, but I waited fifteen minutes more, glancing from my watch to the shaft of light on the floor and trying to ignore my own racing heart until I was out in the hallway once more.

I left the door open, just in case I was summoned back by the next bad dream. But God, how I hoped there wouldn't be another. This one had shredded me, and that poor kid needed some reprieve.

Casting one last glance at his sleeping form, I realized how much in common we had. Poor AJ. I should have been there for him all these months, like I'd promised Xander I would be. I was a horrible friend for having neglected his little boy and his wife.

Swallowing that heavy lump, I made my way back to Karen. We spent another hour or so on the couch, alternately talking and sitting in silence, until she was so exhausted she had to go off to bed.

Again, I had my three shots quickly in a row. The alcohol and my Gray-scented pillow aided me in drifting off to sleep with the light off. When I woke a few hours later, I had to turn it on, but at least it was something. Slow progress, but progress nonetheless.

On Tuesday, Karen arrived at XVenture with AJ late in the morning, bringing him directly back to the astronaut office to see his dad's old friends and colleagues.

AJ beamed when he saw Noah, who greeted Karen with a kiss on her cheek. For that last mission, Noah had been scheduled to go up instead of me. A last-minute health issue had grounded him, but he'd spent years and months training with Xander and me and Xander's backup for that mission.

Noah and I were cordial but hardly speaking these days. We communicated enough to keep things civil when we were socializing and perfectly professional when we were at work. But nothing more than that. The same old tension was always there, that weird dynamic dividing us, like a thick wall between us since Xander died.

I honestly believed he thought that if he'd gone to the station instead of me, Xander would have survived. That somehow the accident was my fault.

Likely because it *was*. And I felt his judgment every time we were together. And now, here, with Xander's family, that tension thickened. I hoisted the boy onto my shoulders. Karen, after hugging Noah and Hammer in turn, shook Kirill's hand when they were introduced. She stood closely beside me, and Noah's dark eyes flicked between her and me several times, his features blank.

I remembered hearing from him that he'd spent a lot of time with the family right after the accident. He'd been the one to break the news to her when she'd been summoned into Mission Control for that last conversation with her doomed husband. Apparently, he'd grown fairly attached to them in the ensuing days.

All the XVenture astronauts had pushed aside our normal schedule for the next few hours in order to accompany AJ and Karen on their VIP tour. We retraced our steps and met Tolan at the entrance to the entire complex—a wide room with high glass bays that let in the light from outside. The inlaid mosaic logo of XVenture gleamed in the glossy stone floor, and twenty-foot scale rocket models were suspended overhead. It was an impressive sight and an appropriate place to start the tour.

Tolan waited for us alongside two other people. My pace faltered only slightly when I recognized one of them as Gray, standing beside a man I'd never met before. They were talking. She was smiling and laughing.

I zeroed in on her, noting immediately how different Gray looked. She wore dressy gray pants, a pink and gray silk shirt and low pumps on her feet. *And* makeup. And jewelry. And her hair—she'd cut her hair. *Short.* It was layered around her ears and wasn't unbecoming. It was actually rather cute and suited her.

But this much change at once. I blinked. What the hell had transformed her so dramatically in just over a week? My gut sank as I realized the answer might be the man standing beside her.

Her smile did not falter in the least when we approached. She met my gaze but pulled her eyes away just as quickly to smile at the kid riding on my shoulders. She even had new glasses with darker frames that gave her more of a sexy librarian look.

My heart raced, and suddenly I grew angry over the demise of *my* Gray to make room for this make-over counterfeit.

My eyes flicked to the man as he was introduced to us. I guessed his first name before Tolan even spoke. This had to be the mysterious Aaron.

Aaron Thiessen, as he was introduced to us, seemed pleasant enough as we shook hands all around. I remembered the brief fantasy I'd had about inventing some way to inflict pain or even death on this man. Whenever I thought about him with Gray, I didn't regret that feeling one bit.

Tolan was explaining the different rocket models, each representing a different phase in XVenture's aerospace development, including the crowning glory, the Rubicon III rocket which would take me into space in six weeks' time inside the Phoenix capsule, designed to carry up to five astronauts into low and medium earth orbit.

Once testing was complete, XVenture would be contracting with NASA, Roscosmos, the European Space Agency and JAXA, the Japanese space agency, along with others, to take astronauts to the International Space Station in the near future.

I wouldn't be one of them. I would not be going to station again. Though at this time, I was the only person who knew that. I'd fly again to keep my promise, but I couldn't go there again.

Thiessen seemed interested in the company, though painfully lacking in knowledge of the space program. He questioned Gray often, tilting his head toward her and pointing out different displays as we passed them. The kiddo on my shoulders was quiet, observant, and his mother seemed more interested in catching up with Hammer and, especially, Noah.

And I had to admit that I tailed Gray and her escort—perhaps a bit uncomfortably close. She cast me a pointed glance once or twice, but that was it. I refused to back off.

Which made me a complete asshole.

I was fine with that. Me and my inner asshole got along just great.

And both me and my inner asshole did not like the idea of Gray getting chummy with this Aaron character—or anyone else for that matter.

Which made things...complicated.

CHAPTER TEN
GRAY

IN THE NINE DAYS SINCE I'D RETURNED TO MY HOUSE, I'D managed to find a task to fill every spare moment of the day. My condo had been completely decluttered. I ended up taking three garbage bags down to the dumpster and five to charity donations—old clothes, worthless souvenirs, way too many blank notebooks and stationery products I'd been collecting but never used.

I'd decided a new look for myself was in order, too. I got that pixie cut I'd been contemplating and bought a few new nice outfits for work. Normally I hated shopping, but browsing store windows sure beat going home and sitting in my empty condo. I even bought makeup, too.

Maybe I owed it to myself after all this time to spend more time on my looks. Maybe if I hadn't been so invisible, so forgettable...

I paused, staring at myself in the mirror halfway through watching and systematically pausing a YouTube eye makeup tutorial on my phone so as to better pick up on the instructor's tips.

Was that what I was doing? Making myself less forgettable? Less invisible, in hopes that by fixing that, I might get back what I'd lost?

I sank to sit on the closed toilet seat, the realization weighing heavily.

Was this it? The next step in the progression of grief processing?

Third Stage: Bargaining

Every day at work it got a little easier. I'd gone pretty much an entire week without seeing him at all. But when we took the tour together, it was at once thrilling and awkward.

I could tell that he was overly interested in Aaron, to the point of almost seeming jealous. Though whenever that hope rose up, I told myself that he definitely wasn't.

On the other hand, watching him so close and happy with Karen and AJ at once warmed my heart and also made me a little sad that I wasn't in on their happy reunion. I had to watch it from a distance, like an outsider.

Because as it was, I had been relegated to the position of outsider once again. As each day passed, those days with Ryan on the inside felt more and more like a dream that had only existed in my head.

I opened up my message app at least once a day to start a long message to him before hastily deleting it. I'd never hit send on a message like that. But it felt strangely cathartic to type it out, anyway. My own version of therapeutic writing.

Perhaps some primal screaming was in order for further expressive therapy.

It had to get better soon, right?

Even if just in increments. I imagined that each new day would be slightly easier than the one before. Or at least that's what I hoped for.

***

The answer to that question came just the next day when I realized, no, things likely weren't going to get better anytime soon.

Marjorie, my soon-to-be boss on the health team, asked me to distribute the monthly mental health questionnaires amongst the astronaut and chief engineering teams. It was the astronauts' turn to get the full interview treatment this month, while the engineers would sit it out until next.

But everyone had to do a questionnaire, and I suspected the astronauts would be as annoyed by this as the engineers had been.

I asked her why she didn't just email them to everyone, and she replied with a smirk. "Simple psychology, Gray. If these personalized forms aren't delivered with a human attached to them who can hold them accountable, the guys will blow them off and let them get buried in their email."

So the task had fallen on me. How lucky.

I drew a long breath and blew it out before pushing into the astronaut office with my papers in hand. The office was more like a medium-sized workshop, in truth. There were square tables set up with tablets and laptops and, a drafting table for sketches and blueprints. Each astronaut had their own corner for a desk discreetly set back by cubicle partitions. There were mockups and models of vehicles and control boards, samples and rolls of plans held in cylinders, and poster-sized checklists pinned to every wall that wasn't covered in a whiteboard. The place was a picture of organized chaos.

And I'd just walked into the middle of a war zone.

Okay maybe *war zone* was a bit of an exaggeration. But for a medium-height, slenderly built woman among a cluster of hulking, athletically-built men yelling at each other, it felt like a warzone.

Noah was bent, insistently tapping a clipboard on the table with his index finger. "It needs to fucking get done *before* we go to Florida. How hard is that to understand? I'm sick of arguing about this with you."

I opened my mouth to say something then snapped it shut again immediately in response to the drama I'd just been drop-shipped into.

Ryan stood across the table from him, fists clenched and staring at Noah like a bulldog about to pick a fight with a pug.

"It'll get done. Get the stick out of your ass," came Ryan's salty reply. I was actually shocked speechless to hear him speak to a colleague like that.

Noah now had a hand on his hip. "If being precise and methodical about our approach to testing is having a stick up my ass, then fine, I'll live with that. Gladly."

"If you want the test done so badly, why don't *you* do it then?" Ryan ground back.

Noah threw his hands in the air, looking toward the other guys as if for support. As if they'd discussed this very subject before when Ryan wasn't around. "For fuck's sake, Ty. It's a lights-out board test. It takes less than half a day to run the sims and their variations."

Shit. I immediately thought about fleeing in the opposite direction, though my feet felt like they'd grown roots into the floor. The old Gray would have done that. Would have disappeared into the woodwork until the big boys stopped hollering at each other.

But I was a new Gray. A very new Gray. And New Gray was not afraid to be seen and noticed.

I cleared my throat loudly to let them know I was there. Four heads turned my way, and four pairs of eyes settled on me.

"I'm sorry to interrupt. I just had your monthly questionnaires for the health office." I brandished the fistful of papers in front of me as if to prove I was legit.

Utter silence. I may as well have walked in there and asked them all to tap dance on the worktables for me.

Ryan glanced at Noah, and in a much quieter voice, he said, "I'll get it on the calendar." Noah nodded, the flush of anger in his features fading. It seemed no matter how much they argued amongst themselves, they were always a unified front versus the outside—most especially against the health team members who had the power to ground them.

I stepped forward and distributed the personalized questionnaire to each one, and, as it happened, delivered Ryan's last. He practically snatched the paper out of my hand, and without looking at me, made an abrupt about face and retreated behind his cubical wall.

I stood there, stunned for a moment by his overt rudeness. However, I found myself taking note of the rigidity of his carriage and the stain of anger, or maybe even embarrassment, on his lower neck just above the collar of his knitted shirt.

Frowning, I wondered about the significance of their argument. What was a lights-out board test, and why was it important? I made a note to dig into that when I could.

For right now, I was awkwardly aware that the other three astronauts were watching me closely as Ryan's back receded. When I glanced up at Hammer, there was some open concern on his face. That sentiment seemed mirrored in varying degree in the expressions of the other two. How much did they know about Ryan and me, if anything at all?

The open pity on their faces said a lot. They knew enough.

I swallowed a lump and squared my shoulders. Was it too late to leave with my dignity intact?

"Okay, well," I said quietly. "Marjorie would like to meet with you all early next week. I'll, uh, I'll let you work out who's going when." My voice was low, husky, and I did this weird sort of pivot maneuver on the polished cement floor in slippery pumps and practically fell over. Grabbing the edge of the table, I recovered in time to not fall flat on my face.

"Are you all right?"

"You okay?" Kirill and Hammer spoke at once.

Without answering, I straightened and left the room, mercifully alone again.

I went through most of the rest of my day by rote, pushing thoughts of that weird encounter in the astronaut office out of my mind.

In spite of my dorky clumsiness, I was still proud of how I'd carried myself, how I'd fought to maintain a calm demeanor whenever I was near him, whether it was during the VIP factory tour or this quick encounter today. I didn't want to let him see how much I was hurting, so I fought to remain calm, serene. To maintain the façade of being unaffected, in spite of all the turmoil inside.

Ryan was already crushed under a mountain of guilt. He couldn't afford to add my heartbreak to that heavy burden. As much as I hated that he'd done it, and questioned constantly *why* he had done it, I couldn't let him punish himself. It ran counter to everything I was about.

That evening, however, I decided to give in to my misery and dive into a pint of mint chip ice cream. Häagen-Dazs with extra-large chocolate chunks. I was five spoonfuls in when the doorbell rang.

I suspected who it might be. She'd texted me pretty much every day since our talk in the hallway to ask if I was okay.

I was wearing pink fuzzy pajama pants with monkeys all over them and a pale pink tank top when I greeted Pari at the door.

"Well, this is a surprise," I said.

Her gaze hardened. "I really don't think it is. It was pretty obvious I was going to crash your one-woman party tonight."

I shrugged. "I may have had an inkling, yes." I stepped aside, letting her enter.

She immediately zeroed in on my carton of ice cream on the coffee table. "Ah, Gray, really? How cliché."

Pari lifted up her hand, holding a plastic grocery bag. "I actually have two more for you in here."

I grabbed her a spoon, let her choose the flavor she wanted, and put the rest away while we settled in on the couch. I was strangely reminded of a night like this two months ago, the night I'd watched the documentaries about Ryan and his interviews, taking notes.

We dug into our ice cream, though I'd almost had my fill at that point. Pari related a random funny story from work, and I listened attentively—the thing I did best.

After I stashed the remainder of my pint of ice cream in the freezer, I asked Pari if she wanted me to do the same with hers.

"Hell to the no, girlfriend. I'm making all this disappear!"

"Are you doing okay?"

She swallowed another spoonful with a wicked grin on her face. "Better than okay."

I smiled. "I take it you and Victoria...?"

She took another spoonful of ice cream as if mulling over how to answer me. "It's complicated. We're taking it slow. Victoria felt hurt because of how I acted after that night we spent together. I've apologized and explained, but I respect her reasons for wanting to go slow."

I rested my elbow against the arm of my chair, my fist against my cheek, smiling.

"What's the goofy smile for?" she asked, darting me a suspicious look. "You're supposed to be depressed."

I shrugged. "Just happy for you. And, you know, you sounded really grown up just then. Almost like..."

She brandished her spoon in the air at me. "Don't say it!"

"An adult!" I finished, laughing.

She overexaggerated a wince as if she'd heard a loud noise. "Damn, you said it. I'm not ready for adulting, Gray. You know this."

"How well I know this," I said with a long sigh.

She scowled. "You will be happy to know that I have no ice cream that I can fling at you in response."

I smiled and shrugged. "Just being agreeable."

We paused again after she trashed her carton and washed her sticky hands. When she came back, she floofed the back of my haircut before sitting down. "I love your new hair, by the way. Was that part of your breakup makeover?"

I put my hand to my hair, remembering how Ryan had run his fingers through it. *Don't ever cut your hair.* I smirked at her. "I was overdue for a cut. No need to call it a breakup makeover." I flicked her a careful glance. Maybe it was one. Even though I hadn't known that was a thing.

Pari peered at me, tilting her head, her eyes narrowing. "Are you that well-adjusted? Or do you just hide it so well it's hard to tell?"

I shrugged. "Maybe both?"

"I mean, how do you not want to wring his neck or at least put your foot out to trip him in the hallway at work?"

I opted not to answer. She didn't have to know that I'd maybe had a fantasy or two about kicking him in the shins while wearing pointy cowboy boots—perhaps as recently as this afternoon.

"Oh, believe me, this breakup is smarting just as much as it hurts anyone else, I suspect. If I seem to be taking it in stride, it's just because I've had lots of practice."

Her brows rose. "With breakups?"

I laughed. "No. No way. Practice with hiding what's going on inside. My parents both nearly had twin nervous breakdowns when my first valve replacement failed. I was sixteen and critically ill, and at first the doctors didn't know why."

"It's hard to imagine your dad losing it about anything." Pari leaned forward, picked up a glossy coffee table book about exoplanets, and began to page through it.

I sat back, thinking, still processing what I'd learned the previous week about my dad talking to Ryan. Dad had threatened to pull out of funding the company if Ryan kept the relationship with me. The more details I'd tried to pry out of Ryan, however, the more he'd clammed up about everything. And I clearly wasn't in a position to confront Dad myself. At least not until after the test flight. My hastily devised plan was to bide my time until after the test flight, minimizing contact with my dad until then, then dropping the bomb. Hopefully with the funding threat out of the way, there might even be hope for a reconciliation with Ryan.

That was assuming the only reason he'd broken things off was because of my dad and his misguided blackmail. With the way Ryan was deep-freezing me, it was hard to tell if getting back together was something he might even want anymore. My stomach twisted into knots.

"Dad can lose millions in a day when the stock market takes a tumble, and you'd hardly know it from his mood at the end of the day. He always left his work at the office. But..." I shrugged. "Family is different. Kids are an extension of the parent, in many ways. He's always been overprotective."

And I'd been a fool to assume that he'd drop that behavior once I became an adult.

Somehow he'd found out about the burgeoning feelings between Ryan and me, and he'd done what he could to quash it. And whenever I thought about what he'd done, I grew so angry I could hardly think straight.

Until I could get that under control, I'd be letting all of Dad's calls go straight to voicemail.

When the doctors told me I'd need a new valve replacement only three years after the first one, I wanted to curl into a ball and cry. Open-heart surgery is one of the most painful things a human body can endure and recover from, and I remembered every bit of that pain from the previous one. I didn't want to go through it again. In my teenage angst, I might have just as soon given up and picked the alternative—no surgery and certain death.

"When your parents are sitting at your bedside day and night barely sleeping and eating and half out of their mind with worry, it's not the best time to fall apart and start crying. I learned to suck it up."

I hid the pain, and the anger, and the *Why me*'s. And I learned to be a brick wall, finding my stoicism. Even then I knew their marriage was hanging by a thread and that only their love and concern for me was holding our family together.

"A 'stiff upper lip,' as my dad would say," Pari said with a nod.

I put my finger to my upper lip as if to test the stiffness. "I don't know why they say that."

"Having a stiff upper lip makes it hard, especially with feelings." She frowned. "I mean, your job is to listen to everyone else talk about their problems and their feelings, but you don't get to have your own."

"I have them. I just keep them contained."

Her forehead wrinkled. "You're the expert, but is that healthy?"

"I guess we'll see." I shrugged. "And maybe, maybe I was mistaken in my feelings for him. I'm still sorting it all out."

Now would be a *great* time for a subject change. Fortunately, Pari was very susceptible to those, especially if I threw in just enough gossip to whet her appetite.

She blinked. "Okay. But—"

"Hey, I had a quick question. What's the lights-out board test?"

She frowned only briefly at having been interrupted then looked at me. "What's the context?"

I related the argument I'd walked in on in the astronaut office without using names of who was arguing what, just to be safe.

Pari absently twirled a dark, glossy strand of hair around her index finger, thinking. "I'm not sure. I think it's one of those mission-critical scenarios they have to run through in order to be able to handle emergencies. I don't work on the capsules though. But I know who I can ask. I'll get back to you on that."

After we watched a little TV and chatted some more, Pari went home and I dove under my covers, having long since felt a weird sort of melancholy settle heavily over my shoulders.

I hadn't been aware of the sadness until it was just *there*. And I wondered if I'd made the transition into the next stage of grief.

Fourth Stage: Depression

The sadness, crying, and excessive sleeping lasted through the weekend. Clearly, I was battling a bout of depression. And when Monday came, I did the unthinkable for the very first time.

I called in sick. Me, who'd had perfect attendance to all my classes as an undergraduate *and* a graduate. Me, who rarely got sick anymore, presumably because I'd already blown through my lifetime share of that, if such a thing were the case.

I wasn't ungrateful for my newfound health.

But now, despite knowing in my head that this was normal, it was a hard decision to make. I needed a few days to recoup, and I couldn't help but feel a little ashamed.

You're not at work today, everything okay? Pari's text came on Monday afternoon after I'd awakened from my second nap of the day. When you're depressed, you go for naps like a hobbit goes for snacks and meals.

Just needed a little break. I'm fine, I replied, opting to keep it as succinct as possible, lest she appear on my doorstep tonight with more pints of ice cream. Ah, Pari, ever my junk food enabler.

I got an answer back re: lights-out board test you asked me about. Apparently, it's a dark test to see if control board for capsule can be completely rebooted in full darkness to simulate board losing power on dark side of the planet.

I frowned, replaying the argument in my head again. Lights out. Darkness.

Ryan refusing to get it done.

A weight sunk in my stomach as I contemplated the ramifications. And as those additional thoughts turned in my head, I found I now had even more to worry about than just the demise of a burgeoning relationship.

But I tried to be disciplined about it. I only allowed myself the weekend and those two extra days to indulge myself in the misery. I slept as much as I wanted to—which was a lot. I ate junk food. I went to the movies.

And when I walked into work on Wednesday morning, I didn't feel much better, but I'd forced myself to dress in something new, wear makeup and fake it.

I was doing fine until, an hour in, I got a text from Marjorie.

Had to run off-site to finish up some training for the new group of engineers today and it's taking longer than expected. I need the last astronaut survey interviews done. Can you handle that for me?

I blinked, my heartbeat speeding up. A real-live interview. Some actual counseling time, even if it was just routine. A break from writing reports, tabulating surveys, and developing training protocols. That actually sounded like some fun. I keyed in my response. *Sure thing. What time and who with?*

Her response zipped right back. *Everything's all set up. Kirill is just before lunch and Ty is right after. I've already got the other two.*

I sank back against my desk chair, deflated. Of course, one of them had to be with Ryan. Because lately, this was my life.

Well...shit.

CHAPTER ELEVEN
RYAN

AFTER LUNCH ON WEDNESDAY, I WAS DUE TO ATTEND my regularly scheduled—and duly annoying—mental wellness check with Marjorie. I'd filled out the damn questionnaire and sent it in, hoping she'd give this one a pass, given how close we were getting to the actual launch of the vehicle test flight. I didn't have time to burn sitting and fielding shrink questions when I could squeeze in some more time in the simulator.

I almost—almost—blew off the interview. I had a plan to offer to Skype with her until Kirill offhandedly mentioned at lunch that Gray had done his interview instead of Marjorie.

All three men's gazes landed on me as I paused, mid-chew. No one had said a thing when I'd rudely blown her off in front of them last week, but they'd gotten the intended message. Not only had I been pissed about Gray overhearing our disagreement, I'd also wanted to make it damn clear to the guys that she and I were no longer involved.

And that they should butt the hell out of my personal life.

Noah, thankfully, recovered first, realizing the awkwardness of the moment. As usual, we were back to coldly cordial and a long way from our former friendship. He cleared his throat and leaned forward. "So, how did AJ like Disney? I heard you took them last weekend."

I swallowed my bite, nodding. "He loved it. Wanted to do every ride twice. At one point, I sent Karen off to shop and just did whatever he wanted."

A strange expression crossed Noah's face. "She's doing well?" he asked, his voice slightly lower. I frowned. There was something weird going on with him and Karen. Something awkward. But far be it from me to pry.

Karen and Noah were grown-ass adults. They could figure it out. Besides, I'd had my own issues with Karen. And they'd improved greatly since she and AJ had been here.

"You are having a lot of fun spoiling that kid," Hammer said with a smile.

I nodded. "Gotta agree that I am. It's tons of fun. It's going to suck when they go back to Texas."

Lunch wrapped up quickly. The guys went back to our office, and I headed over to Marjorie's. The door was closed, and I rested my hand on the doorknob, pausing to take some deep breaths before I opened the door.

Then I remembered that I should probably knock, so I raised my knuckles to the door.

"There's no one in there," a soft voice said at my shoulder.

My head whipped around. Gray was standing just beside me, wearing a creamy lace scoop-neck blouse and a pale blue skirt, simple earrings and a gold chain around her neck, and pale pink lipstick on her lovely mouth. Without thinking, my eyes sunk to her neckline. I could easily spot the top of her scar, which she'd made no effort to hide.

I was simultaneously annoyed and proud of her. Annoyed because she *still* appeared so together, so calm about all of this. It seemed obvious that she wasn't missing me the way I'd been missing her. And I had to admit that more than a little of my recent hostility toward her came from that.

But I was proud that she wasn't hiding herself anymore, trying to blend into the background.

Gray, I'd once reflected, was the blandest color ever, and she'd chosen that name for herself to blend into the shadows. To not be seen.

But gray wasn't the bland, nothing, absence of color I'd once thought. No. Gray was the color of a presaging storm, the twilight sky after an unusually clear day, a foggy beach. Gray was the color of a pristine, uncut diamond, the color of distant, eternal starlight originating thousands of years before we were born.

Gray was the strength of thunderclouds and the tranquility of a shining sliver of a moon.

I swallowed, my eyes meeting hers. The sensation was like a force punching right through me. I struggled for breath reminding myself that I couldn't afford to keep thinking like this.

And yet I couldn't stop.

"Let's go in, and we'll get through this as quickly as we can so you can get back to work." She interrupted my racing thoughts.

I nodded, opening the door and then letting her precede me into the small room dominated by a massive desk that looked right out of a 1950s typing pool.

Instead of taking Marjorie's usual seat behind the desk, Gray sat in one of the two chairs on the other side, gesturing for me to take the chair beside her. She pulled out a sheet of paper from a royal blue file folder and clicked her ballpoint pen, poising her left hand over the paper.

"Marjorie was called away today. But if this is too weird for you, I can have her do it when she gets back. I'd, uh, probably have to give her a reason though."

I released the breath I'd been holding and shook my head. I was going to blow off the appointment with Marjorie, but I wouldn't pass up these few moments to talk to Gray. Maybe deep down I was a masochist.

"Not weird." My voice sounded breathy, and I grasped the arms of my chair, suddenly regretting that I was sitting so close to her. It was difficult to hide much with body language at this angle. I opted to fold my arms across my chest.

Get a hold of yourself, Tyler, I urged myself. I was the one who had broken things off with her. I had every opportunity to take control of this situation.

Why did it feel otherwise?

And for that matter, why was she dressing up all of a sudden? Was it for that Aaron creep? I'd watched them like a hawk the previous week during the tour. They'd done a lot of talking, a little laughing, some joking. He'd never touched her inappropriately, and she'd been friendly but not flirtatious.

I still wanted to rip his head off. As any logical human would want to do.

"How are you?" I finally asked.

Her expression did not even waver, eyes dropping to her paperwork. "Actually, that's my question." She looked up and met my gaze. "I heard you retired from the Navy last week."

I nodded, expecting this question. At least part of the interview would be predictable. "That's true."

"How are you feeling about that?"

My eyes flicked away, reminding myself that I wasn't supposed to find her so adorable when she was in Dr. Gray mode. It didn't matter. My brain was sending the memo, but the rest of me wasn't reading it. And my responses to her were as automatic as they'd always been.

"It wasn't a surprise, to them or me. It was a long time coming. But I drove down to Coronado myself and did it in person. It was a positive experience. Even saw some of my old buddies from the teams."

She nodded. "That's good." Her head tilted slightly, and she gave me a weird look as if something wasn't quite right to her. Of course, it wasn't. I'd pretty much memorized that entire speech in anticipation of that question. "That's, um. I mean, that's great. I'm so happy."

All of it had been true, but it had been carefully packaged and presented neatly without need to express all the bittersweet feelings I'd had about severing that last tie to the Navy. To my Dad. To NASA. To Xander. I swallowed.

She took a deep breath and clicked her pen up and down with her thumb while skimming my questionnaire.

"As a precursor to answering these questions, it's important to remind you that they in no way will be used against you by the company. They are completely confidential and protected under therapist-patient privileges and are used only to monitor your continued general well-being and mental health. Do you understand these conditions?"

I listened as she rattled off the rote preamble without hesitation and not even the slightest hiccup—especially when discussing therapist-patient privileges.

"Yes."

"How is your general physical health?"

I tilted my head to the side. If I hadn't been determined to keep my game face on, I would have been calling uncle and telling her this was too awkward. But astronauts didn't do that. Astronauts never rocked the boat or showed weakness. We never did anything that would in any way jeopardize a chance to fly.

Definitely not during mental health checks.

Even when the mental wellness professional involved *was* my weakness.

Especially then.

"It's fine. I get checked out regularly. I'm working out practically every day."

She scribbled as I talked, and I noted how her tongue tucked out at the corner of her mouth as she concentrated on what she wrote and what I was saying. I'd never noticed that before, how she stuck just the tip of her pink tongue out when she focused. And with a sudden urgency, I wanted to reach over, pull her to me and fiercely kiss her.

She clicked the pen again with her thumb as she held it close to her face and read from the form. "And your sleep?"

"My sleep is fine," I lied.

She didn't move. And she sure as hell didn't write anything down. Her eyes lifted to mine, and we locked gazes. She knew fucking well I was lying. But in normal circumstances, a therapist asking this question hadn't slept with me. Hadn't spent hours sweaty and naked underneath me or wrapped in my arms, using my chest as her pillow.

My throat felt tight.

She swallowed then shook her head slightly.

I raised a brow. "I'm giving you the exact same answers I would give to Marjorie."

She blinked several times, appearing to puzzle over how best to react to that. Then her eyes flicked down to her notes. "Any changes to your appetite?"

"Nope."

"How much alcohol are you consuming and how often?"

"A few drinks a few times a week." So, I fudged the numbers on this one. I clenched my jaw and waited for her to move on.

She paused for a long time, then flicked her gaze up at me. "Are you using alcohol to help you sleep?"

"I don't believe that one was on the questionnaire."

Her face clouded. "I'm following up."

I wasn't going to fucking answer that one, and I didn't like that she was using those mysterious mind-reading tactics again, or whatever they really were. Probably she just knew me too well. Far too well to be doing a routine mental wellness questionnaire.

She knew too much about a lot of things, and I was seeing now that my curiosity about her might potentially lead to danger. But like an idiot, I hadn't seen that coming until now.

"I'm sticking by my original answer. A few shots, a few times a week."

She licked her lips and marked something on the questionnaire.

"What was that? What did you just write down?"

Her brow furrowed. "I was checking off that I asked the question."

I pointed to the mark she'd made on the paper. "That looks like an L to me. Is L for lying?"

She blew out a breath. "It's a checkmark."

"It's backward."

She raised her brow. "Because I'm left-handed. We do them backward."

I folded my arms, now feeling oddly relieved that things had lightened up a little. "Still looks like an L to me."

Her mouth creased. "For liars, I just draw a stick figure with a long nose, like Pinocchio."

My eyes narrowed. Was she serious or pulling my leg? With her deadpan delivery, it was so hard to tell.

She paused again, putting the pen down. "I have to wonder, though, why you're so concerned I might be marking that answer down as a lie."

Uh oh. It's a trap, Tyler. Don't fall for it.

Perhaps I overexaggerated my *casual* shrug. "Just looked like an L to me."

"It could be an L for infuriating."

I made a face. "Infuriating doesn't start with an L."

"Or maybe an L for mystifying." One of her thin brows shot up.

I opened my mouth and then closed it. Now I was on to her. "So, it's a check mark."

She tilted her head to the side, biting her lip. "Or it could be secret therapist code invented to render paranoia in astronauts."

My eyes narrowed. I wanted to laugh, but I wasn't going to give her the satisfaction. "Very funny."

She finally grinned. "Thanks. I thought so."

I darted a look at her then looked away, unable to take much more of this. Her smiling, calm demeanor. Her acting like we were mere strangers or just acquaintances.

I was an asshole for wanting it, but I wanted to see some hurt, some devastation. I wanted to know that I'd had some effect on her.

In my peripheral vision, she picked up her pen, scanned the rest of the questionnaire, then tucked it inside the blue folder once more.

I turned back to her, hands on my knees, ready to push out of my seat. "Great. Are we done?"

Her face was serene, her green eyes hard like marble. Green marble. What was that mineral called? Malachite, that was it. "One more thing, please."

I settled back against the chair, feeling a little wary. "Sure."

"When I came into the office the other day, you were arguing with Noah about the lights-out board test."

My heartbeat sped up, and I was immediately on alert. "It was merely a difference of opinion that has since been resolved. The test is on the schedule now."

She locked gazes with me. "And you'll be the one doing that?"

I tightened my jaw and nodded.

She continued, flipping through a pad with some notes on it. "It involves periods of time in pure darkness so you can practice activating controls by touch and memorization."

I bounced a knee up and down very quickly. "Mmm," I grunted noncommittally.

She fixed her gaze on me, holding perfectly still while she peered at me expectantly as if waiting for me to elaborate. I leaned back, my knee bouncing even faster.

"You're doing this test, Ryan? In the dark?"

"That's what nodding means. Yes." I laced my fingers over my chest and stared down at my bouncing knee.

"You can't stand the dark. You can't even stand to have the room dim. Darkness is a trigger for you. How do you propose to get through that test?"

I turned back to her. "I sleep in the dark now."

Her eyes widened. "You do?"

I nodded again. It was more or less true. More often than not, I had to turn on the light when I woke up a few hours after falling asleep in the dark, but it had been a good start. And some nights, I did actually make it through.

"That's been...your progress has been fast."

I raised a brow at her. "You don't believe me."

She bit her lip. "I'd be lying if I said I didn't have my doubts."

I stood and turned to the window, grabbing the handle to close the miniblinds. I'd mostly done this with vodka to help, but I had also practiced without it. For short periods of time, I was fine. It had taken work to get me there, but I could do it.

I'd show her.

I sat down again. "Go stand by the light switch. Count silently to twenty, then switch it off."

She stood and did what I asked. And with that countdown, I prepared myself. Reminding myself the light would only be off for a short time, that I could relax, breathe through it. I applied everything she'd taught me, focused on where I was in that moment, on the physical sensations of my clothes touching my skin and the chair pushing against my back.

She flicked the lights off. It wasn't completely pitch black, but it was dark enough in that room that I felt my blood pressure rise. Her form was a vague outline by the door.

I inhaled slowly and acknowledged the speeding of my heartbeat. I squeezed my fists tight and then relaxed them.

After a moment her voice came from the other side of the darkness. "Are you all right?"

I nodded and then stopped myself. Of course, she couldn't see me, so I inhaled a breath, released it. Then I let out in a clipped voice, "Yes. I'm fine."

After another long and unpleasant string of seconds, she flipped the light back on.

I relaxed my hands, my legs, my feet, the way I'd practiced and looked at her, the picture of tranquility.

She didn't move, and I stood, tugging on my pantlegs as I maneuvered around the back of her chair and to the door. She was still standing beside the doorway, near the light switch, and she didn't move, clearly shocked.

That's me, Ryan Tyler. I always aimed to impress.

My hand was on the doorknob when she wedged herself across the jamb and came very closely into my space. My heart sped up as I got a whiff of her strawberry scent. I stiffened, pulling back slightly.

"You aren't ready to do this, Ryan. You know it, and I know it."

My gaze flicked away, annoyed. "Do what?"

She let out an exasperated breath. "The test flight."

I waved back to my chair. "I just showed you that I am perfectly fine in the dark."

Her jaw dropped. "*With* a long warning, in a calm, quiet office with just me, and when you know the light is coming on again in minutes or even seconds. That's a really controlled environment, and you still needed to prep yourself."

My jaw clenched, and I released it, looking from one of her eyes to the other. "I'm fine. I'll get the test flight done just—"

"What happens if you're orbiting and the lights go out? The board goes out and you have to reboot everything on the dark side of the planet?"

"In the unlikely event that happens, I'll be ready." I turned the knob to put an end to the conversation.

She responded by slapping her flat palm on the door, the sound echoing in the room. "*No.*" Her voice shook, obviously emotional. "That's not the same thing and you know it. I should have said something weeks ago, but I kept staying optimistic that we'd find a way to work through it together. But this isn't the way. You aren't ready."

My eyes were inches from hers. She swallowed thickly, her eyes dropping from holding my gaze to fix on my mouth. "I'm ready, Gray. And I'm going up."

"Ryan—"

But it was my turn to bang my palm against the door, just inches from hers. "Please move." My other hand turned the knob again.

She didn't budge. "You need to be honest with yourself—"

I jerked back to her. "You first. I seem to recall that you were very enthusiastic about this flight."

She shook her head. "I don't want something bad to happen up there. I don't want you to die." Her voice was audibly trembling now—and my gut tightened to hear it. But that cold wall of determination rose up to fortify me.

I gritted my teeth, my irritation rising. "I'll be fine."

She frowned. "But you're *not* fine. You're not fit to fly."

Heat burned up my spine. I pushed back from the door and ran a hand through my hair, turning a little circle around our chairs, then facing her. "Are you going to ground me? You can't, you know. It's not your call."

She shook her head. "I'd rather you made the decision yourself."

"I have made the decision."

She suddenly looked like she was going to burst into tears. But she didn't.

"Ryan," she said quietly.

"We're done here, right?" When she didn't answer, I stepped forward and grabbed the doorknob again. "*Right?*" I practically shouted so that she half flinched.

She moved aside just as I whipped the door open and left without looking back.

***

"Doesn't it get to you sometimes? The whole celebrity thing? I mean—do you always have to go out in public in a getup like this?"

Karen waved to my baseball hat, hoodie and shades. It was early evening at the beach. We were walking along the shore as AJ ran ahead of us to gather small rocks and throw into the ocean. A light breeze brought the briny scent of the ocean, the earthy smell of seaweed. The sun was at least an hour from setting but still elongated our shadows across the sand.

I shrugged. Gray had once called this my Marvel Superhero Starter Kit. I called it my Get Some Peace While out in Public Kit. Since I was on a quiet beach in Newport rather than in glitzy Santa Monica or Malibu, I was less likely to be recognized. But it still happened occasionally.

"And why are you wearing *that* hat?" AJ pointed to my red Angels baseball cap. "You're a traitor. You used to like the Astros."

I shrugged. "I still like the Astros. I like the Angels, too. I grew up rooting for the Angels."

AJ huffed his indignation and moved to the waterline to throw his rocks while I smiled, watching after him. Karen raised her sunglass-clad face to the sun as the breeze blew her long, dark hair in tendrils snaking out behind her.

I was still shaking off my irritation from earlier today and that infuriating meeting this afternoon with Gray. I'd had things under control until she'd asked me about the fucking lights-out test.

And she'd looked at me with that look in her eyes.

And begged me to reconsider doing the flight.

I'd been too uncomfortably close to wanting to listen to her. Her fear had been that palpable.

I shook my head, and Karen looked at me questioningly. "You all right? You seem a little down since you got home from work."

I rubbed the back of my neck and flicked a glance at Karen. The last thing I needed right now was for *her* to get wind of all this. She'd already expressed her own trepidation about my flying again.

"How are *you* doing?" I fired back at her to keep her away from things I didn't want to discuss.

She smiled. "I'm good. I'm enjoying this. I know I'm on vacation, but California has been good for my soul."

I wrapped an arm around her shoulders when the wind blew an especially strong gust at us and she shivered in response.

"I'm going to run back to the car and grab your sweater."

She reached up and grabbed my arm, smiling. "Don't. I'm fine. I feel *alive.*"

I was happy one of us did. My hold on her shoulders tightened, and I smiled. "I'm glad."

She rested her head on my shoulder until AJ came running up again with a particularly pretty shell to show his mom. When she complimented him, he presented it to her with an adorable courtly bow that had us both laughing in response.

He then turned tail and ran off in search of a stick so he could write in the sand.

As we watched him, she said, "Those first few months were torture, you know. I didn't want to reach out to you because I knew you were also suffering. I think that was a mistake. I think that drove a wedge into our friendship."

I grabbed a wild strand of her hair and tucked it back behind her ear. "I'm sorry, KareBear. I should have been there for you."

She shook her head. "No, this isn't about sorrys or regrets. I shouldn't have even said it like that. What I mean is that this feels nice. It feels comfortable. It's going to be hard to leave when the time comes."

158 | BRENNA AUBREY

I rubbed my hand up and down her arm, trying not to show my concern. Since they had come to stay with me, I'd discovered more details about her life after Xander's passing. She was on anti-anxiety medication now, a discovery which had floored me because Karen had never taken so much as an aspirin when she had a headache.

Suddenly a fresh wave of guilt weighed me down. Not only had I been responsible for his death, but I'd left his family to flounder for themselves. I swallowed, feeling the misery nip at me like the cold water swirling around our feet.

Karen squeezed my arm that she'd been holding onto. "You okay? You're a million miles away."

Two hundred and fifty miles, I thought. Straight up. I hadn't left low earth orbit emotionally since Xander had died in my stead.

"Don't you worry about me, KareBear. I'm good."

Her mouth quirked. "So you would have the rest of the world believe, anyway."

I frowned. She was right on that score, too.

"The dedication for Xander's tree in the Memorial Grove is at the end of September. I was wondering if..."

I already knew, and I'd already been planning to attend. Astronauts, directors and other key employees of Johnson Space Center in Houston were all memorialized in a special grove on the premises. A tree, an elm, was planted with a plaque in front of it bearing the memorialized person's name.

Xander's ceremony was coming up, and I'd been asked to speak. "I already know and I'm going to be there."

She blew out a breath, as if relieved. "Will you stay with us then? AJ would be thrilled."

I quirked a smile at her. "I aim to please, especially if it's for that little guy."

She bit her lip, blinking. "You're so amazing with him, Ty. Thank you."

I shook my head. "No thanks needed. You know I love him. You know I love both of you."

She pulled me into a hug and said, "Damn it's going to be hard to leave. This weather. The beach. All this fun stuff. I'm not looking forward to it."

"Ah," I waved my hand dismissively when she pulled back. "You've got three more weeks. You'll be sick of this place by then." She laughed, and I watched her, delighted by the sound. It honestly did seem like she was doing better. "You have things lined up for the weekend? I'm sorry I've gotta go out of town and be with the *girlfriend.*"

She shook her head. "It's still so weird when you talk about that whole thing. I still can't believe it's all fake."

I laughed. "Believe it."

"Where are you going?"

I adjusted my sunglasses and the brim of my hat. A few women sat up in their chairs as we walked by, and one of them whipped out her phone, appearing like she was going to take a picture. I turned my back to them and faced Karen, just in case.

"Tahoe. It's up in Northern California. Short flight. It's a film festival or some such, so I'm sure I'll have to watch a bunch of artsy crap. I'll try to get home as early on Sunday as I can."

She laughed and turned her head to spot AJ, who was frantically pointing at us and then at the sand. We turned slowly to approach him.

"Hammer and Noah want to spend time with us. We'll have tons of fun."

I suddenly remembered that weird look that had crossed Noah's face during lunch when we'd been talking about Karen. "How's Noah being with you? Is everything all right there?"

Karen shot a look at me. It was speculative, almost if she was trying to figure out why I was asking her that. Then she gave a shrug. "He's fine. Same old Noah."

Her pace quickened as she moved to catch up to AJ.

"Look!" AJ called to us as he stood proudly by the work of art he'd scratched into the wet sand. "I wrote all our names." And as if we couldn't read them ourselves, he pointed to each one and announced the word to us. "Ty. Mom. AJ." Then he bent and scrawled a barely recognizable heart around all three names. "So we'll always stay together."

I paused, and Karen complimented him on his sand-writing abilities. He ran off several yards ahead of us again to begin scratching out a "secret message" for us to find when we reached him.

I watched him, my heart almost bursting with pride. That handsome boy. That poor damaged kid.

"You know..." she said as we stopped to give him more time to write his message but kept watching him from the distance, "even if the studio had not flown me out here, I would have probably found an excuse to come and check up on you. I'd been keeping tabs on you from afar but it's not like it used to be. And now my parents..." Her voice shook.

I stiffened. "What's going on? Are your parents okay?" Jesus, not them, too. I loved Karen's parents. They were also like family to me. Family I'd been neglecting as badly as Karen and AJ.

"Dad's retiring soon. Still says you owe him several rounds of golf once he does." She turned to look at me. "He, uh, he asks after you a lot. Still collects all the magazine articles and records the documentaries and interviews." I smiled sadly. Xander had often joked that Paul Diaz liked me a lot better than he liked Xander, his own son-in-law. I'd laughed it off, explaining the simple logic that of course Paul liked me better because I wasn't the man who was sleeping with his little princess.

Now, after having had my own encounter with paternal hatred from Gray's father, I understood that point-of-view so much better.

Karen's mention of her father drove home to me how deeply this went, how profoundly I'd been entrenched in Xander and Karen's family life and how connected they'd been to mine until I'd forced this separation. No wonder everything had felt so lonely, so isolated out here.

Karen was suddenly blinking back tears. "Dad's planning on moving up north next spring. Mom's not doing so great healthwise, and it will be easier for him."

I frowned. "Is her lupus getting worse?"

Karen nodded. "I know the move will be better for them, but I'm dreading it. It's going to suck not having him there for us. He's been like a surrogate dad to AJ." She hastily wiped the tears from her cheeks with the back of her hand when AJ came running toward us.

A few feet away, he dropped his stick and beelined it for me, hands raised above his head. I obediently stooped and scooped him up, turning him around and around while he laughed. "I wrote a secret message in the sand."

Karen chuckled through the last of her tears that, thankfully, her son didn't notice. "It's not a secret if you tell us about it, silly."

We made it there eventually, after a piggy back ride and a few jests where I pretended I was going to throw him into the ocean. The message said. *Ty + Mom + AJ.* And below it, three stick figures all inside the same house. "We should always live together," AJ pronounced.

CHAPTER TWELVE
RYAN

A	T BEDTIME, AS WITH MANY NIGHTS SINCE THEY'D BEEN
	visiting, I had the honor of tucking AJ in. This had
	steadily become the highlight of my day. He'd been quiet
at dinner and I'd chalked it up to his exhaustion from our fun at
the beach.

I reached for the paperback copy of *Harry Potter and the
Sorcerer's Stone* lying on his nightstand. "You ready, champ?"

He smiled and put his hand out and I thought it was for a
high-five, so I gently laid one on him. But instead, he clasped his
small hand around mine. He looked earnestly into my eyes with
his serious hazel gaze. "Will you come visit us in Houston, Ty?
A lot?

"I will. I'm actually going to come visit you guys at the end of
September."

"And then October? Then November?"

I laughed. "Well, I do have to work. And I don't have my own
jet to fly anymore so I can't just hop over whenever. But I do
promise I'll come."

"You and Daddy used to fly in your T38 together."

I smiled and chucked his cheek, trying to ignore the sharp
pang I felt whenever AJ brought up his father. "Your dad did the
flying. I was his RIO."

"Radar Intercept Officer," he said with a proud smile for knowing what the acronym meant.

I grinned. "That's right."

"But you can fly it by yourself now, right?"

I nodded, then cleared my throat. The thought of flying without Xander made me glad I didn't have to get in that jet anymore. When I worked for NASA we went up in them regularly. I still rode, sometimes, with Noah or Hammer in their back seat.

But that begged the question. Would the test flight be any easier to fly without Xander there? And I had to remind myself that he was the whole reason I was doing it. And I would do it.

I held up the book to change the subject. "Ready to go?"

He nodded, easily diverted.

Unfortunately, it was the chapter where Harry, wearing the cloak of invisibility, wanders around Hogwarts castle and stumbles upon the Mirror of Erised. When he gazes into it, instead of seeing his own reflection, he's surprised to see his dead parents and other relatives within. Because the magical mirror, instead of showing a standard reflection, shows the gazer his heart's desire.

I sat on AJ's bed, trying to rush through the part where Harry looks into the eyes of his weeping mother and proudly sad father.

But AJ made me reread the passage three times before I could continue on, each time reliving Harry's tears as he sees them for the first time he can remember. I was unable to keep myself from thinking about the day that the Navy officers came to my mom's door to tell me about my own father's death.

I was unable to keep from wondering how AJ was told that Xander hadn't survived our EVA. After the fact, I learned that

Mission Control had cut the live feed from NASA to the internet and all other public outlets the moment they'd realized something was wrong. When had they notified Karen? How had they managed to get her into the Space Center so quickly to be able to talk to him during his last minutes?

And when had she told AJ the reason they were going into Mission Control so early in the morning? What was his indelible memory of that time? The time he'd known for certain that he'd never see his father again? That Xander would never teach him how to play baseball or knot a necktie or ride a bike without training wheels?

Or watch him graduate.

Or give him advice on his wedding day.

Or proudly hold his newborn child.

I swallowed a lump, trying not to notice the solitary tear that trickled out of AJ's right eye, down cross his temple.

"I wish there really was a Mirror of Erised," he whispered in a trembling voice.

I reached out and covered his small hand with my own. "So do I, buddy. So do I."

"I don't want you to read to me anymore tonight," he said after a long pause.

"Okay. You want a drink of water?"

"No, I just want to be alone. I need to think about things. Can you leave the light on?"

That request I understood better than anything else he wanted. I held my fist up to his for a bump. "You're the champ in my book, bud."

He smiled weakly. "Thanks."

I replaced the infernal book back on the nightstand, moving the bookmark to the following chapter where, hopefully, he wouldn't notice that we'd skipped ahead. I didn't want to read any more references to the Mirror of Erised.

I stood in his doorway for a few minutes as he lay quietly, staring up at the ceiling. His lips moved as if he was whispering something to himself. An overwhelming and ferocious feeling of protectiveness took hold of me. At that moment, I knew for sure that I would walk through fire for this boy. I'd cross an ocean for him. I'd do anything to keep him safe.

And I wanted to be able to read him stories. More stories. Every night.

And be there to see all of his firsts.

I ducked into my bedroom, splashed some cold water on my face, and took a deep breath. I could have used a drink right then, but I wouldn't do it. I'd been saving it for just before bed.

If Karen could get through this shit every single goddamn night, then I could do it for just one, for her. Without vodka to bolster me up.

I swallowed, thinking about the day as I made my way to the back deck where Karen stood watching the moon rise in the east. It was almost full, and there was plenty of light out here besides.

I came up behind her and wrapped her up in a big hug. She let out a long breath and turned around to return it.

"Thank you," she said. "This has been a good day. A *really* good day. We need more good days. All of us."

I looked down into her beaming face and smiled as well. "AJ needs them most of all."

She nodded solemnly. "Yes, he does."

"I want to help you," I said, my arms still wrapped around her.

She nodded. "You're being a great help, Ty. Just being here with you has done wonders for him. And me, too, for that matter."

I took in a deep breath and summoned up the courage to say what I had to say. "I want to take care of you two."

She smiled sadly, looking up at me with weary eyes. "You're over a thousand miles away from us."

I leaned forward. "So move here. Into my house."

Her brows knit. "What are you saying, like—live together?"

I released her to give her some room and to give me the breathing space I'd need to get this out before I chickened out. "We could get married. I'd be AJ's stepdad. Your family already likes me. AJ is the closest thing to my kid."

She pulled back and turned to take up her wineglass, pressing it to her lips.

I watched her closely. A voice at the back of my head was shouting at me, telling me what a stupid idea this was. But why couldn't I make it work? Why couldn't I fix things this way?

I didn't love Karen—not in that way. And she didn't love me. But many marriages were happy even when there wasn't passionate love. I'd probably never know that kind of thing, anyway. I half believed it a myth until...until I didn't. Until Gray.

But it had been several weeks since I'd pushed Gray away. I felt every one of them every time I thought about her and the hole she'd left—that she'd *torn*—in the fabric of my space-time continuum. And I knew, that if I couldn't have Gray, I wouldn't have anyone. Not like that.

But I could love Karen and AJ in a different way. Karen and AJ needed me *now*. And I wanted to be part of a family. I'd be there for them. In every way. I'd stand in for Xander, the man who had sacrificed his life for *me*.

The solution, so ridiculously simple, filled me with a rush of relief and also joy. With Karen and AJ and the rest of her family, I wouldn't be alone for the rest of my life.

"It just makes sense. We can take care of each other. I love AJ. You know I do," I pressed after she put down her wine glass.

"Yes, I know that." She glanced at me out of the corners of her eyes. "But if I ever get married again—and that's a big if, because I really don't think I will—but if I did, I'd want it to be a real marriage. Not something fake like this thing with you and Keely. Not something to look good from the outside. Not even just for security." She took a deep breath and released it shakily. "I've already met and married the love of my life, and that's probably never going to happen again."

I reached for her hand. "It doesn't have to happen again. I understand that. I love you, and I want to take care of you. And this wouldn't be a fake marriage."

She frowned at me. "And all the womanizing and running around you've been doing? The partying? That's going to magically stop?"

I took a deep breath and leveled her with a serious gaze. "It already has. I haven't been running around or partying for months. I—" I hadn't had the need. The days had been filled with lots of hard work and Gray. And the nights...

I gulped and swallowed. It was best not to think about Gray at all. And especially not while discussing this with Karen.

Karen rubbed the center of her forehead and sighed. "I'll admit it makes sense. It does, but..."

"It's settling."

She nodded. "Yes. It's settling."

I raised my eyebrows. "And why is that bad? We'd be comfortable. We've known each other since we were teenagers. I want to be there for your son. I love him."

She froze, staring at me as if she needed time to process what I was saying. I reached out, removed her wine glass from her hand, and set it aside. Then I took the hand that had been holding it. "Let's do it, Karen."

She sighed and looked away, but her fingers tightened around mine. "There's one major obstacle, even if I was convinced."

I tilted my head, watching her closely. "What is that?"

She leveled her gaze on mine. "You're going up again next month. And, naturally, you have to understand that I have an aversion to marrying someone in a dangerous profession. Even one I understand intimately."

I nodded. "That flight is for Xander. I can't change that. I promised him."

She clenched her jaw and relaxed it. "You also promised him you'd be there for me and AJ."

My insides sank. "Yes. I don't know how to uphold both of those given your conditions. But I'd already decided that I want to move to a more administrative role after the test flight. I'll still work at XPAC, but in a different capacity."

"I get it." She flicked a look at me. "But I still don't agree. You take a lot on yourself."

I shook my head. "No more than I should have from the very start. This is the least I can do for you, for AJ. And for myself." I took a deep breath and let it go. "For Xander," I added quietly.

Our eyes locked, and she nodded slowly. "It doesn't have to be just about you taking care of us, you know." She spoke softly.

"I'd promise to take care of you, too." She reached out and took my other hand in hers, closing her fingers tightly. Then, with a sigh, she leaned forward, touching her forehead to mine.

I pulled back to bring her in for a hug, kissing the top of her hair. Immediately I was reminded of how she didn't smell like Gray. No strawberries. No freshness. No sunlight.

I also found myself listening for her heartbeat, realizing that I was trying to hear the ticking sound that Gray's heart made. I wondered how long it would take for me to stop comparing every woman to Gray. Sooner would be better.

For a long time, we stood like that, with Karen cocooned in my arms. It wasn't a choice of being with Gray or being with Karen. There was no choice that would allow me to be with Gray. Not without destroying her future and what she'd worked toward for so long.

No, this was a choice between being alone or doing what I should have been doing all along. It was long past time for me to man up.

This was me, manning up.

"It does make a lot of sense," she finally said after a long period of silence. "I keep running through my head what Xander would say if he were here, and I can't help but think that he'd be cheering for it. To know that his son wouldn't have to grow up fatherless."

No, he wouldn't have to. Not like I'd had to.

She cleared her throat to speak again. "I propose that we go slow. Let's keep things how they are for now and then after your flight, let's go out on some dates and take it from there."

I pressed my cheek to the top of her head. "I can give you that time. Just don't forget. I will do whatever I can to take care of you both. You can depend on that."

She let out a long sigh. "I know." Then she laughed, a light, ironic chuckle. "So funny. When we got here, I was one hundred percent convinced you were in love with someone else. Now here we are."

"Yeah," I breathed. "Funny." I squeezed my eyes shut tight and forced myself not to think about love. Or about missed opportunities. Or about Gray.

A little while later, Karen started yawning and decided to retire. I cleaned up the last of the straggling dishes and wiped down the counters in the kitchen.

Then I hit the wet bar in my sitting room, downed my triple-shot night cap, and went to my room.

I was all ready for bed and doing my normal psych routine before turning off the lights when my phone beeped. Grabbing it, I checked out the notifications screen.

Gray: Please, can we find some time to talk tomorrow?

I paused. If I opened up the app to respond, it would show that I'd seen and read the message. But if I put the phone down now, she'd assume I hadn't seen it before going to bed.

I paused, remembering her pleas to me earlier in the afternoon, the true anguish in her face—more than I'd ever seen from her when I'd broken things off. *I don't want you to die.*

I had two more days of work. I could avoid her easily enough. Then Tahoe this weekend, then time in Florida training at the launchpad and the capsule facility.

After setting the *do not disturb* feature on my phone, I put it face down on the nightstand and began my deep breathing and visualizations. Every time the image arose of those pleading eyes, that sweet, earnest face turned to mine, I pushed it out again just as fast.

The true irony was, once the lights were off, I pulled her pillow next to me, buried my face in it and slept for hours in the dark.

CHAPTER THIRTEEN
GRAY

I PACED THE FLOOR OF MY FRONT ROOM FOR HOURS THAT night, unsure what to do. My mind had been a whirl since meeting with Ryan that afternoon. How much of a fool had I been to allow things to go so far and for the launch date to get so close? Had I really been oblivious to the question of Ryan's suitability to fly again?

I knew about the PTSD. I knew better than anyone but him about the darkness trigger. I'd thought we could get past it. I'd thought it was a minor issue to work out.

I was an idiot and a really shitty psychologist.

It didn't matter that he managed to represent himself to Marjorie as completely mentally healthy. I knew otherwise.

But I knew otherwise because I'd been sleeping with him for months. So was it ethical for me to act against him on behalf of the psychological team?

I was not his therapist. I'd been pondering these ethics issues and had taken to the internet and my various school textbooks in search of answers since the meeting that afternoon. I was also planning to seek some advice from my academic advisors.

But at that moment, I could hardly think straight. I had a headache, and my hair was sticking out in every which direction from running my fingers through it. Contemplating the possibilities made me ill.

That afternoon, I got a text from Karen in response to one I'd sent earlier asking how everything was going. Though I'd been vague, I was really fishing for info on how Ryan was doing.

Karen: We are doing great, thanks so much for asking! AJ is all settled in and we are fortunate to spend some of our fun time with Ty. I can't get over how well he's doing. Thanks for all the help you've given him. He's like a changed man.

Like a changed man. Yeah. Except he wasn't. He was just hiding things even better now than he had before.

After dinner, I picked up my phone to text him. Before I figure out what to say, however, my phone rang. Keely's ID showed up front and center in my screen.

I hit the button to accept the call.

"Hello?" I answered, sinking down onto my couch.

"Gray? Hey there. Hope I'm not calling too late." She sounded rushed and a little out of breath.

"It's only eight. You're fine. Are you okay?"

"I'm well, but I need to ask you a huge favor. And I hope you'll say yes."

Uh oh. "Is there a problem with one of your events?"

She heaved a long sigh on the other end. "Sharon's deathly sick, and I need an assistant this weekend. Can you do it?"

"Oh, I'm sorry about Sharon. Is there anything I can do?"

"She'll be okay, but she's really contagious and I can't be around her. Are you free this weekend?"

I nodded, though she couldn't see me. "I can help you out in any way you need."

"Good. Then I need you to fly to Tahoe with us on Friday."

Us. Tahoe. I hesitated, wondering and yet also knowing who the *us* was in that sentence. I'd been vaguely aware that they would be doing an out of town event together this weekend. Was there any way I could wiggle out of this? She seemed desperate. "What's the event?"

"It's a film festival and awards ceremony. There's a cocktail party, optional movie screenings, and the main event is on Friday night. The place I got for us to stay in is *gorgeous*. This cozy little artist hideaway guesthouse. It's on a cliff that overlooks the lake in among the trees. Super private. Jeremy Fisher owns it and lent it to me personally."

I blinked. "Jeremy Fisher, the multi-academy award-winning movie director?"

She laughed. "Yep. Him. Cool, huh? Say you'll come and help me out. You don't even have to talk to you-know-who if you don't want to. I'm still mad at him for being such a pig of a male."

Clearing my throat, I said, "I'm a big girl. I don't need to ignore him. I'll come."

We went over the details of where I had to be and when.

After I entered the event into my electronic calendar, I finally texted Ryan, my heart beating in my throat as I did it.

The truth was, we had an incomplete conversation to finish. And we had a little ground to cover before we were going to be forced to work together this weekend.

Please, can we find some time to talk tomorrow?

He never responded.

Not even the next day. And when I went looking for him, he was nowhere to be found.

Either he was studiously avoiding me, or it was a figment of my imagination. I couldn't guess which.

Call me. I mean it. We need to talk. I keyed the message in and hit send the next day on my way to that coffee that Aaron had insisted on. He never went back on his promises, he assured me. And, according to him, he'd promised me coffee weeks before. He even drove all the way out to Seal Beach again just to buy me a cup of joe.

And also to listen to me talk for hours about the space program, past and present.

He was patient. I liked Aaron, and it was clear that he was interested in both me and learning more about space.

Under different circumstances, I might have considered dating him. Maybe in the future I would. As soon as the mere thought of dating someone else didn't sting like a freshly opened wound submerged in salt water.

Regardless, on Friday, with my packed bag, I left work early and headed to the nearby Long Beach airport, where I met Ryan and Keely for the ninety-minute flight to Reno, Nevada. Keely must have informed Ryan that I was pinch-hitting for Keely's assistant because there was no visible sign of surprise on his handsome features.

As Keely and Ty were VIPs, we boarded in First Class after everyone else had been seated on the plane. The two of them sat beside each other in the first row, and I could see the others around us angling for a look or even a not-so clandestinely aimed photo.

In Reno, a car met us and drove the hour to Lake Tahoe and the beautiful retreat home that Keely had borrowed.

The mountain weather on the California side of the lake was fresh and gorgeous, a welcome change from the stifling heat this time of year in the LA basin. But since it was early August, the area teemed with vacationers.

As she pulled into the gated community, our driver flashed ID at the guard gate and then wound her way up a long drive barely wide enough to accommodate one lane each way. Since the plane ride, the three of us had been ensconced in our own little worlds, each hiding in either our phone or personal tablet— or in my case, an e-reader.

I couldn't help darting looks at Ryan, who seemed completely immune to my presence. He'd managed to avoid even the slightest millisecond of mutual eye contact.

But I was not going to give up that easily. We had an entire weekend. There had to be a moment where I could catch him alone and continue our conversation about his suitability for the test flight. It turns out a Navy SEAL-turned-astronaut could be one of the slipperiest creatures on the planet. Who'd have thought it?

The little cabin we were to inhabit for the weekend was literally hanging off a cliff that set back a short distance from the shore of the lake. Above the door there was a sign that read *Glass Lake Cottage*.

Inside, the place was breathtaking. Small, cozy, but ultra-modern. All white and chrome and glass. There were three floors. The bottom held a hot tub and the gym. The middle level had one bedroom, a luxurious adjoining bathroom and laundry, and a cozy, light-filled study across the hall. The top floor was the open kitchen, living room and a dining room with floor-to-ceiling glass windows on three sides that looked out over the trees and the blue, blue lake.

I puzzled. "One bedroom? For the three of us?"

Keely frowned and shrugged, glancing from one of us to the other. "I accepted his favor sight unseen. He did say there was an extra bed around here somewhere, maybe a Murphy bed or a fold-out couch. Gray and I can share the king size bed in the bedroom."

Ryan seemed to fight rolling his eyes. "I'll take the floor if need be."

After a quick look around, we noticed that the couch folded out into a bed for Ryan.

"But there's only one bathroom," I pointed out, knowing how long it took Keely for prep time.

Keely waved her hand. "Oh, all the events are at the big hotel down on the north shore. I'm going to go down there early and have the stylist do my hair and makeup. They have my wardrobe over there, too."

"So we should meet you over there after we get ready?"

Keely gave another one of those mysterious smiles and said. "Mmm hmm." Her eyes flicked to Ryan and then to me. "I'm heading over now. I'll send the car back for you."

In other circumstances, I might have been angry and given her the evil eye for her obvious manipulating. But without knowing it, Keely was giving me exactly what I wanted. Time alone to talk to Ryan.

I checked my watch. But not much time. We had an awards dinner to prepare for. I pulled out my phone and gave Keely the run down on the night's schedule as she hurried out the door.

She thanked me then gestured brusquely toward the house. "Make sure to use your time up here well, Gray."

I narrowed my gaze at her. "Did you do this on purpose? Is Sharon *really* sick?"

Keely hesitated. "She's sick, but I may have overexaggerated how much. Are you mad?"

I rubbed my forehead. "What are you doing?"

She shrugged. "I wanted you to come be with us. Come on, Gray. It'll be fun."

I shook my head at her. "If you wanted your date to be in a good mood, you shouldn't have brought me up here."

She rolled her eyes. "I don't care what kind of mood he's in as long as he manages to smile pretty for the cameras. These astronaut men and their emotional unavailability. It's a good thing that fling with Kirill stayed that, just a fling."

I nodded. I'd heard that they hadn't seen each other in a while. That flame had, as she'd put it, "burned itself out, but damn what a nice fire it was!"

"Listen, Gray, I gotta go, but I just want to say one thing. Sharon gets on my case for all my interfering. I've tried to be better, but whenever I've talked to you or talked to him, I can tell you want to know all about the other one. You ask about him. He asks about you. I figured, why not just give you a little time to, you know, be in the same room?"

With a wink she sank into her seat at the back of the town car.

"But we see each other at work," I said as she shut the door, gave me a sweet little shrug, and told the driver to pull away.

She had no way of knowing that I'd been texting him for two days with no answer. Now that he could no longer avoid me, we might as well clear the air, right? When I got back into the house, the one bathroom was in use. Since Ryan's carryon and garment bag were unzipped and lying on the bed, I assumed that he was getting ready.

Or he was avoiding me.

Or both.

For lack of anything else to do, I pulled my dress out of my case and hung it up, then pulled Ryan's tux from the already-open garment bag and did the same.

My hands shook as I did it. He always looked so amazing in his tuxedo. I'd have to remind myself all night that I was mad at him. Maybe I'd just force myself to constantly avert my eyes.

We switched off using the bathroom and dressing in the bedroom and filed into the town car the minute we were both ready. In the back of the car together, I finally caught his eyes. Surprisingly he smiled and said, "You look nice tonight."

I immediately frowned, confused both by the compliment and his actual attempt to acknowledge me. The plain, dark blue cocktail dress I wore was subdued in order to blend in with the dressy occasion. There would be no danger of me being mistaken for one of the participants.

But with makeup and a little fluff to my cute new haircut, I felt pretty. I raised a hand to my short hair, suddenly conscious of the style and of the fact that I'd gleefully chopped it all off because he'd once asked me never to cut it.

"Thank you," I said quietly. "So do you, but you always look good in that." I gestured to his tux.

He glanced down at his tie and flicked something off his lapel. Then he shifted, appearing awkward.

Another pause

I turned to him. "Are you ever going to talk to me? About the test flight?"

He stiffened and turned away, gazing out the window.

"Ryan," I said.

"I spoke with Marjorie yesterday," he said conversationally as if he hadn't just randomly changed the subject out of the blue. "Had an hour-long meeting with her at my request. I also had a full physical. She says everything looks good for me to go up on the test flight."

I blinked. "But—does she know—did you tell her about *everything* going on with you?"

He turned back to me with a gaze that looked like it could bore twin holes through my body in seconds flat. "What happens between a therapist and patient is confidential, right?"

My mouth dropped. "Yes, but confidentiality is usually for the therapist's end—"

He leaned closer to me. I could smell him. His upper arm bumped my shoulder, and a shock zapped through me. Both his anger and his presence were overwhelming me.

"She gave me the okay to fly. That's what matters," he said with finality in his tone.

I shook my head, but our car turned into the driveway of the hotel before I could push the conversation further.

Once the awards event ended, and we had spent an acceptable amount of time at the afterparty, we left. Keely yawned loudly. "I'm so beat. I hope I'm not getting Sharon's bug."

Instinctively both Ryan and I moved away from her on either side as we stood at the curb waiting for the car to pick us up.

"Good thing I didn't have to kiss you tonight," Ryan muttered. In spite of myself, I laughed.

But of course, on the drive back to the cottage things were awkward and tense. I still couldn't get over Ryan's earlier rudeness, and he, I presumed, was pissed at me for pushing the matter about the test flight.

Keely sat in the front seat, but sent pointed glances back at us quite often, her arms folded indignantly. "Aren't you two going to talk to each other?"

I raised my eyebrows in surprise, then glanced over at Ryan who looked at me in the same moment. Our eyes met, and it almost felt like our gazes collided and then physically bounced off each other.

But to Keely's great frustration, that wasn't enough to break the ice.

The ice was pretty thick and cold between us, actually. And I wish I could have blamed that entirely on him. But I couldn't.

We bunked down according to Keely's plans, the two of us would take the lone bedroom. Ryan the fold out couch, with the requisite amount of grumbling on his part that went along with that.

However, when I woke in the morning, Keely was nowhere to be found. At least not in the bedroom, anyway. Glancing at the clock, I was shocked to see it was almost ten. I sat up and then forced my tired bones out of bed. I did not go to bed after midnight very often. Yeah, they didn't call me party girl for nothing.

Actually, they didn't call me party girl at all.

As I brushed my teeth, I thought it was weird that Keely had no toiletries in the bathroom. After a quick shower, I threw on my yoga pants and t-shirt and went up the stairs to find her.

The only thing I found on the top level was a snoozing Ryan. Come to think of it, I didn't see her luggage sitting around anywhere, either. *How weird.*

I jumped down the stairs again to see if I'd overlooked her suitcase in the bedroom. Nothing. And the closet was empty, except for my few things.

As a matter of fact, it did not appear as if Keely had ever unpacked, and her side of the bed had not been slept in. She'd sent me down to bed the night before, saying she wasn't tired. And as I drifted off to sleep, I'd assumed she'd come down sometime soon.

Apparently, she hadn't. And she was gone.

I snatched up my phone to text her, but I had no bars and the words NO SERVICE glowed in the upper corner. I hadn't noticed this loss in service the night before.

Shit.

I ran back up the stairs again and over to the fold-out bed.

Reaching out toward him, I had to stop myself when I remembered that it usually wasn't a good idea to wake a former serviceman—particularly a special operator—from a dead sleep by touching or grabbing them. It could sometimes be a triggering mechanism.

I'd never had that problem with Ryan before, but I couldn't remember a time in which I'd woken him by shaking his arm. So instead I called in a normal tone of voice, "Ryan."

For a minute he didn't move, and I studied him in sleep. I used to watch him sleep—in a totally non-creepy way, of course—

when we were in bed together. He never looked peaceful in sleep. He always looked contained as if he were silently struggling against some unknown force.

It used to worry me then. Now, it struck a spike of terror right down in the center of my heart. Every time I thought of him in that capsule and something going wrong to trigger him, it made me cold with fear.

"Ryan," I called a little louder, and he sat up, eyes wide open, perfectly awake.

He blinked a few times and then focused on me. "Yes?"

"Keely's gone."

He rubbed his eyes with the back of his knuckle. "Gone? You mean like on a walk?"

I held out my hands palms up in a gesture of helplessness. "No. *Gone* gone. As in I don't even think she slept here last night."

He scratched his jaw, and it made that flinty noise as his nails rubbed at his morning growth of whiskers. In spite of myself, I got goosebumps remembering the feel of those morning whiskers all over my body during a rousing bout of morning sex. In some places, the sensation had left me feeling tingly and tender all day long, remembering how he'd touched me, how he'd felt.

Damn. Random memories like that loved to just pop into my brain at inopportune moments, zapping straight down to my core, threatening meltdown. It wasn't fair. Most women never had to see their ex-whatevers again after being unceremoniously dumped by them.

"She wouldn't just leave like that and not let us know," he said, clearing his throat of the morning gruffness. "That's not Keely.

Did she text you? Let me find my phone and see if she sent me anything."

I shook my head. "There's no cell reception up here at all. And no wifi that I can detect."

He pushed his way out of bed, and I immediately averted my eyes. He was wearing only his boxers, no shirt.

Damn. I didn't need to see him half—scratch that, three-quarters—naked at this particular point in my breakup recovery.

I turned around and headed to the kitchen. Since the entire upper floor was open concept, I could still see him if I turned around. Instead I ducked behind the fridge door and grabbed a chilled bottle of water. When I turned around, I noticed a lined sheet of notebook paper sitting on the counter. It was covered in writing.

My eyes slid to the bottom. Keely had signed it and adorned her name with multiple hearts.

"She left a note. It's here in the kitchen."

He came up to the counter opposite me. In my peripheral vision, I could see that he was yanking a t-shirt over his chest. Once that was accomplished, I held the note up to him as if to corroborate my claim.

He frowned. "What's it say?"

I read it aloud:

Dear Gray and Ty,

So you know, I wasn't lying about not feeling very well last night, so I've had my publicist make my apologies.

If being roped into working with me up here this weekend wasn't going to be enough to get you to talk, then a girl's got to resort to drastic measures. Actually, the truth of the matter is that I was planning all along to move to the hotel and attend the rest of the Film Festival solo.

Reality Keely is going to go home and sleep this off while megadosing on Vitamin C. But Imaginary Girlfriend Keely is going to be snuggled in a "romantically remote glass cottage" while waiting for her beau to pop the question this weekend. At least that's what the press will have been led to believe.

Maybe you're wondering why I'm doing this. Well, I was hoping to help. I love happy endings. I like sappy romance stories and movies on the Hallmark channel. I like to believe that's possible in the real world, too. I absolutely love love and watching other people get there. And especially helping it along a little. It's like being a fairy godmother. Every girl's got to have a hobby, you know.

Should either of you take it into your sweet little heads that you are going to bail out on the magic of the gorgeous glass cottage, think again. By the time you are reading this, I'm sure there are different media outlets and fans alike all jockeying to provide the first glimpse of the shiny new rock on my finger. Let's just say that whispering engagement rumors to the press is like throwing chum in a shark tank, only more likely to lead to the loss of a limb.

The media will only be allowed to come as far up as the gatehouse, so your privacy is ensured as long as you stay on the grounds and away from public eyes. And please try not to be seen outside together because then the jig will be up, and Ty will end up roasted on social media for "cheating" on me.

Therefore, you are both trapped, just the way I like it. :)

There's no wifi. No cell reception. No way to communicate with the outside world except for the landline.

I'll send a car for you at five p.m. on Sunday for your flight out.

I hope you take that time to communicate with each other. The
cottage is fully stocked and very private. There are lovely trails down
to the beach.

Enjoy your romantic weekend together.

Kisses,

K

PS—The Parent Trap is my fave movie ever.

I blinked a few times, rereading the note in my shock. Ryan
had stood stock still and rigid as I'd read the note, getting more
and more visibly tense in my peripheral vision. Arms folded
across his chest. Shoulders back and stiff. When I chanced a look
up at him, his jaw was clenched so tightly that if you'd shoved a
lump of coal in his mouth—wait, I knew that wasn't how the
saying went, but it probably applied to his other end, too.

He closed his eyes and pinched the bridge of his nose between
thumb and forefinger. "What the hell has gotten into that
woman? What did you say to her?"

I scowled at him, setting the note down on the counter.
"Nothing. I just said you decided it wasn't a good idea for us to
see each other anymore. Nothing about you caving to blackmail
or being afraid of a sixty-three-year-old man."

His features darkened. "That's not nothing. Nothing is 'It's
none of your business.'"

I sighed. "I didn't put her up to trapping you into spending
the weekend with me, if that is what you are asking. That would
be the last thing I'd do."

His hand dropped from rubbing his forehead and he glared at
me. "Why's that? Because you wanted to spend the weekend with
Aaron?"

I leveled my gaze at him and glared over the top of my glasses. "Don't even start that shit."

He blew out a breath then crossed the room to his open suitcase on the floor beside his pull-out bed. Grabbing some clothing, he disappeared down the stairs and into the bathroom.

I futilely tried to check cell reception up on this floor. Still nothing. I wished I'd known the night before that we'd be stuck in a communication vortex all weekend. Good thing I hadn't planned on getting any work done.

Ryan emerged from the lower level fully dressed with his hair combed, and he'd procured a pair of binoculars somewhere, probably from the study or a closet.

Before I could even ask, he looked up at me. "I'm going to reconnoiter."

I raised my brows. "Are we fighting a war?"

"I want to verify that what she's saying is true. That we're stuck here."

I frowned. "I doubt she's lying about it. Why would she? If you go out, you risk being seen."

He shot me a look. "I was a Navy SEAL. I know how to do this without being seen. *It pays to be a winner.*"

I rolled my eyes. "You gonna start singing *Anchors Aweigh* now or is that my cue?"

He grinned. "Watch and learn."

"If I can't see you, how am I going to watch?" He left through the back door that led through the garage—as I remembered from my early investigations of the house. As he did so, I called, "*The only easy day was yesterday!*"

"Hooyah!" came his immediate reply as the door shut behind him.

I couldn't resist, I had to admit, so I moved to the front window and glanced out over the top of the driveway. As he predicted, I didn't see him. I had no idea what route he took, but after a few minutes of searching, I decided to pull the blinds in case some photographer made his way up the hill and was, even now, snapping pictures of me looking out the window.

I turned back to the room, hugging my arms across my chest and trying to sort out the jumble of racing thoughts. What the hell was Keely thinking to stick him here with me for the weekend? I mean, I might manage to kill him before he killed me.

Would it just be one very distant and chilly weekend with two people holed up in one place with nothing to say to each other?

Or maybe I could find out what was going on in his head. Maybe—if he tolerated it—maybe I could help him. Wasn't it just tragically me? Gray of the broken heart, selflessly offering up help to the very man who had broken it?

Or maybe, at long last, I could just let myself be mad. Let myself vent the feelings I'd bottled up for weeks. Let them out and let him see...

But would it help?

CHAPTER FOURTEEN
RYAN

WELL THAT SETTLED IT. I WAS GOING TO KILL KEELY. My hand closed around the hard tube of the binoculars, so tense I could probably crush the lenses if I focused just a little bit more. I'd spotted at least one van, a photographer and a vehicle with a satellite receiver on the roof. I'd been able to get close enough to overhear parts of their conversation and they were currently plotting ways to get up past the gate after dark.

Fortunately, they were still unsure which cabin inside the community that "Tyley" were staying at, but several paparazzi were pouring over a tablet that showed aerial satellite photos of the entire community. Time and process of elimination would have them peeking in the front windows in no time.

My recon involved checking out the cabin from all front-facing sides and I noted that Gray had pulled every last shade down against the brightly sunny day. *That's my clever girl.*

I allowed myself the automatic thought for half a second before chastising myself for it. I was still thinking like this. *Still.* All these weeks later...

It wasn't my right to think that way, and I hoped that my tendency to jump to those thoughts would ease up soon. But for the moment, I wasn't going to worry about that. I just needed to figure out a fucking way to get through this weekend.

Her. And me. Under a small roof. In a gorgeous, romantic setting with no internet or TV service or anything else to divert us.

How the fuck was I going to keep my hands off of her?

Last night she'd looked so beautiful that it had been almost physically painful to keep my eyes off her. But I had. I'd been very good at resisting the temptation in public.

In private? I didn't trust myself. I'd have to resolve not to speak with her or even spend time in the same room with her if it was avoidable.

And that fully-stocked mini-bar I'd spotted in the living room was calling out to me. But I couldn't get drunk. That would make it worse. Because this gaping hole inside my chest—the one I'd been nursing for the past four weeks, would demand to be filled. And in certain cases, it would demand to be filled by any random warm body and soft pair of lips I could find.

The true danger was that inside that cottage wasn't just *any* warm body or soft pair of lips. That body and those soft lips belonged to the only woman I currently wanted. The only one I wanted to hold. And as the weeks had gone by, that wanting had only gotten stronger, not weaker.

This was a shields-up, guard-up, locked-heart scenario. I'd already hurt her enough. More than I'd ever wanted to. No need to drive in the knife—for her *or* for me.

I'd keep it distant and professional, like I had been at work, in public, around all my friends. I could do this.

I slipped back into the garage, taking care to lock the door from the inside, then into the house, doing the same.

Gray sat at the dining table in front of the big windows looking out over the lake. She held a giant mug to her face with both hands, and I was reminded at that moment that I could use some coffee and a little breakfast. Protein would be good. Then a thorough workout. That would help clear my head properly.

So I set to work, asking her if she wanted some scrambled eggs. She demurred more with a sound than an actual pronounceable word. Likely she'd come to a similar decision that I had. The less actual conversation between us this weekend, the better.

I poured some coffee then turned to check up on her. When I turned around, I noted how her head jerked from looking at me. I buried a self-satisfied smile in my mug as I tipped it back again. There was no small gratification in catching her checking out my ass.

Seemed I wasn't the only one who was missing it. *Careful there, baby girl. You're showing some emotions.*

Christ. Keely had no idea. Or maybe she had, but this was torture. And I thought this, as a man who had survived the physical screening test, SEALs BUD/S training, SQT and everything else they'd thrown at me during qualifications.

Not to mention those years in the teams. At least during those years, I'd gotten plenty of sex when I was on leave or at liberty. The astronaut lifestyle had been more complicated. It was feast while boots were on the planet and famine while on station.

The past four weeks, I'd been living like a priest. All because of that sweet young thing across the room from me. Resentment burned in my chest. It wasn't her fault and I shouldn't be directing my frustration at her, but goddamn, this was rough.

I tipped the rest of the coffee mug back and then turned to refill it, affording her some time to recover.

After breakfast and with not much else to do, I changed into my workout clothes and descended the two stories to the gym. Some cardio on the treadmill, some lifting on the weight machine, sit-ups, pull-ups would all do me good.

I was determined to render myself exhausted so I would not think about sex. Or Gray. Or sex with Gray.

Fuck, I was doing it again.

Forty-five minutes into my workout, she came down the stairs and entered the gym with a towel wrapped around her. After casting a very brief glance in my direction, she moved over to the hot tub and read the instructions on the control panel. I tore my eyes away from her when she dropped her towel.

But not so quickly that I didn't see her bikini. And the way the bottoms hugged her round ass. And those long legs, that expanse of glowing skin that I knew from intimate experience was even softer than it looked.

I dropped the weights and moved to the salmon ladder for pull-ups. Time to punish myself with some deep, core abdominals. I'd make myself so sore that sex wouldn't even cross my mind. Nope. I was not going to think about kissing her. Or touching her. Or putting my mouth all over her...

Damn it. I was suffering from a classic case of blue balls, and apparently it was now threatening to cause brain damage.

As I pushed my way up and down that salmon ladder, each pull up giving me momentum to push the pull-up bar to a higher level of hooks, I felt myself getting into the zone. I hardly even allowed myself to breathe and forced the pace faster each round until the pain grew too intense. I let myself drop to the mat below, covered in sweat and breathing so hard I could scarcely catch my breath.

I bent, bracing my hands on my knees and sneaked a side glance at the spa. Gray was openly staring at me, her face frozen in something that looked a bit like fascination. When she noticed me looking at her, however, she pulled away and turned her head, sitting back and putting her feet up so she could stare at the ceiling while the spa jets massaged her.

I turned, determined to do another hour with my back to her. After a little while, I heard her get out of the spa, turn it off and go up the stairs.

I finally sat down on the bench and downed a liter of water, trying to decide if I had it in me to do more today. I decided on cool down stretches and slow rehydration.

A half hour later, I climbed the stairs to use the bathroom. The door was open, and the bathroom was steamed up from a recent shower but was empty. Not even understanding the reason why, I turned around to glance across the hall into the bedroom.

Gray hadn't closed the door, and she'd just dropped her bath towel to the ground. And she was standing there naked as the day she was born. Gray was a lovely woman, slim build, curved hips, a smaller than average chest but a willowy, feminine frame marred only by the jagged scar from multiple open-heart surgeries which bisected her chest.

My eyes traveled up from her sweet-tasting thighs—and I knew from firsthand experience— across her smooth belly.

I was immediately hard and aching. And for God only knows what reason, I left the hallway and entered the bedroom.

It was goddamn impossible to not think about what that slight, feminine body felt like pressed up against mine. Naked. To remember what she sounded like when I made her come.

Fuck. I wanted it. I'd wanted *her* every night since the day I ended it.

I wanted to taste her again. All over.

If I didn't get out of here fast, I'd be pushing her onto the bed and covering that beautiful naked body with my own. And now I wasn't just hard and aching. I was throbbing with need.

And it wasn't exactly a secret I could keep from her, given I was wearing gym shorts.

She froze, staring at me wide-eyed. But instead of jumping or screaming or scrambling for her towel she dropped her jaw and actually appeared pissed off. "Do you mind turning around or something?"

I raised my eyebrow. "What's the point of that?" I mean, I'd already seen everything, right? Many times, many hot, sweaty and very, *very* enjoyable times. I folded my arms. "You keep managing to get yourself naked in front of me. Why is that?"

She rolled her eyes and reached for her shirt, which was lying on the bed, and pulled it over her head. My eyes sank down over her belly again and rested just at the top of her thighs. I wanted to taste her *there*.

God, I missed sex.

And I especially missed sex with *her*.

Her eyes flicked downward, and she noticed. And here I was, caught like a fourteen-year-old boy in front of the hot teacher.

Without saying a word, she bent and pulled on her underwear next, sliding them up her legs oh, so slowly. I gulped.

"Nice try. You don't actually think I was lying in wait to stop you in your tracks with my naked body."

"I was only pointing it out as an encouraging gesture. Feel free to do it as often as you like."

Having finished her task, she buttoned the fly of her jeans, sent me a snarky smile and said, "You should be so lucky." Then she exited the room and climbed the stairs, leaving us standing there—me and my painful erection—to ponder what the fuck had just happened.

You should be so lucky, she had said. And she was right. I wished I was.

With a sigh and a hand in my hair, I shook my head and went to shower off the sweat of my workout.

After a late lunch, there was plenty of silence and more awkward maneuvers to avoid each other. She read on her e-reader, and I played an old version of Mario Kart on the PlayStation hooked to the TV.

Just before sunset, Gray emerged from downstairs with her shoes on.

I frowned. "Going somewhere? That's probably not a good idea."

She did not react, grabbing a hoodie and pulling her arms through it. "I need some air. I'm going down to the lake shore to watch the sunset."

Well that made two of us. I set down the game controller on the coffee table. "I'll come with you."

"I'd rather be alone."

"And I'd rather make sure you're all right at this elevation. We are at over 6,000 feet above sea level here. Exertion could have an effect on your heart."

She scowled. "I am perfectly healthy. You know, for all that you despise the man, you do a really good job of sounding just like my father sometimes."

If that was her way of turning me off the overprotective behavior, it was effective. But not effective enough to deter me. As long as Gray was within arms' reach, under the same roof and it was in my power, I was going to watch over her. There was no question about it.

CHAPTER FIFTEEN
RYAN

O
UT THE SIDE DOOR AND DOWN A FLIGHT OF CONCRETE
steps, the path to the lake was a straightforward—if
steep—one. In amongst the tall trees and the golden sky
of early evening, we descended still more flights of concrete steps
and navigated the well-traveled path downward to the shore.

I watched her closely, just in case. Making the jump to this
altitude from sea level of the Los Angeles area was not an easy
one. And whether or not she protested, Gray did have a potential
issue that should be watched.

I'd done high altitude training many times—both as a Navy
SEAL and as an astronaut, so I could acclimate after a day or so,
usually. I noticed her slightly labored breathing, though, and I
had to remind myself that it was normal.

When we arrived at the shoreline, the sun had already set but
the lake and sky were still light enough to provide visibility. But
we'd be returning in the dark, so I'd noted the best possible
pathway back from the lake even as I followed her.

She stood at the shore where the cold azure water lapped
softly against the dark soil in among the trees.

It was peaceful. Birds were singing. A breeze riffled the leaves
in the trees. Nearby, boats in their slips creaked against their

199

moorings. I could almost be happy here, on an evening like this, with *this* girl...

She was talking, narrating some story about an analog study that she was in the process of writing a grant to conduct. "I want to get some real, trained astronauts involved in the study along with civilians."

My brows rose. "To send to Antarctica for the winter? I'm not sure you're going to get many takers."

She raised her head and looked at me. "Even in the interest of science?"

I laughed. "Even astronauts try to avoid holing themselves up on a lone continent without any prospect of a warm body to keep them company only to freeze their balls off in hundred-below weather."

This she found extremely funny. As she bent over to pick up a few pebbles, she actually snorted. "As opposed to going to the ISS."

I shrugged, studying the sky. "Fair point. But there, you're flying in space instead of freezing your ass crack off on the ground."

She was watching me closely, and her eyes drifted toward the sky. I knew what she was thinking. That it would be getting dark soon. She had to know that it was on my mind and perhaps *she* was keeping a close eye on *me*.

But I'd been practicing with that, too. Being outside at night in Orange County was not too difficult because it never got that dark. Here, however, I could see that it would be *very* dark. And if my memory served, we still had a new Moon for another night, so we'd have no light but the stars tonight.

"I don't get these analog missions," I said, baiting her. Perhaps if I got her talking about her passion, it would take her mind off noting any signs of my distress.

She was dropping pebbles into the lake and watching the ripples. *Plop.* And she'd study the ripples, watching them ring out from the center until they faded to nothing. She'd stare intently, as if her life depended on tracing the rings out until they vanished. Then she'd search for another rock and repeat.

"Analog missions are essential for experimental psychologists to gather data, so we can figure out how to best support actual space travelers. And with such harsh living conditions, Antarctica is a perfect analog for Mars."

"Uh huh," I said, tilting my head to watch her. I was mesmerized by the arch of her long neck, the way her short hair shivered in the breeze. She extended her arm and, *plop.* The ripples danced out from their center and she watched, her mouth partially open.

She didn't tear her eyes away from the glass-like surface of the lake, and *I* couldn't tear my eyes away from *her.* I could listen to her speak for hours about analog missions or even the goddamn weather if she was passionate about it.

But not just passionate. Gray was also compassionate, and intelligent, and her *joie de vivre* might even be contagious if I were of the mind to be able to catch it. For the brief period that she'd lit up my life, she'd been like a true ray of sunshine fighting hard to cancel out the darkness.

But never succeeding.

Because I was dead inside. So I could only witness her brilliance from a distance, like a dead black hole in the center of space that sucked all the light from the surrounding stars, bleeding them dry of all their energy until they, too, became lifeless, burnt-out husks.

"So basically, you use lab rats in their more intelligent form."

She laughed. "This is how we learn what kind of support systems we need to help you guys. And the 'lab rats' are enthusiastic volunteers, doing it for science."

Plop. Plop. Plop. Three more pebbles, all one right after the other. The lake was lovely, but she had all my attention.

"The participants have a lot of fun with it, too. I mean you love your job, but you have to do a lot of unpleasant things and take a lot of risks," she added quietly while interrupting her pebble search to flick a pointed glance at me.

Plop. All grew silent again. The wind stirred, and the sky dimmed to a pale purple and gray. She appeared lost in thought, so I just watched her, the vivid, shining young star who had dared to wander too close to the dead black hole and had been locked into my gravity. Who, only by the grace of my pushing her away, had managed to escape and did not realize her own good luck in doing so.

She blinked and turned to me. "I can't stop thinking about that metaphor about ripples in a pond and how simple words and actions spread out from the center and influence so much more. How events in our lives are like that... Things happen that end up causing ripples well into our future."

I leaned a shoulder up against the tree nearest me, folded my arms over my chest and watched her, a skeptical eyebrow raised. "Aren't you a little young to be making philosophical statements like that?"

Her eyes narrowed. "I've been through enough that I like to think it gives me a unique perspective on life. Like I can usually tell when a person is lying to himself—and everyone around him. And how that sends ripples out from their center, too."

Well, well, well. Claws at last. I was wondering if she'd show them. God knew it had taken a lot. She had an excellent command over her emotions. I couldn't help but think that she would have made an exceptional astronaut, had her health permitted it.

I didn't move, just kept that same stance, jammed stiffly against the tree. Despite the oncoming darkness, I could see the judgmental expression on her face. She'd flung a challenge right into my face. Damned if I was going to deprive her of the response she was looking for, in spite of it all.

"Oh yeah? How am I lying to myself?"

"I think you already know the answer to that." She glanced around her, as if suddenly noticing the low light. Her eyes traced the way we'd come.

I shrugged. "I think if you are going to throw out a judgement like that, you'd better be able to defend it."

"I am not your therapist."

"But—"

"Do you think this will work?" A voice called out nearby from the lakeside. It was not close, but here amongst the quiet and the trees, the sound carried well. We both froze and turned. There was a cluster of three people near the boat dock, about three properties away from our own.

"We're not even sure which house they're in! But we've got it narrowed down to one of the five on this side."

Reaching out, I grabbed Gray's arm, and yanked her behind the tree where I was standing. I held a finger to my lips when she turned to me, wide-eyed.

"Are those reporters?" she whispered. I was pretty sure that's exactly what they were, so I nodded and put a hand over her mouth. I mouthed to her, *No talking.*

The voices grew louder as the group walked along the shore, and we angled ourselves around the tree to stay out of sight as they approached. They paused, mere feet from where we had been standing and spoke again. "Either of you bring a flashlight? It's getting dark out here real fast, and I have no idea what we are even looking for. They could be up in that glass one on the cliff right now having wild monkey sex, and we'd have no idea."

"It's definitely not that one. Not big enough. I'm sure Keely has her squad with her."

Much to my frustration, Gray began to laugh behind my hand. Warm puffs of air blew out against my palm, and I shook my head stiffly. I held up my other hand, knuckles out with one finger up, turning it in a small circle. Her dark brows wrinkled together in a frown, clearly mystified by my combat hand signal, *rally point.* Meaning we needed to get the hell out of here and back up to the house before they saw us.

Branches snapped under foot as the small group continued to walk along the shore. "Damn, Joyce, make more noise, please. It's not like we're on a covert operation here."

"I think you're going over the top with this," someone replied. The voices started to grow fainter as if they were moving away. I chanced a peek around our tree, confirmed by the sight of three backs. With relief, I nearly stepped out from behind the tree when I caught sight of a fourth person, someone who was standing on the beach and staring in our direction.

I jerked behind the tree again and pulled Gray tightly against me. When she would have talked, I put my hand over her mouth again and pressed my mouth to her ear. "There's one more on the beach. As soon as he turns his back, we are going up the way we came."

With her this close to me, I felt every inch of that lithe body against mine, the strawberries and mint of her scent. I closed my eyes, drinking it in, nearly delirious with it. Slowly I heard footsteps retreat from our position. But it took a monumental effort to convince myself I didn't need to bury my nose in her hair anymore. She was clinging to my shirt, her hands fisted in the material. It was bringing back delicious memories of our bodies pressed together, touching each other, holding each other. Of me sinking deep into her heat, moving inside of her, making her moan.

With no small effort, I pulled myself away and glanced around the tree to confirm there were no more people on the beach and they were walking away from us. I turned back to her and in the very dim light, pointed toward the house.

I fell into step behind her as she picked her way through the undergrowth and back to the clear path that led to the many sets of concrete stairs. And though we were easily in the clear, she quickened her pace, perhaps conscious that I was right behind her. But she didn't appear to be paying special attention to her footing, nearly slipping a few times.

"Careful," I whispered harshly, but she wasn't listening. Instead moving faster. It was almost dark enough that we should have been using a flashlight—or at least the light on one of our phones, to pick the way. But that would be a sure way of being seen, even from a distance.

She turned to reply over her shoulder. "I want to get up the steps before it's too dark."

And that's when she mis-stepped. The next thing I knew, she went down, her feet sliding out from under her less than a meter from the cleared path. I reached out but wasn't quite close enough to catch her.

She sucked in a loud breath, fortunately falling on her ass instead of bumping her head.

When I knelt down beside her to check if she was okay, she was quietly laughing. "Well, I always did say my dad was an idiot for naming me Grace. Unless it was an exercise in irony."

"You okay?" I whispered as she reached down toward her ankle. "Did you twist your ankle?"

"My foot came down on the edge of that big rock over there. I scraped my ankle and...*oh!*"

She held up the hand that had just touched her ankle. It was wet and shiny. *Blood.*

"You're bleeding?" I said, my heart speeding up.

"It's okay. It's just a graze."

"It's okay for most people. Sure. Most people aren't on blood thinners. Roll up your pant leg."

Instead she was trying to push to her feet. "I'll be fine."

I put an end to that stupidity. "Stop it. Don't move, goddammit." I scooted to where I could reach her leg and rolled up her jeans myself, grasping her ankle. It was now too dark to be able to see much, especially since most of the light was blocked out by the trees and since, out here in Tahoe, there wasn't much ambient light, like there was in the city. It was a clear, starry night. A gorgeous night.

But my girl was bleeding, and I didn't notice much of anything else as my mind raced through how to best manage the situation. She wasn't being cooperative.

"Ryan, stop treating me like an invalid. I'm fine."

"You're fucking bleeding. Don't you dare try to stand on this leg right now. You need a pressure bandage."

"Did you stuff something like that in your back pocket or something?"

In response, I hooked my fingers around the collar of my t-shirt and yanked it off. I began twisting the material around my hands. As I worked, I peered into her face, which I now could hardly see. "Tell me you brought your wound sealing powder with you on the trip."

She hesitated. I checked the wound. She was bleeding pretty badly, even from a scrape. People on blood thinners were at risk even from superficial wounds such as this. I pulled her ankle up to rest on my bent knee and began to wrap my twisted t-shirt around it. "Gray?" I said sharply when she hadn't answered me.

"I forgot to pack it. This was a last-minute trip for me, and I didn't anticipate—"

"*Fuck,*" I spat as I pulled tighter on the t-shirt to give it extra pressure application. "Goddammit! What the fuck were you thinking, going on a trip without it? No one anticipates getting injured."

She blew out a long breath. "Don't yell at me. I don't have a crystal ball. I was preoccupied while I was packing."

Preoccupied? With what? With having to spend the weekend with me? Or perhaps she'd been thinking about that new guy—whatever the fuck his name was.

I pushed to my feet, having finished the bandage. "On your feet. C'mon."

She held up an arm, and I gently pulled her to her feet. "I'm good to walk."

"The *fuck* you are. I'm carrying you up."

"All the way up all those stairs? No, I can make it. I just might need to lean on you."

I had my hands braced around both of her arms. "I'm not arguing with you. You're getting on my back, and I'm taking you up. You're still bleeding, and you know the risks."

She sighed but relented. "Okay."

"You hardly weigh more than my pack and kit, and you would not believe how many miles I had to hike with all that on my back. It will be just like the old days. I'm fine."

Then I crouched down, and she obediently draped herself across my back, hooking her arms around my neck. I clasped her legs behind her knees and hefted her onto my back, piggyback style. "Hold on tight. I'm going to go up the stairs double time, okay?"

"Uh. Okay."

"Don't let go, Gray." I gave her one last command before I turned and picked my way along the path and made it to the base of the long climb on the stairs. Her arms tightened around my shoulders, and I tried not to think about the feel of her against me, or that vision of her standing naked in the bedroom like some kind of sea goddess standing on a wet towel instead of a clam shell. Taking a deep breath, I prepared myself for the physically demanding task ahead.

With a swallow and a deep breath, I let out a "Hooyah!" as I tackled the first steps.

CHAPTER SIXTEEN
GRAY

I F ANYONE HAD TOLD ME FORTY-EIGHT HOURS AGO THAT I'D
be mounted on Ryan Tyler's back and we'd be going up a hill.
That I'd be clinging to his half naked form while his stunning
muscles rippled underneath my hands, I would have laughed in
their face. That haunted sort of laugh that came only from the
hollow chest of a broken-hearted woman.

But here it was, happening. And as I fought delirium from
the delicious smell of his heated skin, I couldn't help but think
that life was so freaking bizarre sometimes.

Ryan all but ran up the concrete stairs, his head bent to watch
the ground in the very low light so as not to miss his footing. If
only *I* had been as careful. I leaned my cheek against the warm
skin on the back of his neck, and his muscles rippled and tensed
underneath my hands on his shoulders. Not once did he miss a
step, and he only paused on each landing for a few seconds to
catch his breath before he began climbing again. I did what I
could not to throw him off balance, and we made it to the top in
no time.

Slowly I slid to the ground, balancing on my good leg and
noting that the blood had pretty much completely soaked
through his shirt. Panting heavily, Ryan opened the side door of

the cabin and peered at me through narrowed eyes. "It's still gushing isn't it?"

I shrugged. "It's not bad."

He shook his head. "Your blood is running down my pant leg, so don't fucking lie to me."

I cleared my throat, the sting of his admonishment nearly bringing tears to my eyes. *Where the hell had that come from?*

I sniffed. "Sorry. Didn't mean to get my blood on you."

He grimaced and hooked an arm around my waist to pull me against him. "That's not what I meant, okay? I'm worried. Let's get that bleeding stopped."

Then without saying another word, he scooped me up into his arms and carried me inside. I tried not to think of the irony of him carrying me across a threshold like a groom with his new bride, but my stubbornly hopeful mind went there anyway.

I leaned against his broad, solid chest and tried not to remember that I'd once dreamed about our forever. Heat and resentment burned in my chest like acid at the memory. If only he'd been as stubborn about preserving our relationship in the face of my dad's threats as he was about preventing me from standing on my own two feet.

How easily he'd given us up. The shame and pain of it still burned.

Ryan took me straight to the downstairs bathroom and laid me inside the sunken tub to keep the blood contained and proceeded to ferociously whip off my shoes, socks, the bandage and then my pants, almost taking my underwear off in the process.

"Chill out for a second," I snapped, pulling the undies back on. Seeing me naked once today was enough.

He didn't respond, instead grabbing my leg, which was now free of his improvised pressure bandage, and inspecting my ankle, pulling it up perpendicular to the ground. Hot blood continued to ooze from the wound and drip all the way down my leg.

"The wound needs to stay up above your heart. You keep that fucking leg up, you understand?" He rasped in a breathy voice that had nothing to do with his taxing run up the hill with me on his back. "I need to get ice."

I laced my fingers together around the back of my thigh to continue holding up my leg. My ankle, calf and thigh were sticky with dried blood, and though I didn't say anything to Ryan, I had to admit that I was starting to feel slightly lightheaded.

Ryan returned in minutes with a clump of ice wrapped in a towel. "The home remedy for stopping bleeding is to lower the local temperature to constrict the capillaries. This isn't going to feel great, fair warning."

I took a deep breath, closed my eyes, and then opened them again. "Lay it on me."

With that go-ahead, Ryan pressed the cold to my wound and held it there, leaning my leg against his thigh. Neither of us said anything, and we avoided each other's gaze during the stretch of time that we waited for the ice to have its effect. Finally, I couldn't take the pain any longer and pulled my leg away.

Grim-faced and obviously reluctant, he slowly pulled the pack away from my ankle and bent for a closer inspection. He turned my ankle this way and that, stroking the skin carefully with his long fingers, seemingly unaware of the shivers he was sending down the length of my leg. Pain or no, this unbelievably sexy and shirtless man bent over me, carefully administering to me, was turning me on in a major way.

"Let's get you cleaned up so I can be sure the bleeding has stopped."

I lifted myself to the edge of the sunken tub and he ran the water. With a washcloth, he slowly, carefully wiped down my leg. And honestly, even that was turning me on.

I was so damn mad at myself for that, too. I'd gone twenty-five years without having sex before Ryan and I had gotten involved. Now I was like a cat in heat every time he looked at me or touched me because I hadn't had any for four weeks.

Of course it didn't help matters when, having finished cleaning the blood off of me, Ryan dropped his pants. He used another wash cloth to clean the blood I'd leaked all over his strong, muscular, hairy legs. I swallowed, my heartbeat accelerating.

I should have averted my eyes. He now wore nothing but his boxers which clung to him and left little to the imagination. Yeah, I'd seen him gloriously naked many times. I'd felt that incredible naked body pressed against me during the only hot sex I'd ever enjoyed in my life, and it had been amazing.

But I sure as heck didn't need a reminder of that now in my wounded, vulnerable state.

After cleaning the gash and slapping some taped gauze on it, Ryan scooped me up to carry me into the bedroom. He ignored my protests, and I tried my hardest to ignore that he was naked except for his boxers.

I had on just my panties and a t-shirt with no bra underneath. We might as well be naked, *and* he was taking us to the bed.

Yeah, *not* a good idea. *So* not a good idea.

Gently, he lay me against the pillows and then blew out a long breath. I studied his face and noted for the first time how stressed out he appeared. He'd been *really* worried about me. I reached out and touched his arm. "Are you okay?"

His cheeks bulged where he tightened his jaw and then relaxed it. He looked visibly shaken. As if, having moved out of problem-solving mode, he was now crashing from the adrenaline rush and reacting to the "danger" I'd been in.

He swallowed and turned to me. "Stop wounding yourself, for God's sake."

Then he jumped up from the bed and left the room.

In just a few minutes, he reappeared with a bottle of vodka in one hand and a shot glass in the other.

The shot glass, I noted, was empty.

"Did you just do a shot of that?" I asked.

He frowned. "Yeah, and I'm going to do another one." And as if to prove a point, he tilted the uncapped bottle, poured a shot and then put the glass to his lips.

"Stop!" He hesitated and turned his head to look at me. "That's not fair. Where's mine?"

He raised a skeptical brow at me. "You want to do vodka shots?"

I folded my arms, crossed my legs and wiggled my foot expectantly. "Yes, as a matter of fact, I do."

"Have you ever done straight shots of vodka before?"

I fought rolling my eyes. "I've had vodka before, *thankyouverymuch*."

"That's not what I asked." He approached the bed slowly with the full shot glass.

I held out my hand, wiggling my fingers. "Just give it to me. I'm not a baby."

He obediently held out the glass to me, and I took it, knocking it back in as convincing a badass manner as I could.

Unfortunately, that involved a little sputtering and coughing after I swallowed. But he didn't laugh. Solemnly, he took the glass back and poured himself another shot, this time with a Russian toast tacked on.

I waggled my hand at him. "Give it here. You're sharing that shit or I'm going to protest."

He sank onto the edge of the bed and poured another shot, passing it to me. I drank that one down too, glad that there was much less sputtering. And we continued like that for a few more shots until, on the fifth one, he refused to pass the glass to me, keeping it just out of my reach.

"You have got to be feeling a buzz by now."

I raised my brow at him. I most certainly *was* feeling a buzz— actually I was somewhat past a buzz. I'd sailed past tipsy, too, and was well on my way to drunk. But, since all I had to do was just sit there on the bed and not stand up straight without wobbling or walk without falling over, I was able to hide that better than I could have in other circumstances.

"I'm fine," I said, meeting his gaze unwaveringly although the rest of the world around him looked fuzzy.

He stared at me skeptically, and I raised my brows at him without saying more. The less I said, the less likely it would be that I'd slur the words.

Slowly he handed me the shot. "That's the last one, so enjoy it."

I only got half of it down before I started coughing and he had to pull it away from me. Then he put the glass to his lips and sucked up the rest, following it by another full one. "You sure you aren't part Russian?" he asked me.

"Nope. Mom's Welsh. Dad is Midwestern, born from English and Irish stock."

"And here I thought he was just pure evil," he muttered. I stared at him, willing him to go on. Willing him to say, *Screw Conrad Barrett. I want you anyway, Gray.*

But he didn't, and my heart took a little dip. Hurt a little more from the sadness, from missing him.

The only thing I could do in response was hiccup. He grinned as if suppressing laughter. "We never had dinner. You drank all that on an empty stomach."

I shrugged and sent him a sloppy smile. "I feel jus' fine."

He laughed, capping the bottle and setting it on the night stand. Then, he reached to chuck my cheek. "You sound just fine."

Under his touch, I froze. He froze. Our gazes locked, and breathing stopped. At least mine did. I swallowed. He swallowed.

Then slowly, he reached out to my cheek again, smoothing the skin there. "You worried me, baby girl," he murmured.

Something in that touch and in those words melted me inside. Not a little, no. Places inside me heated and shifted and warped as if they were actually made of wax. Rearranging the hardened scar tissues around my heart. Those wounds he'd torn so deftly just a month before.

His thumb stroked across my cheek again, and I shivered slightly before turning my head to pull away from that touch.

What good was it to let him speak to me this way, all kind and sweet, as if he still really cared? *Fuck him.*

"Fuck you," I said, echoing my thoughts.

"I wish."

Without realizing exactly what I was doing, my hand lashed out, and I slapped him across the face. His eyes widened, and he caught my right wrist before I could do it again. His hand clenched around that wrist firmly, and when I tugged, the hold tightened even more. I let out a small gasp, and our eyes waged a battle, locked in one another's grasp.

Finally, he swallowed and, without changing his expression, he licked his lips. I watched the mark I'd left on his cheek grow angry and red. "I may have deserved that," he finally conceded.

My breathing came faster, and I was all tension. My body coiled up as if expecting the other shoe to drop—something violent in his response to my violence.

Or maybe he was waiting for an apology.

"My ankle may have stopped bleeding, but my heart didn't," I said in a small voice while our gazes tangled with each other.

He slowly blinked, as if sifting through inebriation to absorb the meaning of my words.

I let out a long and shaky breath that, to my shame, sounded a bit like a whimper.

"Shh," he said, reaching up with his free hand. His head drifted closer as if he would kiss me. I pulled back.

"No, you don't get to do that. You don't get to shush me. You don't get to tuck it away like you never did anything wrong. I'm *angry* with you, Ryan."

He held my gaze, his hand tightening around my wrist, his jaw setting. Those blue eyes, those *gorgeous* blue eyes, like the bluest of blue layer of sky before the black and violent cold of space, something passed through them. Something that looked a lot like pain. "I know that."

I licked my lips. "I may not show it, but it hurts. I'm hurting."

"I'm sorry you're hurting. I never wanted to hurt you."

I blew out a breath in disgust and held up my other hand as if to slap him again. "Do you want another one? I do have a free hand."

Somewhere deep inside, Sober Me was horrified by my own actions. It wasn't like I didn't have control over myself, but rather that the guard I'd always kept firmly fixed around me by sheer strength of will had been let down. I'd given that guard a bit of a vacation. Told him to pack his bags and head to Bermuda until I was sober again.

Besides. I had to admit that it had felt good to slap him that once.

He *did* deserve it. I'd given him my heart. A pure, unadulterated gift. And he'd tossed it away because, as he'd said, he'd "made me no promises."

No promises. And what he hadn't said was that I'd been a fool to expect them.

Ryan grabbed my left wrist before I could make good on my threat. His gaze flew up to mine, and I could see he was not angry. No, he was...guarded.

He cleared his throat and spoke in a low voice. "Is there anything else you want to say to me?"

My hands, where he held them clamped at the wrists, knotted into fists. I settled back against the pillows, regardless.

"You're an asshole."

He nodded. "Yes."

"*Why?* Why would you give up so easily?" It came out all wrong, all guttural and emotional as if it had been torn from me.

His eyes still reflected that same pain. "Because I don't deserve you."

I shook my head. "An easy, trite answer."

"The truth," he murmured. "I never did deserve you."

"Give me a break." I yanked against his hold. "Spare me your *I've touched an angel* BS and give me the truth for once, Ryan."

His eyes were on mine, unwavering. "I've never lied to you."

I shook my head, refusing to be the first one to pull my eyes away. I couldn't accept this. There was no way he hated himself this much.

Or did he?

But why punish me, too, if he did?

He took a deep breath. "You deserve so much—"

"Oh *please!* Shut the fuck up."

Something in his gaze changed, and the air thickened between us. His eyes fell to my lips and he drifted closer, almost as if he were fighting with himself and the part of him that wanted me was winning.

"I decide what I deserve. Not you. Not my father." Enough with these men who wanted to run my life. "*Me.*"

And something in him snapped. Without warning, he was on me. He yanked my hands above my head, pinning them down with one hand while he took my face in his other hand. His mouth was on mine and his kiss was ferocious. He lay on me, his body partially overlapping mine, pinning it down to the bed.

His tongue invaded my mouth. He tasted like vodka and desire.

Desire.

His erection was hard against my leg. His breath came fast, as fast as mine, and we were hot and sweaty and rubbing against each other in seconds. Primal urges claimed us like animals in a frenzy. My free leg clamped around his hips and he ground against me. There were two thin layers—my underwear and his—between us and what we craved most. Union.

My throat was making sounds I'd never even heard before. Somewhere between wounded and delirious with lust.

His mouth left mine and he trailed hard kisses over my neck and down my chest until he was sucking and biting my nipples through the thin fabric of my t-shirt, his cock swelling against my body. My eyes clamped shut, and I couldn't think. Couldn't breathe. *Definitely* couldn't sort out the possible consequences of these actions.

I could only *want* and *crave* and *hunger*.

"Ryan, I need you inside me," I finally rasped when he made no move to take this further. He didn't reach under my shirt. Didn't pull off my underwear like I wanted him to.

He kept at his torture, sucking my nipples until I gasped and writhed. Grinding against me as if he were already penetrating me. But he wouldn't take it further and he wouldn't release my wrists, which he held in a death grip.

His free hand was in my hair, holding my head still, and I had zero control over how this would go. The only thing I had were my words. "Please, I need to feel you inside me." More sucking through that goddamn t-shirt. My lust was so peaked it was almost painful. "Ryan!" I ground out.

He slowly stopped what he was doing, pulled his mouth away and stilled against me. I was hopeful, so I rubbed my hips against his and he groaned in response. But something had changed. Something was cooling him down before this could escalate. His breath came as fast as if he had run up the stairs while carrying me on his back again. His mouth was pressed to the side of my neck now as he struggled to regain control. Suddenly he released my hands and pulled back, looking down into my face.

His own face was flushed with desire. And those blue eyes burned with it. I'd seen that look in them many times before. That look used to precede hours of the two of us grinding against each other naked on the way to multiple orgasms.

But...

Apparently not tonight.

Turning my head, I blinked as the room swam. I was a lot drunker than I'd initially thought. Trying to reframe my perception, I struggled to find the right side up to everything.

Ryan was staring down into my face. He looked far more sober than I felt.

"We can't do this. We're both too fucked up. This is the vodka—"

"Wrong," I snapped. "This is what we *really* want. The vodka just got us to drop our inhibitions."

"It's still not right, and you know it. I know what I want. Even when I'm sober all I want to do is get inside you. I think about it constantly, and some part of my brain is continually plotting it. And I would always wonder if this was me manipulating you."

I squinted at him. "You don't have to make that decision for me."

"Vodka doesn't make decisions for you, either. Yet you slapped me. Something I'm betting you wanted to do but would never ever do while you were sober."

I let out a long breath and looked away. He was right, of course. But damned if I was going to admit that to him. I'd been counting on a good orgasm tonight. *Jerk.*

He relaxed against me, as if seeing that reason had finally seeped through my vodka fog. I could see why Russians loved this stuff.

"Gray, I'm so sorry."

I shook my head. "Don't. Don't pity me."

"I don't. I'm just saying I'm sorry. I—I'm sorry I hurt you and I'm sorry about how I did it."

He pulled back, rolling away from me, but he didn't leave the bed. He reached up and rubbed his eyes. His boxers were misshapen around the huge bulge of his erection. My own swollen arousal was causing no small discomfort inside my panties.

Goddamn him for still having his wits. I could have used a good orgasm tonight. An amazing one. Given to me by *him.*

But he was right. We were drunk and hurting, and this wasn't a good idea from any angle.

To my shock, he started to laugh. It was a quiet, huffing sort of laugh. An ironic laugh. "I have to admit...I was wondering why you were being so nice to me all the time. Why you weren't showing your emotions. I would have slapped me up a few times, too, in your place."

I didn't feel like laughing. I just stared up at the ceiling, blinking, trying not to cry. Trying not to show still *more* emotions. Instead I cleared my throat. "You already carry a pretty damn heavy burden of unnecessary guilt. No need for me to add to it."

He was silent for a moment, and I turned my head to stare into his face. He looked...stricken. As if that hadn't even occurred to him. His brow wrinkled. "You were trying to protect me?" His voice shook when he asked it.

I didn't reply, just stared, just watched as the emotion crossed his features and then was gone. He'd just proven to me that I was right. His guilt was pulling him down and killing everything that was inside, every living piece of him. And the mere belief that I was too good for him was proof of that.

Puzzlingly, he reached out with the back of his index finger and lightly stroked my cheek. "Gray..."

I just shook my head, for once speechless, emotion tying my tongue. Emotion that I wish could show in my face. But the tears wouldn't come. Tears I wished would speak for me, tell him how deeply I felt for him, how much I cared in spite of my earlier anger.

The tears wouldn't come.

My voice was a scratchy whisper. "Please, Ryan...no."

He slowly pulled his hand away, as if reluctant to stop touching me. "Okay."

For a long time, we just lay like that, him staring at me, me staring up at the ceiling, wishing for tears.

"Vodka wasn't such a good idea, was it?" he said finally.

I laughed. "That's the first thing you've said tonight that I can agree with."

"Huh. Okay. Be right back. I need to prep us so we aren't so hungover tomorrow." He left and returned with a huge jug of ice water, two glasses and a bottle of aspirin from the medicine cabinet.

He poured us each a glass and we clinked them. "Down the hatch. We have to do three of these in the next hour. And we should take the aspirin as soon as we can, too. We're at high altitude, so it's going to hit even harder than normal."

I sputtered on the gulp I was currently swallowing. "I am not getting up to pee on my tweaked leg that many times."

"I'll carry you."

"Wow, free rides to the bathroom and I don't even have to date you."

He stared at me for a moment before finishing his first glass of water and then poured us each a new glass.

"Are you?" He asked in a thick, hoarse voice and then cleared his throat and elaborated. "Going to date this dude—Aaron?"

I sat back and stared at him, still comfortable with being blunt with him through the fog of my inebriation. "That depends."

He looked up. "On what?"

"On what happens after the test flight."

His forehead creased and he was at first visibly confused, sipping at his glass of water and staring at me. He took a deep breath and let it go. "Your dad just wanted the best for you."

I shook my head. "He wants to control me. But I'm an adult. And you're an adult. And we do have choices, even if you refuse to see it that way. If we decided to go forward with this after the test flight, he has little leverage. He'll have nothing to hold over your head."

"But he's still your father."

I nodded. "Yes. And my relationship with him is between *me* and *him*."

His face was utterly passive. I could almost see the gears turning in his brain, but his eyes were flat, inexpressive. I couldn't tell whether he loved the idea or he hated it. My heart started double-timing, and of course, the clicking of my prosthetic valve gave me away.

His eyes lowered to rest on my sternum, but he didn't smile. Didn't do or say anything.

He hissed out a long breath and ran a hand through his hair. "Your dad's threat wasn't the only reason I broke things off."

I stared, at once stunned he'd tell me this and yet not overly surprised at what he was saying.

"I don't care what he said to you. What horrible, hurtful things he said. You can't believe it. You can't believe those things about yourself."

His eyes flicked up to me. "He didn't say a damn thing that wasn't true, Gray. That's the whole point."

Something dark and dangerous clamped around my throat. A sudden vicious anger at my own dad. My face flushed, but before I could needlessly rant about him, Ryan took a breath and continued.

"I made a choice because I had to. And that choice told me a lot. I chose to fly again over being with you and that, right there, means he was right. Any man who would make that choice doesn't deserve you."

My hand knotted in the bedspread, and I struggled to find something to say. Speechless and desperately wanting those healing tears—like in the early days when I could sob alone into my pillow. I craved that cathartic release, but I was denied that too, just as I'd been denied the orgasm I'd so desperately wanted.

Ryan seemed to be watching me carefully.

"You don't need to protect me anymore at your own expense, Gray. You can tell me that I hurt you. You can be angry at me. In fact, it makes it easier for me. I understand anger. I don't understand..." He shook his head.

I looked away. My voice, when I finally spoke, was surprisingly even and calm. "Yes, you hurt me. But you hurt yourself more, and I think that's truly what this is all about. Breaking things off was not about not deserving me. It was about your belief that you don't deserve to be happy. That you need to keep punishing yourself."

He sipped at his water and pointed to my glass, silently urging me to follow suit. For long minutes we sat in silence, drinking water, sending each other furtive looks.

I wanted to smash sense into his head. Maybe *that's* what the slap had been about. But my frustrated and desperate actions while drunk would only be something to regret in the morning.

And hopefully we wouldn't have to add hideous hangovers to that regret.

I set aside my final glass of water. "I have to pee," I declared.

Ryan obediently stood and put his glass on the nightstand. Then he bent and picked me up. And though it didn't take a drunk woman to be attracted to this amazingly gorgeous man, I had to admit to myself that my hormones were raging still from that intense make-out session. His arms came around me and pull me to his hard chest. With me in his arms, he made his way out the bedroom doorway and into the bathroom. This only served to ramp up my senses all over again. He gently deposited me near the toilet and then turned and left, shutting the door after him.

And he waited just outside to pick me up and carry me all the way back. Once he laid me on the bed, he checked my wound under the bandage to make sure I hadn't started bleeding again. Suddenly, he yawned. "I should probably go collapse," he said.

"Or you could just collapse here. This bed is big, and it's not like anything's going to happen. And I'm going to guess that the pull-out bed sucks."

He laughed and nodded. "Yeah, it's pretty bad."

I pointed to Keely's untouched side of the bed. "Sleep there, then."

Much to my astonishment, he put up no resistance. Before he settled next to me, however, I crawled under the blanket and slowly, so did he.

"My brains are pickled," I said.

"That's the idea…nice and numb. Feels great, doesn't it? Long live vodka."

"Mmm. Do Russians really drink it to keep warm all winter?" I asked as he settled in beside me and my head fell against his massive shoulder. He hesitated. We were still wearing just a small amount of clothing—him in just his boxers and me in my panties and t-shirt. And we were under the covers together. Everything within my vision and my perception glowed crystal clear and burned hot with the buzz, but I was all too aware of my own fatigue, too.

"Naw, vodka would never keep you warm in a Russian winter. You have never ever known cold like that."

"You spent a lot of time there?" I looked up at him.

He smiled. "In Star City. Where they trained us to go up in the Soyuz."

"Mmm." I closed my eyes, liking the way his shoulder felt under my head. "I wish I could have been an astronaut."

"You would have been an excellent astronaut."

I started laughing. In the state I was in, that was the most hilarious thing in the world. I fell back against my pillow. "You're so funny," I slurred.

His hand came up and he hesitated before he touched me. "You aren't going to slap me if I touch your hair, are you?"

I swallowed a thick lump in my throat. "I'm sorry I hit you. I shouldn't have."

His hand went to its intended target, sifting through my hair. His voice was quiet when he responded. "It didn't hurt—at least not in the way that you think."

He yawned again, covering his mouth with the back of his hand while lightly stroking my hair with the other one. His yawn prompted me to yawn, which prompted another from him.

"So, you're okay to turn off the lights?" I glanced at him.

He was silent for a long time, then quietly he said, "Yes, you can turn them off."

I noticed he had regulated his breathing and was staring up at a fixed point on the ceiling.

With a quick count of three, I flipped the switch on the light and plunged the room into darkness. I listened closely for any change in his breathing. He did not appear to be moving.

"It might be dark, but I have something to focus on. I never get tired of listening to the tickety tock of your heart."

I reached up and sifted my fingers through his short hair, closing my eyes. "I wish..." I said faintly, and even I could hear the extreme sleepiness in my voice. "I wish you could see yourself the way I do. That you're deserving of so much more than this shame, torment and pain."

He did not reply, and I felt myself relentlessly tugged toward dreamland. After long minutes of silence, my hand dropped, and my eyelids fell.

He turned, then and lightly kissed my hair. Then he whispered something I didn't understand. Was it slurred? No. It was Russian. He said something to me in Russian, for some weird reason.

Like why would I understand something he said in Russian?

I fell asleep just as the answer came to me. He said something he didn't want me to understand but that he had to say aloud.

Sleep took me then, mercifully, or I would have been up half the night trying to figure out all the possibilities.

CHAPTER SEVENTEEN
GRAY

MANY HOURS LATER, SUNLIGHT FILTERED IN BRIGHTLY through the window and stabbed my eyes. Only then did I realize that we'd been too drunk to have the forethought to lower the blinds. With a groan, I squeezed my eyes shut again. I was pleasantly surprised by the lack of a pounding headache at my temple that I'd been expecting. Not that I was all that experienced with hangovers, but there was only a vague, dull ache behind my eyes and my mouth was dry with an awful taste in it.

I was certain the real punishment would come when I got out of bed.

It appeared that sometime during the night I'd grown too warm, and instead of being logical and kicking off the covers, I'd torn off my shirt instead. And my legs and arms were inextricably entangled with the larger, heavier body next to me.

The first thing that I noticed was his earthy smell and the feeling of being wrapped up in him. Then the sensations immediately brought back those few weeks in which we'd have sex every night only to fall asleep exhausted—and naked—in each other's arms and wake up that way shortly before having sex again in the morning.

The memory of it, in combination with this current situation, was enough to have that heat of arousal crackle through me as I became more aware of him. His arm lay over my waist, his bare chest pressed to my naked back, the hand cupping my uncovered breast. His steady, slow breath in my hair. His hard erection pressed against my butt.

Damn. *Not good.* Or rather...*so* good. The nipple under his rough hand had long since tightened under his touch. But I couldn't let myself lie there and endure that torture, so I moved, because despite the headache, I was hornier than hell and his nearness was not making it any better.

As I pulled my arm out from under his, the grip on my breast tightened.

Damn. What exactly was he dreaming about? I scooted my butt away from his body, but my legs were both pinned by his.

I wiggled them out from the tangle, and he shifted slightly, giving a small moan.

"Ryan," I called.

He came awake quickly, like he typically did. "Yes?" he answered in a groggy voice.

"I need to go to the bathroom. I can't get up."

His hand twitched. He seemed to be unaware of where it was, and I swallowed, feeling the zing of his touch from my nipple straight down to my core. He stroked my nipple with his fingers and I jumped.

Then I firmly grabbed his wrist and pulled his hand away, pushing myself to sit up as he rolled onto his back and freed my legs from his. His eyes immediately fixated on my chest. As the air was chilly in the room, now, both my nipples were perky and saying good morning to him. I grabbed the sheet and used it to cover up, glancing around the bed and floor for my shirt.

"Why is your shirt off?" he mumbled in a clearly disappointed voice. "Did I miss something fun?"

I raised an eyebrow. "Do you think you blacked out and can't remember sex? Wait—do you remember last night at all?" I bent and grabbed my t-shirt from the foot of the bed and slipped it on. It ended up inside-out, but I didn't bother to fix it.

He was rubbing his eyes through closed eyelids. "Yes, I remember last night. I only had six shots."

My eyebrows rose again. Hmm. I'd only been around him truly drunk once—that time in Houston. He'd been pretty sauced then, but I had no idea how much he'd had to get him into that state.

"Ugh, I feel gross," I said, smacking my lips together.

Ryan sat up then. "Don't go anywhere. I have a remedy."

"It's okay. I'm not that hungover."

He ignored me, getting out of bed. The first thing I noticed, of course, was the huge morning wood in his boxers. Well he *had* touched and looked at my boobs before I'd covered up... *Tit for tat. Literally.* I bit my lip.

"Don't move," he said as he left the room and slowly went up the stairs. He was gone for a good ten minutes and I had to pee. In addition, I was increasingly apprehensive about whatever this "remedy" was.

Just when I was going to go hide in the bathroom anyway, I heard him come down the stairs again. He entered the room with two small glasses partially full of a grayish-yellow liquid. That shit did *not* look appealing.

"What the hell is that?" I recoiled when he proffered me a glass.

"Pickle juice. Raw egg. Ukrainian hangover remedy."

I scooted back when he pushed it in my face, shaking my head vehemently. "No way."

"It works every time. Watch." He tipped his glass to his face and downed it without so much as a shudder.

"You also eat disgusting reconstituted astronaut food while floating around in zero-g, so I'm not buying."

He put his empty glass on the nightstand and sat down. "You have a crappy taste in your mouth and a headache. If you get up, you're going to be sick to your stomach. The salt from the pickle juice and the protein from the egg will restore the balance of salinity and enzyme level in your blood."

I narrowed my eyes at him. "You are shitting me."

He nudged it at me. "Just down it all at once. You won't even taste it."

I gritted my teeth and took the glass from him, peering down from the top.

"Don't look at it," he said. "Like a boss, Gray. Do it. *Do it,*" he chanted.

I narrowed my eyes at him and followed his advice not to look at it. Plugging my nose so I wouldn't have to taste the crap, I slung it back. It was salty and viscous—a little slimy and thick. And though the taste wasn't altogether gross, the texture of the raw egg was. Eww. Worse than a raw oyster, which I'd only had once in defiance of my father, who had forbidden me from eating raw foods for fear it would cause me medical problems.

Unlike Ryan, I *did* shudder. Multiple times. Ryan took the glass from me, watching me closely. I made a face at him. "That is so incredibly vile! What the hell is wrong with you? Jesus, get me some water."

"No, you can't have water for at least thirty minutes. It will dilute the beneficial effects."

I did a double take as I crawled to the edge of the bed to make my escape. "You know, for a man of science who lived for months in low earth orbit in order to conduct important scientific research, you sure do hold to old wives' tales."

"It works. I know from personal experience."

"Anecdotal evidence." I shuffled off the bed in a huff trying to suppress the follow-up gagging as I hobbled on my injured ankle toward the bathroom. It was much sorer today, and there was a fairly large and dark bruise around the area I'd scraped. "And as you know, it's faulty and proves nothing."

"No water, Gray," he called through the bathroom door as I shut it. I opened it up again and blew him a big old raspberry, then slammed it.

Before even going pee—which I had to do urgently—I managed to brush my teeth to get that gross taste out of my mouth.

As I used the toilet and washed my hands, I couldn't help but notice the shambles we'd left the bathroom in last night after Ryan patched up my ankle. The floor was covered in discarded, bloody clothes and towels, including Ryan's pants. The pile included the shirt that had been used as a bandage around my ankle, and was now summarily soaked in scary amounts of my dried blood. No wonder he'd freaked out.

The laundry area was tucked behind a closet door in this very bathroom, so in order to keep my mind off of not being able to drink water, I gathered everything up to put into the washing machine for a good long soak.

I systematically emptied pockets. There was nothing in my jeans, but his pants were weighted down by something bulky. I yanked his phone out of the pocket and it illuminated. Turning to set it on the counter before tossing the pants into the washer, I hesitated, noticing that he had five missed calls and some messages from a contact named Karebear.

Automatically my eyes drifted to the top of the updates while wondering how the heck he was getting texts and calls up here. The reception bar clearly said, NO SERVICE. The top text was dated the day before and read:

KareBear: How's Tahoe? We had a great day, but I'm worried about not hearing from you. Have to admit I can't stop thinking about the other night.

My stomach did a sick sort of dip, and I yanked the phone away from my gaze before succumbing to the temptation to read the rest. Placing the phone facedown on the counter, I tossed his pants into the cold water with the other clothing and the towels. I had no hope of saving the shirt—it was pretty darn bloody—but I threw it in there just in case.

It occurred to me that he must have received all those updates when we were down at the lakeside yesterday evening. Maybe there was a small bubble of cell reception there. I hadn't had my phone with me, nor had I really felt the need to check. Obviously he hadn't checked, or he would have seen *all* those phone calls and texts from KareBear.

A strange lump formed in my throat as I tried not to think about what that text meant. Likely *KareBear* was Karen, who had been living with him for the past three weeks.

And she couldn't "stop thinking about the other night." Had something happened between them? Something ugly clamped around my chest and made it hard to breathe.

Was Ryan seeing Karen romantically?

Part of me was dying to look at the rest of them, but the stronger part of me knew that he deserved his privacy and I was not in a position where I could be snoopy.

I grabbed his phone and left the bathroom.

He was standing in the bedroom in a pair of jeans but was still gloriously shirtless and showing off his flawless male beauty without any effort at all.

I tried averting my eyes as I cleared my throat. "I put all our bloody clothes in the washer to soak, and I found this in your pants."

He took the phone from my hand but immediately set it down on the nightstand without looking at it. Then he excused himself to use the bathroom.

Me? I couldn't tear my eyes from that damn phone. I stood there and stared at it the entire time he was gone, wondering what to do. *Dammit.*

A strange sort of hurt and heaviness wrapped itself around my heart. I hated not knowing about something important going on in his life. I hated being on the outside of what was going on with him.

But...but...

It was none of my business. *Double dammit.*

Then I came to a decision with a sharp nod about three seconds before he stepped back into the room. He was muttering something about trying to get a hold of Keely on the landline so we could make our escape home.

I turned to face him, my fists balled at my sides. "When I pulled your phone out of your pocket, I couldn't help but notice a ton of updates on it. Texts and missed calls. Someone named KareBear is really trying to get a hold of you."

A strange expression crossed his face. Was that concern? I steeled myself as he bent to scoop up his phone. "How is that possible? There's no reception here."

"Probably when we were down at the lake last night."

He unlocked his phone and glanced over the text messages. His face was blank as he returned the phone to the nightstand.

I stared at him expectantly though I had no right to expect anything. When he didn't say anything, I asked, "Is everything okay?"

He flicked a glance at me and then ran a hand through his hair, walking over to the huge windows to glance down at the lake below. "Everything's fine," he replied in a clipped voice.

I blinked, noticing the tense posture, the way he closed himself off effortlessly. Gone was the joking concern about my hangover, the attentive preparation of a remedy, and his cheerful coaxing of me to drink it.

It was like a different man standing here in this room.

It was like standing in the room with the man who'd callously dumped me four weeks before.

That thought pissed me off, so I decided to goad him. "So is KareBear the new trainer-with-benefits?"

His back muscles rippled as he stuffed his hands into the pockets of his jeans. Swiveling at the waist, he flicked me a very annoyed glance over his shoulder. "It's Karen Freed." He confirmed my guess.

"Oh." I swallowed. "I'm sorry." What else could I say? There was a ton of history between Ryan and Karen that I knew nothing about. And he was not obligated to talk to me about it.

I turned, pulled out one of the drawers in the dresser, and dug out a pair of yoga pants, realizing my legs were cold and covered with goose bumps. Though *those* may not have been entirely from the cold, but instead from the strange premonitions I was getting from his behavior and his sparse delivery of this new development.

Bending, I pulled on the yoga pants and wrapped my arms around myself. "Well it's been close enough to thirty minutes, so I'm gonna go grab a glass of water."

And before he could reply or turn around or anything, I left the room and slowly hobbled up the stairs. He was at my side before I was even halfway up, insisting on grabbing me around the waist and supporting me.

Once we made it to the top of the stairs, he directed me to a stool at the kitchen counter and bent to inspect my ankle. I tried to ignore his incredible smell as it wafted by my nose when his body bent over mine. Or the memory of the feel of that body pressed on top of mine. My eyes closed. *Goddamn...*

"I'm concerned by the amount of bruising around this wound. There's a lot of internal bleeding in the tissues."

"Well as a natural side effect of the blood thinners, I bruise easily. Crazy easily, actually. It will work itself out. I've long since stopped bleeding."

He pressed against the bruise with his thumbs to check the swelling and grunted noncommittally. My lips thinned, and I fought to stomp out those flickers of excitement that were stoked by even the lightest touch of his fingers.

I pulled my foot away and recoiled from him. A flash of irritation illuminated his blue eyes, but I ignored it. I slid off the stool and hobbled to the fridge to pull out a bottle of water. I wasn't even remotely interested in breakfast, despite not having eaten dinner the night before, but I felt like I could drink an entire river.

Ryan sat on the stool I'd just vacated and watched me, leaning on his elbows as I downed half the bottle. When I finally came up for air, he asked if I'd hand him one and I did. He uncapped it, took a small sip and recapped it again.

"So what's with this sudden change of attitude?" he asked quietly.

I raised a brow but didn't outright ask the question.

"You closed yourself right off when you came back from the bathroom."

I finished off the water and then tossed the empty bottle in the recycling container. Then I took a deep breath. "Self-preservation, Ryan. I'm guarded."

He nodded. "Because of what you saw on my phone?"

I held up a hand. "I only read the first message, I swear. I tried very hard not to violate your privacy." My voice shook on the last few words, and I could've cursed myself for my weakness.

"There's nothing going on between me and Karen," he said quietly. Then he took a deep breath and let it go. "*Yet.*"

I blinked, and as his words sunk in, I could literally feel the blood drain from my own face. I put a hand on the fridge to brace myself, but every organ in my body felt as if it had just fallen a foot from its natural resting spot.

What the hell did *that* mean? *Yet?*

I watched him with wide eyes and willed him to continue, but his gaze skittered guiltily away from mine.

So I waited.

Chapter Eighteen
Ryan

THERE WAS NO WAY NOT TO NOTICE THE WAY HER features paled as she stared at me expectantly. I'd dropped the bomb, hadn't I? Time to follow through.

It was clear that Gray still had those feelings. She might be good at hiding them but she wasn't *that* good. She'd let it slip a few times for a fraction of a minute here and there. Part of me was gratified to witness that, and the other part of me was horrified.

I also knew that if Karen agreed to my proposal—and that was a big if—then Gray had the right to know what might happen. It all made sense. So why was it so hard to get the words out?

I swallowed. "Karen and I have been spending a lot of time together. We've been doing a lot of talking."

Gray didn't move, just gripped her upper arms looking alarmingly pale.

I took a deep breath and laced my fingers together. It was easier to look at them than to notice the stricken look in her eyes.

"She, uh..." My voice trembled just a little, and I cleared my throat. "She's confided in me. In addition, AJ's not doing so well. He's traumatized and has been having nightmares. He's missing his dad a lot."

241

242 | BRENNA AUBREY

I reached a hand up to rub my forehead, mostly to hide my face from her for a moment. It wouldn't suit for her to see how torn I was about this. She approached slowly until she stood opposite the counter from me, but she said nothing.

I still couldn't look in her eyes, though. "Karen's also been having some issues that I probably shouldn't talk about. But it's been a real struggle for them, and I haven't been there the way I should have been. I promised I would be, but I wasn't. I was too tied up..." My voice died out.

"In your guilt," she continued in a tiny voice.

I clenched my jaw and my eyes cut to look out the window instead of at her. "I've only seen the tip of the iceberg of what AJ's been suffering, but I'm worried. I *love* that kid. I—"

I shook my head, willing away those memories. I'd been there when he took his first step. When he was a baby, his tiny fist squeezing my finger. Feeding him a bottle. Playing catch...

My voice caught when I continued. "I sat in the waiting room at the hospital for a day and a half when he was born. After his mom and dad, I was the first person to hold him. Even before his grandparents. He's like my blood nephew."

I chanced a glance at her, almost expecting her to be angry or even to show more of that strange stoicism she'd been demonstrating for the past month. Instead, her brows were pinched together, and there was nothing but pure concern and sympathy on her face. For some reason, that made me even more emotional. I had to swallow the prickly sensation in my throat.

"I can be a father to AJ. I can take care of them."

"And that means..."

I brought my laced hands to my mouth and watched her over them. "It means I told Karen I wanted to marry her and be AJ's stepdad."

She nodded solemnly, her eyes falling to the cold marble as she considered this information. She brought her hands to rest on the counter in front of her.

"Are you…" Her voice died in her throat, and she cleared it with determination. "So, does that mean you're in love with her?"

Love. There'd be no talk of that fairytale or any other. Not today. I rubbed my lip with the back of my knuckle. My two days' growth of whiskers were getting itchy and yet I had zero desire to shave. I felt protected like this, hidden. *Shielded.*

Ridiculous to think that something so trivial could protect me from the unwitting power Gray had over me.

"I want AJ to have a dad. I lost my dad when I was a teenager. I know how it feels. It sucks. AJ is so young, and he looks up to me. I'm the next best thing to his dad. And I can take care of her, too."

Gray flinched slightly when I said *her.* It stabbed me to see it, but damn it, I had to hurt someone with this, didn't I? I had to hurt *her.* Again.

I couldn't have her, so did that mean I should live the rest of my life alone? I no longer wanted to be alone. I wanted a family. What had changed, I wondered?

The silence in the room was deafening, and I could all but see the defensive wall go up between us. But that wasn't a surprise. What else could I expect from her?

She was watching me with that uncomfortable, unwavering stare she had so often used before. "Do you love Karen Freed?" she repeated.

A deep breath in, my hands clasped together tightly. I blew the breath out and answered, "Yes. I've known her since we were teenagers. She's a dear friend. I do love her."

Gray wasn't looking at me now, just very closely studying the surface of the marble in front of her hands. Then she cleared her throat, and when she spoke, it was in a quiet, low voice, as if it were more of a struggle than normal to keep her own emotions in check.

"If you choose to be with them, it should be for the right reasons. You should make the decision as a way to guarantee your own happiness along with theirs. If you do this, will you be happy?"

"There's more than one right reason to choose to be with someone, Gray. This is as right a reason as any other."

I didn't give the answer that was hovering on my lips because the words would prove her right. *I don't deserve to be happy.*

I'd made the decision to break things off with her. It was heavily influenced by her shitty father forcing the issue, sure, but ultimately, it had been my call.

I buried my face in my hands. What I wanted and what I should do were two entirely different things. Two entirely different women. Two entirely different futures.

Fucking hell.

"Ryan," she said, pulling my attention back to her. She pushed her glasses up her nose. "You deserve to be happy. You need to fight for that, for yourself and your future."

"If she agrees to it, I think we'd be happy."

She finally flicked a glance back up at me. "So she didn't answer you?"

"We're on hold until after the test flight. She wants to take things slow."

Something I said there—about the test flight, probably— seemed to hit her hard. She flinched and moved back from the counter, turning and going to the fridge to open it only to stare for long moments and then close it.

She laced her fingers through her hairline, pulling roughly. "You're making a mistake."

I hissed out a long breath, then took a pull from the water bottle. "That depends on how you look at it."

She shook her head in stunned disbelief.

"Does she know? About Xander's tether? Did you tell her that her husband defied orders and released his tether so he could get to you and help you?"

I stared at her, speechless. Something vital coiled around my insides and squeezed. I couldn't believe that she would use the knowledge I'd given her against me.

Why had I even told her in the first place?

Anger tightened my spine and flushed my face. I stood from the stool. "It's my life. My decision."

I turned to go, but her voice, suddenly forceful and no-nonsense, stopped me. "It *is* your decision. But it's *not* just your life. It's Karen's life. It's AJ's life." She halted and drew a deep breath and added in a trembling voice drenched in unshed tears, "It's *my* life."

It gutted me to hear and I was thankful that my back was to her. I closed my eyes and fought for control where she couldn't see me.

"I don't see you running right over to confront your dad about his interference in your life." I returned in an equally forceful voice. And when she said nothing, I left the room and went downstairs to take a shower.

I had barely stepped through the threshold of the bedroom when the loud clatter of shattering glass halted me in my tracks. My heart also nearly stopped. Had she cut herself again? Cold fear streaked through me, and I darted up the stairs and was back in the kitchen in an instant. She'd moved to the other side of the room, stooping to look at something.

When she reached out, I noticed what looked like a shattered drinking glass right in front of her on the floor. *Oh, hell no.*

"Get the fuck away from that," I yelled, and she jumped in shock. Standing, she looked at me over her shoulder. There were tears on her cheeks. I tried not to notice them, but that was damn near impossible. Had I ever seen her cry before?

Once...in Houston. She'd cried because she'd felt empathy for me.

But I'd never seen her cry for herself. Not even the day I'd ended things with her.

She turned away from me and once again bent over the broken glass. My vision blurred as my blood pressure shot through the roof. Unable to think logically, I stooped and grabbed her, yanking her off the floor without a second thought.

"Did you drop it?"

"I threw it."

She jerked in my arms, clearly shocked. I hauled her into the living room. "You are not touching that glass," I ground out. The last thing I needed was for her to cut herself again. "Don't be stupid."

"Oh, too late for *that*," she spat, violently pushing away from me the minute I set her down. "I *am* stupid! I'm so *fucking* stupid."

I took in a deep breath and tore my gaze away. "I'll clean this up. And then you can find something non-breakable to throw. And you can throw it at me this time."

She turned from me and hastily wiped her face with the back of her hand, obviously mortified that I'd seen her tears. I grabbed the broom and dustpan and hastily swept up all the broken pieces, dumping them into the garbage.

Coming back into the living room, I approached her slowly. She was staring out the window now, eyes fixed determinedly on the lake. Her eyes were red, but her cheeks were dry.

"You all right?" I asked.

She cleared her throat. "No."

That wall was up again. I rubbed the back of my neck and tried to think of what to say. How could I make her understand? How could I soothe her pain?

The answer was that I couldn't. She'd continue to bury it under her calm façade and suffer in silence for months to come.

"I knew there had to be something more," she said in a low voice that trembled. "I knew it. Otherwise we could have put our relationship on hold. You could have come to me and told me about my dad's threats. We'd wait for the test flight to come and go. Then I'd confront my dad and tell him he couldn't do this."

I frowned. Those thoughts had run through my mind as well. But they hadn't added up, not in the end. I didn't want to be the man to come between her and her father, to break up what little family she had left. I didn't want to be the man who forced her to choose.

And I didn't deserve her.

"I made the decision to end this thing between us before Karen came back. My being with Karen has nothing to do with you and me."

"You gave up so easily," she said in a wistful, quiet voice, as if she wasn't really speaking to me at all. "Didn't even give us a chance to work through it."

I stared at her, my fists clenching and unclenching as I fought for a response. I didn't have one.

She jerked her head toward me. "Do you think it's going to be easy with Karen? You're already planning to keep secrets from her. Isn't that right? You believe her husband cashed in his life for you so now you've gotta do the same for him."

Her words penetrated like a knife's blade, and my skin flushed hot. I held out a hand in warning, to tell her to stop. "*Enough,* Gray. Grab something else to throw. Throw it at me if you want. Let it all out and finally show an emotion for once. It might be good for you."

"*Finally* show an emotion?" she turned to me, the color in her face deepening.

I reached up and rubbed the back of my neck, wondering if I should be worried about the way those green eyes sparked when she looked at me. "You have to admit that you've been rather— stoic—about it all."

She blinked. "You're criticizing me for being too stoic? That's rich. That very emotional stability is what you've relied on in the past—to your benefit." Her face flushed and she dramatically waved a hand in the air. "Just because I'm not falling on the ground tearing my hair out and wailing at the top of my lungs doesn't mean I don't care. Or were you expecting me to beg you like your trainer-with-benefits did?"

Wow. Well, if she'd been holding back before she certainly felt no hesitation in letting it all out any longer.

"I just—" And I cut myself off when she dove for a huge ceramic vase on the coffee table and held it in the air as if she'd throw it at me.

I held my hands out, ready to catch it in defense, but she was shaking from head to toe. Shaking like she was blowing in a storm or being carried away by a rocket. Her hands dropped, and she let out a sob.

I went to her and took hold of the vase and pulled it out of her hands. It was heavy. Had she actually thrown it, that would have hurt. I set it back on the coffee table and turned back to her. She was still shaking so hard I couldn't resist pulling her into my arms.

With a snarl, she violently pushed away and smacked me across the chest as hard as she could. She seemed to be trying to push me back but had nowhere near the leverage to do it. I remained in place, nevertheless. She was a lot smaller than me, but she was surprisingly strong. *In more ways than one...*

"You are *unbelievable*," she huffed at me. "You are so quick to play the martyr. Lay down your life and sacrifice yourself for Karen and AJ because that's what Xander did. Isn't that just perfect?" She practically spat at me. "You'll be the hero of everyone's life but your own."

I gritted my teeth.

She didn't seem to notice my lack of response because she was in full rant mode now, gesturing stiffly with her hands.

"*You* are an asshole, Ryan Tyler!" she screamed. "And fuck you for taking something delicate, something precious like my feelings for you, and shitting all over them. You *suck*."

New tears sprang from her eyes and I stood there and took it—just as I'd learned to do during my years in the military.

But somehow this was worse because it was on an emotional level, one I'd never learned to properly deal with. Watching my sweet, beautiful girl suffer because of me was no easy feat. And to think that she'd hidden that hurt all along. What kind of strength had it required to do that?

It only added to that same feeling of worthlessness I carried. Yet another thing I'd touched had turned to shit.

"You're right. I'm sorry." My reply was faint, hoarse.

"No, you're not fucking sorry. You're going up again when you clearly aren't ready to. You're in denial about every single goddamn aspect of your life. Because you're reckless and you don't care." She gulped another deep breath. "Because you want to die."

I could take her anger, and I would. If she needed a punching bag, I could be that, too. Still, those words hurt. She knew exactly where to throw them, like darts sinking in to all the most vulnerable places. The places where I doubted myself.

"Your life is a shitshow. You think you've fooled everyone by rehabilitating your image, because no one knows about the PTSD or the real reasons you're doing any of this—the flight, the proposal to Karen. You can still be there for them and care for them without giving up your life for them."

"Gray—" I growled through my teeth in warning, but she rode right over me.

"You've only regretted one thing in the past year and that was surviving the accident. You've made your mind up that you'll get exactly what you *deserve*." She emphasized the words with air quotes and eyes that flashed with fury. "There's no need for you to play the martyr because you're *already* dead inside. You died the same day Xander Freed did."

I swallowed, and every muscle tensed in anger. She was pulling no punches now.

She swiped indignantly at the corners of her eyes as if the tears were a hindrance to her rage. Then she stepped toward me so that we were standing very close. Her scent—I could smell those delicious minty strawberries. Memories of her body and mine and being wrapped up in that lovely, lovely scent were awakening other heated sensations inside me besides anger.

"I told you I loved you, and you couldn't love me back because you're dead inside. So you pushed me away. My dad was just a convenient excuse." Her eyes narrowed at me. "He made it so easy for you."

A violent breath expelled from my chest like she'd punched me on my sternum. "What the fuck makes you think anything about this was easy, Gray?"

She held my gaze, staring me down like a mad dog about to go toe to toe in a death match. She said I was dead inside. Maybe she was partially right. But a part of my heart certainly didn't feel dead—the part that simultaneously ached for her and wanted to push her even further away because it hurt so goddamn much.

The night before, when I'd held her in my arms as she slept, I'd whispered it to her. Allowed myself that one moment of weakness, that slip in my control. And just to be safe, I'd told her in Russian. *Ya tebya lyublyu. Navsegda.* I love you. Forever.

A man who wasn't broken beyond repair would shout it from the rooftops, share it with all his friends and loved ones, rejoice in what he'd found. This brilliant ray of light, this brazen hope, the perfect period to end all my sentences, the mirror for my thoughts, a once in a lifetime kind of love. A cause for celebration...

...For a man who wasn't broken beyond repair. A man who wasn't me.

She shook her head, her eyes sad and her lips tightening against her teeth. "You gave up, though. You took the easy way out. If you cared—"

"I do care. A lot. More than—" I shook my head and looked away, running a hand through my hair. What purpose did it serve to tell her this now? Wouldn't it be easier to let her just hate me and get on with her life?

That thought punched through me hardest of all.

No. Because I didn't want her to get on with her life. The thought of it made me simultaneously want to go on a killing spree and want to puke. I was a selfish bastard.

Our gazes locked and tangled, heat and tension simmering between us. And as pissed as I was, I wanted nothing more than to grab her and pull her against my body and make her understand how much she really did matter to me. How much I craved and needed her, even though I couldn't have her.

After a long, tense moment, she shook her head, folding her arms over her chest. Unshed tears glistened in her eyes. "Well, I can't say it wasn't a learning experience," she said in a husky voice. "I gave my heart away too easily with you, apparently. I won't do that with whoever else comes along next time."

Next time. With another man.

I closed my eyes, instantly disgusted by the thought of another man's hands on her. "Gray," I groaned.

"Life may have stopped for you because you don't feel you deserve more. But it doesn't end here for me." She gestured to the center of her chest, her chin coming up defiantly. "I want to live, and I want to be happy. So I will move on. Just like you're moving on. You'll marry Karen. I'll date other men, and I'll sleep with them if I want. Aaron—"

My hand shot out and grabbed her upper arm, squeezing it. "Stop."

She pulled against my hold and I wouldn't release her. So she continued to talk while my hand tightened. "Maybe I need a rebound relationship. Aaron's a nice guy. Not too old for me—"

My other hand swooped up and grabbed her hair and I pulled her against me. I wouldn't listen to another word of this, and I knew of only one way to shut her up. My mouth landed on hers forcefully, covering it and smothering her diatribe. *Thank God.* My mouth fused to hers, lips sealing against lips.

She'd refused my words. She would refuse my claim on her. But *this*...could she refuse this?

She swayed toward me and then away, though not forcefully enough to convince me she was trying to extricate herself from me. My tongue slid into her mouth, and she let out a whimper that ignited my blood to boiling in less than five seconds flat. Oh God, how I'd missed this. This might be a huge mistake, but it felt so good, I didn't fucking care.

My cock was hard in an instant, and I fought every instinct to pull her down on the couch and have my way with her right then.

When my mouth freed hers, we were breathing fast and I hesitated, waiting for her to voice an objection or tell me to let her go.

"I'm so fucking pissed at you, Ryan," she panted, her face against mine.

"I know," I answered.

She shivered against me, and I bent and kissed her neck, sucking the soft skin there. She shuddered again, her body falling against mine. Her hands clamped onto my shoulders, and her head fell forward. Her mouth was on my neck, and hot pleasure zinged through my body. The feel of her hands and her mouth were making me drunk with need for her.

Pain flared at my neck where her mouth worked against it. Her kiss had quickly transformed into a bite, her teeth sinking into my skin. This was no light nip. No, she meant business, maybe even to draw blood. I let out a gasp, and she clamped down harder.

"Ah, fuck," I rasped. My cock swelled. So she was pissed, and she was trying to inflict a little pain. It was only serving to turn me on even more. Her hand slid from my shoulder to smooth across my chest, my belly, all while keeping my skin clamped between her teeth. Her hand slipped beneath the waistband of my jeans and into my underwear, grasping my erection without hesitation.

"If you start using your fingernails, we are going to have words," I warned with a light laugh in my husky voice. The pain from her teeth eased up. I used my hold on her hair to yank her head back and look into her face. Her eyes were filled with tears again, her skin was flushed an angry red, and her jaw was clamped shut.

"I want to fuck you, Gray. Right now."

Her eyes roamed my face. "Do it, then." Her hand tightened around my cock, stroking it boldly, and I could barely keep my eyes focused. It felt so good, I wondered for a ridiculous moment if I was going to come in my pants.

'I don't have a condom."

"I'm on birth control."

I blinked, stiffening. Every part of my skin was burning with sudden fury. She hadn't been on birth control when we had been fucking constantly, but now suddenly she was? Had she been serious about wanting to go out and start sleeping with other men? The thought enraged me, and my fingers tangled in her hair, pulling it tight. She let loose a gasp and another tear leaked out of her eye.

"I don't want you to sleep with other men," I suddenly ground out, surprising even myself.

She stiffened. "Who the fuck do you think you are? You just told me that you want to marry another woman, and in almost the same breath, you say you don't want *me* to sleep with anyone else? So I should take holy orders and live in a convent? It's none of your business who I fuck."

Oh, she knew how to push my buttons all right. She wanted to play rough? I could play rough. She thought she was taking control, but she was only making me want to ride her harder.

"It's my business who fucks you today." I grabbed her t-shirt by the hem and dragged it up over her head, tangling her arms in it. When I pushed her against the wall beside the floor to ceiling windows, I raised her arms over her head, using the tangled t-shirt to hold them together with one hand.

In seconds her nipple was in my mouth, beading and puckering obediently for me. Yes, I knew...I knew how much she liked that. Sometimes I loved to just spend an hour doing nothing but touch her and suck on her sweet tits while she moaned and begged for my cock. I loved making her wait for it.

But that wouldn't happen now. I couldn't wait that long to get inside her. My mouth moved to the other one and nipped it before sucking it completely into my mouth. She yelped and swayed against me. I rolled my tongue over her nipple continuously while she rewarded me with her moans. My free hand slid into her underwear, between her legs, stroking her sex.

She was *very* wet. I summoned my last shred of control from God only knew where to keep from tearing those panties off of her and burying myself in her heat. Quickly, I found her clit and slowly rubbed her there, eliciting sound from her like a harpist plucking strings on his instrument.

I knew her body—better than I knew any other woman's body. She didn't know it, but I'd never made love to any other woman as many times as I'd made love to her. A man might think he'd get bored from the same woman over and over again. But not her, not this. It was hot every time, and I could never get enough of her.

I knew from the quickies that had us going from zero to climax in less than ten minutes while parked in my car in a secluded spot at the beach. *And* I knew from the long, slow sessions that had me spending hours concentrating on the most sensitive parts of her body and making her come as often as I could.

I *knew* this beautiful body of hers, like the star maps I had to memorize in astronaut training. I knew which spots elicited which sounds from deep in her throat. Like music. And like an instrument, her body obeyed my hands, my mouth.

Now, her spine pressed against the wall, she was wet and begging me to bring her to climax.

"Ryan, please," she gasped when my hand had slowed, prolonging her ecstasy. "I want to come."

"Shoulda thought about that before you slapped and bit me, little tigress."

She thrust her hips forward to press against my hand where I stroked her clit and I pulled it away. "Nope. No baby girl. Not yet."

I unbuttoned my jeans and stepped out of them and my boxers, then discarded her yoga pants and underwear. She lowered her arms and freed them from the t-shirt. When she stepped toward me, I stopped her, winding my hand in her short hair again, pulling it hard.

Her head shot back, and I devoured her neck. "I haven't forgotten how naughty you've been." Then I pulled harder, until her knees buckled obediently, and she slowly sank to the ground in front of me.

"I think it's time to start asking me for forgiveness...on your knees."

"Or I could use my teeth again."

I drew back, and we locked gazes. She raised her brows. She didn't look any less angry than she had before. In fact, she looked even more pissed since I'd denied her an orgasm. She reached out and grabbed my cock, holding it at the base, and I froze. Then she pressed her mouth to it and began to lick and suck me. Raw pleasure seared through me, and she began to move her head pulling it back and then forward again quickly. Too quickly.

I pressed my hand to her head again to slow her pace. "Yeah," I ground out between gasps as her tongue slid down my length and I lost all sense of my surroundings, sinking into the warmth of her delicious mouth. "Just like that, baby girl."

Oh man. Gratification and heat spread out from where her mouth was holding and sucking me. My eyelids drooped closed, and I could only feel the suction of her mouth, her lips and her tongue. Pure pleasure. I began to feel the familiar build to climax and for a moment considered how amazing it would feel to come in her mouth.

When she pulled away and stood quickly, I was jolted back to reality but not surprised. It figured that she'd try to get me back for my stunt. Her mouth trembled, and a small smile appeared, though I could read in her eyes that the hurts of earlier were not forgotten. She reached out and raked her nails down my chest. I gasped and grabbed her wrist to stop her.

The other hand repeated the action. And the pain and pleasure mingled, stirring my body to even greater arousal. If I didn't get inside her soon, I was going to explode from the tension.

"If I'm a tigress, I better act like one." I grabbed her other wrist and looked down across my chest. She'd left two sets of dark red tracks. How? Her nails weren't even that long.

Still holding her wrists, I flipped her away from me and pressed her front to the window. She moaned and gasped and wriggled back against me, complaining that it was cold. I closed my eyes and relished every second of it.

I took the top of her ear into my mouth and this time it was my turn to use my teeth. She tilted her head away, catching her breath suddenly, and I hooked my hand around her hips pulling them back against me. Returning my mouth to her ear, I murmured the question, "What do you want?"

"I want your cock inside me," she said without hesitation.

And without hesitation, I gave it to her. In one smooth, firm, satisfying stroke I sank into her heat with no barrier between us for the very first time.

Holy fuck, it felt...amazing. To feel her heat, her wetness wrapped around me naked and soft, like silk. Snug-fitting silk.

Was there any part of this woman that wasn't exquisite?

And it wasn't just her body, no. It was her voice, her laugh, her brilliance.

It was the fact that she made me laugh. She made me think.

I moved inside her, and she whimpered and writhed, her ass pressing against my pelvis, making me insane with desire. I pushed myself into her over and over again, not sparing the pace or the force I used. She gasped and grunted, her face pressed against the window, my mouth pressed against her temple, I closed my eyes and fantasized that I was speaking to her...

That with my body I was telling her the things I wished I could say with words—

That she held my heart in her hands.

And she could crush it at any time.

That there wasn't a day or even an hour that passed when we weren't together that I didn't think about her, want to talk to her, ask her an opinion, share a joke with her. That I didn't want to feel her skin, her body, her hands on mine.

I pushed faster, feeling that coveted climb to release. She moved backwards against me, matching her movements perfectly to mine. My hand came around her front to rub her clit while I moved into her from behind.

The sound of her moans told me she was close to climax. I slowed my pace so that she'd get there first. Despite her little hellcat act, she deserved it. And I loved feeling her tighten and convulse around me when I was still inside her.

Just a few more seconds, and there it was. Her head fell back against my shoulder and her back arched as she tensed, the orgasm ripping through her body. During those minutes, I stopped my movements and just concentrated on her, her pleasure, her moment.

She started breathing again when her orgasm faded away, and I pushed myself into her again, this time harder. Her hands found the window sill and she pushed back against me. I took her by the hips and worked my way to the finish doing as I'd promised—riding her hard and enjoying her moans as I did.

I stilled, the orgasm washing over me like a crashing wave on the beach, pulling me with the force of the sea and pounding down on me, stealing my breath. Tension washed from my muscles as I emptied into her, pushing in as deep as possible.

When I finally came back to the real world, I almost lost my balance, but pulled her up against me. We turned and collapsed on the couch and I lay back for a moment. She settled against the other arm of the couch. It was only two feet away, but it may as well have been miles.

Without a word, I stood once I'd regained my bearings and gently pulled her to her feet in front of me. Planting a kiss on her forehead, I swung to pick her up.

Her head lolled against my shoulder, and I carried her down the stairs to the bathroom. After we cleaned up, I took her hand in mine and led her to the bed. Without a word, she sank down beside me, and I pulled her flush against me.

I have no idea how long we stayed like that until we dozed off, wrapped up in each other. But I remember thinking that this was how I would love to go to bed every night. Wrapped up in her after we'd exhausted ourselves with sex.

But I knew it was not to be.

We had today and that was it. Once we went home, everything would change again.

CHAPTER NINETEEN
GRAY

WHEN I WOKE UP FROM MY CAT NAP, HE WAS nibbling on the back of my neck. Of course, the feeling was evoking the most pleasant tingles all down my spine, down my legs, down to that warm place between my thighs.

My eyes closed again almost as quickly as they'd cracked open. It was about noon on Sunday. We didn't have much time left. His mouth slid to devour my ear, which reminded me that I was utterly famished.

I leaned back against him. "Are you hungry? I sure am."

His mouth slipped lower onto my neck and he spoke in between placing his mouth in all the right spots that he knew made me crazy. "I could—eat a—bite or two. Before..."

"Before what? Before we leave?" I teased, knowing exactly what he meant by 'before.'

He grinned. "That, too."

"Mmm. I haven't eaten a bite since...well we never ate last night so I haven't eaten anything since lunch yesterday. Then you decided to get me drunk on vodka."

His head came up and he looked into my face. "Wait, hold the phone, what? I didn't get you drunk on vodka. You got yourself drunk."

I raised my eyebrow. "Who brought the vodka down here, hmm? You're a bad influence."

Ryan pulled away and fell against his pillow, staring straight up at the ceiling, thinking. I rolled over to plant a kiss on his cheek, surreptitiously examining the dark red and purple bite marks on his neck. Wow, I'd been savage in my rage.

Well in truth, he deserved every one of those bite marks and scratches and slaps. Okay, so maybe I'd gone a little bit overboard.

I pushed my way out of bed, guilty at the thought. I never lost my cool like that. Ever. But hearing those things from him—his plan to not only continue with the test flight but to also pursue Karen.

I'd called out his tendency to live his life for everyone else—becoming a SEAL for his dad, becoming an astronaut on a bet, flying again for Xander—and he'd then doubled down on it. Now he was going to marry Xander's widow and take care of his son. The thought of it still made me sick inside. I hoped, rather than knew, that I'd get through to him and make him realize the big mistake he was making.

"I'll warm us up something for lunch, if you want," I said.

After using the bathroom, I did just that. We sat at the table and stared out over the lake and ate in silence. Thick, meaningful silence. A silence that meant there were numerous conversations we needed to have, but in that moment, we didn't possess the desire or wherewithal to have them.

Finally, once our plates were empty, I reached across the table and covered his hand with mine. "I'm sorry I, um, bit you."

An eyebrow shot up, and a cocky smile curled on his lip. "I'm not." He laughed. "It was really hot."

My eyes darted away, and my hand retreated only a few inches before he reached out and caught it, squeezing it inside his strong fingers. Our eyes met and held.

He swallowed and shook his head. "How can such a sweet and calm person like you have a gaze like that?"

I frowned. "Like what?"

He sobered, his focus dropping to the table. "Sometimes it feels like you can burn a hole right through me with your eyes. Like a magnifying glass in the sun zeroing in on a dried leaf."

I raised a brow. "Like Cyclops from the X-Men?"

He laughed. "I meant on a figurative level. And I think you perfectly understood that."

I snickered. "Pari calls it my *look*. That night before I first went to your house she told me 'don't do the look.'"

He frowned. "Did she think you'd scare me away?"

I shrugged, remembering that night, remembering how simple and uncomplicated my life had been before I fell for him. Swallowing what felt like a mountain inside my throat, I took our plates to the sink, filling it partway with warm, soapy water.

After a few minutes of being lost in his own world, staring at the glass table top, he also got up and followed me into the kitchen where I was cleaning off the plates with a sponge.

He came up behind me, pressing his solid body against mine and reaching around me to take hold of my wrists. Instant desire flared in every corner of my body that I was aware of. My eyes drifted closed and I savored his touch. His fingers, as they lightly caressed the sensitive skin inside my wrist, the feel of his lips against my ear as he murmured to me.

"Can't risk you having another accident. It's a pain to get you to stop bleeding."

My heart jumped at the feel of him against me, the sound of his hoarse whisper, the light touch of his hands as they cupped mine and guided them through the motions of washing the dishes and rinsing them. The feel of his warm skin against mine.

This commonplace task that I did every day was now turned into something more. Something sensual and connected. My back shifted against him and my shoulder blades pressed into his hard pecs. I could've spent the rest of my days washing dishes if it was like *this*.

I leaned my head against his shoulder and let out a contented sigh. "I just want to enjoy this moment. Be in this moment with you and not think about anything that happened before or what's going to happen next."

There was a long pause as his hands on mine slowed. Then he turned off the faucet, grabbed the towel and slowly, attentively wiped my hands dry with the soft cloth as I relaxed against him and relied on his sturdy form to hold me up.

Then his arms came around me, wrapping around my torso, holding me fast against him. His lips skimmed against my neck. "There's only this moment, Gray. There's only you and me."

He held me tight, and I kept my mind firmly grounded in the way it felt to be wrapped up by him.

I hated him because he was giving himself to someone else instead of me. I hated him because of the hold he had over me when he touched me, when I smelled him. I hated him because he was so screwed up he didn't know what he deserved and pushed away any chance at happiness.

I hated him.

And I loved him.

Tears came. Leaking from my eyes silently. They came so easily now despite the old habits rising up in the back of my mind to try to suppress them. I fought to ignore those voices and let the tears flow. It was tougher than it should have been.

He was kissing my neck and holding me tenderly, and I put those thoughts out of my head. I didn't fret over yesterday, and I didn't stress out about tomorrow.

It was only today. It was only *right now*.

Slowly, he turned me, still in his arms and I had no time to wipe those tears away. Two thin, salty streams cut paths down my cheeks and clung to my jaw. He dried them with his hands and kissed a trail down each cheek.

I shivered in his arms, and a small sob sounded at the back of my throat.

"Shh." He kissed my temple and rocked me against him. We swayed in unison as if dancing to unheard music. As if dancing...

To the persistent click of my heart.

I buried my face in his shirt and inhaled. Soap and *him*. His smell. Warm awareness sluiced down my back like the spray of a comforting shower.

We stood like that for a long time, just holding each other, swaying. And as I'd hoped, my thoughts narrowed down to this moment, to the awareness of only him and me. I was warm and melting against him. Every inch of my skin burned for him.

And judging from the hard feel of his arousal pressed against my stomach, I knew he felt the same. I didn't even have to ask.

His arms tightened, and I pulled my head back to look into his face. "I want you," I whispered.

He smiled. "You want me? You want to ride on my Saturn V rocket all the way to the Moon?"

I laughed—not just a little. Maybe it wasn't the funniest joke, but it came at a moment when I needed to be reminded why we had so much fun together. He could always make me laugh. And I could do the same for him.

"Yet another cheesy one-liner to add to the collection. Only a man like you would compare his equipment to the largest rocket ever to launch into space."

Now it was his turn to laugh and his arms gave another instinctive squeeze, as if his entire body was laughing, not just his eyes, not just his mouth or his throat.

"Only a woman like you would get the joke."

Suddenly his mouth was on mine, and I wasn't laughing anymore. He hitched me against him and I jumped, wrapping my legs around him and crossing my ankles at the small of his back.

We kissed while he walked us into the living room, our tongues tangling desperately, speaking in a language that we couldn't express any other way. A language that didn't need words but communicated all the things we needed to say at that moment.

He stopped walking when we hit the couch, releasing me so that I slid slowly down his body. He groaned roughly when I rubbed up against his prominent erection, and without hesitation, he reached out, snatched the bottom of my t-shirt and pulled it off of me in one swift move.

So I returned the favor and pulled off his shirt—with a little help from him, given his height advantage over me. Next, he pushed down my yoga pants with no small urgency, then I pushed *him* onto the couch before he could do anything else. His eyes flew wide open when he landed, sitting on the couch, and I climbed into his lap, straddling him.

He grabbed my butt and scooted me forward so that I was resting right on top of his erection with only the layer of his sweat pants between us. I ground my hips against him and his eyes glazed over.

He cupped my breasts, rubbing his thumbs over my nipples until they stood, taut and peaked. Then he put them in his mouth, in turn, making me crazy with the attentions of his hot tongue. When he straightened, we sat for a long, tense moment imbued with anticipation. Nose to nose, we stared into each other's eyes.

"I don't know how to make a moment last longer than it takes to pass," he said. "But I know what a big memory is when I see it. And these moments will be a future beautiful memory for both of us."

I bent forward and kissed him, then pulled back. "There's no future. Just *now*."

Pulling the waistband of his sweats down, I freed his cock, then carefully lowered myself onto him, with his large hands on my hips, guiding me.

My movements were frantic, urgent at first. I couldn't get enough of him, marveled at the feeling, every thrust, the sensation of him filling me up. The way we seemed to fit so perfectly. His hands tightened on my hips, slowing me down. And each of us jockeyed in that way for control.

We were both breathing fast and with that slower pace, fell into a natural, intuitive rhythm. I hooked my fingers around the frame of the couch behind his shoulders to brace myself to move faster.

It was a continuous struggle, me wanting to move faster, to reach that relief, and him wanting it to last. But I took his advice and concentrated on the moment to make it a memory that I could savor later.

When I came, he pulled me forward, locked his lips on mine and pressed a hand to the small of my back to hold me still. And it was mere moments before he came, too. I leaned forward, and he squeezed me tight in his arms as the skin of our chests, clammy with our mingled sweat, adhered to one another.

For a long time, we just held each other like that. Fused together. Perhaps we were searching for more moments to collect and preserve and store away. If only we could keep them, like a snow globe we could shake to evoke this bubble in our own little world whenever we wanted to. Or maybe we were just procrastinating against the inevitable.

Later, we caught our ride—a limo with all the windows blacked out—to the airport. I quietly held Ryan's hand the entire way, but we didn't talk. He was texting someone, presumably answering Karen from earlier in the weekend. I tried to ignore the sick feeling in my stomach and the burning curiosity about what he was saying to her.

I had a few texts from my Dad's assistant and some missed calls from the man himself. I'd been putting him off with claims of being sick or working. I knew I'd have to respond to these new inquiries soon.

A text from Keely lit up my phone a few minutes later. She told me that she'd made it clear to the press that she was nowhere near Tahoe by showing up on a very public shopping trip in Beverly Hills that morning with no ring on her finger. We were all off the hook.

Our seats were a row away from each other on the short flight home, so we had no chance to speak. During the flight,

Ryan had his head turned away from me and he barely moved, which told me he was likely napping.

We returned to Long Beach—the airport from which we'd left on just the Friday before. But if felt like weeks had passed. So much had happened this weekend that my sense of time had folded in on itself. And the moment I'd been dreading was there before I knew it.

Keely had sent a car to take me home, but Ryan had parked his car in the long-term parking lot, so we would not be traveling together from that point on. Generally, the paparazzi did not stalk this smaller airport looking for celebrities like they did LAX, but to be safe, Ryan pulled me toward a corner shrouded in shadow while the driver loaded my bag into the car and waited.

"Gray," he started with a quiet voice, "I wish it didn't have to be like this."

I blinked, but thankfully the tears stayed safely behind my eyeballs, prickling to get out. "It doesn't have to be."

Without another word, he pulled me into a tight hug. I buried my face in his shirt, inhaling him. He kissed my hair, and my heart hurt with every beat. We'd found something here. Something precious in each other. We'd connected and touched hearts.

How could it have led to this moment? To us saying goodbye? Again.

He was kissing me, my temple, my cheek, my ear. "Gray," his arms tightened instinctively, "I need to tell you. I lo—"

But I pushed back from him, laying two fingers across his mouth. Now the tears were dotting my eyelids. He frowned at me in confusion.

I shook my head. "Don't say it. *Don't*. Please."

With my fingers across his mouth, he could hardly answer, but he looked from one of my eyes to the other then slowly nodded.

My hand fell away, and I cleared my throat and endeavored to speak through the tears. I'd say my piece, then I'd walk away. I'd spent the entire time on the plane getting up the courage to express what was inside, searching for and finding the perfect words.

"This hurts. It does. I won't lie. But you know, hurting is a part of living. And not taking risks isn't living. Before this I hadn't really been living. But with you, I took the risk. I gave you my heart, and I don't regret it. You'll always have a piece of it. Always."

He swallowed and looked away, but did not speak.

I put my hand on his chest to draw his attention back to me. "Ryan, promise me. Promise me you'll fight to forgive yourself. I can't stand to see you suffering from these self-inflicted wounds. The guilt and the shame. It has to end. You are keeping poison in your soul, and you'll never heal as long as it is there." I took a deep breath and swallowed. "You need to be whole. You need to live your life for yourself."

His hand came up and wrapped around my hand that rested on his chest. "You've been a bright ray of sunlight in my life..." His voice faded, as if overcome with emotion. I bit my lip to prevent a new onslaught of tears. They stung and injured me like thousands of tiny needles. Harmless and unseen by themselves, but together, they evoked agony.

"Hold on to that light," I whispered. "Don't let the darkness take over." I met his gaze and held it. "You were right. I do need to stand up to my dad. I do need to fight for what I want and not be afraid to show him—or the world, for that matter—what I'm feeling. I will. I'm going to do better. I need for you to do better, too."

He closed his eyes, took my hand and kissed it. I brushed his whiskered cheek with the back of my hand. Then I pulled away.

Maybe this was the stage of grief that brought acceptance. This backing away to the car, holding his eyes, refusing to actually say the word *goodbye.*

Maybe acceptance was knowing that he was right. He didn't deserve me. Not until he pulled himself out of that dark pit and forgave himself. Only he could extricate himself from what haunted him. Only he could fix himself.

I turned my back and walked to the car, getting in without looking over my shoulder.

Hopefully the river of tears I cried on the way home would help bathe the wounds. I would not call this weekend a success— at least not in the way that Keely had intended it with her dubious scheme.

But there had been closure. And disclosure.

And once the wounds were less raw and painful, I'd be ready to move on.

CHAPTER TWENTY
RYAN

I T WASN'T EASY TO WATCH GRAY GET INTO THE CAR AT THE airport after our weekend together. Saying goodbye without knowing when and where I'd see her again was worse. It took every bit of control I had not to run to my own car and follow her home.

It was like tearing a fresh wound in my soul.

But I ignored those instincts and watched her go, feeling hollow, with only those parting words to keep.

I spent my forty-five-minute drive thinking only of that conversation, replaying it over and over in my mind, her words, the way she said them, the look on her face, the way she'd felt in my arms. Over and over again, as if trying to imprint it in my mind. Feeling the finality of it.

And I arrived home tired, dirty and badly in need of a shave.

But I washed up quickly, and after checking on AJ, who was sleeping peacefully, thank God, I went to the kitchen and grabbed a beer. Karen was sitting at the counter, so I took the stool beside her.

"We missed you."

"Did the kiddo have lots of fun with the guys?"

She smiled, nodding. "Tons. He wore them all out."

I leaned my head back to take a long pull from the bottle. When I straightened and swallowed, Karen was staring at my collar.

"What the hell did you do to your neck? Did you cut yourself shaving or is that—" She leaned closer. "It's a bite mark."

I reached a hand up and rubbed it, perhaps the only existing reminder of some of the hottest sex I'd ever had. Then I flicked my gaze back to Karen, who was frowning at me. I took a long breath and let it go. Earlier in the day, I'd decided that Gray had deserved to know about Karen. Well the reverse was also true.

"I thought you said your romance with Keely Dawson was fake?"

"This, uh," I dropped my hand. "This wasn't Keely."

Her brows twitched up. She reached for her glass of wine, staring at me expectantly. How honest should I be with her? If I told her too much, would she back away from my plan?

Then another side of my thoughts questioned, *would that be such a bad thing?* The image of that kid sleeping peacefully, content under my roof was incentive enough to go through with my plan to marry Karen.

"Before you came out to California, I broke up with someone I'd been seeing—for real, not fake like with Keely."

She waited on me to catch my breath, her face completely neutral, so I trudged on. "She was there this weekend, and we had a short-lived relapse."

She looked away then back at the mark on my neck and gave a little laugh. "Damn, I'm kind of jealous. Remembering the hot kind of sex that gets you marks like that is… Ah, well I miss sex, and it's been months since I had any."

I commiserated. And I'd only gone weeks without sex after having broken up with Gray the month before. And wait, what? Did she say months? Wouldn't it have been over a year? I sent her a brief glance and then looked away. It really wasn't any of my business.

Besides if she had found comfort with someone else in the interim since losing her husband, who the hell was I to judge?

She swirled the wine around in her glass and studied it. "Are you in love with her?"

I reached out and started peeling the moist label off the front of my beer bottle. I could lie, yes. I could give her a safe answer that would make her feel better.

But I didn't want to. Because every time I thought of Gray, every time her name popped up in my mind or there was a smell or texture or scrap of memory that reminded me of her, *every* damn time, a pang of longing cut right through me like a razor-thin blade. There was no disguising it. No denying it. No eradicating it.

I gave her the simplest, most honest response I could. "I am."

"So then, why aren't you together? Does she not feel the same way?"

"She's not…available to me. It can't happen, for reasons I can't go into now, mostly because it's a long-ass and depressing story. I promise I'll explain it all to you soon but…"

The other part of the reason I didn't want to elaborate was because I knew Karen's romantic side well enough to know that she'd be bolstered by hearts in her eyes and the airy-fairy romance behind the story. The star-crossed lovers of it all.

Karen expelled a quick breath and practically leapt off her stool. "Oh, Ty! Damn it. I'm so sorry." She wrapped her arms around me, squeezing tight, and I took one of her arms in my hand, holding her there in her awkward sideways hug.

She pressed her cheek to my back, and when she spoke, it was in a voice full of her own emotion. "I'm sorry. Why does love have to hurt so much?"

"I guess that's why people write songs and poetry and books about it."

I leaned back and wrapped my arm around Karen's waist and pulled her in for a proper hug. Karen was a hugger. I'd known that since we'd first met, and while I used to make a game of avoiding her hugs when we were in college, I'd realized long ago that letting her hug me was letting her express herself. So I'd grown to tolerate it when she initiated them.

But this time I initiated, and she seemed shocked.

"This doesn't change anything, okay? I still want to take care of you and AJ. And you know what? You can take care of me, too."

She blinked, frowning, and avoided my gaze. Uh oh. Not a great sign.

"How the hell could it not change anything? If you love her, you should be with her."

I let out a huge sigh and stepped back. "I *can't*. And she can't. I—"

Now she looked even more confused. "So it was mutual?"

More or less. If those words she'd spoken at the airport were any indication. "She understands. I told her about you. That I wanted us to be a family."

Her jaw dropped, and she stared at me like I was a crazy person. "Ty, what the hell are you doing? I don't need you to take care of me. And as for being in our lives, we don't have to be married or even seeing each other romantically in order to do that. Just be there for him like you have over the past three weeks."

"But AJ needs a dad. I *want* to be his dad. I don't want him to have to go through what I went through. You know I lost mine when I was a kid—"

She held up a hand. "AJ is still going to grow up without his dad whether or not I get married again."

"You know what I mean."

She sank back down on her stool, staring at me with a troubled look. "How long is it until your test flight?"

"Just over a month. But Karen—"

She held up a hand. "Hold the phone, okay? This is all becoming clearer to me now. You came up with this plan on the rebound."

I plopped onto my stool in front of her and ran a hand through my hair. "Settling…we agreed that it was settling. But it would be comfortable. We're friends. We've known each other for almost half our lives. I've known that kid since his birth. I'm ready to settle with you and AJ."

She shook her head. "You just broke up with someone you're in love with. You're in *pain.* Good God, Ty, stop putting all this out there. There's plenty of time down the line to maybe explore something later. But not now. Now let's just be close friends. Confide in me."

I swallowed. "Yes, I can do that."

Lies. Liar.

Does she know about Xander's tether? Did you tell her that her husband defied orders and released his tether so he could get to you and help you?

I could tell Karen right now. I could confide in her about that. I could make that choice, summon that courage.

But there was nothing to summon, because I was a coward. A coward who had turned his back on Karen and AJ for months during the hardest part of their grief.

Taking her hand, I leaned forward and looked into her eyes. "Xander..." My voice faded, and my gaze seemed trapped by her dark brown eyes.

She nodded, encouraging me to continue.

But I swallowed, the words stuck in my throat. She would hate me if she knew. She'd scream and cry. And worse, she'd hate Xander for the decision he'd made. The decision to leave his wife a widow and his son fatherless, all to save a worthless human being, friend or no.

I couldn't.

She shook her head again. "I don't understand. What about Xander?"

I cleared my throat. "Xander would want me to watch over you. And being with the two of you makes me feel close to him. It makes me happy, Kare."

She smiled sadly. "This isn't something you do out of obligation. And it's definitely not something you dive into, and we certainly shouldn't. You need time to get over your heartbreak. And honestly, I'm not over my own heartbreak."

I took her hand in mine. "Then we do it together."

Her smile grew as she met my gaze. "Maybe. But that's not a decision we can make now, okay?"

My mind scrambled to find something else to say to convince her to change her mind. At the same time, I couldn't help but wonder *why* I was so desperate to lock this up now. Maybe because if I were committed elsewhere, I wouldn't be pulled back to Gray?

That seemed a futile hope.

Karen broke the silence with a long sigh. "You must be exhausted, and I've also had a long day." She pulled back. "I think we should turn in."

She pushed up on tiptoes and kissed me on the cheek. "Night."

Then she turned and was gone. I watched her go and ran a hand through my hair again. She'd certainly tried her best to stir up my doubt, but I closed my eyes and squeezed a fist, determined that this would be a step in the right direction of making things right.

I'd dedicate my entire life to it, if that was possible.

That was the plan, anyway.

***

The following Wednesday, my fellow astronauts and I boarded a small plane for Florida for launchpad tests and to watch the last unmanned rocket launch carrying the twin of the capsule that I would be riding in next month. An uncrewed full-systems test. I sat across from Noah. He leafed through a technical manual while I did some work on my tablet to pass the time.

We were the only passengers who didn't sleep on the flight.

I threw a look over at our snoozing colleagues. "I guess the pilots have to sleep if they're not the ones flying the plane."

He laughed, and then there was an awkward pause where we both stared out our respective windows.

"How's Karen?" he asked once he pulled his gaze away from the window and looked across the small table at me.

I set down my tablet and clicked it off. I'd been studying the new checklist that had been pushed through to us from operations. Suppressing a frown at his puzzling question, I wondered why he'd ask since he and the other two had spent the weekend with Karen and AJ. He already knew the answer to his own question.

And Noah was never one to force idle conversation.

"Good," I adjusted my seat and glanced out the window. We were over the Gulf of Mexico, where astronauts usually ran maneuvers in their T38 training jets. I pointed out some of our familiar haunts to Noah.

Like me, Noah was not a pilot astronaut, though we had both been taught to fly our trainer jets. Noah had also come to NASA from the special forces, though he'd started out as an Army Ranger so we'd had that familiar Army-Navy rivalry. And we'd been AS CANs—our nickname for an Astronaut Candidate— together.

Most importantly, throughout all the many hours and days of grueling training for our job, we'd once been good friends.

Until ISS Expedition 53. The fateful mission that had changed all our lives.

"You and Karen seem...close." Noah said after sitting back, throwing me a speculative glance.

I nodded. "We've been close. And we're getting there again."

He once again glanced out the window, but he seemed tense, his fist clenched into a knot in his lap. I frowned. Something about this upset him. Maybe Karen had confided in him about my proposal?

That would make way too many people who knew.

"Are you taking her to the dinner reception?" he asked.

I thought for a minute and then scratched my jaw. "Oh, you mean that private dinner that Adam Drake's putting on for us next weekend? I have to take Keely. But damn, Karen shouldn't go alone. Why don't you be her date?"

Noah seemed to pale under his tan and flicked me another unreadable look. "I'll do it. But only if you ask her if that would be all right first."

I laughed. "Why wouldn't it be all right? She knows you, it's all—"

He shook his head. "Ask her first, and then if she doesn't have a problem with it, I'll do it."

I shrugged. "Okay."

Another long, awkward silence stretched out, and I snatched up my tablet again. Noah interrupted me by clearing his throat. My eyes flicked to him as I settled the tablet in my lap.

"I owe you an apology about riding you so hard on the lights-out test. Thanks for getting it done."

I nodded. It had gone smoothly. I'd spent a lot of time preparing for it, and the fact that the duration of the test itself was short had helped. I'd ticked off the time left in my head to keep the panic at bay.

"I'm sorry I kept putting it off. Just didn't seem as important an issue as some of the other things we had going—and still have going. But it didn't take nearly as much time as I thought it would."

Noah rubbed his jaw and studied me, tilting his head. "Was that the only reason? I mean, it just seems..." He shrugged.

I paused for a moment to allow him to find the words. When he didn't, I was tempted to drop it and pick up my tablet. Instead, for some stupid reason, I prompted him. "Seems like what?"

"Like there's something you're not telling me. Well not just me. All of the rest of us."

My shoulders tensed, but I did not change my posture. "Listen, I know you've blamed me since the accident—"

He shook his head. "You're wrong. I don't blame you. But I feel you're not being one hundred percent honest."

"Well," I said, raising my hand to get the attention of our in-flight attendant to ask for a drink, "last I checked, you didn't have mind-reading powers or a way to innately detect lying."

He rolled his eyes in exasperation. "I know you're not a liar. But I wish you'd just be more open with all that's going on with you." My eyes flicked down to the way his hands gripped the armrests. Admirable, really, considering our past, that we weren't shouting at each other or coming to blows.

"You mean, like with my emotions? Do you want me to share all my woes with you?"

He laughed. "Okay, that's not what I meant, either."

Conversation successfully deflected. I mentally breathed a sigh of relief as we talked of other things. And in spite of our various differences, I did know that past misunderstandings or not, Noah had my back. They all did.

We were a brotherhood. We always would be. We had each other's backs.

And our brotherhood had a hole in it. A missing man whom we would never forget. Not if I could help it.

Chapter Twenty-One
Gray

Victoria was giving me a to-do list a mile long, rattling off items faster than I could scratch them down on my legal pad when my phone buzzed for the third time. I'd only been sitting here ten minutes.

I met Victoria's gaze across the desk. "I'm sorry."

Her perfectly arched eyebrow came up. "Why don't you take care of that. I have to go run and do something anyway. "Be right back."

She grabbed an envelope that looked like it held a card in it and jumped up from her desk with spry movements. I also noticed her face was glowing.

As she came around the desk on her way out the door, she must have caught my expression because she stopped and turned back to me. "What?"

I blinked. "What, what?"

"You just got this big smile on your face."

I bit my lip and hedged. "Uh, yeah. You just look happy."

Victoria's eyes widened and she tilted her head at me. "Let's not be coy, okay? I know that you know. But mum's the word, okay?"

I laughed. "Mum is my middle name."

She pivoted on her perfect heels and called to me from down the hall. "I know your middle name is Grace."

I laughed, knowing she was jumping out to put a card on Pari's workstation. Pari was off site for the day, doing some training, so Victoria had the opportunity to surprise her.

I stared unseeing at my list for a long moment, basking in the happiness-by-proxy I could feel radiating off of Victoria. Hopefully they wouldn't have to keep the happy secret much longer, but Pari didn't want to jinx anything and Victoria was insisting they take it slow.

But by all reports Pari had given me, so far, so good.

I was being such a goofy sap that I almost forgot to check the text messages, the entire reason Victoria had decided to give me a break.

Gray, your dad would like to nail down a date for dinner. He's getting a bit feisty about it.

Teresa, my dad's assistant, was a nice woman and didn't deserve the kind of grief she was getting from dad because I was giving him the cold shoulder.

And there went all the joy-by-proxy I'd been feeling for Victoria and Pari and their burgeoning relationship.

With a deep breath, I responded. *Tell Dad to keep his blood pressure down. I'll see him at the XPAC dinner reception next weekend.*

Her response was immediate. *Got it. Will let him know.*

I sent her some emojis in response. I'd come back ready to have a confrontation with my dad, only to find out he was in New York on business until the weekend. And since the dinner reception was also during the upcoming weekend, I'd have to wait until after to have my day. But I'd been preparing. I'd made bullet lists of what I wanted to say and even practiced in a mirror.

Not surprising that the nerd girl would take the nerdtastic approach to this problem, too.

My eyes went back to the checklist on my notepad. The title was, "Exit Strategy for Keely/Ty Public Relationship." Underneath were a list of strategies, a series of tidbits to leak to the press and some things we needed to do on social media. Keely would stop posting pics or even mentioning Ty later this week, maybe even delete a few of her more recent photos with him and stop following him.

Ryan would unfollow her from his dummy Twitter account that had been mostly run by Victoria's assistant under her close observation. Keely would then start taking female friends to her next few public appearances, and finally, she'd be seen out somewhere casual with a mystery guy.

Then, in about a month, she and Ryan would release a joint, heartfelt, and cordial statement about their amicable uncoupling and their well wishes for each other.

Even though I knew it was fake, it still choked me up to read through the list. The fake relationship was the thing that tied me to Ryan. And with it being dissolved, it felt like my connection to him was also being terminated.

The list also reminded me of my own personal breakup drama, all the hurts we'd exchanged in Tahoe and the beautiful memories there, too. And that good-bye at the airport made my heart hurt whenever I thought about it.

Thank God he'd been in Florida for the week. I wasn't sure I'd be able to take passing him in the hallways or making casual eye contact in the lunchroom.

Of course there was the dinner reception coming up over the weekend. The very thought of it made my stomach dip. Key investors, all the astronauts and the entire support team—and their dates—would be attending. It was not something I could back out of no matter how much I wanted to.

**

"Not having a proper dress is not an excuse." Pari shook her head, arms folded as she sat in my passenger seat one afternoon a few days later on our way to the mall. I had just listed every way I could think of to back out of the dinner.

"Sudden very drastic case of E. coli poisoning?"

She gave me serious side-eye. "I'm dragging you into every single store until we find something appropriate. And as much as I despise buying anything at the mall, that is the true testament of my friendship."

I nodded. "That *is* a true testament of friendship. I can honestly say I wouldn't do the same for you."

She scowled and jerked her head sharply toward the door. "Let's go."

The next evening, I modeled my purchases for my Mom in front of the laptop. She was over the moon. The dress that Pari had encouraged me to wear was beyond any risk I'd ever before taken at a public function. And I needed all the moral support I could get, even if my mom was over five thousand miles away.

"*Cariad!*" she exclaimed the Welsh endearment she used for me. "Your haircut is adorable. And that dress!"

It was seashell pink satin, and while not exactly low cut, the dress was strappy on the shoulders and had a V neckline that did not cover the top part of my scar.

"You're going to be a knock out. Do you have a date?"

My smile faltered as the image of Ryan flashed unbidden in my mind. He'd have a date, definitely. Would it be Keely for one last public appearance? Or would it be Karen, whom he was determined to pursue once the test flight was done?

And what would it feel like to see him there with her?

I'd been tempted to invite Aaron. He'd asked me out on a date, and I'd declined. Asking him to go with me to this would be sending him mixed signals. Plus, it wasn't fair, and it felt like using him if I just went out with him to make someone else jealous. He was too nice a person for that.

"You okay? You went silent all of a sudden." Mom was Skyping from her kitchen. As it was late for me, it was very early morning for her in Wales. She was chopping up vegetables to put into a giant pot of soup to cook for the day.

I smoothed the cool fabric of the dress over my stomach and nodded, plastered on a fake smile. "Yeah. Yeah I'm fine." I held up my new shoes to distract her from picking up on my sudden nervousness. "I got some new shoes to go with the dress."

Her mouth dropped. "Those are so glamorous! Like Cinderella slippers." I glanced at them. They were glittery-silver, strappy heels.

"Eh, I wear tennis shoes and Doc Martens all the time, so I figured I'd splurge on one pair of designer shoes. These are Jimmy Choos."

Mom nodded but didn't say anything. Despite having been a billionaire's wife for decades, she was not one who cared much for designer labels. Her style was too boho for that.

"I'm proud of you for not being afraid to show your scar. I know that's been an issue for you in the past. But you're gorgeous."

I fingered the scar self-consciously but didn't respond. She took a break from chopping her onion in order to wipe her eyes and sniffle. "Are you getting someone to do your makeup?"

I laughed. "I can do my own makeup now. I learned it on YouTube."

"Brilliant!" She beamed.

I explained that the dinner was in honor of the last successful unmanned launch before the real deal in just three weeks. The officers, astronauts, support crew and key investors were all invited. Which meant Dad, too.

Which meant an awkward mix of people in that room. And a whole lot of high tension.

My stomach knotted just thinking about it.

The weekend arrived far sooner than I wanted it to. Thankfully Pari helped me get ready. She was mostly there for moral support, but I did need someone to help me put on the jewelry. These were pieces that I never wore, given to me by my mom.

"Wow, Gray, diamonds. You look so glamorous. All that time you spent with Keely Dawson must have rubbed off."

I laughed at her in the mirror as she fastened the clasp of the lovely diamond necklace. The earrings, matching diamond studs, already adorned my ears.

"These were a gift from my dad to my mom not long before their divorce. She called them his 'last ditch effort.' She promptly gave them to me instead of selling them when they split."

Pari smiled. "These look like something Vic would wear. She'd look amazing in diamonds."

I twitched my eyebrow at her. "Well you make rocket scientist money, don't you? Christmas is coming, and you have a special someone to shop for this year."

Try as she might, Pari could not hide her goofy grin. She was clearly falling hard and fast. And Victoria's equal excitement in her office the other day had told me the feeling was mutual. Maybe the L-word was in their future?

"Don't tease me about it, or I'll have to do something drastic."

I laughed. "Don't make empty threats, Pari."

Pari came around the front and adjusted the necklace, which hung right above my scar but didn't cover it. "This looks great. All of it." She met my eyes, and I knew she was giving me extra reassurance due to my insecurities.

Open heart surgery was painful, demanding on a body, and difficult to recover from. Every time I saw that scar in the mirror, a brief memory of the months of pain after the surgery flashed through my mind. But that evening the twinge was not of physical pain; the pain in my heart was purely emotional.

I was literally born with a broken heart. But the figurative one was the one that was aching as I prepared to walk into that restaurant alone.

Pari moved to the window to look out at the late afternoon sky. The trees and bushes outside swayed heavily in the background. "Good thing your hair is nice and short, but take a brush. It's really windy out there and hotter than hell, too."

It wasn't quite fall yet but the Santa Ana winds had come early to Southern California, and with them came that constant feeling of thirst and desiccated skin. I grabbed a tube of lotion and smoothed it over my poor dry hands and elbows.

Pari gave me another once-over and smiled, shaking her head slowly. "I would give anything to see Ty's face when he sees you tonight."

"I'm not going to think about that. At all. I'm already way too far out of my comfort zone."

She nodded. "Time to kiss that comfort zone goodbye, Gray, and take the risk. With risk comes reward, and nobody ever did great feats by playing it safe. Would we have even gone to the Moon playing it safe? No. So just focus on that tonight."

I smiled. "I will."

What she said was true. My horizons would never expand if I kept myself safe and protected. It was the way I'd been raised, to be wary and afraid of the world instead of excited and anxious to go out and explore all of its splendor.

To find my own natural limits instead of living by imposed ones.

I now had a lifetime of lessons in caution to counter.

Here went nothing.

CHAPTER TWENTY-TWO
GRAY

ORTY-FIVE MINUTES LATER, I WALKED INTO THE VENUE for our gathering. The restaurant was an upscale French boutique-style establishment high in the Orange Hills overlooking the sprawl of city lights all the way to the Newport Coast. We had the entire place reserved for our group. In attendance were our host and hostess, CEO and entrepreneur Adam Drake and his wife, Mia, an aspiring doctor. They greeted me at the door with big smiles on their faces.

Being my father's daughter, I'd crossed paths with many people in this echelon of wealth, and I had to say that they were two of the nicest people I'd encountered. They were still young, only in their mid-to-late twenties, and both of them were incredibly good looking. The type of good-looking couple that made you wonder immediately what their babies would look like once they started having them.

Next came my boss, Tolan, with his date. He'd been deep in conversation with the host couple when I'd arrived. But now he greeted me with a huge smile and took my hand, bending to kiss me on the cheek. "Your Dad just got here and has already asked about you. He's over getting some canapés."

I glanced across the room and saw that the paternal unit was talking with one of the other astronauts, Hammer. Dad's body

293

language was stiff and formal, uncomfortable, but he seemed engaged in whatever it was that Hammer was saying to him.

Even as they spoke, Dad's eyes were skimming the room, searching. Most likely for me. Maybe for Ryan. I turned away from him and began my own search. Ryan was nowhere to be seen, and I surmised he hadn't arrived yet. The place wasn't big enough to lose a six-foot-tall, brawny astronaut.

As I scanned the room, however, my eyes halted on a familiar female. Petite height and build, long dark hair, very pretty, as I remembered. She was chatting intently with Noah Sutton, likely having arrived with him. So, she *wasn't* Ryan's date tonight.

My gut twisted tight. Jealousy instantly sank its heated claws into my chest, constricting so that I could hardly breathe. I once again felt the ache of saying goodbye to Ryan at the airport, of knowing he was going home to Karen, of the chance that something might start between them. Nausea bloomed with the thought that Ryan in his own misguided way was actively seeking that out.

These thoughts rendered every beat of my heart a painful one. What if Karen thought it was a good idea too? What if she felt she needed someone to take care of her? Was it my place to tell her that Ryan was motivated by shame and guilt and loss?

I couldn't interfere. It was none of my business what two consenting adults decided, even if it affected my future, too.

This was so damn frustrating and confusing. As I stood, alone with an icy glass of mineral water in my hand, stewing in all the possibilities, I heard a small commotion at the door. Ryan entered with Keely on his arm.

I immediately turned to watch Karen observe their entrance, hoping to glean a little of what might be going on in her head.

She seemed keenly interested in the couple who had just entered, taking in Keely and her gorgeous emerald green designer cocktail dress that offset her red hair superbly.

Karen's gaze bounced from one to the other of them, as if intently studying them, wanting to see their interaction. Karen had to know by now that they were a fake couple. And honestly there wouldn't be much pretense here at this dinner. They'd arrived together for the benefit of the photographers outside.

But everyone in here knew that it was just performance art for the masses. In a few short months, Ryan's image had been successfully rehabilitated, and people were shipping *Tyley* all across the internet and news outlets everywhere. I turned to get my second glimpse, noting that they looked so amazing together that it was hard to believe they weren't really a couple.

Keely's gaze met mine, and her eyes widened. She let out a loud. "Oh, Em, Gee, Gray! You look ah-mazing." She nudged her date, who was already staring at me very intently. "Doesn't she look amazing, Ty?"

He didn't reply. Keely pushed off his arm and made a beeline straight for me. "Gray, you—"

I rolled my eyes but beamed at her. "—Look amazing, so I heard." We locked gazes and then both started laughing.

"I love that color on you. I can't wear pink because, you know, red hair. So I'm jelly that you do that color so well."

"Well you just look gorgeous all the time so maybe I really shouldn't even mention it, though you do tonight, too."

She shook her head and grinned. "Oh, I never get tired of hearing it, babe. Tell me anytime. My hair looks okay? In spite of that crazy wind out there?"

"We've all got big hair going on today. You look great."

Keely glanced over her shoulder then took my upper arm and herded me away from the center of the room. "Have you forgiven me for Tahoe?"

She'd already asked me this by text. I'd been terse in my replies and told her she'd way overstepped her bounds, and she'd apologized profusely.

The next day a bouquet of flowers had shown up on my desk at work. I turned to her. "I already told you we were cool. Just don't strand me with a hot hunk again—unless it's someone I wasn't seeing before." I grinned.

She laughed. "I read you loud and clear. Ugh the thought of getting back in the dating scene is kind of making me wish for only fake relationships from here on out."

I puzzled over the possibility of dating someone else. I hadn't even thought that far ahead.

"Ty is still pretty pissed at me. Barely spoke on the way over. I didn't think sending flowers would help."

I followed her gaze to watch Ryan. He stood in a huddle with Adam and his wife and Tolan, and they were talking about something, but Ryan's eyes were on Keely and me. "Yeah flowers probably wouldn't work. Or cupcakes, either."

She blew out her breath. "Men are so funny. They are mad for like two seconds, and then you distract them and they completely forget what they were pissed about."

I opened my mouth to reply when I detected someone at my shoulder. Keely pulled back, and I turned to see my Dad standing there. He placed a hand on my back. "Well now, Gracie, do I get to meet your friend?"

I stiffened where his hand touched between my shoulder blades, and he frowned. Then I stepped away from his reach under the pretense of taking Keely by the upper arm as I introduced them. "Keely Dawson, this is my dad, Conrad Barrett."

Keely beamed at my dad, and he smiled wide back at her. "A pleasure. I don't go to the movies very often, but I saw you in that World War II movie—"

"*The Edge of the Shadow.*"

"Yeah. I just loved it. You are one talented young lady."

Keely beamed at him. "Gray you never told me your dad was such a sweetheart with such wonderful taste."

"My dad is a sweetheart with wonderful taste," I intoned robotically. Our gazes met, and though he smiled, I didn't. The moment grew awkward, so I cleared my throat. "Excuse me, I'm parched. I'm going to go grab a drink. Be right back!"

Or better yet, I wouldn't be back at all, I told myself as I made my way to the bar and ordered a Dr. Pepper with extra ice. Smooth, Gray. Nice and classy. I was dressed like I should be carrying a flute of champagne, but I couldn't stand champagne.

Maybe it was mean to leave Keely stranded with my dad, but he was a charming guy and could hold his own in a conversation, even with a beautiful starlet. His holding company had backed a few sure bet movies, so it might even be to her advantage to forge the connection.

Anyway, I just wanted him off my back. I was still beyond pissed at him and frustrated that I wouldn't be able to confront him until later. I wandered over to the trays of canapes that were artfully arranged in several tiers. Glancing over the offerings, I opted not to take anything because my stomach was doing flip flops. Between Dad's presence and Ryan's, and the combined animosity between the two of them, it would be a miracle if I could get—and keep—anything down tonight.

"How are you, Miss Gray?" a voice at my shoulder spoke. I'd been staring at the tray, seemingly in a trance, lost in thought and savoring my solitude against the futile hope the isolation would last.

Nevertheless, the interruption wasn't unpleasant. I looked up at Kirill. "*Dobriy vyecher.*"

He smiled. "Good evening to you, too. You are learning Russian?"

"One word at a time." I smiled.

He nodded his approval. "Exactly how I learned it. It's very useful language."

"Especially if we get more cosmonauts on the team."

His blond brows raised. "That might be interesting prospect. Not many want to move to US from Russia, though."

I smiled, remembering an earlier discussion with Ryan. "We'll just do all our recruiting during the winter and show posters of California beaches in January."

He laughed and shrugged. "It might work."

Just then, the lights very noticeably flickered off and then on again—an interruption so brief that, though noticed by all, it only served as a mere reminder of the wind outside. Things like that were ubiquitous when the Santa Anas were blowing—as ever present as the arid heat, persistent dust and smoky air from wildfires. We both looked at each other, startled as others in the room around us let out noises of surprise

"Can I refresh your drink?" he asked. "I need another."

I held up my glass which was half full—yes, I was still being an optimist in spite of it all—and he smiled, drifting away to the bar. There he met Ryan, who was just coming away from it with his own fresh drink. The two of them exchanged a few words, and Ryan glanced up as if inspecting the lighting. Likely that brief power interruption had set him on alert. I noticed his forehead was a little shiny from perspiration and his shoulders were tense.

I didn't want to notice these things and I most certainly didn't want to feel this urgent pull of empathy and worry for him.

I wanted to be free of him. Just like it appeared that he was free of me.

I turned away, feigning intense interest in the appetizers. I'd have them all counted, catalogued and memorized by the time the night was through. But I'd never hope to be so lucky.

I nearly jumped out of my skin when I felt a body suddenly standing near me, a shirt sleeve brushing against my bare arm. A familiar smell and a warm presence.

When he spoke, his voice sent parts deep inside me vibrating. And like a strike of lightning searing right through me in seconds, I realized how much I'd missed him.

Ryan uttered his words quietly. "You've been staring at those for fifteen minutes now. Why not try one?" As if to demonstrate, he picked up an artful piece of sashimi and popped it into his mouth. My eyes zeroed in on his mouth as he chewed, suddenly awash in warm desire for him. I wanted to lean in closer and smell his smell, feel his body's warmth near mine. Instead I took a step back.

"Not very hungry tonight."

His eyes traveled from my face, over my neck and chest, and down the length of me, and that warmth inside me heated and steamed my skin. Then his gaze rested noticeably on my chest, on the prominent scar there, before returning to my eyes. "You look absolutely beautiful tonight." It was little more than a whisper but said in such a way, with such conviction, that I could not in a million years discount his words as mere flattery.

My mouth opened and my lips parted as if I were preparing to say something, yet I didn't know what to say. My throat tightened, and all I could manage was a thin, "Thank you."

He was quite the image of gorgeous himself. Black jeans, tan blazer, dark blue dress shirt that matched his eyes unbuttoned at his throat. He wore no tie but had his golden NASA astronaut badge pinned to his lapel.

I wasn't exactly angry with him, but I was definitely on my guard. I was in defensive mode, keeping a distance to protect myself. But I couldn't be indifferent to him, either. Not when he was standing so near me. Not when he was looking at me like that.

Not when I still loved him.

At that moment, we were interrupted by Karen, who appeared on Ryan's other side.

"I got my wine. I've got a babysitter with the kid tonight and I'm ready to rock and roll. Anything good over here? I'm starved," she said to Ryan.

"There's some cheesy puff pastry thingies you'll love, since you're such a cheese freak." He flicked her a look and a grin that made that heat of jealousy flare to near irrational proportions. I took another step back, needing to get my bearings.

But Karen stepped forward. "Hey, Gray. Great to see you."

I plastered on a smile. "Yes. How are you enjoying your stay? Enjoying California and our freaky weather?"

"I thought I was going to get blown away like a tumbleweed coming in. Hope this weather clears up before the three of us go down to Legoland next week."

The three of us. I looked at Ryan. The three of them. A new little family. That was actually...so sweet.

And it might just be good for him to have someone else to take care of. Shit, what was wrong with me? Why was I starting to think this might be a good idea too?

I could barely breathe around the tightening of my throat. "Sounds great. I hope you all have a lot of fun. Especially AJ. I, ah, have to go check on something."

Before either of them could say anything at all, I was gone, fleeing to the bathroom and trying to calm myself down enough to face dinner with all these different players at the same table. I resolved to sit near someone safe like maybe Mia Drake or Tolan. Or better yet, in between the two of them.

That would be perfect.

By the time I got out of the bathroom, our long table was ready and most people were seated. As there were no assigned seats, I headed toward the far end before Tolan hooked his fingers around my arm. "Sit by me?"

I nodded, only hesitating when I realized that the person on the other side of me would be Ryan.

Keely had mentioned wanting to talk to Mia about medical school for a part she was going to take later in the year. So that left Karen on the other side of Ryan. Now I was suffering from full blown nausea and almost turned around that second.

Only when I took my seat did I realize the depth of the screwed-up seating. Dad sat across from Ryan, intentionally, no doubt.

If ever there was a time to mentally conjure up new and interesting four-letter words, it was now.

Dad's cold eyes landed on Ryan. "Well, Commander Tyler. How goes the training for the flight? You all ready to start your short and pointless voyage to the center of nowhere?"

Ryan pulled his napkin off his setting with a sudden snap, laying it across his lap. "Very excited for it, actually."

I sent a warning glare at my offensive parent, and he glared right back at me. "Aaron told me he's been trying to get a hold of you. Did you get his voicemail?"

Yeah, that little barb was meant to get at Ryan, too. I could tell by the way Dad's cold eyes flicked toward him when he said it. I flushed like a cherry tomato, thankful that most of the table were engaged in their own little pockets of chit chat. "Are you doubling as Aaron's personal assistant now, Dad? How sweet! And here I thought you were busy enough already."

Dad's mouth pursed, but he didn't look particularly angry. More like he'd expected me to make some kind of snarly reply and I'd satisfied his expectations. Well, so much for self-control. I took a deep breath and let it go. I would be the picture of adult togetherness tonight, even if it killed me.

The lights flickered once more, this time blinking off for half a second longer, definitely a noticeable pause. Beside me, Ryan tensed, his napkin falling off his lap. I tilted my head to see that he was white-knuckling the side of his chair in a tight grip.

"You going to be okay?" I muttered the question so that only he could hear. Then I bent, swiped up the napkin and stuck it back on his lap before he could even move.

He slanted a gaze at me out of the corners of his eyes. "I'm fine," he intoned through gritted teeth.

Ryan was hemmed in, by me on one side and Karen on the other, the wall at his back. If he had to make a quick escape, he'd be screwed. Obviously, he hadn't thought this through when he'd come to sit at the table.

The salad course was uneventful, as was the soup. Dad regaled the table with folksy and humorous stories, as was his specialty. I stifled my irritation by refusing to look at him, and though Ryan did watch him, he never participated in the ongoing conversation. I would have given a large sum of money to know what Ryan was thinking or how he was even managing to control his anger toward my father.

I looked again at Ryan. He had his head tilted toward the diner on the other side of him, toward Karen. There was no time to dwell on my jealousy, though. The servers were bringing our entrées, and Tolan was trying to engage me in his conversation with Adam Drake about a possible Moon mission.

Since I was left-handed, Ryan and I bumped arms when he started to cut his steak and accidentally elbowed me while doing it. He turned to murmur an apology and our eyes met. I hadn't planned for it to happen, but when it did, something sizzled and practically popped between us. Suppressed emotion on both of our parts?

It was more than awkwardness. It was connection. I caught my breath.

The lights flickered once more, slowly on and off again like a teasing child had flicked them to get the attention of the room. Apparently, it was the one last virtual gasp before staying off. In the darkness, people sighed or exclaimed surprise, and utensils clattered against dishes. The wind had kicked up, and high-pitched wails and bits of dust rattled against the windows.

But the occupant in the seat next to me panicked. Maybe I was the only one who heard his tight gasp, the clatter of his chair against the floor as he pushed away from the table, the sound of his silverware and plate hitting the floor with a crash. He was on his feet trying to push past Karen when I stood up and grabbed his arm.

"Ryan!" I said, and it may have been lost in the conversation around the table as people laughed and joked, and someone asked a server to bring candles while others fumbled for their smartphones.

Ryan ran smack into the wall behind him before doing an immediate about-face and turning toward me, every muscle in his body tense. I could hear the rush of his breath, feel the heat pouring off his body in waves. "I can't get out. I have to get out. Where's the opening for *Quest?*"

I frowned. That was the name of the airlock on the ISS.

He was experiencing a PTSD flashback, and the panic in his voice was evident. But how on earth was I going to convince a 200 pound, nearly six-foot-tall man to calm down when he was hemmed in on both sides?

I took hold of his biceps, squeezed them hard, and leaned in toward him. "*Breathe,* Ryan," I said in a harsh whisper.

I hoped like hell I could pull him back from where he was stuck in the past with a minimal amount of damage. Then I realized the room had gone silent.

CHAPTER TWENTY-THREE
RYAN

D ARKNESS AND TENSION AND PAIN SWIRL AROUND ME IN a dizzying blur. I can't see a damn thing. It's my worst nightmare. I'm trapped in the dark, and I can't breathe. I drag in a labored breath through my nose. It sounds like people are talking all around me, but the suit is dropping pressure and I can't find the fucking opening to the airlock. It's like a block wall in front of me, and my legs are pinned down as if by gravity.

Is this a symptom of the dangerous loss of suit pressure? Am I hallucinating now?

I open my mouth to answer Houston's question without even remembering what it was. "I can't—*I can't see.* I can't breathe."

The voices around me hush, or is that the static over the comms? Is the CAPCOM at a loss for words? I'm out of my mind with worry for Xander, but they've cut me off from him, ordering me to get back to the airlock, telling me they have his situation handled.

Why don't I believe them?

My SAFER is functional and it was designed for this. The jetpack was specifically for rescuing astronauts who had somehow gone off tether. I could go get Xander, bring him back. I know I could do it before I pass out from the loss of suit pressure. *Work the problem.* It's what we're good at, right? What all those years and years of training were for?

Stars and darkness are all around, and I can't see the ever-present gleam of earth below me. We must be on the dark side of the planet.

"Houston, I did not copy your last. Comm check." My voice comes out strangled, on the thin edge before panic. My mind is racing. What's going on with Xander? Why won't they let me talk to him?

There are hands on my face. It feels like it anyway. Is this a hallucination? Am I dying?

Strawberries and mint. That's what I smell. It reminds me...reminds me of *her.* Sudden confusion clouds my thoughts. Sounds and voices reach me as if through a long tunnel. Her forehead pressed to mine.

Did I know her—Gray—yet? Obviously I did, because I was thinking of her this very moment. Confusion swirled in my thoughts as nightmare and reality mixed together. My lungs clawed at the air. Which meant—which meant I wasn't in my EMU, losing pressure and struggling to find the way into the station.

I was boots-down on the planet, which explained the reason my legs wouldn't move like I was in microgravity. Which explained so many things.

Still struggling for breath, I focused on a sweet voice. *Her* voice. "Close your eyes, squeeze them tight. Think of something else. Think of something that makes you happy, something beautiful, like the lake."

Something that makes me happy. That was easy. Before she could even finish, I leaned in toward her, toward that intoxicating strawberry smell. My lips closed in on hers, and I did as she asked; I closed my eyes and concentrated on that feeling. Grounding myself, literally, focusing on the sensation of gravity holding me down.

Flashes of dim light illuminated the world beyond my closed eyelids, but I kept my eyes closed and kissed her. That sweet taste. That sweet girl. I never wanted to come up for air. I didn't need to. *She* was my air.

But as the light grew brighter and voices spoke up around us again, I felt her pull back. I wasn't ready yet. My hand came up to hold her head to mine, to continue kissing her.

Behind her someone whooped and whistled, clapping their hands. "*Yes!*" shouted Keely. That's right. I was at a restaurant. An awkward dinner party I'd rather not have attended. My heartbeat was still thready, still panicked, but I could feel myself coming down off that adrenaline rush. My eyes cracked open. The dim, bluish light around us came from several flashlight functions on smartphones. And the waiters had set candles on the table.

"Sir, we'll get you a new plate," someone said.

"What the hell do you think you're doing?" another voice ground out. A harsh voice full of anger and hatred. I knew that voice. Conrad Barrett.

Slowly I relaxed my hand on the back of Gray's head, and she pulled back from me. Her body trembled against mine. Our eyes locked, and for a long moment I ignored everything else around us but this. Her.

Only she had noticed what was happening to me. Only *she* had known.

But now, they *all* knew about my fear of the dark. I could feel their eyes on me.

Her dark brows crinkled together in a frown of concern. "It will be all right," she murmured to me, and I had to believe that. I *wanted* to believe it.

CHAPTER TWENTY-FOUR
GRAY

A S WE'D BEEN STANDING VERY CLOSELY TOGETHER, Ryan widened the gap between us by a lot. His hands slid down from where they had held my head to his and he stepped back—stepped away. He backed up against Karen's chair, but he never tore his gaze away from mine. He swallowed visibly, but neither of us seemed willing to sever the connection—physical or otherwise— forged between us.

Several people cleared their throats loudly from the end of the table where my coworkers sat.

Karen was staring at him with the same expression the others wore. Eyes wide, mouth agape. Her chair scraped loudly as she scooted in toward the table, eyes avoiding mine. "Do you need to get by?" Without a word, he took a step around her.

The other astronauts were all watching him, and he studiously avoided their eyes. I didn't even bother to hazard a glance to where Tolan and Adam sat, but I imagined them equally glued to the proceedings as well.

Dad had stood from his place and was staring at me wide-eyed. He hissed the question at me through clenched teeth. "What the hell is going on?"

Ryan turned on him with burning eyes and clenched fists. "Sit down, Barrett. And don't speak to her that way. She was helping me."

Dad scowled back at him. When I opened my mouth to speak, he cut me off, gesturing with a stiff finger at Ryan. "The problem here is that you weren't man enough to walk away. You're destructive and dangerous. I don't want any of that near her."

"Look—" I began, but this time Ryan interrupted me, hissing at my father.

"And *you* weren't man enough to back off and let her live her life like the adult she is."

My blood boiled, my face flushed, and that little voice inside my head that was always telling me to calm down and take a deep breath, control myself, that voice was shouting now.

"She's my daughter, you bastard."

"She's a grown woman."

"Stop!" I yelled at both of them. Every head in the room had jerked toward me, like they were watching some kind of three-way tennis match. It might have been comical had it not been about me and my life. Steam could have been shooting out my ears for all that these two alpha male assholes had noticed me— even while *discussing* me.

"I am *right here!*" My fist struck the table, rattling the dishes and the silverware. "Don't talk about me like I'm not present or I don't have my own goddamn voice."

If my cooler head had prevailed, I would have left the room. But there was no way I could walk out after demanding to be heard.

"And for God's sake, stop making decisions about *my* life as if it is out of my own hands."

Dad opened his mouth to say something, but I cut him off. "You are driving me away. Is that what you want?" My entire body shook as the words flowed out of me, tears rushing down my face. "To drive me away like you drove off Mom? And everyone else? You can't run our lives. You can't dictate to us how we live them. We aren't dolls on the end of a string to parade about for your amusement."

"Gracie." He held out a placating hand. "Please calm down. Your heart—"

My face flaming, I landed a fist on the table again. Silverware clattered to the ground. "*You're* breaking my heart, Dad!"

I detected movement from where Ryan stood. He had shifted his stance. He looked restless, as if plotting to wrangle me out of the room somehow. As if considering how to herd me into some private place. But I had things to say to *him* too. Things that wouldn't be easy to hear.

Catching my eye, he gestured to the exit, and I turned on him, fists clenched, nails digging into my palms.

"And *you*," I hissed. "You are just a *liar*. You lie to me. You lie to everyone around you. But worst of all—saddest of all—you lie to *yourself.*"

With a pang in my chest, I stopped to catch my breath, rubbing at my collar bone and noting how my dad gasped when he saw it. Naturally he assumed I was in some kind of cardiac distress.

Ryan stepped toward me. "Gray. Let's take this—"

"No one can fix what's wrong with you, Ryan Tyler. I can't." I gestured to the other astronauts on his team. "They can't." I resisted the urge to point to Karen. It was just too painful. Instead I struggled for a breath, my entire body vibrating with emotion. "The only one who can do it is *you*. But you can't even acknowledge there's a problem. Good luck to you, though, on getting through this. Nobody wants it more than I do. But I'm done trying to beat any sense into your head. I love you, but I just can't anymore."

Dad stepped toward me, and I turned on him with a sharp gesture. "Don't follow me."

Squeezing around Keely's chair, I turned when I saw Ryan take a step toward me. I made an abrupt chopping gesture at him. "*You either!*"

Fortunately, Noah had stood up to block him and I took advantage of that to get the hell out of there without meeting the eye of anyone else. Making a beeline for my car in my high heels, I awkwardly dodged dust and garbage scuttling about on the wind. Then I tore open the door to seek safe haven inside.

I didn't know where I was going—certainly not *home*. Being trapped inside those four walls with all these thoughts and feelings racing through my mind would drive me crazy. I'd feel helpless. Instead I needed to take charge.

Before anyone could come out into the parking lot to try to stop me, I pulled out and headed north on Chapman Avenue toward the summer-bare hills and away from the freeway. I hoped that just driving aimlessly and thinking would help me gain some clarity.

It was the strangest thing, really, how heading nowhere could suddenly force your mind along paths you'd never seen or considered before. My hands were on the wheel and my conscious mind was checking mirrors and the road and the bright headlights of oncoming traffic.

Feelings stabbed at me like thousands of little memory-knives. Remembering the feel of Ryan's arms around me, the taste of his lips when he'd reached for me in his panic.

The way he'd listened to me when I told him he'd be okay. *And he was okay...*

Goose bumps blossomed all over my skin, and my eyes stung with tears, knowing that now, more than ever, he was lost to me. Nevertheless, I savored those fresh feelings, that rush of joy at being his everything, if only for a few moments before reality came crashing back for us both. They faded and left emptiness and pain in their wake.

Again.

I couldn't keep doing this to myself. Over and over again. Opening my heart to him only to have him rip a fresh chunk out of it. My emotional heart would start looking like my physical one had, deformed and ill-functioning, before brilliant doctors had repaired it. But as far as I knew, there was no such thing as a prosthetic heart valve for the emotional heart.

No. If I cared about my own emotional wellbeing as much as I apparently kept wanting to give all of my heart to the same unavailable man over and over again, I'd have to practice self-care.

I'd have to close myself off, take myself away. Learn how to heal. Look out for myself once and for all.

And I'd have to fix this mess I'd created with my father, too. Fix the damage that he had done to the company by becoming involved and then throwing his weight around. It was time to stand up to him, too. I didn't have to be the one suppressing my own feelings in favor of helping everyone around me.

I could fight for me, and that was just fine.

After meandering through twisting roads up in the hills for almost half an hour, I came to a pull out overlook off the main road, a tiny twisting two-way residential neighborhood of upscale homes that overlooked the lights of north Orange County. Off in the distance, I spotted the giant lit-up A of Angels Stadium in Anaheim, the looming boxy Honda Center nearby, and the brilliant coordinated light show at the brand new ARTIC train station. My eyes skimmed these sights, dazzled by beauty and yet not really seeing them.

Without another second's hesitation, I pulled out my phone and scrolled through my contacts, clicking on the message app. I glanced at the time—just after 8:30.

I keyed in my message and waited.

Me: Hey there, I was wondering if we could meet up. I really need to talk.

I stared at the phone screen for a minute, willing the reply. The telltale three dots appeared, indicating that he was reading the message. I swallowed. It might seem sudden. It was definitely late and out of the blue, but maybe, just maybe...

The three dots disappeared, and a new message popped up on my notifications screen.

Aaron Thiessen: Sure! Coffee house? Or you are welcome to come over here if you'd like.

I bit my lip, considering, then replied.

Me: I'll come over to your house if you don't mind. Promise I won't impose long.

Him: Never an imposition. See you soon!

I swallowed the lump in my throat and started the car, the words that I wanted to say to him already speeding through my mind.

CHAPTER TWENTY-FIVE
RYAN

WATCHING GRAY WALK OUT OF THAT ROOM WAS like watching my heart tear itself out of my chest.

And though she'd warned her old man off, I took a step to follow her when I was very deliberately blocked from doing so by Noah. I didn't resist his interference. I owed him an explanation, after all. I owed them all. My undershirt was still soaked with the cold sweat of that episode in the dark. And they were likely reeling from the revelation.

None of them could possibly be as sick as I was to have revealed it, though. And yet also, I was oddly relieved.

She'd been right, and I'd been too blind to see it. I was unfit to fly.

And now, they *all* knew the truth of it.

I spun on my heel and headed for the men's room instead. I took a moment to catch my breath, splash some cold water on my face, and try to come up with a plan.

But after a few minutes of procrastinating and knowing the rest of the guys would soon follow me in here, I left without a plan, only the gnawing need to go find Gray, to apologize to her. To hold her close if she'd let me.

That desire was soon thwarted when I saw who was waiting for me on the other side of the restroom door, leaning up against the wall, arms folded and staring at the ground, lost in her thoughts. Karen.

I owed *her* an explanation, too.

"Hey," I said softly so as not to startle her out of her daydreaming.

Her head came up, and the curtain of dark hair fell away from her lovely face. To my surprise, there was a soft smile on her lips. "Hey."

I froze, and we awkwardly stared at each other for a long moment. "So, we should talk," I said.

She let out an explosive breath as if she had been holding it. "Yes, we should. There's a small room just off the hallway here. It looked empty. Maybe they won't mind if we borrow a seat. We'll make it an ongoing tradition."

I nodded and followed her to the room in question. It was a small sitting room set aside for special gatherings. There was a large sofa and chairs and a fireplace that was now dark. The lights were dim. Karen took one of the chairs, so I sat on the sofa, facing her.

Karen laced her fingers together and settled her hands in her lap. "So..." Her eyes narrowed, searching my face. "I have something I think you need to read."

I frowned, struck by the oddness of her words. Had she written me a letter? While I was in the bathroom? I puzzled over that while she pulled her purse strap off her shoulder.

She produced a plastic envelope, undid the button-and-string-tie fastener that held it closed, and produced a folded letter from within. It was clearly something she treasured—and something that had been unfolded, handled lovingly, read and reread, and refolded. Over and over again. A letter not quite tattered but definitely affectionately worn along the folds of paper.

She cradled it carefully in her hand as she unfolded it and handed it to me. "Read this now. And we shouldn't talk again until you're finished. Okay?"

With a profound frown, I took the paper from her and laid it out on the coffee table in front of me. In the dim light, I squinted to make out the words. It was clearly in Xander's handwriting. I would have recognized it anywhere.

And I soon realized, after seconds of staring at it, what this was. Every astronaut, before going up, was encouraged but not required to write one or more of these, depending on the number of people waiting for him at home. A letter to a parent, a child, a domestic partner, a best friend. A *just in case* letter.

My eyes flicked up at her, and she nodded. "After witnessing what happened at dinner, I realized that he never wrote you one because you were going up together. But arguably, you are the one who probably would have benefited the most from reading his thoughts on the mission. His hopes and fears. Read it, Ty. You need it."

I sat back for a minute and stared at her, my chest tight and my vision a little hazy. "I can't..."

"*Please.* If you won't do it for me, do it for Xander. Read it."

I felt like I was invading her privacy, even though she was the one who handed me the letter. But I dove in, skimming through the personal message he wrote to her—the brief collection of memories that stood out to him in their relationship. When he first met her, their engagement, and so forth.

I found a message in his words—like a secret code hidden, as if for me—almost three-quarters of the way down the page.

...You know how much I've wanted this, and I can't help but admit to being thrilled about this next milestone in my life. I'm the luckiest man in the world, and you are ninety-nine percent of the reason for that.

I'm also lucky because I'm doing this with my best friend, my brother. If I believed in it, I'd say it was providence that Ty and I are going up together. It means so much. I know that you rely on him a lot when I'm not around, so this will be extra hard for you. But you've never complained. Not once.

If I don't come back, you'll have many questions. And the one I most need to answer is what do I want you to do?

Live, Karen, live your life. Live it without fear and sadness. Live it in a way that you can cherish the memories of us but still make brand new ones. Fill your life with love and happiness and share that with our son. Treasure what we've had together, but please, for my sake, move on.

You've given me so much, and I feel like all I've done is take. With every breath I take, I love you. I love you. I love you.

Yours always,

Xander

I read and reread those lines at least three times, unable to move past them. Unable to *hear* them in anything other than Xander's voice. That voice I hadn't *actually* heard in over a year now. The voice which still haunted my dreams.

His voice leapt off the pages and declared *I'm doing what I love...I'm the luckiest man in the world...I'm doing this with my best friend.*

Xander. My best friend. My brother. The man who gave up everything to save me. I bit my lip and pushed the letter back toward her, blinking back the tears. I couldn't let his widow see me like this. I had promised to take care of her, not force her to be strong for me.

But those words. My eyes returned to them over and over again, scanning and rescanning the lines, hoping to brand them into my memory. Hoping the message would sink in when knowing that in reality I wouldn't allow it to.

I knew why Karen had wanted me to read this but...

But I couldn't let go. The guilt, the shame, they were all I had left.

"Ty," she whispered, leaning forward. "Don't you see? He'd wanted this his entire life. He died doing the job he dreamed of since he was a little boy. He—"

"He died trying to save me." I cut her off in a dead voice, no longer able to hold it in. That secret—that shameful secret that I'd only divulged to one other person until now. "He had everything to live for, and he gave it up for me. Because I was in danger."

She frowned, and her gaze fell to the paper in front of me, then flew to my face again, a question apparent in her dark eyes. "I don't understand," she said quietly.

"I'm saying that Xander defied my orders and Mission Control's and knowingly released his tether. He put himself in danger because my suit was breached."

I shifted, sitting back and meeting her eyes. I didn't deserve the luxury of avoiding her gaze. I stared into her eyes while I told her how her husband—her everything—had wasted his life, had willingly put himself in danger to save my undeserving skin.

The look on her face, the hardening of her eyes, the drawing back and sinking into her chair as I continued to relate the facts to her, broke my heart into a thousand pieces. I closed my eyes finally, rubbing them as my voice shook, hating my own weakness. Hating myself like I knew she must hate me upon learning the truth. Upon learning that I was here, sitting across from her, instead of how it should have been. Instead of it being Xander.

The divot between her dark brows deepened, and I wondered if she would start crying. And if she did, I wondered how I would be able to handle it.

"Good God, Ty," she finally said when my voice trailed off. I couldn't speak another word for my throat closing and preventing speech or even breath. "Have you been tormenting yourself about this for a year? Telling yourself that you don't deserve to be alive because he isn't?"

I didn't answer. I just continued to stare at her, not quite yet knowing where she would go with this. Her fist closed in her lap, and she reached with her other hand to pull the letter back to her. Oh, so it was to be anger.

Good. She deserved to be angry at me. She knew the truth now.

"You fucking idiot," she ground out. "Did you not absorb a word of this? How can you be so dense?" She took a deep gulp of air and held the page in front of her again, her eyes scanning the page as she read out key phrases. "*Treasure what we've had together, but please, for my sake, move on.*" She swallowed, looking at me with dark, accusing eyes before returning to the paper again. "*Live your life. Live it without fear and sadness.* These are *his words* Ty. If you disregard them, you disregard the last word of a man before he died. Your best friend. Your *brother*. You needed these words as much as I did."

"But don't you see—"

"No!" she shouted, waving a tiny fist. "I *don't* see. When we lost Xander, the world lost an amazing man. You lost your best friend. But I—I lost the love of my life. My *partner*. The man I co-parented my son with. And I don't resent you. I don't value his life over yours. In fact, by doing this, by keeping this secret, I resent you for not revealing to the world what a true hero he was. And if you continue to claim that your life means nothing, then you are saying that my husband died—*sacrificed himself*—for nothing. So cut it with this bullshit, Ty! You're above this. Xander was above this. Don't do it. Stop devaluing his sacrifice." She sucked in a deep breath and let it out again to calm the trembling in her voice. "And mine."

I stared at her in shock. With a light shake of my head, every molecule in my body seemed to vibrate. "I—"

"No." She shook her head right back at me. "We have nothing more to say to each other. You know where I stand. Xander was a hero. Xander was the best man to walk the face of this planet as far as we are both concerned. And Xander died because he couldn't live with the thought of being here on this earth without you. Got it? So you owe it to *him* to live your life and be happy. To not make his sacrifice a vain one. He died an astronaut. What he *always* wanted to be. He's a hero, and his heroism will make him immortal. What more can we ask for? What more can you ask from him? To demand more would be selfish."

I was speechless. The words and all sense had been knocked out of me as each truth from her mouth landed like a blow.

With jerky movements, she snatched up the letter and refolded it, slipping it carefully back into its plastic pouch. I stared at her in disbelief, taking in her angry gestures. What could I say to that? Had I been denying Xander's heroism because I couldn't accept the sacrifice he'd made for me? And what the hell right did I have to do that?

If she could accept it, then I sure as hell had to, didn't I?

I rubbed my forehead. How was it possible that this had never occurred to me before? Perhaps because I'd been too pigheaded, too caught up in my obsession to blame myself and treat myself more cruelly than I'd ever treat my own worst enemy.

Perhaps because *I already was* my own worst enemy.

With her task finished and her precious letter tucked back into her purse, her eyes flicked up to mine again, still smoldering with anger. "Now, are you going to explain to me what all that was when the lights went out? You have PTSD. And Gray was able to talk you down from it really quickly. Are you getting help?"

I ran a hand through my hair and looked up at the ceiling. Oh, how I didn't want to be here, but how could I walk out on her? There was no denying my issues, though I'd made a good show of it when Gray had showed up at my door that first day and thrown that in my face.

I could make up all the rules I wanted for Gray, but I couldn't push back on Karen.

"I had been making a lot of progress, mostly thanks to Gray. But I was obviously deceiving myself about how well I'd been coming along."

She nodded. "And, obviously, Gray is the woman you were talking about the other night. The one you're in love with?"

My tongue darted out to wet my lip, and I laced my fingers together to study them in my lap, because for this at least, I couldn't look at her. I'd tried to tell Gray how I felt but she'd stopped me. When I found her to talk to her again, I wasn't sure what words I could possibly use.

I just knew I had to find her.

I nodded in answer to Karen's question.

She let out a long breath. "You dumbass, Ty. I can't believe you were going to do this to yourself."

"Before you say anything, I had to break it off with her, okay? And it had nothing to do with my offer to you. Her father was going to pull the plug on the entire program if I didn't. So he—"

Her sharp gesture cut me off. "Oh my God. Do *not* give me that bullshit. The old Ryan Tyler that I've known since we were eighteen years old would never have let an old fart like Conrad Barrett stop him from going after what he wanted."

She paused for a breath and looked me in the eyes like she could see right through me. "And I saw the way you looked at her. I saw. I never in a million years thought I'd ever see you look at any woman that way. I honestly didn't think you had it in you. But goddamn, you love her. You love her like she was your next breath. That was pretty damn clear."

She might as well have taken a two-by-four and slammed me across the face with it. I sat back, stunned, exposed. My shoulders slumped, defeated. She was right. God, she was right. What had I done? What had I given up?

All in the name of satisfying Barrett, keeping the money flowing. Desperate to hang on to a goal that wasn't truly mine, to a promise I'd made under duress to Xander, who'd never known what it would cost me to keep.

The fight seeped out of me. I'd let Gray get away...not once, not twice, but tonight for the third time. I was pretty certain that meant I'd lost her forever.

She'd be a fool to come back a fourth time after all I'd put her through.

"Don't be an idiot. And for God's sake don't spend the rest of your life punishing yourself because of Xander's sacrifice. If the roles were reversed, you'd never ever expect the same of him."

"Because he had everything to live for."

She leaned forward as if wanting to get in my face but stopped short. "And *so do you.* Be happy. Go get Gray and tell her how you feel, and don't break her heart again. Tell that man to go fuck himself because you love his daughter and you're going to take care of her and let her live her life on her terms. And there'll be no more talk of you and me, okay? You can still be in AJ's life and my life. You're family. And you can damn well stop avoiding us because of your own guilt, because there *won't be* any more guilt. Xander wouldn't want it. You read that in his letter. His own words."

I lightly shook my head and stared at my clamped hands, completely lost for what to say. But I did what I should have done months ago. I sat and listened.

"I knew and he knew—just like all of you know when you strap yourselves in on that rocket—that you take your lives in your hands. It's what you trained for, for years. His job was dangerous. Just like the crew of *Columbia.* Just like the seven of *Challenger.* Or the three of Apollo I. All of them knew the same thing. Stop tying your entire life to that one moment in time." Her brow furrowed in conviction. "As long as it's in my power, I will fight against you doing it because you are family, and I need you whole."

I stared at her in awe, tears smearing the bottom of my vision. I allowed them to spill over onto my cheeks. "You are one amazing woman, Karen Freed," I finally choked out, the emotion overwhelming me.

She smiled sadly, demurring with the shrug of a shoulder. "Of course, I know that already. And *I* deserve to find out if I can be happy again, maybe with someone else. It had been a while since I'd read Xander's letter, and you know, agreeing to your plan would have meant *I* was continuing to live in the past. But I'm going to live, and I'm going to move on. And you should too."

I shook my head. "I'll do everything in my power to be there for AJ and for you."

Her smile grew. "I consider that a promise. You better not flake on me, Tyler. I know where the bodies are buried. And I know how to get you where it hurts."

I huffed out a laugh while swiping at my eyes quickly with the back of my hand, struggling to reign the emotion in along with it. "Isn't that the truth."

Her brows came up. "Now go, goddammit. Don't waste another moment. *Go get her.*"

Inspired by her words, I was bowled over by a sudden rush of—what was it? Energy, determination. *Joy?* Freedom...freedom to admit how I felt. Freedom to know what I wanted. Freedom to pursue it.

"I haven't even told her—"

"Tell her now. Tonight. Don't waste another moment. You of all people should know that life is short. Our time is limited."

I stood from the couch and weaved around the coffee table to get to her. With a huge grin, she followed suit and leapt at me, arms wide and tears springing from her eyes. "I'm so fucking happy for you. You can't even know."

I turned and kissed her hair, feeling those same tears pricking at the back of my own eyes. This time, I was able to suppress them. "I owe you so much."

"Enough. You don't owe me a thing. But for God's sake, go get her or I will consider it a crime against nature and I will never forgive you. *Go.*"

I pulled back and turned to leave, but she grabbed my sleeve. "Hammer's sister is watching AJ tonight, and I was going to spend the night at their place tonight anyway. So when you find her, take her home with you. I won't be there."

I bent forward, kissed her on the forehead, and left.

CHAPTER TWENTY-SIX
RYAN

I N SPITE OF KAREN'S ENCOURAGEMENT TO GO OUT AND GET Gray now, I knew I had unfinished business I needed to take care of first. Likely, business she would approve of, or at least I hoped so.

The other three astronauts were waiting for me in the dining room. They filled me in on what was going on now. Adam and Tolan had gone out front to converse with Conrad Barrett—likely in an effort to cajole him out of bolting from the entire program.

I didn't even care what was being said out there. But I did care about my team members. This was a critical time, and we'd have to proceed carefully.

When I approached them, they clustered around me. Noah folded his arms, wearing a sober expression. "Ty, we have to talk about this...episode you just had."

I nodded. "Yes, of course. I realize none of you are idiots, and I know you are fully aware of what that was."

Noah turned to the other two. "Guys do you mind if we have a word alone?"

They met each other's gazes uneasily before Noah turned back to me. I nodded my agreement and told them, "Tell Tolan that I'd like to speak to all of you in a few minutes. This shouldn't take long." They nodded and left.

Noah shifted on his feet and stared at the ground for a long moment before bringing his gaze up to meet mine. "Being in the dark, that's a trigger for you?"

My face burned with shame, but I couldn't say whether the shame came from admitting I was afraid of the dark like a toddler or that I'd strived so hard to hide it from everyone. That I'd lied to them all and put our program at risk.

"I can only beg for your forgiveness—" I began in a shaky voice, but he cut me off with an outstretched hand.

"I was there that day, too. I also still have nightmares about it. I may have been sitting on the ground in Mission Control, but that day changed *all* of our lives." He gritted his teeth and shook his head. "All this time I thought you were gliding through life, just racking up all the accolades and enjoying the star treatment."

I gave a small shrug. "Well, it does have its perks."

He half-smiled. "Don't blow it off with a joke, Ty. Trauma is serious shit. We're all military men. You and I are special forces. We've seen this before in many different circumstances. You are no better or worse than any of them."

"Thank you."

"Hiding this shit from us was not cool, but I'd be a hypocrite and an asshole if I said I didn't understand."

I rubbed my jaw, hanging my head in shame. "I wanted it for all the wrong reasons. And I was lying to myself as much as I was lying to all of you. But I don't have the heart for this mission anymore. So I need to ask if you're willing and able to go up in my place."

His brows pinched. "Of course. That's my job. As your back up, I'm supposed to step in for you. These are special circumstances, however, with all the press, and everything."

I met his gaze. "I'll do whatever it takes to keep this program going. I'll run the astronaut office and help train the new recruits, get you up to speed on all your training. But..." I let out a long sigh, realizing that it was physically paining me to get all this out. "I was doing it for him. Because I'd made a promise to him in haste. And I swear to God, that if he'd asked me to saw my own arm off that day. I would have done it without hesitation."

Noah nodded and leaned forward, placing a hand on my shoulder, but said nothing, allowing me to continue.

"And it goes against everything we are, and what we train for, and all the hideous competition we put ourselves through, but I gotta admit this. I have to take one for the team this time and admit that I'm not fit to fly. Not now." *Maybe not ever.*

I bit my tongue, though, and didn't say the last part.

Though I meant every word I was saying, my heart wasn't in this admission. My heart had followed Gray out the door a half hour before and was frantically searching for her in every place I could imagine she might have gone.

Because damn, three times crushing someone's heart was three times too many. I had to make things right with her before another hour went by, but I couldn't leave Noah and the other guys hanging like this, either.

I ran my hand through my hair.

"I'm not walking away. I'm just doing the right thing. I'm stepping back and letting someone else fly the mission."

"You've been working through this, though, right? With Gray? She didn't seem that surprised when it happened."

I hesitated, unwilling to discuss Gray with him. "I'm going to be there as much as I can to support the mission. It will go on as planned. And before you ask—I'll be fine. So let's go talk to the others."

"One last thing... I owe you an apology. I thought you were just being an asshole and sleeping with her." He shook his head. "Clearly, that isn't the case."

I stiffened. "It isn't the case. I love her."

"Then I'm sorry I was a prick to you about it. I hope things work out with her."

I shook my head. "It's not looking good at the moment, but I'm going to go find her as soon as we speak to Tolan and the others."

He nodded. "Yeah. And you know we have your back."

I clasped his shoulder in return. "And I have yours."

I found the others outside, clustered around the entrance. Barrett had left but Adam and Tolan and my fellow astronauts were waiting for me. The next ten minutes saw me repeating most of the same things I'd said to Noah to the rest of them. Tolan listened with sober features, clearly not happy with the turn of events. But everyone could agree that my flying was not the answer.

We decided to meet the next day with Victoria to discuss how best to handle it with the public. I could not have asked for better support, especially from my astronaut colleagues who all shook my hand and told me individually that they were there for me.

Finally, finally, over an hour after she'd left the restaurant, I was out the door on a mission to track her down. But I had no idea where she'd gone.

The most obvious place, her condo, was where I went first. Her car wasn't in her parking space, but I practically banged the door down anyway until her neighbor popped his head out and did a double take. I'd usually visited on the downlow, avoiding neighbors and wearing my usual disguise.

Now, his eyes widened. "Hey, you're—"

"Gray—your neighbor—has she been home tonight?"

He shook his head, and when he opened his mouth to say something else, I did an about-face and bolted down the stairwell back to my car, my mind racing with the possibilities of where she might be.

Work was the next place to go, but after scanning the parking lot and not seeing her car, I texted Pari and asked if Gray had gone to her house.

Pari got back to me almost immediately but couldn't help me. I asked one of the night time security officers, and he didn't even need to check in the building. Gray had not gone into the building tonight.

From there on out, the search got more frantic. I checked the place at the beach where we'd often gone to walk, but her car wasn't in the parking lot. I went by the tiny diner where we occasionally got a discrete meal during our time together. No luck there either.

Since Gray and I had conducted the majority of our relationship undercover and hidden by the false pretense of my fake relationship with Keely, we really didn't have that many usual haunts.

I drove through her neighborhood again and saw nothing.

I was starting to lose my mind with worry.

Where could she have gone? To someone's house I didn't know about? Checked into a hotel somewhere? To her father's house?

If I knew where he lived, I'd be on my way already. But I didn't have his address and had no way of finding it out any time soon.

Sitting in her parking lot, I finally did the most logical thing. I texted her.

Then I called her.

Neither got me an answer, not even the little dots that said she had read the text. The call went straight to voice mail, which told me her phone was either turned off or out of power.

I ran my hands through my hair a few times, scrambling to think, then decided to regroup at my house and figure out a new tactic.

Obviously, she didn't want to be found. And who was I to violate her wishes? Especially after all I'd done to her.

But goddamn it, I wasn't going to let things go unsaid. The stream of thoughts ran through my head constantly as I sifted through the north Orange County and Long Beach areas in order to find her.

Over an hour later, I pulled into my driveway, exhaustion gnawing at me. It was after eleven o'clock and past my normal bedtime, and the adrenaline from the incident at dinner had long since worn off and left me weary to my bones.

I was depleted, empty, and utterly bereft at the thought of going to bed and waking up not knowing where she was or what she was doing. And even more so, not having her lying beside me in bed.

I'd allowed too many of those nights to pass already.

I'd been such a fool. I thought I was doing the best thing for her when I'd let her go. I'd *known* I was doing the worst thing for myself.

At that time, I firmly believed that I only deserved the worst. I'd hated myself that much.

But now, intuition, which sounded a little like Xander's voice, was whispering to me otherwise. The words from that letter. The thought that, as Karen had said, he might have cheered me on from the other side.

I was ready now, ready for this next step in my progress. Ready to do it for myself as much as I wanted to do it for her.

But I couldn't find her.

Pulling up beside the garage, I parked and got out. As usual, all the lights had come on at sundown, so the pathway to the front door was well lit. I hopped up the steps, key out to slide into the lock.

Halting mid-step, I spotted the figure propped up against my door on the brightly-lit doorstep. She was slumped, eyes closed as if she had dozed off, her blond head lolling over her chest, her bag by her side.

She'd been waiting for me to come home and fallen asleep in the meantime.

And for some reason I couldn't move. I could only stare at her, feeling a strange sort of thickness in my chest and a lump in my throat. Blinking at the stinging in my eyes, I jerkily moved to the door and unlocked it, then without a word, I bent and hefted her sleeping form into my arms and took her inside the house.

I took Gray into the spare room that served as my office and laid her gently on the couch. When I reached for a nearby folded blanket, she was already stirring restlessly.

"Shhh. Go back to sleep," I whispered when her eyes cracked open, even then knowing it was futile to suggest it. I didn't want her to go back to sleep. I wanted to talk to her and tell her everything that had been running through my head as I'd scoured the city searching for her.

But she looked so tired, so small. So worn out.

So overwhelmed by everything that had gone on this evening.

Despite my encouragement to go back to sleep, she opened her eyes and blinked, getting her bearings. She reached her arms above her head and stretched all the way down to her toes.

I took in her slightly disheveled hair. At some point she had changed out of the beautiful pink dress and into jeans and a t-shirt, but her skin glowed from her brief nap. She reached up and touched my cheek, and I could hardly breathe.

She was beautiful. So beautiful. Her green eyes were clouded with concern, the slight crease between her brows deepening as her gaze focused in on me.

"Are you okay?" she asked, smoothing her slender fingers across my cheek. "I came because I was worried about you and I had to know if you were okay."

And that ache in my chest tightened and released, suddenly letting loose a flow of warmth and emotion, like a dam breaking. I let out a breath mingled with an ironic laugh. Trust Gray, my beautiful, sweet Gray, to worry about someone else when she'd just undergone an incredibly stressful event.

"It's almost midnight, and I just spent hours turning the county upside down looking for you. I got home and didn't even see your car. Where'd you park?"

"In the street. I figured you and Karen would be pulling in soon." She frowned. "I went to meet with someone, then I came here. Then I waited because my phone was dead and I didn't have a charging cord. And I gave you back your key."

I knelt beside the couch as she sat up, rubbing her eyes. We stared at each other, eyes on the same level. Then she cleared her throat.

"So, if you were looking for me, you must have had something to say."

I nodded. "I have a lot to say. A lot of important things."

"So do I. Like about you doing the test flight—"

I shook my head. "That's taken care of. I can't do it. You were right."

She stared at the ground, not exactly looking happy at this news. She was probably still upset with me, concern or no. It was so like her to set aside her feelings of being hurt in order to see if I was okay despite whatever she was feeling inside.

"Are you okay with that call?"

I sat back on the floor beside the couch. "It was my call. I know they would have probably decided against me anyway, but I didn't fight it. It should have been this way from the beginning."

Her eyes flicked to me. "But you helped the program so much with all the publicity you did. None of that was a waste. Thank you for thinking of our jobs."

We were silent for a moment, then her gaze flicked up to mine. "I'm glad you're doing better. But I hope you talk to someone. Open up in therapy. It can help you." Then, to my astonishment, she pushed up from the couch and pulled her car keys out of her pocket, stifling a yawn with the back of her hand.

"I should go. But I want you to know I met with Aaron Thiessen tonight after the meeting."

A dark sense of foreboding hung over me. "Oh?"

She nodded, seeming to fight a smile. Shit, had she decided to move on? That quickly? Maybe she thought we needed a clean break. But to rush to his house right after the restaurant? My mind spun.

"I pitched to him. He wants to buy in. And if we're lucky, maybe he can buy my dad out. So the good news is that we still have a program even if my father decides to throw a toddler tantrum. The bad news is that you and I are going to have to reach a place where we can work together eventually."

As she talked, I found myself going Mach 4 through a myriad of emotions. Concern and foreboding, first at the mention of Aaron's name. Then relief to hear that she'd gone to his place to pitch to him. Then disbelief that she was discussing the future of our jobs.

I didn't give a fuck about our jobs at that minute.

Xander's words ran through my mind, over and over again. *Live your life. Move on. Be happy.* Find my future. That's exactly what I had to do.

I still wanted that family. I still wanted that belonging.

And I knew that the woman standing right in front of me was the key to that dream.

"I owe you an apology. A lot of them, really. But tonight, especially. When I was arguing with your father, I—I didn't want to take away your voice, Gray. I'd never knowingly do that."

She stood still then nodded perfunctorily. "Apology accepted." Then she turned to go.

But my hand shot out to gently clasp her upper arm. I was reminded of that first day after the investors meeting when I'd followed her in the hall and she'd been evading me. I'd reached out then, too. She'd dressed me down for it.

But this time, she paused.

"I can't let you go yet," I said. "Not before I say what I have to say. Then, then unlike before, I'll leave the decision for your own future up to you."

She shook her head. "I don't think either of us is in a position to talk about our future right now."

I tensed, not liking her answer at all. She seemed...depleted, spent. Like she'd given up.

She'd once accused me of giving up on us so easily. Maybe she had, now, too.

"Hear me out, please? Then if you want to leave, you can."

Her face looked troubled. "You only have to apologize once, Ryan. There's no need to dwell on it."

I sent her a sad smile—tinged with maybe a little hope. Maybe more hope than I had the right to hold onto at that moment.

I took a deep breath before stepping off the cliff. "I love you, Gray." That thickness returned to my throat in a rush. The stabbing behind my eyes. That emotional rush only got worse as I witnessed her eyes immediately filling with tears. I cleared my throat. "I love you more than I ever thought possible to love someone. I can't begin to imagine what the rest of my life would look like without you. More than just loving you, I *need* you."

I watched as she processed my words, the tears rising quickly in her eyes and a thin stream spilling over. "You'll understand if

I only accept those words with a heavy heap of caution after all of this, after Tahoe. And what about Karen?"

I let out an explosive breath and shook my head. "I told her everything. I didn't hold back. About the real reasons I wanted to go through with that plan. About the accident, the tether, everything."

Her brows buckled. "How did she react? Did she take it hard?"

I shook my head. "She called me a dumbass and an idiot for not going after you. She said I deserved to find love and she did, too."

Gray nodded, her features sober. Despite having red eyes and tear-stained cheeks, she appeared remarkably calm and composed.

"Here's the thing, Ryan. I decided that getting my heart stomped on twice was unacceptable. I can't do that again." Her voice trembled, and she swiped at her cheeks with the back of her hand. "I can't take the risk a third time."

I looked away, trying to disguise the icy disappointment that showered down on me. It hurt. It sucked just as much as before. Even when I'd caused it, it had been wretched. But could I blame her?

"How do I know that one little thing isn't going to send you spiraling and pushing me away again? It was an act of sheer providence that finally convinced you that you couldn't fly. If the lights hadn't gone out in the restaurant, then what? You'd still be set to fly that mission. You'd still be determined to pursue Karen. No one but me would be aware of your PTSD. None of what happened tonight was a result of a decision you made. You were exposed and now you have no other choice to make."

I tensed as she spoke, as if her very valid points were like punches landing on my torso. She was right. Had it not been for the shitty weather and the blackout, I might still not know.

I rubbed at the base of my neck. "You're right. It was luck. Plain and simple. I was an arrogant fool who wouldn't listen to you or anyone. I had no business near that flight. And the incident happened here on the ground instead of up there. All I could focus on was myself and my pain and my need to make it up to Xander without having the wisdom to realized that this wouldn't have been what he wanted anyway."

She adjusted her glasses and looked away with a frown, appearing confused. No, scratch that, she appeared more conflicted than confused, which caused hope to spark inside of me.

"I got lucky tonight, yes. And I'm grateful. I'd be hoping for luck beyond what any one man deserves by asking if you could take a chance on us again."

She froze, stared at me for a long time while I hoped for a glimmer of some clue about what was going through her mind. Then she slowly shook her head.

"I won't willingly put myself out there to get hurt again," she stated in a low voice, as if it might be the last argument she had left.

I nodded grimly. "It's a risk. Whether it's the first time or the third time or the tenth, it's always a risk. But where there's a risk, there's also a reward."

"This is a high-risk situation, and I'm a little gun shy."

I took a tentative step toward her. "And I don't blame you. The crux of the problem was that I didn't feel I deserved you. And you know what? I still don't feel like I deserve you."

Now *she* looked crestfallen, her gaze dropping to the floor. But I put my thumb and forefinger on her chin and lifted her face to mine. "I don't deserve you right now. I'm broken. But I'm not done. I can do this. I can become the man you deserve. And I'm willing to do what needs to be done. I'm willing to fight for it."

She blinked several times. "I'm not going to make you fight for it, Ryan. But on the other hand, the things you'll have to do, the work you're going to have to accomplish with yourself, it's not going to be easy. And you have to do it for *you*. Because you want to heal. Not for me. And not for the program or Karen or AJ either. But because you deserve to be whole."

My prospects with her were looking worse and worse by the minute. My stomach dipped, and the rest of my internal organs threatened to follow it right down the drain. "Can I at least ask you to be patient and wait while I work through it? I want—I need the chance with you." My hands slipped to her shoulders and she wavered where she stood, appearing to search for her words.

If she made me beg, I'd do that too. Easily. My back knee bent but she seemed to anticipate what I was doing. Grabbing my shirt, she pulled me forward. "Ryan, stop. I'm not trying to torment you. These are all important questions. You already know how I feel about you."

I hesitated while she was quiet, staring down at the floor. Then she reached for me and pulled me into a hug. I wrapped my arms around her and tightened my hold, pressing my cheek to her hair. Was this goodbye? Was it *not now*? I held my breath and waited.

"I can't fix you Ryan. I told you that the day of the investors meeting. And you've got a long road ahead of you. But you don't have to walk it alone. I can't fix you. But I can love you. Flaws and all. Because that's what love is."

I stroked her soft hair. From this angle, I couldn't look into her face, but I could feel her relax against me. "I love you, Gray. I'm such an idiot that when I told you in Tahoe, you were asleep, and I was so scared you might hear anyway, I said it in Russian."

In spite of her tears, she laughed. "I heard you. I wondered why you were speaking Russian to me."

"I wish I'd said it in English, then. I wish you'd heard it then and you didn't have to go this entire time thinking I didn't care. I've been so stupid in so many ways that asking you to forgive me feels like asking you to perform some sort of impossibility."

She laid her wet cheek on my chest. "It's not impossible. Carl Jung once said that it's easier to go to the Moon than it is to penetrate one's own being." She sniffed heavily. "Which means you're in for one hell of a journey."

I reached down and laced my fingers through hers. "Could you be there with me? I'll be the one doing the hard work, but the thought of not having you beside me..." Her head came up and I cupped her cheeks in both my hands.

"I said I love you. That means I love you at your worst as well as your best." She turned and kissed the palm of my hand.

I bent and kissed her. She tasted of salty tears and sweetness. The sweetest lips I'd ever tasted. My heart hammered like it might burst from my chest. "I love you. I'm going to say it to you every day for the rest of my life—in a language you understand."

"I love you, too," she said, fresh tears pouring down her face. "And I want to be here for you on your journey. We've past the Rubicon now."

My mouth twitched up at her familiar reference to the ancient river once considered the point that, once crossed, marked the true commitment to the voyage. The Rubicon was the point of no return. "I'm all in, Gray. I won't turn back from this, from *us,* ever again. Doing it before almost finished me. I won't be an idiot again."

Her arms came around my neck, and she pulled me to her. The familiar surge of desire for her rose up and took hold of me, but I was also excited to have her close to me, hold her in my arms, sleep beside her peacefully. I wanted these for all our tomorrows.

So I took her by the hand and led her to my bedroom. We undressed. We kissed and held each other tightly. And then we fell asleep, wrapped firmly in each other's arms.

In the dark.

Chapter Twenty-seven
Epilogue
Gray

O NE WEEK LATER...

Cameras clicked furiously as Ryan once again faced a bevy of journalists and important media influencers from the stage set up in the XVenture assembly building. An actual section of the Rubicon III rocket, painted white with red detailing and lettering, provided the perfect background.

After the succinct announcement by Tolan, an even briefer statement by the new prime crew member of the test flight, Colonel Noah Sutton, Ryan took the podium and the room quieted.

He looked serious, composed and much less nervous than both of his predecessors. Wearing a dark blue suit, green tie and the shiny gold astronaut badge on his lapel, he was stunningly handsome. My heart even did a little flip as I snapped a few photos with my phone.

That silence practically echoed through the room as Ryan straightened and grabbed each side of the podium in his hands and looked straight ahead. He had no notes and there was no teleprompter. He'd apparently, completely memorized what he wanted to say.

"Astronaut Alexander Freed was my friend, my brother. But he was also the hero who saved my life. And because of circumstances beyond either of our control, I returned safely home from our last mission, but Xander did not." He paused and took a long breath, appearing to brace himself for what came next.

As clearly and as succinctly as possible, Ryan described the accident and how Xander had freed himself from his tether in order to get to Ryan once he noticed his suit was breached. Agitated mumbles from the crowd rose up as Ryan continued to narrate the accident in the simplest terms.

But the press had never heard this version before, so this was big news.

No one had heard this version until Ryan had told me, then Karen.

"I'm still coming to terms with the ramifications of losing Xander. He made the ultimate sacrifice to save his friend. Every day, I endeavor to find meaning in his decision." Ryan took another long pause to collect himself. I squeezed my fists tight in front of my mouth, wishing I could somehow fortify him from afar.

"It's been a long road back from that day last year when we lost him. And I've struggled privately and in the most profound ways. I've needed a lot of help, but I've learned a lot. Enough to know that I'm not ready to return to spaceflight at this time. But the XPAC has my full support and devotion. I'll remain working with them and helping to run the operations at the astronaut office for as long as I am of use there."

He licked his lips, his eyes flitting about the room until he seemed to locate what he was looking for—or rather who. When Ryan's gaze met mine, I smiled and flashed him a thumbs-up to encourage him. He gave the slightest of nods, as if to indicate that he understood.

"Xander Freed died a hero and it was his sacrifice that saved four other astronauts and the International Space Station. It is my hope that his sacrifice will be forever remembered and that we further our missions from earth orbit, to the Moon, Mars and other destinations in our solar system. We shall not forget the brave, strong and courageous people—those of Apollo 1, Soyuz 1 and 11, *Challenger*, and *Columbia*—who like Xander Freed, gave their lives to further these missions. We owe it to them to continue our venture into space travel.

"I'm eternally grateful to Xander for each breath I take and each day I am permitted to live out my life. I know that Xander would want those whom he loved most in the world to live a happy and fulfilling life. And every day I'll strive to live up to that."

Despite the myriad of hands and overtures for his attention made after he concluded his speech, Ryan retreated not long after. Noah and Tolan were left to field the remaining questions about the change in the mission. Both Noah and Tolan gave Ryan their utmost support, but I only heard a fragment of it as I left. Using my pass to get back into the main building and my best hunch, I found Ryan quickly. He was sitting at his desk in the astronaut office.

In the dark.

"Hey," I said, standing in the open doorway while waiting for my eyes to adjust. "Want company or would you prefer a little alone time?"

There was a slight shift from his corner and I heard him get up from his chair, maneuver around the tables until stepping into the shaft of light from the doorway. He stopped there and looked at me. "Depends on the company."

I smiled and walked toward him. The door slowly slipped shut and by the time I reached him, it was dark again. He pulled me into his arms.

"Is me, myself and I acceptable company?"

His arms tightened, pulling me flush against him and he landed a hard kiss on my mouth, opening it in seconds. His tongue entered my mouth, dancing against mine, stoking those familiar, pleasant flames.

When his head finally came up, he breathed against me. "It's the best company."

My arms slid behind his neck, bringing my mouth to his ear to whisper, "Your speech was amazing. I'm so proud of you."

His mouth slid down to my neck, nibbling there. "I meant it, you know. About letting go. About trying to live a happy life."

My hands came up to his cheeks, framing his face. "Good. Because that's what you deserve," I said as I looked into his eyes. It was hard to read his exact expression in the dark. "You were right to say that's what he'd want."

We kissed again and swayed against each other. "You know that means you're stuck with me, right? Because I will never be happy without you." I could hear the grin in his voice.

"Really. Even though I break all your rules?"

"*Especially* because you do."

He left my side to move to the door. I heard the bolt snap closed in the lock and he returned to me in moments.

"Now, I feel like taking some risk."

"Right here?" I asked as he lifted me against him and I locked my legs around his waist.

He walked us over to his desk in the back corner and set me on top of it. I leaned back and rested against my arms and raised my foot to trace his torso feeling simultaneously silly and sexy for posing this way.

Ryan gently grasped my ankle then quickly slid his hand up my leg to palm my calf. Heat surged everywhere.

"How glad am I that you wore a skirt today?"

I smiled as I unbuckled his belt. "I have a feeling you're about to show me."

His hands were on my panties, tugging them insistently. "I have a lot to show you."

I belted out laughter in the darkness, lying flat on my back.

"What's so funny?"

"That's another one of your cheesy one-liners, isn't it?" I lowered my voice to mimic him. "*I have a lot to show you.*"

He freed himself of his boxers and scooted me to the edge of his desk. "You already know by now that it's not a one-liner, it's a promise."

He moved to stand between my knees, his palm sliding up the back of my neck. Then he laced his fingers into my hair as our mouths reconnected, sucking breath from one another. His palm rubbed over and over my nipple until it ached.

I was gasping when he pulled away. "The guys could come back at any moment."

He slid into me hot and firm, letting out a sigh of pleasure as he did so. "That's a risk I'm willing to take."

Approximately One Year Later...

I'd always loved Griffith Park Observatory. When I was young, my mom brought me here. She liked her long walks and we had the hills and the huge park behind our neighborhood to wander and explore. The world had seemed so huge to me then. And the observatory had expanded that understanding out into the vast universe.

It was there that as a child, I'd fallen in love with the stars and dreamt of visiting strange planets. And it was here that, this night, I sat in the audience in the planetarium as the man I loved read an excerpt from his newly-published autobiography and answered questions from the crowd.

He was stunning in his casual button down shirt, blazer and dress slacks. No flight suit tonight. None of the typical astronaut accoutrements aside from his ever-present gold astronaut badge, which winked under the lights whenever he moved.

Pari sat on one side of me, Karen and AJ on the other, though we took turns having AJ sit in our lap so he could get a better view of Uncle Ty.

Hands shot up, people calling out every few minutes as the moderator took new questions. A teenage girl stood up—as unlikely a space fanatic as I must have looked when I was her age, aside from all the nerdy shirts I wore.

"Commander Ty. I really have to ask. Will there ever be any hope of you getting back together with Keely?"

My gaze flicked to Karen's and we shared a laugh. Ryan hid his inner cringe phenomenally well and only those of us who knew him well could have known he was mildly annoyed by the question.

He moved the mic away from his mouth as he gave a small cough, then answered. "Well, I have a great deal of respect for Keely and we remain good friends. And I hate to disappoint you but there's been someone else in my life now for some time. She makes me happy and she's definitely the one. So I think my search is over."

My breath sucked out of me like I'd suffered a blow. Certainly, a blow of surprise. The most pleasant surprise I could possibly imagine. Blinking, I tried to absorb his words but there seemed to be this weird sort of static in my ears.

"Well for the sake of all us girls who've been shipping a Tyley reunion, you should definitely put a ring on it."

The room erupted in laughter. Ryan shrugged and said. "You know, maybe I should."

Karen's hand immediately landed on top of mine, squeezing it hard. She gave the tiniest little squeal that only I could hear. And from my other side came a knowing nudge in the ribs from Pari.

"He loves you," she muttered.

And all I could do was sit there and feel all these weird sensations rush through me. Which was weird to my logical brain because I already knew he loved me. He had made good on his promise to tell me that almost every single day.

And it wasn't just with his words. He'd shown it in actions too. He'd encouraged me to reach out and try to repair the shredded relationship with my father. And after months of cold freeze, I had.

And even recently, they'd spent an evening in the same room together without a single barbed remark exchanged. Ryan, for as much cause as he'd had to hate Conrad Barrett, had quickly allowed the détente. Because he loved me.

And I sure loved him.

Later we stood in little groups while Ryan signed books, sitting beside his assistant and co-author, Lee, and managed by the publicist in charge of the book tour. Hammer, Noah and Kirill soon joined us, all looking handsome and attracting the female gaze wherever they stood.

Victoria approached with a stack of signed books hooked under her arm. She slid her free one around her girlfriend's waist. Pari turned to her. "You could not possibly like the book so much that you had to buy five copies."

Victoria laughed. "These are going out as gifts to some of my peeps."

Pari grinned. "And here I thought you were just sucking up to Ty." She leaned forward to land a kiss on Victoria's mouth, but swerved at the last minute and kissed her cheek instead. "You've got lipstick on."

Kirill held his hands out to AJ who enthusiastically jumped forward for a ride on the cosmonaut's shoulders. "I should have been up here when Ty was reading his book," AJ said. "I can see everything from up here."

Hammer tugged on his foot playfully. "Ty's book wasn't boring though? Not even a little?"

AJ shrugged. "He needs more pictures in his book. There aren't any pictures of me in it."

Karen and I looked at each other and smiled. There were, however, lots of pictures of his dad in the photos section.

Karen and AJ had moved out to California this past summer and were now living near enough to us that we could call them neighbors. This happy circumstance had led to all of us spending time together regularly, and for Ryan to stay close with his "little buddy."

The group soon dissipated as we exited the building to wander the grounds while we waited for Ty to finish up. Hammer and Kirill were horsing around with AJ, doing some kind of weird tag game that I didn't recognize. Pari and Victoria had gone to the car to stash her stack of books. Noah and Karen were walking to the lookout to watch the city lights.

I waited by the open door, peeking in every so often and more than once snapping photos of him looking all scholarly while he signed books.

All he needed was a tweed blazer with leather elbow-patches and he'd have that sexy professor thing going on. *Rawr.* Until that idea had popped into my head, I'd had no idea whatsoever that I might have such a fantasy.

The publicist, Lee and Ryan emerged from the building not long after. Ryan's head swiveled as he scanned his surroundings with purpose. When his eyes landed on me, his smiled widened. He excused himself to his companions and walked quickly to me.

I tilted my head and gazed at him out of the corner of my eye. "Should I be seen with you? I mean, I heard you have a special someone now."

"Come with me, please," he said, taking hold of my arm and heading out toward the lookout. There were people there, but he steered us to the side where we stood alone. Most of the book event people had left and it was mostly just our friends and family in the area.

I turned to him, straightening his lapel. "Well, Commander Tyler, you certainly looked handsome tonight. And I have to warn you that I might attack you the minute we're alone."

He dropped his arm from around my waist and looked oddly stiff for a moment, then gazed out at the lights as if trying to make some sort of decision, his brow furrowing.

I frowned. "Are you okay?"

He turned back to me and took my hand. "I'm more than okay. I'm in love with an amazing, incredible woman and am feeling a sudden urge to follow a teenager's advice."

I blinked. "What?" *You should definitely put a ring on it.* Gulping, I opened my mouth to ask more when I noticed that he was taking a knee on the grass in front of me.

What? Um. Was this real life? Was he playing some kind of joke on me?

"Her advice was to put a ring on it, but I don't have a ring to put on it right now. I think I have something almost as good..." He reached up to his lapel and unpinned his astronaut badge, fitting the clasp back on the pin before taking my hand again. He put the badge into my palm, cradling it with his other hand. "Angharad Grace Barrett, will you be my wife?"

Breathe, Gray. Breathe. In with the good out with the bad.... Click click clickety click.

My heart raced and he was well aware. I expected to see sardonic amusement at my reaction when I looked in his face. Instead, he looked pale and like he might fall over if I didn't answer him soon.

But in order to answer him, I needed to fucking remember how to breathe first.

My fingers closed around the pin in my hand, and I swallowed, finally sucking in some air. "I—I—"

His brows went up, and he was now starting to look worried.

"Yes," I finally choked out. "Of course."

His shoulder slumped in relief.

"But only if you never call me by those two names again."

He laughed and pushed to his feet, standing before me. "Well I'll have to say them once more at the wedding, but after that, you're on."

He leaned in for a lingering, affectionate kiss that was suddenly disrupted by cheers and applause. We broke away from each other and turned to stare. A group had formed and had been watching us from about fifty feet away. The astronauts, employees from XVenture, including Tolan. Even some stragglers from the book signing and other random visitors to the observatory.

Karen had her phone up, snapping photos to document this milestone, no doubt.

As they continued to whistle and applaud, Ryan pulled the pin out of my hand and pinned it to the bodice of my dress. "There," he said, straightening it. "That looks perfect. Soon to be replaced by a proper engagement ring."

I raised my brows at him and put a hand over the pin on my dress. "Hell no. I'm not giving this back."

He slipped his arms around my waist and pulled me in for another hug as he laughed at me. Soon AJ broke with the crowd and came running to us, ignoring his mom's calls to stand back. He tugged on Ryan's pant leg and Ryan obediently lifted him up to our level.

"What just happened, Uncle Ty?"

Ryan looked at me and smiled. "Gray is going to be your aunt."

AJ looked at me as if to confirm and when I nodded and smiled, he held up his fist toward me to exchange one of our customary fist bumps. "I totally knew that was going to happen," he said with a solemn nod.

"This calls for a group hug!" Hammer said with a laugh.

Ryan jerked toward him. "Back off, jackass," he grunted but they were already on him. The three guys surrounded him and Karen came up beside me and suddenly we all did this weird sort of huddle. Everyone reached for someone else and Ryan and I were buried somewhere in the middle of that tangle of arms and legs, being smooshed even closer together.

"Group hug!" Everyone shouted and other friends and coworkers came and joined in the fun.

I reached up, hooking my arms around my future husband's neck and pulled even closer to him to say loudly into his ear, "Here's to starting a brand new adventure. Together."

ABOUT THE AUTHOR

Brenna Aubrey is a USA TODAY Bestselling Author of contemporary romance stories that center on geek culture. Her debut novel, At Any Price, is currently free on all platforms.

She has always sought comfort in good books and the long, involved stories she weaves in her head. Brenna is a city girl with a nature-lover's heart. She therefore finds herself out in green open spaces any chance she can get. She's also a mom, teacher, geek girl, Francophile, unabashed video-game addict & eBook hoarder.

She currently resides on the west coast with her husband, two children, two adorable golden retriever pups, a bird and some fish.
More information available at www.BrennaAubrey.net

To sign up for Brenna's email list for release updates, please type this link into your browser:
http://BrennaAubrey.net/newsletter-signup/

Want to discuss the Gaming The System series with other avid readers? Brenna's reader discussion and social group is located on Facebook
https://www.facebook.com/groups/BrennaAubreyBookGroup/

or Goodreads
https://www.goodreads.com/group/show/180053-brenna-aubrey-books-geekery-gaming.

Made in United States
Orlando, FL
05 May 2022